WOODEN WOLVES

ELEMENTAL WOLF BOOK 1.5

A.B. HERRON

Soaring Herron Press

Soaring Herron Press

Wooden Wolves
©A.B. Herron 2025

ISBN: 979-8-9929150-0-6

Proofing by Owl Eye Edits
Interior Formatting by Platform House
Cover Design by Ravven

To those whose dreams
have come crumbling down,
roll up your sleeves with me,
and let's build something new.

Dear readers,

Welcome to the Elemental Wolf world. This novel, **Wooden Wolves** is a tangent, a quick sidestep back in time to follow what happened to Tobin after that pivotal night in the cemetery at the end of **Watching Water**. What was supposed to be a short story to set the stage for Nora's third book became a monster, demanding to be given its own volume. Seriously though, it's Tobin, what do we expect? This book is happening in sync with **Hearing Wind**. While Nora is working through her own mysteries at Crater Lake, Tobin is in these pages building his new and improved life apart from the rest of the group.

All this to say, if you have read **Watching Water**, you will be continuing from there. If this is your initial introduction to the Elemental Wolf series, then welcome, and enjoy your first taste of what lurks in the magical community existing right alongside us. Have fun, and remember, if you don't believe, you will never see, and you might be safer that way.

May your reading be Wild, -A.B.

CONTENTS

CHAPTER I

A Graveyard Escape

Tobin

T he one thing Tobin hadn't planned for was needing to drive while being a werewolf.

"Shit," Tobin growled, untangling himself from the subcompact. He violently paced around the car, willfully ignoring the screams echoing from the deep trees. With his heart racing, he mentally tackled the puzzle again. Yet, no matter which angle he assessed it from, the cramped metal space refused to accommodate his new shape. And those screams were definitely getting louder.

Tobin snarled and snapped at the air with his new fangs. There had to be another solution! Sure, he hadn't fully believed in this outcome, despite his hopes and hard work. Yet here he was, covered in fur, twice his normal size, and running for his life from a graveyard.

The need to escape had clearly not been on his agenda.

But it worked, he thought, *it really fucking worked! Nora's magic changed me. We should be back there together howling at the moon in celebration.* The wild notion scampered around his brain as he attempted to problem solve, nervously rubbing the fresh scars on his ribs that ached with betrayal.

The distant screams broke, the night going still.

Tobin wheeled around, his new fur standing at attention. Nothing moved in the dark trees. He paused, erect ears pivoting, but all he could hear was his brother's labored breathing beside him. The silence consumed them, stretching into tension. Tobin's newly minted instincts insisted they had to depart. Now.

"Matrix?" The huge black dog looked up, a whine escaping with each breath. Guilt stabbed at Tobin, and he mentally dodged the painful emotion. His brother's stolen soul was still trapped in the body of a dog. It was his brother that was supposed to have been changed tonight, to regain his human form. But it hadn't worked that way. *Someone had to test the magic,* Tobin wildly reasoned. *I risked myself for Max's benefit, it was all for him. It's not my fault we were betrayed before he could be restored.* The words echoed hollowly within his head.

Tobin squatted down to run his clawed hands carefully over the beast that contained his brother. He could analyze the mistakes later, right now they had to flee. "Can you get up? I need you in the car."

The big dog struggled to stand, cried out, and slumped back to the ground. His impact with that tree clearly had consequences. Dog versus Bone Wraith was not a fair fight, but if Matrix hadn't acted, hadn't attacked, Tobin might still be enslaved to that malicious creature.

"I'll fix this," Tobin choked as he scooped up the one hundred and fifty pounds of canine and carefully settled his brother in the back seat. Part of his brain thrilled at his new strength, the move was effortless, while another part of him swore at the difficulty of prying open a pill bottle with hands that were now more paw-like and tipped with half-inch claws. He gave up and bit the top off the bottle, scattering a few pain pills in front of Matrix, adding beef jerky as a chaser. The dog complied, gulping the pills and the meat before crumpling back into the upholstery. *He must be in severe pain to check out like this,* Tobin thought

Closing his brother securely into the car, Tobin scrambled to the front and attempted to again, wedge himself into the driver's seat. Contorting his muscular torso into a c- shape, he tucked his tail between his legs and managed to smoosh himself into the subcompact. Slamming the door caused him to shred the vinyl with his claws while bashing his head into the roof, his furry knees now wedged uncomfortably around the steering wheel. There was no way he could force the seat back any further without ripping it out of the car entirely, and his tail was protesting being sat on.

One problem at a time. Tobin thought, attempting to subdue his anxiety. Frantically, he fumbled for the keys, bumping his wolfish snout on the rearview mirror, the sting making his eyes water. He checked out the window again, his hot breath fogging up the glass and his wet nose streaking across it. Nothing in the woods moved, but Tobin's imagination provided images of rust-colored bears, bathed in firelight and blood, charging towards them.

"Damnit," he snarled, trying again to fish the keys out of the cup holder where he'd left them. The keys refused to be subdued, escaping his claws to retreat under the seat, mocking his predicament. Tobin dropped his head to the steering wheel and swore colorfully. He felt like he was trying to jam a G.I Joe into a Hot Wheels car. The physics weren't in his favor.

"I'm a fucking werewolf," Tobin muttered to himself, his new enhanced sense of smell registering the odor of fear drenching the interior. This couldn't be happening. He was supposed to be the biggest, baddest creature in the forest now. He was supposed to have freed his brother from being a dog, shown Nora that everything he'd done was to help her, and triumphantly broken the bonds of magical enslavement that had fettered him for the last four years.

He was supposed to be powerful.

Yet here he sat, crushed into a cheap Kia like a discount sardine. Matrix was still a dog, Nora was probably ready to destroy him, and a bear the size of a Mack Truck had killed the creature responsible for Tobin's misdeeds. All Tobin had done was get himself turned into a werewolf and run away. But at least he was free.

This night was not going to plan.

Why hadn't Nora just listened to me? Why hadn't she trusted me? I wasn't trying to hurt her. Tobin rationalized to himself. *It's not betrayal if I'd had no choice. It was the only chance to save Max!* Tobin's eyes slid unbidden to the back seat where his brother sagged, panting in pain, furry ribs rising and falling with each hitch of breath, still cocooned in the body of a dog.

I had no choice!

A rumbling cry reverberated from the distant cemetery. The bellow of a bear in pain. Tobin jerked away from the uncomfortable feeling growing in his stomach while fear bloomed anew. He could pick apart his actions later, but now they needed to leave. And yet, as he reassessed the car problem, all he could feel was delight at his transformation. His life was going to change for the better now, he just knew it.

⋅ ∘ ◉ ∘ ⋅

MATRIX WATCHED HIS BROTHER THROUGH A HAZE OF RED PAIN and blue drugs. The area on his left side sent lightning crackling into him with each breath he took, but it was starting to mend. He didn't know what the Wraith had done to augment this dog's body to house his human soul, but he was faster, stronger, and smarter than any canine. Yet even with enhanced healing, this body remained a prison muting the man he'd been. Only magic, or pain, could stimulate his full ability to think.

And right now, he relished how his thoughts shown in bright shards of reason and understanding. Yet poor choices had led them to this moment. He appreciated that his little brother had attempted to restore his humanity, but his methods? Stalking? Drugging? Kidnapping? Magical transformation, not only of an unwilling victim, but then of Tobin himself? What had happened to his goofy little brother? Who was this monster that now held the other end of his proverbial, and literal, leash?

That monster unfurled from the car to reassume his pacing, attempting to solve a size problem. Sometimes bigger wasn't better. Matrix chuffed to himself, but the joke hurt too much, both physically and emotionally. Instead, he studied the werewolf. Standing upright at about six feet five inches, Tobin was now as broad and muscular as any linebacker, and linebackers didn't drive fuel efficient sedans.

Tobin swiveled towards him, yellow eyes glowing pewter in the starlight.

"What?" Tobin asked.

Matrix pawed slowly at his face, like he was trying to scrape it off, then shook his head, mindful of the pain that punctuated each movement.

"Huh?" Tobin blinked.

Matrix repeated the action.

Tobin cocked his head to the side, then his ears pricked up. "You want me to shift?" Matrix nodded. "I'm not sure how…"

but he closed his eyes and seemed to try. Nothing happened at first, but then Tobin began to pant like he was running.

"It…hurts." He growled, then dropped out of sight behind the car.

Wet noises, grunts of distress, and a scent close to lightning and green growing things flooded the air. Magic, he was smelling magic. The next odors were those of human sweat, wet wolf, and pain. The last faded quickly, transforming to the tingling aroma of elation.

"I did it." Tobin gasped and drew himself back onto his feet and into Matrix's view. "I fucking did it!" he whisper-yelled, pumping the air with his fists before diving back into the car, starting the engine, and gunning the little Kia down the forest road. "Let's get you home M. You're going to be okay, and this is all going to work out great, I can feel it." Tobin reached behind him, gently ruffling Matrix's fur. The dog could still smell the subtle scent of magic winding into his brother's normal musk, augmenting it and becoming something new.

Tobin was no longer human.

"This is amazing, I can see in the dark now."

Despair engulfed Matrix. Even with this second chance, he'd failed to protect and guide Tobin. Suddenly, it was all too much, he let his head fall to the seat and closed his eyes, giving in to the drugs and releasing his meager responsibilities. What else could a dog even do? He was practically powerless to help and now his little brother's life would never be the same.

CHAPTER 2

Desire Dashed

Neoma

The sound of snuffling filled the semidarkness of her dreamscape where trees towered over her and the unseen creatures melted like fog as soon as she sensed them. Neoma shuddered in anticipation, face down as warm breath puffed along her naked spine. Conjured magic tingled over her skin as a monster crept closer, her favorite fantasy making her toes curl in her sleep. Her senses expanded and contracted the sensual moment as her body responded in the waking world, longing rising as she slumbered. Heat drifted over her skin in little waves, goosebumps rippling after them. She smelled pine, rain, and male as a light touch traced her ear, a breath moving her tight curls across her cheek.

A warm body shifted around her as desire peaked and the dream tore away from her greedy mind, evaporating the sexy monster to mist, and plunking her down firmly into an unfulfilled reality. Even in sleep she couldn't get lucky.

Neoma snapped awake, her heart racing as tiny tremors rode her nerve endings like broken promises. She wanted to cry a little, she had been so close! What had happened? She was home...in bed...but—she wasn't alone. Caleb Warren had happened.

The arm twined around her embodied all the reasons she couldn't leave this little town. Something always held her back, restricting what she wanted, rewriting her life despite her best efforts. This muscular limb might as well be her chain, and the body attached to it a pretty consolation prize in lieu of her goals.

Or maybe Neoma wasn't a morning person. Either way, she had to change her current situation.

Being awake brought her attention to the pain in her elbows and hips. It had surpassed annoying and was now flirting with mild agony. Why had she said yes to Caleb last night? This went against their arrangement; fuck buddies were not supposed to include sleepovers.

This is not good for you Nae, she berated herself as she attempted to shift out from under Caleb's massive bicep. *He's not even that fun to play with. When was the last time you actually got your needs met?* The answer was too depressing to entertain. *Besides, he's never been what you're looking for, you know this.* But did she? Some days, Neoma wondered. Caleb was cute, accessible, but couldn't find her clitoris if she shaved a big arrow down there pointing it out. What was worse, he didn't seem inclined to learn, and kept thinking his manly member was enough of a showstopper. Maybe he was all that was available to her, and she should just accept her fate.

Her internal voice disagreed, and the pep talk continued. *There is more out there than cute farm boys and broken dreams. Don't settle. If you settle, you're giving up. And if you give up, what are you going to do? Sit around and rot? Rotting is not an option. Reframe your future, rediscover your purpose. There are new goals, you just need to find them.*

Now her internal voice sounded like her best friend Megan. Did that mean the brainwashing was working? *Damnit Meg, why do you have to be in my head first thing in the morning?* But Neoma knew why. Megan Logan, Meg, had moved out of this little Washington town, gone to college, and was currently living her best life as a wildlife biologist in Canada. Neoma was…well…stuck. Her ambitions of dancing in New York had lasted four years. But before she could get a firm grip on her future, that reality had wilted, shriveled, and died, forcing Neoma back home. And here she sat, trapped, trying to build a life with the dried-out pieces of desiccated dreams.

Yep, she thought, *I'm all sorts of cranky pants this morning. Heavy on the cranky, light on the pants.* And with that, she slid out from under the offending arm and slowly sat up, batting her curls out of her face as they tried to shield her further from the world and its lackluster opportunities.

"Where ya going, beautiful? Come back and snuggle, I think this spooning position might have some fun opportunities." Caleb murmured, his face still smashed into the pillow, his hand reaching out to rub her back carefully, trying to tug her gently under the covers. She had to give him that, even when he was insistent, he was always careful with her. She hated that her body needed it.

"Caleb, I have to meet Mom for breakfast. I warned you last night that if you stayed over, it would be an early start." Neoma strove to keep her crankiness in check but could tell it was leaking out around the edges. Coffee would shore up her mood, but the coffee was next door, and she was not. "Besides, you said you needed to get up early to work out, so this is your golden opportunity." She tried out a smile, it didn't crack her face, so she continued with her forced optimism.

Turning on the bed, she looked down at him. How to begin? Damnit, he did look cute in the morning. That puppy quality he possessed was accentuated with his tousled hair and big goofy grin shining at her. Maybe this arrangement wasn't as bad as she thought?

"I love waking up to you, Nae," he said while she again itemized his positive attributes. "We should do this more often, getting lucky in the morning is my favorite." He shuffled his big body closer to her. "If you want, we can finally do it doggy style this time. I mean, missionary really lets me in deep, but we should both be enjoying ourselves." He looked like he had just offered to grant all her wishes.

Cute and then he opens his mouth.

"Caleb," she warned him, her hand covering her face, "we've talked about this."

"I know, but come on. We're good together, the sex is amazing."

At least one of us thinks so. Neoma had tried talking to him several times about what she wanted and needed. Her adventurous list had been slowly truncated down to one thing: an orgasm. And he seemed unwilling to even explore that with her.

As her exhausted thoughts circled, Caleb stroked down her arm. She watched the contrast of his tan skin pale against her darker flesh. There was no warm rush at his touch, a pleasant tingle perhaps, but not the sense of connection she needed. Besides, she'd always wanted a partner who would challenge her in and out of the bedroom. Caleb was sweet, end of story. Sweet was good for cravings, but not for regular consumption. Neoma required a man who was a full course meal, able to see beyond his own pleasures, who wanted her for...well, her. Flaws included. *I'm such a cliché,* she thought bitterly.

Yet this dissatisfaction was more than skin deep. When Caleb had asked her out, she'd been lonely, and he'd looked good in his farmer's tan and tattered baseball cap. The date was nothing special, and she'd known they didn't have more than high school in common, and even then, those classes were a stretch. She'd hoped they could at least talk about books, or movies, but Caleb hadn't picked up a book since English with Mrs. Artist, and he only watched sports. For a bookstore owner, this lack of literary addiction was hard to overcome. And she couldn't care less about the batting average of a player she'd never heard of.

But the sex had scratched an itch, so she'd proposed the current, no strings attached arrangement. Simple, it was supposed to be simple. They could explore a little of what he wanted, a little of what she wanted, and everybody wins. Except, it never seemed to work that way. It was always about his needs in the moment. They would get to her later, and yet *later* never seemed to arrive.

Maybe I'm just being picky? Neoma sighed and shifted gently away.

"I gotta get ready, we can talk later." She got up slowly, shuffling towards the bathroom, her hips tight and throbbing. Neoma paused and dropped a few fish pellets for her Betta, Tugman, as he wiggled around in his bowl, excited to see her. Because a dog was not an option, Tugman was her work-around. His elegant fins flashed reds and purples in the weak light, following her finger as she pointed to his food. He was a pretty cool fish, and she smiled at him as he puffed out and danced for her. Turning away, she entered the bathroom and grabbed a toothbrush. As she scrubbed, a warm bulk materialized at her back right before arms encircled her like an anaconda.

"Caleb," she murmured, mouth full of foam.

"Come on Nae, come back to bed. Your mom lives right next door, a few minutes isn't going to make you late. I've really missed seeing you this last week, I'll be quick, promise, it'll be fun, and maybe tonight we can get together after work and go to the game." She could feel the smile on his lips as he kissed down her neck, hands holding her against a body that worked hard every day and reaped those benefits. For a moment she softened, letting her imagination take her back into the dream world that involved darker things. Taking her away from innocent farm boys trying to seduce her, giving her a whiff of pine where creatures listened to her when she told them what to do. That *wanted* her to tell them what to do.

Neoma spit out the toothpaste and locked eyes with Caleb in the mirror. "I have a schedule, please respect that." Hurt flashed across his face, and she felt his joy behind her wilt. Now she'd done it.

"Okay, sure, that's fair...I guess. But what about tonight? I'd love to take you to the game." Apparently, he didn't get discouraged easily. Neoma sighed internally.

"I feel like I'm repeating myself here. Thank you for the invite, but no. I didn't enjoy high school, and one of my great pleasures of graduating was never feeling obligated to go to another game." She wiggled past him and started pulling out clothes for the day.

"Is that because you feel awkward?"

What? She shifted to look at him. "Excuse me?"

"Well, you know, there was that big falling out you had with the rest of the dance team." His eyes darted to her and away. They both knew at least half of her old team would be at the game tonight, cheering on sons, brothers, or just for the love of football. "Then you left for New York, never contacted anyone." Clearly, he'd been listening to gossip. "And for obvious reasons, you had to come back, and you still haven't reached out to anyone." Yep, small town rhetoric was spilling out of Caleb. He stalled, struggling with his line of thinking, "But you...well you are..." he fumbled, cheeks going strawberry.

"What Caleb? I am what?" She whirled around, crossing her arms over her chest *Wow, could I get any more annoyed this morning?* Maybe it was the lack of satisfaction last night that had her on edge, coupled with her destroyed dream dalliances. She didn't want to think about that as she snatched up her dress and fumbled it over her head.

"Fine, you know what, you're a bit of a loner." Caleb spit out and leaned on the doorframe of the tiny bathroom, arms crossed, studying her as if he'd just realized she was in a bad mood, and he wasn't interested. *Huh, was he annoyed with her now? A loner? That's why he thinks I don't want to go to the game with him? As if it were that simple. Does he not get that I'm grieving? That everyone got to move on with life, and I'm having to recalculate daily. But why would he get that? He's never bothered to ask.*

So now he was exasperated by her antisocial behavior? *Well at least we're on equal footing*, she thought, irritated by everything since her dream melted away. She returned his stare with interest. Too bad her imagination got away from her again.

In the gray filtered light of morning, he looked unearthly, inhuman. An Adonis carved by gods, naked and wanting as he leaned on the doorframe. It was as if a fictional creature had stepped out of one of the paranormal romances she enjoyed. All he needed now was a sexier than sin smile, eyes to glow, or to flash a little fang. *If only,* she thought as her imagination painted that scenario, giving her time to think while pulling on leggings under her dress. The brief fantasy didn't improve matters.

Desire must have crossed her face because he came to attention like a hound scenting a rabbit and took a step towards her. *What? No, no no no no!*

"I don't think so, Caleb. This *'loner'* is going solo," she stressed his adjective. "Don't worry about locking up, and enjoy your day," her voice was tight. They looked at each other across the small space before Neoma shrugged into a light jacket, stepped into sandals, and grabbed her keys. Shuffling towards the door was as hasty an exit as she could manage with her joints grumbling at her, but at least he didn't try to stop her retreat.

Outside, the damp spring air prickled her skin with goosebumps as she made her way to her mom's house. But she couldn't walk away from this problem. No matter how hard she tried, her imagination was not going to round Caleb up to the monster, or man, of her dreams. *Shit, I really need to end this.* The bird song seemed to agree with her.

————— • • ● • • —————

NEOMA SAT AT THE KITCHEN TABLE EMBROILED IN A STARE down with a cupcake. The cream cheese frosting twinkled as the morning sun caressed its artful grooves and swirls. A delicate purple flower, encrusted in sugar, was perched on the white castle of frosting like a precious gem. It was begging to be eaten, really, truly, she could practically hear the little voice in her head calling her forward. I mean, why roll around in sugar if you didn't want to be consumed? The creator of this cupcake was trying to kill her. Neoma glared at the sparkling flower like she could make it wilt.

"Oh there it is!" Neoma's mom, Kristin, plucked the cupcake from her eye line, effectively ending the stalemate. "Neoma, you weren't going to eat that were you, honey? You know what it would do to your arthritis. That much sugar," she shook her blonde head, "your joints would hurt for weeks from the inflammation." Her mother tsked gently, not realizing she had flour on the end of her nose.

"No Mom, I wasn't going to eat it." Neoma said quietly. *Although I might have if you hadn't found it sitting there.* She carefully sat up, her body complaining softly. At least her hips and elbows had calmed down a bit after she started moving. Today was a manageable pain level, hence the temptation of the cupcake. Or perhaps she wanted to fill in that need for something satisfying after Caleb's failure to deliver, *again*. What's the use of a fuck buddy if they never got to the fun stuff?

Shoving that unappetizing thought aside, she conceded her mom's assessment of her diet. Adding inflammatory food to her system made her rheumatoid arthritis worse. The last five years had been an experiment in dealing with this disease, which had had the audacity to show up in her mid-twenties. She'd been at the New York Dance Academy for four years, and her career had been about to take off. Ballet companies were starting to take notice, and then the universe had given her RA as a graduation gift. Too bad it didn't come with a return policy because she was more than ready to kick it to the curb.

Neoma slowly crossed to the stove and prepared to make oatmeal, giving the enchanting cupcakes on the kitchen island a wide berth. "Mom, why are you doing this here? You have a whole bakery and staff who'd have done this for you. Or is there another reason? Have I really irritated you so much that you're now torturing me with your evil confections?"

Kristin snorted and dipped into the bowl for more frosting. "Oh, I could have, honey, but I really wanted to make these at home. It feels less like work and more personal." Her mom gave the cupcakes a gentle smile and finished frosting the last one, anointing it with the teasing flower. "And don't you remember? They're for Trisha's baby shower today. Aren't you coming?" Her mom raised her big sky-blue eyes to blink at her daughter, causing Neoma to quickly drop her gaze to the slowly heating pot of water.

"Mom, you know I don't really feel up to socializing…" she scrambled for a word that didn't sound so depressing. "Lately?" She should have been suspicious when her mom asked her to come over for breakfast. Why hadn't she remembered Trisha's baby shower? She wanted to blame the drugs, but her pain was low, so she was clearheaded, her joints not all on fire and swollen, just cranky, like her. She could go. Well, she could if she wanted to see all her old high school friends in one place, shooting her pitying looks while celebrating a new baby coming into this world. *No thank you.* Neoma thought, *I'd rather try and straighten my hair as I set it on fire.* Why was the universe pushing high school down her throat this morning?

"Kjære," Oh boy, Mom was getting serious, she was using Scandinavian pet names. "I'm just worried about you. All you do is go to work and come home. You don't even go to movies anymore."

"Mom, I just took Lukas last weekend."

Kristin looked down at her daughter until Neoma shrugged. "That was your little brother, not your friends, and you take him regularly. That's not what I'm talking about, and you know it."

"Mom, I know. I just…I just want some space to come to terms with all this. Ya know? It's hard enough moving back to this small town and…"

"And being a proud, beautiful, bi-racial Black woman?" Kirstin slid in there before Neoma could finish her thought.

"Yeah Mom, and that." Neoma rolled her eyes and wished for the millionth time that her dad hadn't died when her mom was pregnant with her. She appreciated her mom's undying support, but when you were the one family member who wasn't a Scandinavian Viking throw-back, it got old when people pointed it out. *Yes, my dad was Jamaican, and yes, I noticed, thank you.* Neoma rolled her eyes a second time at her internal commentary.

"I'm sorry, Kjære, what were you going to say?" Her mom reached out and tucked a stray honey-brown curl back behind Neoma's ear.

"It's nothing, really. I would rather hole up at the bookstore and work on my blog, and not have to be overwhelmed by blathering women who can only talk about marriage, babies, or what's trending on TV."

"As if you don't ever watch TV." Kristin's smile took the sting from her words.

"I know, but I don't watch reality TV. I watch dark fantasy, and no one has any idea what I'm talking about."

"Megan would." Kristin said softly, carefully squeezing her daughter's shoulder and then returning to the cupcakes.

"I know, Mom, but she's in another country, and she swore she was never coming back to this hick town. I'll send her an email later." Neoma poured in the oats, added the organic dried fruit, and began to stir. At least this disease forced her to eat healthy. She would hate to think what might happen if she could self-soothe with junk food. "You want some?"

"Only if you have enough, I went right into baking and forgot to eat."

"You always do, Mom." Neoma returned to her task, wondering if her best friend was enjoying her internship studying the migratory habits of caribou and how climate change was affecting them. At least Megan got to pursue her vision of saving the world. Neoma was still trying to pick up the fractured pieces of her dream with bleeding fingers. She often wondered if having RA would continue to shatter her remaining endeavors, or if the disease would leave her one path towards something she loved.

"Oh, and honey, I noticed Caleb's truck outside this morning. You two getting serious?" Kristin's tone was aimed at casual, but Neoma knew her mom was fishing. "He's a sweet boy, you could do worse."

"Mom!" Neoma cheeks reddened. Why was there never a pause button on life when she wanted one? Or better yet, a rewind? "You know what our," she choked on the word, "relationship is. Stop trying to make it more."

Kristin shrugged and retrieved her cupcake travel box from the top shelf. "You're playing with his heartstrings, Nae. You know that boy's been in love with you since first grade. And sure, he isn't the sharpest crayon in the box, but he has a brightness to him all the same."

Neoma's shoulders dropped, and she wiped away the condensation gathered on her face from the boiling oatmeal. She knew Caleb wanted more, but not more of what mattered. This morning had made that pretty clear. She was already stuck in this town, did she really want to be tied to a man who barely connected to her on any meaningful level? Seriously, that wasn't even a question, but what choices did she have left? She was no longer the young woman with a dance scholarship to Juilliard. The vibrant creature who'd knocked down every barrier in her path to make her dream a reality was long gone. She was a broken person now, with a body that no longer felt like it fit, twisted by rheumatoid arthritis, unable to do more than shuffle some days. Her dancing dreams were cold ashes, scattered to the winds of fate which were supposed to have carried her far away from this town and the narrow-minded people living in it. She was supposed to have found freedom. Supposed to have found her people.

At this point, she'd given up on kinship with individuals who'd share her cultural roots. She simply yearned for a group that might understand and accept who she was, where she'd feel safe, where she might belong. Megan and the blog helped with her sense of isolation, but they weren't tangible, and her mental health needed flesh and blood people, not echoes. *Is that spark for connecting dead? Do I even have it in me to keep looking for something that probably doesn't exist in this community?*

Neoma dabbed water from her face again and straightened her back as far as it was willing, steeling her resolve with every centimeter of height she gained. "Mom, I think the oatmeal's done. Want to grab me some bowls?" She would make the best of this. She had to.

CHAPTER 3

Not Top Dog

Tobin

"Matrix, do you think we lost them?" Tobin asked, a slight tremor in his hand as he pulled his new truck onto a dirt logging road, taking them deeper into the national forest just outside Portland. Two weeks had passed since the cemetery, and a full moon was due to rise any minute.

"I think Benji and Nora are trying to see if I turn tonight. That's the only reason he'd be waiting for me outside of work. Right?" Adrenaline still pumped though him as he parked the gently used Toyota Tundra up against the tree line where the road came to an end. "This place looks pretty desolate, no one should find us way out here."

Matrix pulled his head back inside the vehicle, giving a soft affirmative *woof* of agreement. Tobin glanced behind him at the nearly invisible road. There was no sign of headlights, their backtrail was clear. After turning off the truck, they got out and looked around.

"Thanks M. If you hadn't smelled Benji sitting in his truck, I would have missed him. That must be a new vehicle for him too. I don't remember it." Every night, Tobin checked the office security cameras before leaving work. He kept expecting Nora or Benji to ambush him. It's what he'd do. But nothing had happened. No contact by phone or otherwise.

Hefting a small backpack, Tobin locked up the truck and hid the keys behind a rock. Precautions taken, he looked for a game trail to lead him into the twilight dusted trees.

"Do you think it's weird that we've heard nothing from them?" he asked, but Matrix just grunted. Tobin rubbed the bite scar on his forearm, the teeth marks smooth white lines that resembled shooting stars across his skin. Nora's bite, the gift that changed him, that he'd manipulated her into unknowingly bestowing.

He traced the ridges with a finger, his thoughts about Nora still conflicted. *Would she answer the phone if I called? Does she understand why I did what I did? Or does she hate me even after I helped her unlock her true potential?* He didn't know, and he wouldn't if he kept skirting every possibility of seeing her. But manipulation and kidnapping didn't exactly paint him in the best light, and he wasn't ready to face those consequences, especially if she could undo what he'd become.

Nope, I won't let that happen. I've wanted magic my whole life. I'm not giving this power up now. Tobin thought, clenching his fists until his knuckles cracked. *Please let this work.*

Everything seemed to be riding on tonight. Had Nora's magic really changed him into a werewolf permanently? Or was that one transformation all he got? Dread flooded his throat with bitter bile, and he choked it back, pushing the thought aside. The last four years had been hell. The Bone Wraith had used him as its toy, forcing obedience by holding Max Baxter's soul hostage within Matrix's body. To restore his brother to human, Tobin had been willing to do anything, including testing Nora's new powers on himself.

Unfortunately, the Wraith had betrayed him when that magic had worked. The deception had destroyed all his careful planning, and a murderous bear had shown up, preventing Tobin from explaining to Nora why he'd needed to capture and drug her. Retreat had been the only survivable option, forcing Tobin to abandon Matrix's chance at humanity. And now Tobin needed to know if he, at least, had gained something that night.

I'm sure that's why Benji was waiting for me. They don't know if this worked either. We are all in new territory. But what does it matter to them if I can shift? Fear rushed through him as his brain spun out options. *Maybe I'm a threat to them. Maybe they need to stop me from changing?* It seemed like a reasonable possibility. Tobin got the impression that the magical community didn't like to share power. But they wouldn't track him out here. Ignoring the fear, he smiled, pushing aside a tree branch as he wove deeper into the gathering dusk. Once he knew what his new abilities were, he

A.B. Herron

could tackle the Benji problem, for now he needed to discover his potential.

Jittery, he readjusted the pack and kept going. All day he'd felt like he'd been drinking Red Bull and Rockstar on an empty stomach. The moon was coming, and his heartbeat was rising with it. An impending sense of joy infused him, carrying him forward with ravenous expectations. He just needed to get far enough into the woods to be isolated. This had to work, the moon had to make him shift.

Tobin had been trying to ignite the transformation for the last two weeks, and no matter what he did, nothing materialized. No fur, no fangs, nothing. However, things were different—he was different.

A downed log blocked their path, Tobin leapt over it without thinking, his eyesight unbothered by the encroaching dark. This deer trail smelled of musk and broken pine, and he took big gulps of air, tasting the spring growth as if he was chewing on grass stems. *I fucking love this*, he thought, listening to Matrix tracking at his heels with quiet steps while crickets hummed around them.

Nora couldn't possibly want him to give this up. Could she? Yet why had Benji been at his work today of all days? Revenge? Tobin had gotten Benji locked in a silver cage with Nora after all. *But the Wraith ordered that cage built, then ordered me to place them in it. I didn't know how powerful he was, heck, I didn't know what he was! How was I supposed to plan for bear shifters? His involvement wasn't my fault.* But the mantra was losing potency with each denial. He shuddered, checking the surroundings for movement.

If Benji was out for vengeance, all the guy had to do was shift and eat him in a place where Tobin least expected it. This abandoned swath of forest would qualify nicely. Good thing Portland traffic was a bitch.

Something tingled in his awareness. Tobin paused, acutely aware of the eastern horizon as his linear thoughts disassembled. Distracted, he looked around, his skin starting to feel too tight. This could work, the woods were thick here, no convenient meadow or clearing to give him space, but he didn't need space, he needed cover.

"M, I feel…I feel odd." Tobin quickly removed his small pack, stripping down to his boxer briefs, then stuffing clothes into the bag, securing his boots as well. The April air licked the gathering sweat from his skin in cool lingering strokes. He dumped out a package of beef jerky on a tree stump and opened a bottle of water. He didn't know what else to do. Would this be fast? Would he be able to think like the last time? *Will I be a rampaging monster?* A small part of him questioned, *Will this even work?* He shut that voice down as his stomach heaved, gooseflesh skating over his arms.

"Shit," Tobin gasped as he hit the ground on his knees. He clutched his gut, a hot sensation cutting deep across his spine. The pain twisted things inside him, and he started to tremble, moisture leaking from his pores like tree sap.

A.B. Herron

Moonlight sliced through the branches in silver swaths. Where they touched his skin, it blistered, broke, and boiled forth chestnut fur that raced over his flesh like a frothing ocean. Tobin tried to scream, but his throat contracted in a choking gasp of spasming muscles. The air throttled from his lungs as his vision swam, flashes of bright heat bursting behind his eyes. Pressure built in his skull, forcing movement, sounding like a cracking glacier, sharp and deep. Pain, his world was pain. And pleasure. Endorphins kicked in, twisting his perceptions until he couldn't tell what he was feeling, just that he *was* feeling. Sensations burned every nerve ending and made him question his ability to ever be human again.

He was drowning in the rich agony of magic as it remade him, and Tobin relished every moment.

• ◦ ◉ ◦ •

MATRIX SHUFFLED BACK FROM HIS BROTHER, A LOW, CONFUSED growl ruffling his lips. What was happening? The black and silver shadows surrounding them made him bristle, lifting the thick guard hairs off his shoulders and ruff. He couldn't protect his brother from this twisting of self, this power that Tobin had invited into his body and soul. Matrix felt helpless.

The air stank of magic, wolf, and pain. The big dog retreated further, watching as Tobin writhed on the ground, a high keening silencing the tree frogs and crickets and leaving behind the whisper and creak of branches tossed in the wind. The leftover soundtrack accentuated the creepy feeling that bled further into the area around them. Matrix didn't know where to turn, he didn't want to take his eyes off Tobin. Yet something else was moving in this silent forest, watching them. The presence had a weight, like inclement weather, prickling the dog's instincts to run for shelter. But there was nowhere to go.

Tobin gave a final grunt and lay still. Matrix crept forward only to leap backwards when Tobin sucked in a breath like a bellows inflating. One, two, and at the third inhale, Tobin rolled onto his hands and knees then shakily got to his hind paws, teetering like a newborn deer, triumph pulling him upwards.

Yellow eyes glowed in the moonlight, and Tobin braced his legs and rocked his muzzle towards the sky, clawed hands falling to his sides as his chest puffed out, lips puckering.

No mighty howl erupted into the night, instead, a rough coughing fit shook Tobin, making Matrix pin his ears back as his wolfish brother tumbled down onto his butt with a wheezing yelp. The new werewolf looked at Matrix and dropped his head, still trying to catch his breath on his claws and knees. The pungent scent of embarrassment filled the gulf between the two brothers, making Matrix sneeze with displeasure.

"Maybe..." Tobin coughed and tried again, his voice rough. "Maybe I need to take this slow." Instead, he reached for the beef jerky with a shaking claw. Matrix watched as his brother made short, slobbery, work of the food and water, the man unaccustomed to eating with an elongated snout and jagged teeth.

The big dog looked away, scanning the darkness for signs of the earlier presence. Nothing flavored the breeze, no twigs snapped, no undergrowth moved. Had he imagined the silent watcher? Matrix shook his head and veered back to Tobin, approaching slowly, and nudging the werewolf with his nose.

"I'm ok M, really. Actually," Tobin paused and got to his changed feet, towering over the black dog, "I feel fucking fantastic!" He took a few tentative steps and bounced on his paw-like toes, warming up, shaking out his upper arms, flexing and opening his clawed hands before pulling out the snug waistband of his underwear and giving a relieved nod. "Everything accounted for." Tobin grinned like a maniac, and Matrix puffed air in agitation.

Tobin laughed, lurched into a shaft of moonlight, and froze. Matrix watched as his brother went still, his chestnut fur making him look black in the undergrowth. An almost slack-jawed expression flowed over Tobin's face, the werewolf's body going liquid.

"I hear you." Tobin whispered. "I'm coming." And he bolted deeper into the forest, running like a whisper through the trees. Matrix growled and took off in hot pursuit, following Tobin's silhouette that seemed to glow with the moonlight as if he were a reflection on water. The big dog snarled as he ran, his protector duties were being put to the test.

THE ASCENT UP THE SMALL MOUNTAIN WAS SURPRISINGLY effortless. Tobin bounded over downed trees like they were bumps in a sidewalk, moving through thick brush as if it were tissue paper. The trail he left behind him didn't cross his mind. He was a tank with fur, no obstacle was going to stand in his way. *She* was calling.

The top of the hillock was bare, the tree line receded from past harvesting. Yet here, the moonlight fell unfiltered. It brushed over Tobin's new fur coat with the caress of a lover. He wiggled with unabashed joy, his tail wagging as he dashed up to the tippy top.

"Yes," he cooed, his snout tipping back, baring his throat to the moon. "I'm here." He spread his muscled arms wide, feeling the moonlight as if it was a presence that he might embrace, or a liquid he might imbibe, a cosmic tractor beam that he could de-atomize into and fly up to the stars to live forever in her light. Now this—this was a fitting place to howl his love song to the heavens. How could he have thought otherwise?

Again, he pulled air into his lungs, feeling his vocal cords start to vibrate in anticipation.

CRACK!

A hard object impacted the side of his skull, tearing the tip of his sensitive ear. The force spun him like a football, the world going dizzy until he landed in a crouch.

A.B. Herron

"What the fuck?" He growled, holding up a clawed hand to the wound. The smell of copper perfumed the air as liquid splashed his palm. What had struck him? Something moved at the edges of the trees as another object punched his nose and sent a blinding burst of pain up his snout and behind his eyes.

"This territory is not yours, man-wolf." A high-pitched bleat cut the darkness. "You dare to trespass here without permission?" Another projectile struck Tobin in the ribs, and he yelped, backing away from the voice.

"Who are you? Show yourself, coward!" He snarled as another shot landed in his vulnerable stomach. "FUCK!" Enraged, Tobin spun, attempting to get back to the woods, but every direction he tried was met with another strike from nowhere. The impacts were making him bleed, but he was healing almost as fast as the damage was happening. It didn't make them hurt any less, the pain lingering in his tissues like noxious fumes.

"What do you want!" he wailed at last, tucking into a tight ball to protect all his tender bits. "How can I be trespassing? This isn't anyone's land!"

"You assume, you trespass, you think like a human." The piercing voice spit venom as something struck Tobin's butt, slicing through his underwear and thick fur. "You are not human anymore, man-wolf. Your ignorance will not protect you."

Fear flooded Tobin, his mind blinking back to the cemetery as a Kodiak bear rampaged towards him in a killing frenzy. He had known that bear in human skin and never guessed that Zayden had been any more than ordinary. What else was he ignorant about? Had he made a terrible mistake coming this far out into the woods for his first transformation? If he'd stayed closer to the city, would other magical creatures be deterred by the sheer mass of humanity? What if this attacker was worse than the Bone Wraith? What if it could enslave him too?

He hunkered down tighter, trying to breathe through the panic while his limited knowledge of mythical creatures tumbled through his brain, each one more fearsome than the last. Logic, he had to use logic to fight this, but scenting the air wasn't working, every time he tried to raise his nose to the wind it became a target. Besides, a scent ID probably wouldn't help him, he had nothing to compare it to.

Inexperience be dammed, since when did a werewolf have to hide? He fumed, fury kindling deep in his belly, slowly eating away at his terror as another object ricocheted off his spine and plunked down in front of him. He sniffed it, it smelled like goat. This wasn't magic striking him, these were ordinary rocks. His brain made a connection, he knew what was attacking him. *I'm going to make this creature pay.*

MATRIX REACHED THE EDGE OF THE CLEARING IN TIME TO SEE the first strike make Tobin bleed. Instead of lunging out into the open, he carefully prowled the tree line, creeping as only a shadow could through the dark. Whatever was attacking, it was moving quickly, and seemed to be using the trees to get from one vantage point to the next. Matrix smelled musk, magic, and violence. Whatever this thing was, it was happy to assault his brother. It was having fun.

⚬ ⚬ ● ⚬ ⚬

"Forgive me," Tobin affected a grovel, hoping the lore about Fey pride held true. "I didn't know I trespassed on land held by one as formidable as yourself. You're right, I'm unaware of the magical creatures out here, I'd like to learn." His deference burned, but maybe he could lure this assailant out into the light. He needed his suspicions confirmed if he was going to have a chance.

A snort sounded to his right, and he dared to glance that way. "You are overawed by me?" The nasally voice sounded amused. "I am but a servant to a great master. If I make you quake, you will not live long in this world. As to what prowls in the unknown? I see no reason to teach you, but I will give you this. Man once knew but has relegated us all to children's stories and myths. Humans are blinded by your gods, shielded by ignorance alone. If you do not remember that we exist, we cannot harm you. A simple and terrible spell, one that no longer protects *you*. Learn fast man-wolf, or you will be prey."

The insult did not need translation. Tobin lurched to his feet growling and leapt in the direction the voice had originated. "I'm not prey!" he bellowed, and his claws swiped through what he thought was a warm body, only to feel his nails biting into thick tree bark and sticking fast.

A tsking sounded to his left. Tobin whirled his head, his claws immobile. Something climbed out of the shadows to stand on a fallen log. The figure was only three feet high, but as the moonlight illuminated it, Tobin gasped and tried to wrench his arm free without success. The creature was stunted, spiked horns sticking out of a tangled head of hair and a wrinkled face that scarcely passed for humanoid. The skin on its upper body resembled a browned and bruised apple, while it's lower half was covered in curly pelt, knees bent deeply, and black hooves instead of toes.

"Stop," the creature spit. It turned to the side to look past Tobin and addressed the shadows. "I will not harm him further if you do not intervene," it bleated.

Tobin's eyebrows rose and surprise skittered down his spine as Matrix stood up, two feet from the small creature.

"My master's ire is not with you. You are becoming. He," and the creature indicated Tobin, "is a blundering fool with no power, no protection, and no pack. The man-wolf was not invited, he was invented, and he has no place here."

Tobin blinked as Matrix slowly sat down, a low rumble trembling the air.

"I understand, I will get to my point. But," warped hands rubbed together, "this man-wolf is so much fun to play with. All that potential and no control. I can make him twist like greenwood in a fire." A cruel smile split the melted features of the creature, making it look even more alien than it first appeared.

"You're a faun." Tobin snarled. The goatish figure bobbed its misshapen head in assent.

"How nice of you to name me, as if I were of feeble mind. I know well what I am, and my place. I guard these woods. The trees, they told me you were here. They drank in your pain and pleasure as the moon's magic made what it would of you. Just because you wear fur tonight, you think you belong here." It sneered, its almond-colored skin wrinkling around a flattened nose.

Blinded by fury, Tobin couldn't respond. This pint-sized creature, this grass-eating abomination of twisted goat was lording over him like it was some woodland prince. Tobin was a fucking werewolf! This thing should be running in terror. "My fangs are bigger than yours goat-boy." As insults went, Tobin needed to do better. "Come closer and see how powerless I really am." He threw all his weight into pulling free as he snapped his slavering jaws like a rabid wolf in the faun's direction.

Lances of red pain filled his world as the tree held and his shoulder yielded, ligaments snapping, burning with the enthusiasm of a lit fuse. Tobin fell to his knees, sniveling, tears and snot coating his face in a sticky morass as he struggled to stay conscious in a world washed red. Two breaths passed, ten, then the red haze cleared. With a sickening *pop*, his shoulder sucked back into place. This time, the fireworks glittered blue, the pain easing as his flesh molded itself whole. The tightening of ligaments flashed yellow through his head, and he struggled back to his paws to give his shoulder more slack.

The little creature was laughing at him.

"You are as bad as a wolf in a trap of cruel iron. You do not take heed of the danger you are in. You are only concerned with wrenching yourself from that which holds you." The faun's judgment of Tobin's intelligence stank of fetid scat. "That tree will not release you until I ask it to. You have no authority here. Remember that, man-wolf."

"What do you want from me?" Tobin ground out, spitting away blood from where he had bitten through his tongue. Breathing heavily, he slumped against his wooden prison.

The faun leaned forward, gnarled fingers resting on its furry knees. "My master wants you to leave." Its eyes danced in wicked delight as Tobin blinked.

"Leave?" Tobin was indignant. "Fine, fine. Let me go, and I'll head back to my truck and drive away."

"No no. Again, you think too simply. You must leave the city."

"What? No, I live here."

"Here? Come come man-wolf, here you do not live. I live here. You only trespass when you think you are wild. We both know the truth, you are but a human wearing fur, pampered and tame."

"I am a werewolf! Look at me! Magic sings in my veins." Tobin screeched, gesturing at himself, desperate bloody spittle flying.

"The only magic you hold, you stole."

The cold words hit Tobin in the chest like an ax. He flinched away, yellow eyes squeezing shut to block out the truth. The faun cackled as Matrix growled.

"You want me to leave Portland? Where would you have me go?" Tobin whispered.

"Awe, intelligence blooms like mushrooms. At last." The small creature rubbed its hands together and addressed Matrix. "I knew if I broke him in the right spot he could bleed reason."

Matrix jumped up and barked, snarling at the faun who leapt to its hooves with startling speed and held out a steadying hand. "Peace." It swung back to Tobin.

"You, cross the river, go into unclaimed territory. South of the river belongs to my master. The North side…" Its smile was a slash of darkness. "That side is for those that do not belong, who have not proven their worth or their loyalty. That should fit you well man-wolf, that is, if you can survive there alone."

Tobin's head was spinning from this creature's convoluted instructions. Go north? Washington? And do what? Would Vancouver be far enough? He didn't want to leave Portland, it was his home, his job was here, his friends. He glanced at Matrix, the only family he had left. The big dog looked back at him and slowly wagged his tail, his head tilting to the side in a doggy shrug.

Matrix was right, what choice did Tobin have? If the very trees could be used against him, he couldn't stay here and risk pissing off whoever this "master" was. He fumed, hating being powerless once again.

"What about Nora?" he spat. "She's been living here for years."

"Nora?" The faun tipped its head sideways, one thick nail tapping on its bearded chin.

"The other werewolf, the one who made me," Tobin snarled.

The faun rose slowly, moonlight casting its shadow long and dark across Tobin, obscuring the misshapen creature's features. "Go north man-wolf, pack-less one." The voice made fur rise all over Tobin's body. "Your ignorance and weakness offends these woods. If the trees hear you here come the next full moon, there will be no leniency." The faun snorted and with a twitch returned to the gloom under the trees.

———— •◦◉◦• ————

MATRIX WATCHED THE LITTLE CREATURE SCAMPER INTO THE ferns, muted greens and browns moved along in its wake like ripples on a pond. The trees around them seemed to sigh, and Tobin suddenly fell to the ground as his claws came free. The big dog lumbered over, nudging his brother with his nose, a questioning whine pulling at his throat.

A.B. Herron

"What are we going to do?" Tobin's yellow eyes still glowed softly with the moon's light. Matrix stepped forward until his shadow eclipsed his brother's face, lest the werewolf fall under the moon's spell again. "Thanks M." Tobin roughly got to his paws, teetering for a moment before catching his balance and rubbing his newly healed shoulder. Matrix beheld spots of glowing red where the pain lingered in his brother's tissues.

With a wet nose to Tobin's hip, Matrix gently encouraged the werewolf back the way they'd come. The dog could still smell the faun, still feel the creature's malevolent intent trained on them as they made their way to where Tobin's pack was stashed. It wasn't until they reached the edge of the clearing with the truck did Matrix's hackles fall. The wild magic of the forest seemed to pull back from the edge of the road as if repelled, and they stepped onto ground that felt somehow malnourished. It was a hollow feeling that diminished Matrix's human thoughts. He almost ran back to the woods. Instead, he accepted the inevitable and trudged forward. After all, he was only a dog, he'd have to make the best of it.

"Well M, I guess we wait here until the moon sets." Tobin looked defeated, his tail and ears drooping as he sank into the shadow cast by the truck, avoiding the moon's light. "Do you think it would be safe to…?" With a furtive glance around, he tipped his head back to try one more howl.

Something whizzed out of the forest and sliced Tobin's cheek, ricocheted off the truck, and spun into the night leaving a scratch in the gray paint.

"Fucking damn it!" Tobin screamed.

Matrix sighed and laid down to wait. Watching as a werewolf threw gravel at the surrounding woods, kicking and swearing, until the sky lightened, and the moon gave up her dominion.

CHAPTER 4

Balloons and Bitches

Neoma

N eoma tugged on her dress as she stood with her mother in front of the bright purple door. A garish wreath of taffeta festooned with baby bottles, rattles, and ribbons hung in front of her nose announcing the sex of Trisha's "bun in the oven." Balloons that flashed, "It's a girl!" fluttered in silvers and pink all the way from the mailbox to the ornamental shrubs guarding the stoop. The sun bouncing off the mylar left spots dancing in Neoma's eyes.

"I can't do this," she muttered under her breath.

"Yes, you can." Kristin took her daughter's arm gently in hers, balancing the cupcake box to the side. "Your friends will be pleased to see you. Besides, you and Trisha used to dance all the time. She misses you." The wild yapping of a small dog punched through the wooden door, reassuring the occupants that the doorbell did, in fact, ring. Just in case they hadn't noticed.

"Do you think they're having a boy?" Neoma asked sweetly.

"Nae!" The door flew open releasing a small white dog that resembled a cotton ball as Kristin choked off her laugh. "You came!" Miss Mache, Trisha's mom, nearly yelled as she stifled Neoma in a hug. "I wasn't sure you would."

"Thanks for having us." Kristin smoothly interceded, handing Neoma the cupcakes and leading Miss Mache back into the house while deftly avoiding the exuberant dance number being performed around their ankles. Neoma trudged in behind them, closing the door. *I wonder if hell is decorated with mylar?*

The sounds of giggling and gossip led them down the hall and out into a backyard fluttering with crepe paper streamers in every shade of pink. More balloons tugged at their tethers, trying to reach the sky, and a table overflowing with gift bags almost groaned as Neoma added the small card and children's book to the onslaught. A few bags dared to be individuals, populating the pink with hints of purple, yellow, and green, but someone had tucked them deeper in the pile. Neoma looked down at her light blue dress and cringed.

"Well hello stranger," a high voice said from behind her. Neoma swung around to come face to face with Miranda, the former head of the cheerleading squad.

"Miranda, good to see you." Neoma worked hard to make her hug seem effortless as she embraced the other woman. She noticed Miranda's dress was white with little pink flowers drifting across it.

"Well, it's been a minute. What have you been up to? Dating anyone?" Miranda gave a polite smile. "Mark and I are going to be celebrating our seven-year wedding anniversary this summer. Can you believe it? It seems like only yesterday he was leading our team to State, and now he's coaching. That man of mine, you just can't keep him down."

"Congratulations. You must be very proud." Neoma ran out of things to say. High school was so far from her mind, she barely remembered that Mark had taken the football team to State their senior year, let alone been aware of what the current team was doing. Last time she'd seen Mark, he'd been crossing the street to the local bar with some other guys. They appeared to be recounting their glory days by tossing around invisible footballs, while shoving each other like teenagers.

"So when are you going to settle down and start kicking out your own brood?" Miranda asked, then her hand flew to her mouth. "Oh, I'm so sorry. Can you still have kids? You know, with your condition?"

Neoma wanted to drag her hand down her face. "Arthritis doesn't prevent someone from having kids. It's not like it petrified my uterus or something." She thought about adding more but stopped.

"Oh, you sure? Well that's great to hear. Mark and I are thinking of having a third. You know, it's so much fun to try." Her nose wrinkled with her smile as she sipped her blatantly alcohol-free soda from the can with a straw. "Of course, I would have to take maternity leave again from the junior high school if we don't plan this right. You know, they just can't seem to run that office without me. Good thing too, it ensures they can't get rid of me." She winked, "Not that they would want to. But I don't know what we'd do without that great insurance package. Kids are always falling off something. But enough about me, what are you doing nowadays? Still working at the bookstore part-time?"

"Full-time. I own part of the business."

"Really? Well, that was super nice of your mom to let you do that. I'd imagine having a job makes you feel useful." Her smile blazed as Neoma fumbled with what to say, the barb sinking deep.

"Well, between running the store, and maintaining a few blogs, I don't have much time to eat bon bons or wallow in self-pity," Neoma said, her smile brittle.

"Blogging? Really? How interesting. That's great to hear, I mean you know what they say about idle hands." And she winked again. "Glad you're busy, although that seems surprising. Aren't bookstores a bit of a sinking ship? I mean, doesn't everyone just order books off Amazon these days?" Miranda took another sip, rubbing her belly and swaying back and forth as if rocking a child.

"Actually, we have a very loyal following." *You bitch.* "Did you know we also showcase local and Pacific Northwest authors? We have a great author coming in next week. You should stop by. Bring your mom and she can pick up the books she ordered." Neoma smiled innocently. "Oh, but I should warn you," Neoma said, dropping her voice, "the author writes adult romances. Your mom loves them, but they're quite spicy and a bit above the eighth grade reading level to be sure." Neoma reached forward and patted her arm. "Excuse me, Miranda, it was nice to see you. I gotta go say hi to Trisha before things get started. Be sure to tell Mark I said hello."

Neoma swirled and glided away, begging her body for every bit of strength and grace she had previously possessed. Her body, for once, didn't let her down, and she could almost feel Miranda's hot eyes burning into her back. Because ballet was no longer her full-time obsession, her physique had changed since senior year. But she hadn't gone quietly into this dark night of depression and disease. Nope. When she could, she continued to push her physical limits, trying to stay strong and keep moving. Today she refused to shuffle, today she would dance.

However, her triumphant glide of escape came to an abrupt halt as she nearly collided with another woman dressed in pink cotton with white polka dots. *Was the dress code in the invite and I missed it?* Neoma wanted to groan but the woman turned and made eye contact.

"Neoma, oh, you *actually* came," Paris's tone implied she didn't care.

"Apparently," Neoma stalled as Paris's dark eyes moved over her like a slow-motion security camera.

"Huh, you still don't look sick to me. Pity. Oh, and before I forget, so sad about your health affecting New York. But maybe you just weren't as good as you thought." Paris looked down as a small child grasped her leg and tugged at her skirt.

"Momma, can I go play with Billy on the slide?" The little girl was the spitting image of her mom, dark hair and eyes, milk pale skin, and a polka dotted dress.

"Not today Starla, you might get your dress dirty. Go join Honey at the crafts table." The child stuck out her lip but didn't say anything, her eyes snagging on Neoma.

"Hi," Neoma gave a small smile and held out her hand. "I'm Neoma, nice to meet you Starla."

"Momma," the kid whispered out of the side of her mouth, "is that Princess Tiana? Are you friends with her?" Starla's eyes were wide even as she moved her body further behind her mom until her little fingers and face were the only visible parts of her.

Neoma watched Paris's back stiffen, and almost chuckled before the other woman snapped, "No, Starla, Neoma is no friend of mine, and definitely not a princess." Her eyes blazed brown fire before adding, "But give her a few more years and perhaps this town will finally have its Quasimodo." The little girl scrunched up her forehead, clearly confused. Neoma, however, had just been verbally slapped by a Disney insult. *When was this high school shit going to end?*

"Paris," Neoma placed her hand on Paris's arm and the woman's head spun to her, almost shaking off Neoma's touch.

"How about we call a truce today, ok? I won't call you words that start with a *B*, and you won't act like you're the best color in the rainbow. Deal? I mean, it's been what, over ten years since we've even spoken? Let's bury this hatchet."

"Momma, what's a hatchet?"

Paris stepped in so close that Neoma could smell the strawberries on the other woman's breath. "You stole that scholarship from me, and then you wasted it. You're not the only one who wanted to escape this hellhole." Her voice was all strawberry frost, slicing Neoma like icicles.

"I wasn't the one who showed up for the audition pregnant." Neoma muttered back. "You made your choices, that's not my fault," she hissed, but guilt bloomed anyway. *I'm not responsible for Paris losing the baby. I'm not. I didn't push her to train that hard. I earned that scholarship regardless of her condition.* Neoma shoved hard at her remorse, forcing it into the past before it could gain a foothold. Yet she couldn't help but wonder if Paris would have secured the dance scholarship if Neoma hadn't been there. Hadn't interfered? Her gut clenched. *If I'd known what was going to happen to me, would I have made different choices?*

She tried to flinch away from that internal dialogue but one more thought echoed through her mind, *How many other people's lives have been derailed by this disease?* Neoma's blood boiled, and her stomach dropped. She didn't want to think about all this, she knew she shouldn't have come.

"Neoma!" A vibrant voice cut through the tension making Paris jerk backwards. Her dark eyes continued to smolder with fury before she spackled on a friendly smile. The transformation looked painful.

They both turned as a petite blonde woman waddled forward, her large belly splaying her feet sideway like a duck's.

Neoma couldn't help herself, she laughed, tension leaving her in a rush of exhausted breath. "Trisha, is that really you?"

"Better believe it." Trisha chuckled and rubbed her bulging stomach. "I keep asking if there are three kids in here, but the doctor assures me there's only one. I'm so glad you made it." She gave Neoma a warm, but awkward hug. There was a gauche distance between them, but if it was caused by the baby bump or the years of neglected friendship, Neoma couldn't tell.

Miranda had joined the small group and seemed to be whispering with Paris as Trisha inquired about the bookstore and Kristin's bakery. Miranda broke up the friendly conversation by ringing a small pink bell and announcing to the group it was time to play games and then open the presents.

"The first game will be Guess that Poop!" Mothers all around started laughing as everyone made their way to the chairs on the lawn. Miranda linked arms with Trisha, pulling her onwards as the pregnant mom-to-be shot an apologetic glance back at Neoma.

Paris spoke, surprising Neoma. "I know what you're doing with my cousin." *You bitch* was implied. "Don't fuck him up like you do everything else," Paris said and kept walking, not even acknowledging she'd spoken to Neoma as she stalked away. The chill of her passing prickled Neoma's skin, the words leaving a hole in her gut as the temperature of the spring day seemed to plummet.

Neoma blinked rapidly, turning her gaze skyward, trying to find an inkling of calm in the sea of her rolling emotions. *Mom, you gotta get me out of here, or inflammation be damned, I will eat that cupcake.*

※ ※ ※

STARS SPARKLED OVERHEAD LIKE SNOWFLAKES CAPTURED ON black velvet. Neoma sat back and let her body swing lazily in the hammock, the movement lulling her into dreams of endless ocean and boats to faraway lands. The stress of her day melted, letting her mind drift into the sky, her aches and pains going with it.

Tonight was the full moon, the weather obliging with markedly decent visibility and low temperatures. Clouds amassed in the west, leaving the east a transparent window into the heavens. Suspended between trees, Neoma mimicked a caterpillar inside a faux fur cocoon, awaiting the rising sun to hatch. Even as the cold threatened to lock up her joints, she relished the sensation. Cold always brought her comfort, a soothing touch that turned her breath to crystals, and tasted like snow as it nibbled at her lips with frigid teeth. She smiled and licked at the frosty flavor.

"Nae, are you even listening to me?" The voice chuckled into her ear. Neoma adjusted the phone. "Or have you been abducted?

"Will you believe me if I claim the latter? Or should I just plead the fifth?" Neoma watched a satellite make its noiseless sprint across the black.

"You know I love you to pieces, otherwise I wouldn't bother answering when you call." Megan sounded tired, her humor slightly forced.

"I hear a 'but' coming."

"But," Megan snorted, "you're avoiding tackling the real reason for this call. And I know it has nothing to do with sugar flowers and Trisha's baby shower. You don't reach out so late unless something's bugging you."

"The baby shower sucked."

"I can imagine. Was Miranda there?"

"Yep. In all her inflated, small town, holier-than-thou, glory."

"I bet you knocked her down a peg at least."

"Yeah, but Paris was right behind her. I almost ran into her, literally."

"Oh, I bet she loved that. I'm surprised you're still alive."

Neoma gave a small snort of laughter. "Did you know she has a daughter?"

"Yep," Megan sighed, "Facebook stalking is my hobby when the internet is up. She looks like a little carbon copy of her mom."

"She's going to think the same too, with the way Paris is raising her."

"Nae, you don't know that. Kids always have a chance of becoming their own person. Don't assign this kid her mom's biases, it just unfairly stacks the deck against her."

"You're right, I'll give her a chance if we ever run into each other again. But I'm not sure I can handle round two with Paris, it was pretty brutal."

"She brought up the scholarship again, didn't she?"

"Yep."

Megan gave an exhausted sigh. "Nae," she admonished, "beating yourself up over something that happened in high school, that you—dang it, Nae, we all make stupid mistakes, it's how we learn not to make them again. Have you thought about just talking to Paris? Maybe try clearing the air and your conscience?"

"Nope, no way, we are not going there, Meg. I only brought it up to tell you I didn't fold and run away this time, I stood up to her. Not that it made me feel like the better person." Neoma worried at the edge of the blanket.

"Nae, what happened back then wasn't your fault."

"Sure, whatever."

Megan sighed.

"It just wasn't the same without you to back me up, that's all. We were unstoppable, the two of us, and I miss...us."

"We still are us, Nae, we're just further apart."

"I miss you." Neoma whispered across the lonely distance. "I look up and think about you out there doing what you always talked about and, it just...Megan, I still don't know what to do with myself. How do I find my true north when I feel like I've dropped my compass?"

The quiet that stretched between them filled with moonlight as the moon crested the neighbor's rooftop, carving black shadows with sharp edges. Even the stars dimmed with her arrival. If only the moon could shed light on what Neoma should be doing.

"You're still writing." The reply was soft, and Neoma could hear the whisper of wind over the phone.

"Yes."

"Well, that's something—something worthwhile. I've been reading your blog." Neoma tensed. "It's good Nae, it's really good. And more importantly, it sounds like you're helping out other people with RA, giving them more of a community, a support system. Why are you not following your own advice and leaning on them in turn?"

"I, well, it sounds silly." Neoma stretched out of her cocoon and pulled on the rope to get her swinging, before tucking her arm back inside the faux fur. She watched the sky sway. Megan waited patiently while she absorbed the pendulous movements, letting them soothe her. "If I reach out and join the rest of them, I feel like I'm giving up. Like once I admit I need help, there's no going back. I'll never be rid of this disease, and every year it's stealing a little more of my life and my independence."

"Oh Nae," the sigh was filled with pain and understanding. "You can't do this alone my friend. And you know I'm always here for you."

"When you're not out chasing caribou."

"Well, yeah, that. But seriously, you need to find a community there. Maybe even Portland? You're still driving ok, right?"

"Yeah, mostly, but some days I can't. However, the heated seat in the car helps, so I make it work. But it isn't something I want to do regularly." Neoma's back ached just thinking about it.

"Any chance one of the new medications worked?"

"Nope, not a one." Neoma sighed, her body seemed to reject every arthritis drug out there except for over-the-counter drugs and cannabis. She couldn't take the regular anti-inflammatories daily because they were hell on her digestion. At least the CBD products offered her some small relief, even if they didn't treat the cause.

"That really sucks." Megan rarely said she was sorry; Neoma hated that response and was grateful for her friend's discretion.

"Well, hey, I still have my sense of humor." She chuckled weakly.

"Yes, don't lose that. But back to my point about support systems." Neoma groaned. "Hey now, I'm just saying be open to new things. Communities change, even ones the size of Kelso. I mean come on, you tried swimming and that worked out ok, right?"

Swimming was the one activity that seemed to keep Neoma mobile, and she appreciated the feel of the warm salt water moving over her skin. The people at the pool were pretty kind, and the retired women's water aerobics class had adopted her with open arms. Still, putting on a swimsuit and bobbing around with the White Haired Wonders, as they called themselves, left her feeling self-conscious. Despite that, she'd forced herself to go twice a week. Her athletic tendencies not allowing her to become a lump on the couch.

"Yeah, it did, but Meg, no one understands me."

"You think it might be because you don't let anyone in?" The response was gentle, but it still landed like a blow.

"Ouch."

"You're wallowing. You told me never to let you wallow." The moon now hung suspended like an opaque soap bubble lifting off into the night.

"Point." Neoma steeled herself for the next subject. "What do I do about Caleb? Turns out, Paris knows I'm sleeping with him."

"OooOooo. I bet she didn't like that. How'd she find out?"

"I'm sure he told her. They've always been more like siblings than cousins, especially after Paris's mom passed. I think she practically lived at Caleb's house after that."

"Well, Paris's dad was a piece of work."

"Yeah, he was." They both fell silent, the past tightening around them for a moment. Neoma shook it off and refocused on the present. "Anyway, I can't stand that she knows. It makes this even worse. What do I do?" Neoma clutched the phone harder, Paris's parting words still stinging.

"Oh Nae, Paris's feelings don't get to dictate your actions with Caleb. And if he isn't taking your needs into account, then that's selfish. You can't change that, so don't try, he has to. He's sweet, but it sounds like he has this rosy vision of you and him that he's labeled as love, but it's hollow. If he was really able to be a fuck buddy, and you know deep down that he isn't, then I'd give you my blessing. But his heart, as it is, wants you, and your heart is still floating out there with the moon." Megan knew her so well. "You can't be who you wanted to be. So be who you are. Let the world behold that amazing, creative, incredible human. Live like you used to, large and loud. Caleb is only seeing what he wants to, don't settle for someone who can't see you."

"I'm not sure how to do that. That's the problem." Neoma hated how small her voice sounded.

Megan scoffed. "You're kidding me, right? You just faced down two of the most passive-aggressive bullies from school and you stood tall. That fire is still in you. Besides, words remain yours to command, they haven't been stripped from you. Come on, Nae, the internet is your playground, and the potential there is unlimited." Neoma could hear frustration crackle in her friend's voice and pulled the blankets closer around her as if they could shield her from Megan's ire.

"You are more than your body. You remember this right? Your imagination is worth a second look, and no one ever gets to glimpse that. Ever since high school, you have filled up notebooks with stories. Okay, so you don't have the future you planned on, but you still have a gift that you can use. So, use it and write. At the very least write the world you want, because I know if you don't write, your heart is going to start bleeding ink."

"That sounds dramatic," Neoma said dryly, even as she appreciated the visual.

"Shut up, I'm talking." Megan huffed and kept going. "So what if you don't get to dance on stage in New York? You could still have a book reach the top of the New York Times Best Seller list. That will get you seen. That will help you find more of 'your people,' so you can stop lamenting about how alone you are. *Where* you are no longer defines *who* you are. There are no more borders. Not with the world being so connected nowadays. Now stop acting like you're trapped by this disease. Your body might be limiting, but your mind still has room to grow. Don't hobble it with your fear." Megan finished with a woosh, almost breathing hard. Neoma blinked, the moon looking fuzzy.

"Have you thought about a career as a life coach?" Neoma finally asked.

"You can't afford me," Megan chided.

"No doubt, woman. Where did all that come from?"

"We still have a lot of snow up here, and the last occupant left philosophy and self-help books lying around. You know me, I get bored. I read things."

"And then you know things."

"It's so true." They both giggled like kids.

"Thanks Meg, I needed this."

"Sure, sure. You can thank me by actually doing something with this priceless advice." Megan's voice softened. "Please Nae, try?"

Neoma heard the depth of her friend's worry for her in those little words. Her heart cracked at the fear that undercut the conversation. The worst part was that fear echoed her own. Was she more than her ability to move? To dance? RA seemed to eat her identity day by day. Each swollen joint a pyre, the vestiges of her active life burned slowly away by inflammation. Her deteriorating mobility shackling her further from her joy with each flare. Would there be any of herself left when it was done? Or would an empty husk of pain and drugs be all that remained? If she didn't at least try, she would be stranded with the latter.

"For you, Meg, I'll give it a whirl."

"Not for me Nae, for you."

Neoma watched the moon twinkle through her lashes as she disconnected. Enough of this wallowing. She'd cried twice today, and she was stronger than this. Tomorrow, she would send out the short stories she'd been working on, then she would have that talk with Caleb. The hammock rocked, as if in agreement, making the moon wobble on its course.

CHAPTER 5

Doublewide Disagreements

Tobin

T obin took Benny's offered hand, trying not to grip too hard but noticed the other man wince anyway. He let go quickly.

"This is really it then? You're seriously going to leave Portland for good?" Benny asked while Marsha embraced Tobin in a quick hug, sniffling slightly into his shirt. Tobin awkwardly patted her shoulder as she released him.

"I guess so. Umm, thanks guys, for everything. You really made me feel welcome here." Tobin ran out of words. He had no family to say goodbye to since his parents and grandparents had died when he was younger. His closer friends were few and online, and he'd been avoiding the runners since he'd become a werewolf. His social life really had boiled down to work colleagues. *I guess I really am a lone wolf. That does make keeping my secrets a lot easier.*

Tobin shrugged at the realization. *Besides, people are messy, distance is always simpler.*

"Well, it won't be the same at the shelter without you." Benny gave Matrix a final scratch on the ears as the big dog lowered his head out the truck window for Marsha to kiss. "You've been one of our best animal control officers these last six years, I guess all that recreational running was good for something." Benny laughed, the man wouldn't break out of a walk if his pants were on fire.

"You have no idea," Tobin agreed placidly.

"If you come back through town, be sure to stop by," Marsha sniffed. "I'm so sorry that you developed that intense cat allergy, you were always so good with them. But your health is important. I love that you found an exciting opportunity in Washington, I knew your computer skills were being undervalued here." Pride gleamed in her eyes as she gave him a final hug. "Keep in touch, okay?" Marsha's attempts to mother him were continually unsuccessful, but he had to admire her doggedness.

"I'll do my best." Tobin promised, knowing he would probably never see his coworkers again. As for his fictitious cat allergies, that was prudent lying for survival. Ever since his change, those razor blade wielding furballs had all decided he needed to die. If the faun hadn't forced him to leave his job, the cats would have.

"Okay, well, off to my new adventure. Bye."

FOUR HOURS LATER, TOBIN TOOK STOCK OF HIS NEW LIFE. The rental house, and house was generous, wasn't much to look at, but it wasn't the interior he was interested in. The important features included proximity to the woods, isolation, and that the owners leased to someone with a giant dog and asked no questions. For what he needed, it was perfect.

"Well, brother," Tobin addressed Matrix, "home sweet home, I suppose. Want to go for a run?" The dog huffed out a huge sigh and shook himself. It wasn't the most enthusiastic of agreements, but Tobin would take it. The preparations to leave Portland seemed to have sucked the joy out of Matrix, his brother becoming more distant with each packed box.

"Come on, M, talk to me. What's eating you?" Tobin asked. Matrix shifted his head to look at Tobin, his eyebrows raised. "Really, I mean it. What's wrong?" Tobin sat down so he was eye to eye with the canine, leaning forward, elbows resting on his knees.

Matrix's body posture changed, perking up to look around as if excited. He trotted over to a box and snuffled through it, pulling something out, then bringing it to Tobin. It was a map of Portland.

Matrix barked, wagging his tail and twirling in circles.

"No, no way. I already explained this." Tobin's voice got cold, and he sat up straighter on the couch. "We can't risk it. That fucking faun said go and don't come back." Matrix sat down and looked blandly at his brother. "We need to stay here until I can figure this out."

Matrix whined at him, nudging the scar on Tobin's right forearm where Nora's bite had transformed him. "I already told you, M, I'm not asking Nora for help. What makes you think we can even trust her? What if the Bone Wraith got her? What if she's the bait and as soon as I reach out, she'll take me back to it? Take us back to it. I mean, we don't know if that bear destroyed it." Tobin suppressed a shudder remembering the charging grizzly. That bear had been a nightmare on four legs, sending Tobin's instincts screaming to escape. "But I have a feeling he didn't banish the Wraith, and I'm sure not going back there to find out." Being enslaved for five minutes felt like a lifetime. He unconsciously rubbed the burn scars on his ribs where the silver tattoo had shackled him to that horrific creature. This scar was not pretty white lines like Nora's bite, but shiny red melted flesh that still resembled a spider's web. *Never again,* Tobin promised himself. *I bow to no one now.*

Reflexively, he scratched Matrix behind his floppy ear. The dog let out a suffering sigh, leaning his big head into Tobin's touch, offering up doggy comfort.

Tobin flashed back to the cemetery, to the moment when he'd provoked Nora into biting him while she was drugged. The Wraith had instructed him to force her to attack in order to release her new power. If that power granted Tobin's longing to become a werewolf, then it would confirm her magic's ability to change Matrix back to Max. Tobin's desperation to restore his brother made him reckless, and his avarice for magic made him brave. Unfortunately, the Wraith had played a deeper game, knowing Tobin's silver tattoo would enslave him as soon as he transformed.

Matrix was the only reason Tobin was free. Buying his brother the precious seconds needed to rip the silver from his skin before the Wraith could order him not to. The dog had suffered broken ribs for his efforts, forcing Tobin to carry him when they'd fled. But they'd managed, against all odds, they *had* escaped.

A shiver passed through Tobin at the memories of the Wraith's dead hands touching him, caressing his "new pet." Nightmares didn't get better fuel. With that nightly reminder, he wouldn't risk encountering that creature again. Not even for a second chance to help his brother. Shame twisted deeper, and he dropped his trembling hand.

Matrix got up and trotted across the room again. Grabbing the cell phone, he came back, laying it gingerly in Tobin's lap. He sat, placed a big paw on Tobin's knee and looked imploringly up into his brother's hazel eyes. He pawed at Tobin's arm where the bite shimmered white in his suntanned skin.

"You want me to call her, don't you? You think she'll forgive me for kidnapping her?" The dog gave a very distinct nod.

"Well, you're an optimist." Tobin rolled his eyes.

Matrix gave a small growl and nudged the phone again, flexing his nails to scratch Tobin's bare leg.

"Look I'm sorry M, I just can't risk it." Tobin reached to scratch the dog's ears, but Matrix dipped his head and moved away. "Come on, don't be like that, I'm thinking about our safety here. There's just too much we don't know, and I need some time to figure this out," Tobin begged.

Matrix began to walk away, then paused and picked up each paw deliberately studying them, then his tail, casting his eyes down each side of his furry body. He returned his gaze to his brother. Tobin could almost hear words in his head. *I'm still a dog, and Nora could fix that.*

His shoulders slumped. "Max, I'm sorry, I'll figure it out," he whispered as something painful built inside him. He hadn't used his brother's real name since Max had been killed four years ago in the line of duty. Naming the dog Matrix had put some insulation between Tobin and his loss. Even though Max wasn't technically gone, the man he'd been wasn't fully present either.

The big dog, a vessel the Wraith had chosen to preserve Max's soul, padded back. He nudged the phone resting in Tobin's lap. Anguish flashed to anger in a hot heartbeat at the dog's persistence. Leaping up, he threw the phone without thinking. They both jumped as the device impacted the drywall with a sharp crack and stuck, dust trickling down the dingy wall.

"Damnit!" Tobin yelled as he stormed over to his phone, yanking it free and inspecting it for damage. The expensive case was barely scratched. *Huh, werewolf proof,* Tobin thought, but the distraction didn't last, his anger sparked again, and he kept yelling.

"I'm done having this argument with you!" He rounded on the dog. "I need to get myself under control first, learn how to use these new abilities. Don't you understand? If I go and talk to her now, she'll see me as dangerous, what if...what if she can undo what she did? The Wraith said she was different, what if she's a werewolf that can take away this gift? I can't go back to what I was. I just can't!" He howled the last words, breathing hard, feeling the wildness inside him roiling under his skin—it felt amazing, inhuman, unstoppable.

Matrix gave him a scathing look, lifting one lip in a snarl and stalked out of the room. Tobin didn't notice, too caught up in the feeling of feral power surging through him like an electric current. He closed his eyes and tipped his head back, calling the change to him, begging the magic to break the surface of his skin and remake him. He was so lost in the moment that he almost crushed his phone in his hand. But in the end, the sensation drained away, leaving him buzzing and alone.

Without the full moon as his catalyst, Tobin still couldn't shift. He growled in frustration. There had to be a way around this. Nora could change without the moon present, he'd seen it twice, so why couldn't he? Yet she could change into a full wolf, and so far, he hadn't managed that either. More research needed to be done, but hell if he was going to just call her and ask. He'd been trapped by his ignorance once with the Wraith, he refused to be caught again by a woman, even if she was everything he'd ever dreamed of.

• •◉• •

THE ALARM DIDN'T EVEN SOUND BEFORE TOBIN'S HAND reached it, clicking it off. Rolling out of bed, he hit the floor and started his push-ups, switching from diamond push-ups to one handed and back again until he had cranked out about a hundred. Getting off the floor, he went to the chin-up bar inserted in his doorway and started his next round.

Working on moving through the house in the dark, Tobin found his running shorts where he'd left them, dressed and stopped in front of a large dog bed in what passed for a family room in the tiny house.

"I'm going running, do you want to come?" Tobin asked the darkness that stood up and shook himself, resolving into a roughly dog shaped blob. "Great, it will be nice to have company. You think you can keep up?"

Matrix sighed, dropped into a downward dog stretch, reversed direction until his spine was in full extension down to the last tail vertebra, then shook off as if emerging from a lake. There was no waiting for Tobin as he trotted out the large dog door and into the yard to take care of his own business.

The tiny house rested in the outskirts of Kelso, Washington. The small town clung to the I-5 interchange like a leech, feeding off the artery of travel between Portland and Seattle. Kelso had once been a hotbed of fishing and timber abutting the Columbia River. Those days of abundance were deteriorating, the industries throttled by environmentalists and bureaucrats. However, its location, touching the Mount St. Helens wilderness, was perfect for Tobin who wanted to be within reach of major cities, but still remote. He'd succeeded; the tired rental was surrounded on all sides by uninhabited forestland which stretched for miles.

Morning still masqueraded as night. Twilight waited in the shadows, the sky studded with stars preparing to twinkle their last before the sun stole their glory. The tranquil air held the scents of fall like a heavy shroud, cradling the odors of dying leaves, dampness, mildew, smoke, and an edge of frost. Tobin breathed deep, savoring all the nuances he could now appreciate with his elevated senses. *Humans have no idea how blind they really are,* he thought as the scent of owl, fresh blood, and rat lit up his brain. His new wildness started to build within him; the need to run intensified. His vision sharpened, giving grays to the understory's previous inky hues.

Restless, he bounced on his toes, the gravel drive crunching under his bare feet. Each passing week changed him more. His feet had toughened so he could practically walk over broken glass without damage, but it was the feel of the naked land that encouraged him. The earth seemed to ground him, connecting right into the fresh wildness within. Now he understood why Nora ran barefoot so much. It calmed and excited him in equal measure. Shedding the shoes had led to discarding more human trappings while in the forest, especially the cell phone. The only apparel he indulged in was a pair of loose shorts made of natural fibers since synthetic fabrics smelled strange to him now. The faun had accused him of being too human, he would show that warped creature how wild and connected he could be.

Matrix glided up to him in the dark, touched the back of Tobin's knee with his wet nose, eliciting the desired yelp. "Ack, why do you keep doing that?" Tobin pushed the dog away from him. Matrix wagged his plume of a tail and smiled a doggie grin, looking satisfied.

"Fine, glad I amuse you. You about ready?" Tobin tried to sound more pissed, but after getting the cold shoulder for almost a month, he was grateful to have his brother teasing him again. Matrix had even gone on a hunger strike for about a week to show his displeasure. It started with him ignoring his food, touching Tobin's bite scar, then retrieving the phone and staring. Tobin had gotten so frustrated, he'd put his phone where Matrix couldn't reach it. The dog started sleeping in another room and going out at night without Tobin. The rejection stung.

"Let's go through those south trails today, I keep feeling like there's something down that one deer path that I want to look at." Matrix didn't wait for him, he just turned and shot off the gravel road and into the gloom of the forest. *Okay, Tobin thought with a painful stab of irritation, maybe M is still a little pissed at me.*

• • ◉ • •

MATRIX RUSHED AHEAD INTO THE DARK THEN DOUBLED BACK, crisscrossing his track until he knew Tobin wouldn't be able to untangle the scent trail. He was pissed at his brother's decisions, frustrated at his own limited communication, and angry at his inability to actually help with anything. The sensation of uselessness kept gnawing on him. Existing with a dog's capacity for thought had been an unrealized gift. As he regained more of himself with the constant exposure to Tobin's magic, the clarity of his situation had started to feel like a curse.

Growling at his feeling of impotence, he crept to the edge of a log and waited, his hours of practiced stealth rewarded. Tobin soon materialized. He was getting better at running quietly, but he still didn't move like a wild creature. The scuff of his feet on the bare patches of earth, and the occasional snap of a twig let Matrix follow his progress with ease. His brother ran too much on his heels, hitting the ground with more of a thump than necessary, and his breathing was too heavy.

Tobin passed and Matrix lingered until the footfalls faded before regaining his paws. Something other prowled this new forest, giving off echoes of the watcher from the Portland woods. The sensation made Matrix's hide twitch each time they entered the trees, and today he wanted to uncover the source of his disquiet. Not that he could do much. He snapped at the negative sensations and shook them off.

A small sound made him pause. He listened, his upright ear pivoting to catch the slight vibrations, his nose teasing out the air around him.

The noise repeated. It was the tiniest sob Matrix had ever heard, and if he hadn't been so still, he would have missed it entirely.

Sniffing down the side of the log, he caught the whiff of saltwater and magic. A small cry of distress hissed through the leaves as he lowered to his belly and carefully moved the dry fern frond aside with his nose. Something wiggled in the duff, about the size of a baby mouse, trying to bury itself deeper in the near darkness of the log and debris. It smelled so young.

Matrix whined gently, moving his nose to the side to peer in without looking like he was going to eat it. The small creature stopped moving, its muffled cries of dread fluttered around it like moths. The dog shifted again, placing a huge paw within reach, but not going any further, waiting, radiating kindness with every atom of his self.

Finally, the small being unwound from the nest of darkness, and stumbled forward, the dusky light of dawn a gray thing that brushed the little creature, giving it form. It was covered with down like a baby bird. A small, wrinkled face the color of mud peered at him, and in its sticklike fingers, it clutched a bit of tattered wool in the vague shape of a bird. Tracks of tears smudged its creased face, and terror was bright in her big black eyes.

"Are you going to eat me?" Her voice was the twitter of a chickadee, English so garbled that Matrix experienced the meaning more than heard it. He attempted a comforting whine and swished his tail gently behind him.

The little girl froze. He dropped his tail, flattening himself further. The little thing let her gaze wander over him. From her perspective, he must appear mountainous, but she clutched her toy tighter and stepped forward.

"I'm lost." Her bottom lip trembled, but she bravely held his gaze. "I fell out of the nest. Eike and I were wrestling, and I tripped. Eike is always pushing me around when Ma and Da are gone. Flick didn't see. When I hit the ground, I heard bogeys so I ran. Ma said if you hear a bogey, run, always run, and hide. Hide deep in the dark. They are stupid, and if you smell like leaves, and look like leaves, they will think you are leaves."

Matrix had no idea what she was talking about, but with each word, the little girl moved closer until she had a tiny hand on his paw. A thrill coursed through him. Something told him to protect this mite of a creature as dim colors of yellow and green emitted from her.

"You promise you won't eat me?" Her voice was stronger. Matrix wagged his tail again, and this time she seemed to understand it was a part of him. "Good. My nest is up there."

She pointed to a lower branch in a Bigleaf maple. Matrix could just make out a small lump of something. "Ma says that good creatures can see it, and nightmares will avoid it. Please take me home, the bogeys…the bogeys will come back."

Matrix twitched his nose, indicating with his eyes for her to climb on. It took some doing, and some whisker pulling, but the child finally perched as if she belonged there. The big dog got up slowly, taking great care not to topple her like dandelion fluff in a stiff breeze. She was so light, he couldn't tell she was there except for the shadow of yellow she made in his vision when he crossed his eyes.

The next part was harder. The stretch up would have been beyond a smaller dog, but on his hind legs, he was able to balance and nudge her into the nest. She squealed with excitement and suddenly there were three little faces peering at him from the tightly woven twigs. A wren swooped down and trilled a warning, trying to cover the children with her wings as her wicked beak plunged for his sensitive nose.

"Flick, no!" The little girl whistled and put her small hands on the bird. "He saved me!" The bird stopped and chirped at Matrix but continued to fuss. The girl looked back at him and waved, then shrieked and pointed. "Bogeys!" And all the little faces disappeared into the nest, the woven home going silent.

Matrix swiveled and saw five creatures, the size of toads, and looking eerily similar to the lumpy amphibians, oozing over the log. When they stopped, their warty hide would meld into the surroundings, giving them perfect camouflage. They became visible with movement, small piggy eyes flashing black, and large, flared, noses snuffling the air. They drooled in anticipation of a meal, one with downy feathers hanging from the corner of its mouth, all draped in drab energies that slithered in his vision.

Matrix's ruff bristled as he lunged without thinking, not giving the creatures a chance to spot him in the gray light. With two snaps of his jaws, all five bogeys were crunched and swallowed whole. They tasted like frogs and bitter green magic. He halted, a little shocked. Somehow, he knew he had just eaten fairy folk, small ones, but still beings of magic. The woods wobbled for a moment as energies around him pulsed, then steadied, feeling more balanced.

Cries of triumph erupted from the nest behind him, disrupting the odd feeling. Chirping accompanied the clapping of tiny hands. He moved to watch as a different bird, a chickadee, landed next to the nest, a stick-like creature dismounting from the bird and rushing to her brood. Matrix identified her as a sprite from the library books Tobin was studying. Tiny heads were counted before the sprite turned, clasped hands over her heart and bowed deeply to Matrix. Ushering the kids back, they vanished into the nest as both small birds took flight.

A glimmer of satisfaction filled Matrix. Maybe he wasn't completely useless as a canine?

The belief shattered as a sharp whistle split the morning air. Matrix jumped, he'd left Tobin unguarded, the one thing that lent him purpose. Fear drove his paws as he frantically dashed to catch up with his brother. If carnivorous toads were roaming these woods, what else might prowl beneath the trees? Matrix swallowed down his failure along with the last alluring taste of bitter green magic, a hunger for something more taking root within him. He thrust the feeling away. Right now he had a job to do.

CHAPTER 6

Between a Wall and a Cold Place

Neoma

Neoma would be the first to admit this felt, and probably looked, awkward.

"Why exactly are you doing this?" the young voice asked. Neoma refused to open her eyes, trying to focus on her breathing.

"Because if you can master your body, you can master how your body feels. But first you must get to know your body."

"Didn't you already do this through dance?" Neoma's half-brother broke into her silence. Again!

"You know, he brings up a good point." Kristin cut in as she entered the family room, her slippered feet making swishing noises on the carpet. "With the way you pushed yourself with dance, I'd imagine you'd already have that body-brain connection." Neoma could hear her sipping coffee, the strong fragrance of bitter dark roast filled the room like aromatherapy.

I have a new body now, Mom, one that no longer feels like mine. And no matter what I do, I just can't make it fit anymore. Neoma thought, stomping down the painful words before they could erupt. Evoking sympathy was not her style.

"You know, you guys don't have to sit in here and watch me. You could both do something else. Anything else." Exacerbation crept into Neoma's tone. "I wouldn't have bothered coming in here, except there's not enough room on my floor to get a really good stretch. And I thought it would be quiet."

"What family did you grow up in, Kjære?" Kristin asked her daughter with a chuckle. Scandinavian endearments were Kristin's love language, especially when her children were amusing her.

"A nosy one apparently," Neoma huffed.

"Well, if you didn't set up a yoga studio in my family room, I wouldn't interrupt you." Kristin laughed as she passed her son, mussing his light brown hair. Lukas was Neoma's half-brother, the results from a one-night stand during Kristin's birthday trip to Seattle. Kristin maintained he was the best present ever. Dave, the unexpected father, offered to help Kristin relocate, but she was unwilling to give up her bookstore, bakery, or her baby. She also hadn't wanted to transplant Neoma right as she was starting eight grade.

So, in true Kristin fashion, Neoma's mom had taken on the challenge of raising another kid, this time with a teenager as support instead of her late parents, who'd both passed the year before. Despite their loss, Kristin's infectious joy and laughter endured, even though the hard parts. When Dave wanted to give Lukas his last name Kristin refused, insisting all her children would have the family name of Lund, tracing back to the Vikings, according to Grandpa. Lukas Lund arrived just as Neoma became a freshman. He was pink, screaming, and proceeded to turn Neoma's life upside down in the best of ways. Dave stayed involved with Lukas, pulling him up to Seattle whenever possible, but mostly it was the three Lunds together in Kelso. Neoma didn't regret this part of having to live close to home. She adored her goofy little brother, even when she wanted to swat him.

"Is this right?" Neoma cracked her eye to see Lukas on the floor trying to copy her. His twelve-year-old hyper-flexible limbs bent in directions that made her twenty-seven-year-old limbs cringe.

"Dude, you went past right and into the realm of superhuman. Here," she unbent herself carefully and untangled her brother's extremities, "let's try this again, and if you go beyond a straight line with your knees or elbows, you've gone too far."

Lukas rolled his eyes, but paid attention and finished stretching with Neoma while Kristin watched. Somehow, the group participation made things easier, and Neoma found herself sinking deeper into the stretches and coaxing a bit more length out of her swollen joints. The breathing and exercise did help.

Kristin reached out and rubbed the back of Lukas's head with her foot while he laid prostrate in Child's Pose, a wicked twinkle in her blue eyes.

"Mom!" Lukas complained, "I'm focusing here!"

"Touchy little Zen master you're becoming, Hjort en." Kristin grinned like a satisfied cat as she sat and savored her morning cup and watched her "little deer." The coffee scent brought up nearly forgotten memories of Neoma's Norwegian grandparents. She missed the constant smell of roasted beans that had clung to their lives.

"Are we going to the movies now?" Lukas asked, popping up and doing a spin just because he could. His slate blue eyes sparkled, light brown hair framing his face as he waited for the answer.

"If you get ready, I'll consider it." Neoma responded, and Lukas dashed up the stairs humming the theme song to *Star Wars*, with volume.

"You sure you're up to taking him?" Kristin asked as Neoma slowly got to her feet. "I think he's having a growth spurt and has the tendency to go from easygoing to demon in moments."

"I'll keep him fed. It'll be fine." Neoma smiled at the sounds of Lukas vigorously brushing his teeth.

"Yes, food, the answer to most childhood meltdowns." Kristin said with a sardonic smile as she answered her beeping phone. A look passed over her face before she made some affirmative noises and said goodbye. Unease prickled Neoma's scalp.

"That was Stewart, he needs you to swing by the store before you two head to the movies. Apparently, there's a small problem." Stewart was their bookkeeper, accountant, go-to person, and stand-in manager so Neoma could have time off occasionally, and Neoma adored him for it. This was her Saturday off, and she used it to spend time with Lukas. It was a precious gift as far as she was concerned.

"What's the problem?" Stewart was quite capable, Neoma couldn't imagine what had happened that would make him call her on Saturday. "Is the place on fire?" Her stomach did a sideways flutter-step.

"No, he assured me of that as soon as I picked up." Neoma's shoulders relaxed. "But he wouldn't tell me, said you needed to see it, and he didn't want me going all, and I quote, 'mamma bear and trying to fix it,' end quote." Kristin raised one pale brow as if challenging her daughter to confirm that accusation of her protective instincts.

"I'm not touching that." Neoma sighed and rolled up the mat.

"I'm ready!" Lukas crowed as he bounded down the stairs like the deer from his nickname. "Let's go watch *Star Wars*!"

"You remember this is the original one, right? It's not the new one, that doesn't come out until next year."

Lukas rolled his eyes at his sister. "They're always better at the movies, it feels like the ships really fly over your head." Lukas made star destroyer noises and bolted for the car.

"Well, Kjære, better catch up." Kristin winked.

"I guess I better." Neoma's lips quirked as she hefted her bag. "Need anything while we're out?"

"Nope, just take pictures of whatever the problem is so I can rage in my private space before you get home."

"Not a chance, Mom." They both laughed.

— • ◦ ◉ ◦ • —

NEOMA PULLED THE CAR CAREFULLY INTO THE BACK PARKING lot behind the store. She made sure to park with the driver's side facing Stewart's cherry red, mint condition VW bus, lest Lukas get too excited opening his door and scratch the museum relic. Lukas, for his part, continued to hum the theme to *Star Wars* and bounce on his feet as he waited for Neoma to unlock the employee entrance.

"Hey Stewart, I promise I left my mom at home, what's the problem?" Neoma called as she made her way through the spacious back room that still managed to be cluttered. Boxes of books and other merchandise lounged in piles, expanding into every stitch of available space. On the far wall, bookcases hoarded their ever-expanding valuable used books cozied around a couch. A collection that Neoma added to with each library closure and estate sale she visited. The promise of "someday" draped heavy in dusty layers over those shelves. With the proper application of time, the area could be organized and even used to expand the store, but that desire always seemed to take a back seat to the day-to-day demands, an idle thought that had yet to bloom into a dream.

Neoma paused to carefully pick a box cutter off the floor, closed it, and put it back on the desk, wondering if Lukas had hit it while running through, or if Stewart had left it there by accident. What was this problem that would have a careful man like Stewart so distracted?

"Oh shit!" Lukas yelled.

"Lukas!" Neoma admonished as she rounded the corner out of the stacks of books and into the light from the front window. "Oh shit."

"That about covers it." Stewart calmly replied from behind the front desk. "Sorry Nae, I hated to bring you in on your day off, but…" He let the sentence drop and indicated the front window, which still dripped fresh spray paint in little rivulets of white and orange. Large letters filled the small shop window proclaiming "Burn books" with swirls of flames licking at the bottoms of each word. It also appeared someone had tried to start a dragon but been interrupted.

Neoma was dumbfounded. *Is this aimed at me?* Although racism and microaggressions were not an unknown experience in her life, the encounters with it tended to be more face to face, like with Paris. Yet attacking her business felt premeditated and targeted. Never had anyone been this outwardly aggressive. And why now? She had worked here for over ten years. Fear began to tingle at the back of her neck, making her feel vulnerable in a space she considered safe a moment before.

"It's not aimed at you." Stewart supplied before she could ask. "I think it's foolish kids trying to impress their friends with their artwork. My guess is that someone lost a dare." Stewart's voice was compassionate, and Neoma could see Lukas nodding his head in the corner.

"Lukas Lund, what do you know?" she asked, feeling the ill taste of fear start to mutate. Cold rage filled her ears with white noise, freezing her blood. The strange feeling engulfed her, making her head spin as she put a hand out to steady herself.

Who would attack my store? Why? Is this some cruel game? Her internal questions incited the anger in her chest to spread, becoming a cold balm that coated and hardened her fear. She embraced the feeling, wrapping it around herself like brittle armor, shoring up her defenses, her weaknesses. This store was her livelihood and now it was sullied. *Someone is going to pay for this, somehow.* Neoma startled out of that strange cold as Lukas spoke.

"I think Stewart's right." His voice broke with his age and anger. Neoma nodded and turned back to Stewart.

"We actually have them on video, Nae." Stewart tapped the computer. "They're wearing face masks and hats. However, it wouldn't be too much of a stretch to ID them, especially since you can see the artwork on the back of their skateboards. But if you have an idea of how you want to address this, I'm all ears."

"Good. I don't want to call the cops," Neoma said.

"Fair. Besides, businesses have been getting tagged all over town, and the cops haven't done much to stop it."

"That's because it's Carter doing most of it." Lukas piped up. Both adults swiveled their heads in his direction.

"The mayor's kid?"

"Yeah…he's trying to make a point that he's as bad ah—hard core, as anyone else." Lukas quickly amended his language as Neoma narrowed her eyes at him. "Some kids were giving him flack about being a momma's boy. That he'll do anything she says."

"And his mom is looking the other way because it's her precious baby that's destroying property," Neoma finished. "Just great, and now it's my problem." A surge of icy fire went through her. If she didn't handle this right, her store would continue to be a target for tagging, and with as bold as Carter had been to brand her front window, that would just encourage one-upmanship. Her anger crystalized into sharp purpose. Suddenly, she saw solutions instead of blind irritation at the boys who'd done this.

"Lukas, how do you know all this? You're not even in high school yet."

"Bradly's in my art class. He talks about his brother all the time. Carter's teaching him to do cool things with spray paint and layering effects." Lukas shrugged.

"I'm going to throttle someone." Neoma looked around the store and her eyes alighted on a book. "I have an idea." She straightened her back and marched out the door, calling over her shoulder, "You guys stay in here, and out of sight, I'm going to handle this."

Neoma launched out the door and whirled around to confront the defaced window. She crossed her arms over her chest and tilted her head to one side, then the other. She backed up a bit until she was standing in the street to take the whole thing in.

As she studied it, her anger seemed to focus, and she was able to look at the mess of her shop with a critical eye. Carter's art was good, really good. His line work, shading, and potential dragon actually had merit.

Neoma whirled and strode down the street, turning the corner at the bar. Behind it was a skate park, a dished-out pit with cement hills and valleys covered in a kaleidoscope of spray paint. It looked like modern art met Monet and had children while doing crack. A few boys' rode boards in lazy circles while a cluster of kids lurked up against the wall of the public toilets smoking in the shade as if no one could see them.

"Carter," she bellowed into the park. A shadow at the corner of the wall jumped and jerked back deeper into the group of kids. Neoma grabbed her cold anger and poured it into her voice. "Carter, over here *now* and let's have a conversation like adults. Or would you rather involve your mom?"

The shadow detached from the huddle and stepped into the sunlight, becoming a teenager. His dark hair was slicked back underneath a backwards ball cap, dark shirt, baggy jeans, with a flannel tied around his waist that completed the ensemble. His backpack hung loose from one strap, and he carried a skateboard. *If this boy uses the word "Dude," I might have to destroy him,* Neoma thought. *Save the world from this walking cliche.*

"If you have any friends back there, egging you on, better tell them to get their butts out here too unless you want all this glory for yourself." Carter flashed belligerent eyes at her but motioned to the lagging group, and two more shadows became disgruntled teens.

Neoma waited until they got closer, then spun on her heel and marched them all down to the store. They followed like depressed ducklings, hanging their heads and scuffing their feet until everyone was standing in front of the shop window.

"So, what do you think of this?" she asked, her hands on her hips.

They all looked at her like she was nuts. "Huh?"

"You heard me, what do you think of this? Did you rush it? Are you happy with the final product? What would you change if you had the time?" The two lackies blinked, but Carter caught himself and looked back at the window.

"Really?"

"Yes, humor me. I want your artistic…*critique*."

"Huh, well," he fumbled his words, "obviously, it's a work in progress, so it's not bad per se…I mean, if I'd done it, I would've spent some more time on the shading to make the flames pop. And clearly that dragon's not even outlined yet, so like, yeah, the full effect can't really be…appreciated." His gaze slid to her and back to the window. "The dragon would have been the bomb."

"I'm sure." Neoma's words tasted like winter. Carter flinched. "Wait here." And she walked back into the store and grabbed a large book, returning to the teens who were fidgeting in the street.

"Now look," she started to flip through the pages showing off different pictures of street art. "Each one of these are made by someone I would call an artist. These people got to take their time, build their craft, and actually put out something that added to the landscape of the city. Their work makes people stop, look, and remember. This," she indicated the window, "is the work of a spoiled child trying to get his mommy to pay attention to him."

Carter, whose eyes had lit up when she started showing them the pictures, visibly deflated, his cheeks reddening.

"However," Neoma said, and three sets of eyes rolled up to fix on her, "if you want your mom to take your art seriously, I have a proposition for you." The strange cold that Neoma had been feeling chimed like a bell, she had them.

"Like what?" Carter asked warily. He looked ready to bolt at any moment.

"Clean this window. Now. Today. I don't want to see a smear of paint left behind…"

"You've got no proof it was us," Carter blustered.

"I have you all on video, with those tatted up skateboards clearly visible. It wouldn't be hard to get someone to ID the board art as yours," Neoma said, ice frosting her tone again.

"But that will take hours!" Lackey number one moaned, his expression melting like a Munch painting. Carter elbowed him, and he shut up with an "oof."

"Allow me to finish." The boys snapped back to attention. "I will give you my permission, as the store owner, to use the wall on the side of my shop as your practice canvas." Their eyes widened. "If, and only if, you produce something that actually advertises the bookstore, and that I consider presentable street art, I will allow it to stay. I will also use it as advertising on social media, and credit you in the process."

"Yeah but," lackey number two spoke, his nasally voice stretched like bubble gum stuck to a desk. "Seems like we should get paid if you're going to, like, use it to promote your store. Paint's not cheap." He tipped his chin, trying to assert himself as a legitimate business negotiator. Peach fuzz frosted his cheeks, unable to hide his acne while greasy hair dangled in his eyes.

Neoma put her finger to her chin as if considering his words. "Well, it has got to be cheaper than what you'd pay for the window to be cleaned. Then there's the potential lawsuit I could hand to your parents for willful destruction of private property."

"No, no!" Cater stepped between them. "That's more than fair. Please, I would love the chance to paint your building." He held his hand out, looking more like an adult and less like a skulking teenager for the first time.

"Okay, deal." Neoma shook, happy the kid didn't have a firmer grip as her arthritis throbbed. "I would suggest whitewashing the wall first before you get started. And if that paint is not off the window by tonight, this deal is null and void."

"Yes ma'am, I understand."

Ma'am? Whatever, I'll take the respect right now. Neoma pursed her lips, nodded her head, and went to strut triumphantly back into the store, her anger starting to melt into satisfaction.

"Neoma, ma'am, wait." She turned back. "Umm, could I buy that book?"

Neoma looked down at *The World Atlas of Street Art and Graffiti.* She laughed and the last of that odd cold rage left her. "All right, but come inside and pay for it, I have a movie to get to."

CHAPTER 7

Talking Trees

Tobin

T obin checked Matrix's collar with the ID tag stitched on. Today was about stealth and taking the right precautions. Over the last week, he'd sensed a presence watching them from the trees. He was done with being ambushed, he was going to flip the script and find this thing first before it made its move. But he wanted to be smart about it. He double checked the dog collar; it was loose enough that Matrix could slip it if needed. Should they be forced to separate, Tobin wanted to ensure Matrix could find human help and make it back home. His brother's safety ensured, he was ready to hunt.

"Let's go." Tobin whispered and took off down the deer track that had become their entrance into the forest.

The darkness lifted as they passed under the canopy. The space between trees opened slightly with the mature growth but the understory continued to be thick and congested. Tobin allowed his body to guide him, feeling the air on his bare skin, his breath moving in and out of his lungs as he pushed his pace, Matrix panting close at his heels. An inner sense, which Tobin guessed was wild instinct, awakened. Suddenly, he perceived the forest as a complex living organism, not separate parts. Bats fluttered through the predawn picking off the lingering summer insects. A tentative bird called in the distance, questing for the sun. Tobin smelled the musk of the male deer who must have run this trail before him. Each creature belonged here, had their place and purpose. Did he?

The rank smell of bear assaulted his senses as he crossed another game trail. The pungent odor made him sweat, and he sped up to avoid any mistaken encounters. After watching the giant grizzly tear Chaz apart like a stuffed toy, his fear of bears was deeply rooted. Even with his new strength and speed, Tobin didn't trust that he would be a match for a bear, and he didn't need to find out.

Up ahead, the trail followed a rise, and Tobin could just make out the crest of a hill as dawn washed the ink out of the night and gave silhouettes to the trees. Soon, color would mingle between the trunks of the pines as morning bloomed rosy and golden in the clear sky. Tobin increased his pace so they could catch the sun before it breached the horizon when he saw something move.

It was a shadow, and it slipped from tree to tree as a wisp of cloud, the darkness of one trunk seeming to reach for the other as the gloaming gave definition to the forest. It was not an animal, and the wind was blowing from behind Tobin, so he couldn't catch a scent. He slowed slightly and glanced at Matrix, who with his shorter stature, seemed unaware of the moving darkness.

Again, Tobin let his eyes wander the ridgeline, keeping them soft, looking out of the sides of his vision instead of trying to focus too hard on one thing. He was rewarded as the shadow detached from the last trunk and merged with another. Almost like watching an octopus hunt on a reef, oozing from spot to spot and changing color and texture to blend in seamlessly with their surroundings. A chill went down Tobin's spine; they were being stalked.

Matrix growled softly, not a warning, but more "I see something." Tobin brushed the dog's back in acknowledgment, and they both softened their footfalls, ready to react to whatever this new thing might be. Now more than ever, Tobin wished he could call his shift forward at will, to have claws and teeth worthy of respect. He was currently stronger than a normal human, but strength could only do so much.

Maybe I should start running with a knife? The errant thought was filed away for contemplation later. His brother had taught him how to fight with a knife, but Tobin hadn't practiced since Max's death. And would a knife even do anything against something not human? *If it was iron, it would work against Fey.* He answered his own question, the babble of his human mind continuing as his hindbrain assessed the situation. *But I could never carry a silver blade, I wouldn't want something that could be used against me.* Since becoming a werewolf, Tobin had found he was extremely sensitive to silver, fortunately, he didn't run into it often in his daily life.

They were now on the ridge that bordered a clear cut, the view to the east open and empty of trees. The denuded slopes dropped away and down from where Tobin now stood. This was not ideal for standing his ground, and yet the trees, whose cover he needed, might be used against him. The idea of standing out on the exposed earth made his skin twitch, and he growled softly.

"So it does affect you?" A silky voice asked, seeming to come from the trees themselves.

Tobin didn't jump, but let his peripheral vision continue to follow the strange shadow that slipped from a tree about thirty feet from him. The light was now hitting the creature directly, but still it remained amorphous. His few books on Fey lore hadn't covered a being like this.

"What?" he asked the trees. "The light?"

"No," the sound was the softness of rustling needles in the wind. "The sight of all the slain ones, their bodies gone to feed the hunger of the humans."

Tobin blinked. *Did it mean the harvested trees?* Matrix had left his side and was casting around for scent on the ground like a normal dog, slowly zigzagging his way towards the shadow. What was he thinking? Tobin spit out an answer to keep the creature focused on him. "What makes you think I'm not human?"

Laughter filled the trees; their branches seemed to sway with the sound.

"If you were human, you never would have seen me, felt me near you. Besides, I have been watching you. I know what you become when the moon is full." Mirth danced around Tobin like milkweed fluff, the lightest of touches against his bare skin.

"Then what am I?" Now he was curious.

"Werewolf," the voice said, then paused. "Or at least that is what you believe yourself to be. But no, you...you are something new, something made. Like wood from a tree, you have been shaped into something by the whittling of sharp magic. And yet..."

The voice continued to be everywhere, but the shadow crept closer, Matrix almost on top of it.

"And yet?" Tobin prompted, his heartbeat loud in his chest. What did this creature know of him? How could it know it?

"And yet, you retain your humanity, infused with something more. A flower pollinated, dreaming of being fruit. You hear the forest now, do you not, man-wolf? It calls to you, pulls you in, and you yearn to answer it, even in skin. But you do not know what you really are, or even what you can do."

"Yes," Tobin breathed. Fear started to rush through him. What if this was another creature like the faun? Could it ban them from these woods? Or something like the Wraith? What if it could enslave him and Matrix? A vine wrapped around his bare ankle and Tobin yipped.

Suddenly, a scream reverberated through the trees and the vine that had started to climb Tobin's leg fell limp. The shadow was no longer a shadow, but a woman dressed in a sleeveless gown made of vibrant fall leaves that fluttered around her as she fell. She tumbled to the ground thrashing and kicking, but Matrix had her bare ankle in his mouth and easily overpowered her smaller body, pulling her hips off the ground. Blood glowed amber as it oozed from where his teeth sunk deep into her flesh. A pattern of vines and flowers twined around her bare arms and legs as she fought, their colors brilliant against her darker skin.

"Matrix, drop her!" Tobin barked as he leapt forward, scooping the wounded creature into his arms. Matrix finally released her, and Tobin understood, his brother was keeping the Fey visible until he had her, otherwise, she would vanish into shadow again.

Some deep instinct made Tobin pin the wiggling creature against his bare chest, keeping her from the earth. "What are you?" He spat into the dark brown hair as it obscured his vision, her head nearly colliding with his nose.

"Let me go!" Her voice commanded as she struggled. This time, the words came from her mouth and not from the forest. He almost loosened his grip.

"No, not until I know you won't hurt us." Tobin growled, bringing as much wolf into his voice as he was able. She went limp.

"I am not for you to have, man-wolf. Release me," she said clearly. Her body began to heat within his grip. "This is my last warning."

"Give me your word that you will not harm me or my dog. You were hunting us, and I want to know why." Tobin growled back, then squeezed her a little harder, twisting around one of her delicate arms as he did so.

She hissed in pain, but her voice remained strong. "Fine. I mean no harm to you, or yours. So mote it be." The forest seemed to shudder with her edict, and both Tobin and Matrix looked around at the quaking trees.

"I have given you my word, man-wolf, now let me go."

"Will you vanish again if I release you?"

She scoffed, "I feel we are past that, don't you?"

Suddenly, Tobin felt stupid. He put her down, backing off a few steps but not letting her out of his sight. The cold of the morning seemed to slap his bare chest where she'd been pressed against him, the skin red as if sunburned.

"Why were you following me?" Tobin asked, watching as she bent down and inspected her ankle. The bite mark there was already healing, and in the bright light of morning, Tobin could clearly see her blood was the color of tree sap. Matrix sat to the side, licking his lips, an unreadable doggie expression on his face, and the sharp smell of sweet maple heavy in the air.

The woman straightened and glared at Tobin with eyes the color of cherry blossoms framed in a face seemingly chiseled of a rich hickory heartwood. She was slight in build, about 5'5" with small heart shaped leaves along her hair line. They looked like an emerald crown nestled within her russet curls. Tobin thought her a wingless fairy, carved from a living tree, angry at being earthbound.

"What are you?" he asked again, her strange pale pink eyes assessing him.

"You humans, always wanting to know what things are, but never able to feel the truth of what is in front of you." She sighed as if disgusted by his ignorance, smoothing her leafy dress. "You could call me a dryad, if you must label me."

Tobin filed the name away to look up later. He thought it meant she was a type of Fey that lived in a tree, and her connection with the woods only added weight to that guess.

"What do you want with me?" Tobin asked again.

"I watched you move into that rotting box. Have been watching as you set about making this your territory." She laughed at him like he was a small child playing house. "At first, I thought you were simply another lost human trying to be connected to the forest. But then the moon showed her face and the truth. You let the surrounding trees taste your blood while your hands dug hard into the earth. Your skin split and sprouted a pelt, wild magic surging through you and twisting

A.B. Herron

you into another shape. It looked painful. Yet you seemed to bear it well enough. I was surprised you did not howl like a fool, announcing your presence. Still, the forest knew you were here, and its predators wanted to hunt you. I could have let them have you, but I decided not to."

Unease washed though Tobin followed by a spike of rage. "I'm a predator, I can hold my own." He showed her his teeth as if he were a rabid dog, and she met his expression with a condescending smile.

"You are a babe, believing you are a monster." She closed her eyes and rotated her face to the sun, drinking in the morning light before continuing. "It is no matter, we all have to start somewhere. What I want to know is," she opened those soft rose quartz eyes and glanced back at him, "do you want help with what you have become?"

CHAPTER 8

Stalking Answers

Tobin

"Matrix, you ready? We're going to Portland." Tobin said, grabbing his keys.

The dog looked up, narrowing his eyes suspiciously, his one ear flopping to the side while his erect ear flattened. Two weeks had passed since encountering the dryad, and Tobin had been glued to his computer doing research ever since. Heck, he'd barely gone outside.

However, he finally had a lead, and the information he needed to proceed without undue risk. He could understand Matrix's sudden wariness, especially due to the faun's warning to leave Oregon. But that creature wasn't likely to plague him within the city, especially in daylight with humans milling everywhere. *At least it seems very unlikely. According to fables, Fey don't tolerate human cities, and besides, I'm not going to linger, I'm going to get in, get what I need, and get out before the sun sets.*

"Don't look at me like that M, seriously. What was it you always told me? When trying to figure out a hard case, know the players and start at the beginning. Well, that's what I've been trying to piece together all week and now I'm pretty sure that Shawn, Nora's ex-boyfriend," Matrix growled. "Yeah, that guy was a dick, but I'm pretty sure he's the one who changed her, so I think we need to go pay him a visit. He seems like enough of a self-righteous prick that I'm guessing if I flatter him and show submission, he'll talk to me about being a werewolf. What do you think?" For a moment, Tobin was unsure, the little brother asking for approval.

Matrix tilted his head, scratched his ear, stretched and stood, before sauntering over to Tobin's side. "Does this mean you have my back?" Tobin asked, ruffling the dog's one tall ear. Matrix snorted and huffed. Tobin took that as a yes, and they walked out the door together and jumped in the truck.

The drive to Portland didn't take long, the weekend traffic surprisingly light going into the city. Tobin had timed things well and navigated his plain gray truck into a parking space outside a tall office building near the river. He'd gotten here early to survey the landscape before making his move.

"Ok," Tobin spoke while checking his rearview mirror. "I've been following this guy for weeks on social media; he seems to be all about business and getting a leg up in his firm. They work late and play hard but seem to do it with style. He appears very deliberate in his social posting, no 'look how drunk I got with friends Friday night', or any of that career ending crap I keep running across in people's feeds." Matrix groaned. "I know, I don't understand it either. You kept telling me how you would catch people from what they posted online, well Shawn is being smart. He posts about his work schedule and his overtime. Dry, but informative."

Tobin smoothed down his brown hair, put on a nondescript gray baseball cap, shrugging out of his dark, lightweight jacket. He was dressed all in shades of gray, nothing to stand out and be memorable. "I know he's working this Saturday because of some big case he keeps calling attention to, saying how if he isn't doing dinner at the office, he isn't doing his job. Kiss-ass. But that's good for us, he's working alone, and the parking garage should be empty. I checked this out the other week, and they have light security, more video cameras at the entrance and exit, and only about one or two per floor. Lots of places to be out of sight." Matrix wagged his tail, Tobin thought he looked proud of his little brother.

"He drives a red BMW sport 28i, so it shouldn't be hard to find." Matrix nodded. "I'm going to approach him from the side, upwind, so he can smell me and won't just attack when he realizes what I am. If he knows how to change without the moon, maybe we'll get our answer, but I have a feeling he won't be that dumb, it's too risky in the middle of the city. I'm really hoping he'll just talk to me."

Tobin took a swig of water, giving some to Matrix. His palms were sweating slightly, and he realized he was nervous

A.B. Herron

and excited in equal measures. With any luck, he would get some answers today. If things went badly, he might be walking into an unintentional werewolf turf war. This was like gaming, assessing risk and reward, only this time it was for real with consequences that could actually hurt. Still, the thrill of meeting another werewolf had his endorphins flying.

They got out of the car and took a walk around the block, stopping for some food, taking their time to move around the building and surrounding areas before finding a bench and taking a seat. Matrix sniffed for signs of magic, and Tobin studied the people milling around them from under his hat brim, his non-prescription glasses in place. He kept checking his phone, noticing another update on Shawn's social media. "Going to be working late again, good thing there is plenty of take-out nearby."

"I'd think, well, damn, this guy really does live in the office. Weird for a werewolf, I'd have thought he'd head outside as soon as possible." Tobin sighed and fidgeted on the bench, feeling his own need for movement, the forest calling to him. "M, do you mind hanging out in the truck for a bit? Keeping an eye on the lot? I need to stretch my legs, and if I keep walking you around, someone is going to start to notice."

Matrix snorted, looking offended.

"What? I mean, you don't exactly blend. You're not a golden retriever or some little white scruffy thing."

Matrix sighed and got up, pointing towards the truck. "Thanks bro, I owe you." Tobin walked him down to the vehicle parked in the shade, lowered the windows, and watched his brother climb in. He made sure there was water in the travel bowl and re-upped the meter. "Okay, I won't be gone long, just don't let anyone hijack you, okay?"

Matrix rolled his eyes and turned to diligently watch the garage. Tobin wondered if his brother missed doing stakeouts and other detective activities. Until now, he hadn't thought about it. How much did Max miss being Max? Miss his old life? How much did he really remember? A fresh surge of regret and loss for a brother he might never get back threatened his focus. Blinking quickly, he shrugged it off, concentrating on the moment and the mission, letting himself be pulled into the pedestrian traffic heading towards the river, blending into the humans like a shadow.

CHAPTER 9

Book Dragon

Neoma & Tobin

T he roads were quiet as Neoma guided her car carefully onto I-5 south towards Portland. It wasn't often she had the opportunity to get away on her own, but this was the book fair weekend when Powell's and the local libraries all combined for a massive book sale in conjunction with the downtown Saturday Market. Usually, Mom and Lukas would have driven with her, but wedding cake disasters had called Kristin into work unexpectedly, and she'd dragged Lukas along. They'd catch up later. So, for the next few hours, Neoma had Portland, and books, all to herself. It was heaven, and she suspected her mom had known that.

An hour later, Neoma pulled into a parking structure and shut off the car, rubbing tenderly at her elbows and grateful for the seat heater keeping her low back and hips warm. Her body protested more and more when she took this drive. She didn't want to think about walking back with armloads of books after standing on concrete for half a day. Nope, that was what little brothers were for, hauling heavy things. With that in mind, she shot her mom a quick text about where she parked so they could find her then negotiated herself from the vehicle.

Waterfront Park of Portland's Old Town district meandered along the Willamette River. White tents with sharp points were clustered everywhere on the brick paths; everything from jewelry makers, food venders, to flower sellers enhanced the sensory experience as she made her way through the bustle.

And suddenly there they were, tables and tables of new and used books, waiting in neat and chaotic piles to be pawed through and fawned over by rabid bibliophiles. Neoma practically rubbed her hands together with glee as she inserted herself into the madness, the scent of books surrounding her.

Two hours later, she was enjoying her book time along with a strange cat and mouse game between herself and another enthusiastic shopper. The guy had snagged her attention a few stalls over as he'd pawed through a bin of older fantasy novels like a dragon inspecting his hoard. Other than his ardent behavior towards literature, it was his outfit that drew her eye. He wore darker hues against the market's background of loud colors and summer vibrancy. Everything from his hat to his jeans were faded grays, and he moved like a shadow through the booths, slipping between tables and customers alike without disturbing the messy surge of human commerce.

The clothes were not the only thing Neoma noticed. Nope. The man was built in all the right ways as far as she was concerned. Whereas Caleb was a bulldog, this guy was like a Belgian Malinois, lean, athletic, and potentially dangerous. A sinful smile slid over her lips while pretending to read a dust jacket, eyes following his movements. All her years of dancing had given her a deep appreciation for people's refined physique, and this man was worth appreciating.

Neoma could practically hear Megan in her head commenting on this stranger, "See Nae, there are men out there besides farm boys. And look, this man likes to read, go talk to him!" Neoma chuckled. She'd call Meg on the way home and share her stalking tendencies, if her friend would pick up the darn phone! Of course, Meg would probably chide her for not approaching the guy and asking for his number. *Maybe I won't share this.*

Returning to the books, Neoma tried to keep her eyes from unintentionally tracking the tasty stranger. After all, what would she do with some guy's number from Portland? She sure wasn't going to be driving down here for weekend hookups. And what guy would want to come spend weekends in Kelso when he had all of Portland to cavort through? She couldn't imagine her sarcastic wit would be enough of a draw, and someone that athletic probably wanted to spend his weekends climbing mountains. Not her thing anymore.

Neoma sighed as her phone vibrated. She fished out the annoying device, stopping her perusal of the old books containing folklore and fairytales. Lukas's name popped up, his text letting her know they were parking and would be hunting her down in the next twenty minutes.

Neoma sighed again. *Well,* she thought to herself, *the bright side is my hired help has arrived. Downside, my alone time with all you lovelies is almost over.* She let her fingers trail over the slightly ragged spines, realizing that her daydreaming about Mr. Tasty would also have to be put on hold. *Well, at least until I get home tonight.* She smiled wickedly to herself, she had plans for this mysterious book dragon. Continuing her slow pace, she idly crafted names for him in her head along with a slightly skimpier wardrobe. *And perhaps, a sword, yes definitely a sword.*

A dark chuckle escaped her as she tucked her phone away. Her gaze returned to the books, her eyes alighting on an older title barely visible beneath its brethren. Her hand reached, but another hand swooped in and grabbed the same book at the same time.

"Excuse me," the male voice said, but didn't release the book. Neoma followed the broad hand, up the well-toned arm, to the tight gray t-shirt stretching across a firm chest, coming to rest on a face hidden behind dark rimmed glasses. It was her book dragon, Mr. Tasty. She licked her suddenly dry lips.

She'd assumed he was younger, yet up close he appeared to be about her age. His face was slightly sculpted by experience, and a confidence that few twentysomethings possessed radiated from him. Now that he wasn't thirty feet away, she could clearly make out light brown hair under the baseball cap. The dark rimmed glasses framed intense hazel eyes that met her gaze and fell back to the book they both grasped.

"I hate to be a pain," he spoke again, "but I really need this book."

It was the use of *need* that made her hesitate to let go. That, and the fact that he hadn't released the volume. Besides, he had great arms and watching him flex while maintaining his grip on the book wasn't getting old.

"How do you know I don't need it too?" she responded, her snark jumping out before she could censor herself.

The man looked baffled, read the title of the book again, his brow knotting as he studied first the book, then her. He pulled back slightly, nostrils flaring, then something in his posture seemed to relax.

"Why would you need something about old myths and legends from Europe? Nothing in your current collection, and you have quite a few," he indicated her woven carrying basket that was already too heavy, where ten books lay nestled up against some fresh veggies, "speaks to your claim. Heck, half of them appear to be romance novels and the other half are hard to find classics. Nowhere in that bundle do I see mythology," he concluded as if presenting an argument in court.

She bristled. "And you think, based on ten books, that you can assume my reading preferences that quickly?" Okay, he was nice to look at, but possibly an ass. She held on tighter to the book.

Surprise flashed across his face, and he blinked as if really seeing her for the first time. A shadow of uncertainty tugged at his mouth, wrinkling his brow. He seemed at a loss.

Neoma took a breath, reminding herself she had been combative first. *Or,* she amended in her head, *he could just be hyper focused on whatever mission had him scouring the tables with such intent. I don't know this man, and I'm supposed to be working on being open so perhaps that starts with me giving him the benefit of the doubt.* It hurt a little, but she flexed her mental muscles and attempted to rein in her snap judgments.

Viewing what he'd said through a new lens, she set aside her offended feelings, knowing they were within easy reach, and considered the dialogue anew. The man didn't appear to be judging her selection, not really, only stating it as fact. *I bet he's not used to someone standing up to him after he's laid down his truth. Perhaps I can give him a new perspective on things.*

Teasing obstinate men was a secret hobby of hers. However, she was reluctant to chase away Mr. Tasty. Conjuring up amusement, she laughed, "Clearly, you're not a book addict. This book isn't seen around much, and I've been hunting for a copy. I have more folktales and such at home and this would augment the set nicely." She squinted at him. "Why do you need it?"

A.B. Herron

The man narrowed his eyes and stood up straighter, he wasn't that much taller than her, but with her back hurting, she knew she was slouching. "I'm a folklore major and doing my thesis on European mythology." He didn't break eye contact, but something told her he was lying. *Oh, he is going to be wily.* Neoma smiled, *let the fencing begin.*

"Really? What university?"

"University of Washington."

"Okay, what's the focus of your thesis?" His eyes did a quick jog, telling her he was thinking creatively. In other words, lying. She knew she had him and let her grin become predatory, enjoying the verbal game between them. "No academic has to think that hard about their thesis, I say you're bluffing."

The man snorted. "Why would I do that?"

"I'd assume it's because you're embarrassed to tell me why you *need* this book."

"Other than it costs a fortune online?"

"Oh, point to you, you've done your research. Color me impressed."

"Well then, does that mean you'll let go now?" He gave a small tug on the book.

"Nope, I want a real reason from you if I'm going to relinquish *my* book." She smiled at him and slowly pulled the tome back towards her. His hold didn't let it go far.

Those intense eyes sized her up, as if judging her commitment to this strange dance. "Okay, you guess my reasons, and I'll consider letting go."

"Nice. All right, I say you want this because you're either working on a fantasy novel, or you're creating backstory for a multiplayer game of some sort. Maybe a live action RPG, or an online version, I'm not sure. How am I doing? Have I hit the mark?"

"Huh, I like those answers. Yet now I'm curious, how did you know I was lying?"

"Easy, because if you'd wanted to find this book in the UW library, it's probably there." He blinked as if he hadn't considered that, calculations building within his gaze. "I mean, if *you* were a student and were *really* studying there." She released the hardcover, satisfied with her victory and willing to give him a consultation prize for his quick thinking. The man took a partial step back, his head tilted to the side, studying her.

The penetrating look he was giving her caused her breath to hitch in her chest. There was interest there as if he was trying to figure out what made her tick. Her natural shield of snark and antagonistic banter, which tended to put people into fight-or-flight mode, hadn't chased him away. She wanted to squirm a little under his attention.

"Look," she continued, mentally shaking off her discomfiture and standing a little taller as an idea came to her, "if you're not going to keep that volume for all eternity, let me know." Neoma dug around in her basket and pulled out a business card. "I'm serious, I'd like to add it to my collection, and if you need other references, I can probably help you out." She handed him the card. He took it slowly, like it might bite him, eyes never leaving her gaze before unceremoniously shoving it in a pocket without apparent interest.

Neoma frowned. *I'm really not sure how to read that. Maybe he will actually look at it later?* she thought as her eyes rolled. *Whatever, I tried, and gave up a good book for a guy, Meg can't ride me for zero effort.* Yet he hadn't run away, instead, he lingered in front of her, seeming to contemplate his next move.

He's not walking away. She swallowed, her pulse ticking up another notch, still racing from the excitement of the exchange. That, and the way his regard felt a little like sunshine.

• • ◆ • •

TOBIN WAS COMPLETELY BAFFLED BY THIS WOMAN IN FRONT of him, and he didn't like the confusion. He needed to understand people, their motives, their reactions, how they saw themselves so he could get what he needed. She seemed to be a collection of contradictions. At first blush, she appeared around his age, but she moved like she was older. Her back was slightly stooped, and he could smell pain on her, the scent of deep inflammation muddled by topical eucalyptus type products that burned his nose. Yet the way she spoke to him, her voice was young and strong, belying his previous assumptions about age.

Then there was her attitude. He found that most people couldn't meet his eyes for longer than a moment when he pushed. She stared him down, she challenged him, not giving in when he pulled his wildness forward to get her to drop the book. She hadn't cared, but had continued to test, practically daring him to engage with her further. It thrilled him.

If it weren't for her scent, which smelled human under all the menthol, he'd have been worried she was Fey and leading him into a trap. But scents didn't lie, at least he didn't think they could, so he had to conclude she was simply a very confident human.

Part of him respected that, while another part was petulant that his body language hadn't worked. He'd hoped for more of a reaction. He was a werewolf after all, able to intimidate normal humans on a subconscious level, right? Or at the very least, make them wary? She'd just rolled her eyes, dismissing him.

Why was that interesting to him?

Tobin realized he'd been quiet for too long trying to unravel her personality. He reached for something to say, anything to keep her for a moment longer. Maybe buying time would gain him answers to this unexpected mystery.

"Why were fantasy author and multiplayer games the only two options you gave me? Why not podcaster, or…" he trailed off, at a loss for who else might go to battle for an old book about Fey lore.

She snorted, her eyes leaving him to peruse the waiting piles. He watched her pick up a volume and discard it with a careful grace. She gave each book the same attention she'd given him, studying it, making a decision, and forsaking it back into the sea of literature.

"Huh, stumped you, did I? Well to answer your question," she turned to him, and he noticed her light eyes had little flecks of brown in them, "those are the two most common people I run into who are motivated to get their hands on older mythology. I suppose if I were closer to UW, I'd see more folklore majors, but I'm not. Besides, if you'd been studying up for writing game scenarios, that would've been kinda cool." A small smile bloomed on her lips before evaporating back into distracted concentration.

"Do you play?" Tobin asked, he hadn't had time for online gaming friends since his transformation, and he missed it. Maybe this risky trip to Portland would be more successful than he'd gambled on. If this chance meeting netted him a new gaming contact, he would be more than satisfied. And stumbling upon this book fair? It was a gift. He'd been having a hell of a time finding what he wanted online while studying up on Fey lore, and the old book selection actually had possible answers. This could be a win-win type of trip. One werewolf, an informative book, and a possible gaming prospect? And no one had thrown a rock at his head. Things were looking up.

She spared him a sideways glance and picked up another book. "My little brother games." This time, it was Tobin's turn to smell a lie on her. But she hadn't said no, just deflected. He wondered why.

"Neoma!" The voice rang through the stalls and the woman in front of him snapped her head in that direction.

"Here!" she yelled, waving one arm high. "Well, I guess they found me. You might want to go pay for that and make a hasty retreat unless you'd like to be questioned by my over-inquisitive mother." Neoma smiled with real warmth while she said it.

Tobin saw a tall, pale blonde beelining for their location, with who he assumed was said younger brother in tow. The duo looked Nordic to him, but family relationships were complicated. He wondered briefly at Neoma's honey brown hair and deep tan skin, but decided sticking around for answers wasn't that important. Besides, he'd left Matrix in the truck for too long. It was time to get back.

"Thanks for the advice," he said, tipping the tome at her. "And I appreciate the book." And he found that he did, the words were not just polite window dressings. Too bad this woman lived in Portland; she was the first person he'd been curious about in a long time. But he let her mystery go, what prowled around his new home took precedence and this book would help. After all, knowledge was power, and Tobin was very tired of being looked at as weak by the supernatural community.

"Take good care of it," she said, still shuffling through the piles, apparently nonplussed as he retreated. Yet as he paid for the hardback, he couldn't help but feel as if he were being watched, his instincts tingling over his arms like spiderwebs.

CHAPTER 10

Simple Human

Tobin

A few hours later, Tobin returned to his stakeout bench, his new book open on his lap, flipping through it. The weekend rush was subsiding as people moved towards evening activities. Lights began to glow in different offices as dusk settled in, making the building before him look like a partially lit up circuit board against the fading sky. "Any magic?" Tobin whispered from behind his cheeseburger. Matrix huffed twice for "no", only shaking his head slightly as he dove into the box of fries Tobin had given him. The need for calories had increased with Tobin's higher metabolism, requiring food about every two hours. Good thing his new tech jobs were paying well, or he wouldn't be able to feed himself. Also, Shawn had been right, there was great take-out around here.

"Ok, I think it's time to get in place. Shawn mentioned on his feed earlier about wanting to watch a game tonight, so I think he'll leave soon to make that happen."

After stowing the book in the truck, they both jogged across the street and into the parking garage. With lazy care, they trotted slowly up the ramp inside the structure, looking like they were working on interval training. Not the best place for it, but it gave a steady incline, and Tobin had known people to do it before. After about three complete up and down tours, they went up to the third floor where they found Shawn's shiny red car and moved behind a pillar. Tobin let Matrix off his leash and the huge dog made his way downwind of the elevator doors and dissolved into the shadows.

Tobin tried not to shuffle his feet as he waited, his patience rewarded by the ding of the elevator. Shawn stepped out and glanced around the lot before looking down at his smart watch as he hustled towards his car in determined strides, briefcase and jacket swaying.

Silently, Tobin stepped from behind the pillar into the breeze blowing through the parking structure and straight towards Shawn. The man didn't ease his stride. Tobin shuffled his feet, loud enough that a werewolf in human form should hear him. Shawn didn't react. Was he just playing with Tobin?

"Hey Shawn?" Tobin called, his voice nervous, then he remembered that he was a predator now too, and he should own it. Squaring his shoulders, his muscles bunched beneath his tight shirt as he strode towards the man, raising his hand in a familiar gesture of greeting.

Shawn stopped and looked at him, squinting his eyes, then glancing around. "Do I know you?" Tobin could almost see files spinning in the other man's head, trying to assess if Tobin was a client or not.

"Well, I was hoping you might remember me. I used to run with Nora Westfir, from the running group?" At Nora's name, Shawn's face went cold and hard.

"I can't imagine we have anything to talk about. I'm sure I don't have time for whatever this is. If you're having a legal problem, call my office and make an appointment. Right now I'm off the clock, and I have plans." Shawn turned back towards his car with abrupt dismissal.

"She bit me."

Shawn froze. "Excuse me?"

"You heard me, Nora bit me, and now I want answers." Tobin let a little growl into his voice, making it echo in the nearly empty garage.

Shawn whirled back around. "I don't give a shit about what you and that freaky-ass fuck-tart are up to. She's your problem now, and why the hell would you think I would have answers for you?" he spat at Tobin, hitting his key fob and making the car beep, his face reddening.

Tobin tilted his head to the side, feeling his wildness welling up. This man was weak, he smelled like prey, not predator. Tobin breathed in great gulps of air and tasted Shawn's anger and rising fear on his tongue. It was delicious.

"I broke up with that fucking head job, so you can have her. I offered her everything, and she chose to go play in the mud, in the dark. But then what should I expect from her kind?"

Shawn opened his truck, tossing in the briefcase and jacket he was holding. When he turned, Tobin was right behind him, a golden sheen covering his eyes.

"The way I heard it," Tobin whispered, "was that she left you standing in the dark alone. Unwanted. And scared. You couldn't control her so you tucked your tail and ran." He leaned in and sniffed along Shawn's neck in one long stroke. Shawn hit Tobin's chest with both hands but only managed to back him up one step.

"Get the fuck off me you freak. You're as bad as she was!" Shawn's eyes rolled in panic, but he didn't take them off Tobin as he fumbled for his door handle.

"You're not a wolf, are you?" Tobin took half a step forward, but to do what? Matrix dodged between the two men, slamming his front paws into Tobin's stomach and knocking the wind out of him. Tobin went down gasping.

Shawn didn't waste the moment but dove into his car, revved the ignition, and peeled out of the spot and down the ramp backwards before turning his car around and squealing down towards the exit. The foul exhaust filled the air, making Tobin cough while he struggled for breath. Matrix sat, anxiously looking at him, waiting for him to recover.

"I got it wrong." Tobin finally gasped out. "Shawn didn't turn her." He took another deep breath, the coughing subsiding. "M, thank you, I don't know what came over me. I wanted to...to break him." Tobin scrambled to his feet and reattached Matrix's leash before they jogged to the stairs. They needed to get out of here.

Safely back in the truck, Tobin tossed the hat into the backseat, removed the glasses, and pulled out of the spot, heading for the bridge back to Washington.

"So now what? If Shawn didn't turn her, then who did? Or was she turned? Could she be a born werewolf? That would explain some of her unique abilities." Tobin mused as they made their way home. Matrix reached his head through the seats and touched the scar on Tobin's arm with his wet nose.

"No, I'm not calling her. Stop asking." Tobin snapped. Matrix retreated to the back, grumbling. The rest of the ride was silent.

A.B. Herron

CHAPTER 11

Accept the "No"

Neoma

*T*his *phone needs to come with more of a warning system,* Neoma thought as she held the thing slightly away from her head wondering at the compulsion to pick it up. *It's not* like she hadn't seen the name on the screen, but the impulse to answer the ring had overridden her better judgment. *Maybe a good electric shock would teach me to leave it alone.*

"Well, how are you feeling?" Caleb asked her again, her silence stretching into awkwardness.

"Surprisingly okay, actually." Her words scampered out, and she cringed. *Where the hell is my mind today? I might as well spread my legs and ring the damn dinner bell!* She wasn't sure she wanted Caleb to come over, but her lack of forethought had just made the decision for her.

"That's great! I can be there in an hour as soon as I finish loading the barn." His enthusiasm hit the brick wall of her silence and crumpled. "I mean, well, only if you want me too, Nae." His sudden reticence fed Neoma's guilt.

"No, that's fine Caleb."

"Fine doesn't sound good," Caleb said.

"You're right, I'm sorry. I'm just feeling a little unfocused." Thoughts of Mr. Tasty lingered in the background, proof that there were other men out there. Ones who liked to read. She blinked and tried to concentrate on what Caleb was saying.

"Are you still mad about something? Come on Nae, I haven't seen you in weeks. Can we just move on from whatever that business was? We've got a good thing going here, I'd hate to lose you." His disgruntled pleading made her skin itch.

Lose me? You don't have me. Yet she hadn't done anything over the last few weeks to fully disabuse him of this. Her dance of avoidance was an epic performance lately, so why had she picked up the phone tonight? *Clearly, my subconscious wants me to be a better person. Or the loneliness has poisoned my reason, and I want to give this one more try and see if there's something there to salvage.* She was afraid it was the latter. *Would a transparent conversation even work?* She worried at a stray curl, pondering the options.

"I guess it couldn't hurt to have company for a little bit. Besides, I'd like to talk to you." Neoma relented.

"Talk to me? About what?" Suddenly his enthusiasm vanished, replaced by wariness.

"Us, Caleb, that's all. You know, what we mean to each other, and what we're getting out of this arrangement."

"You mean relationship, right?" he asked.

"See, that's a great example of what we need to discuss."

Now it was his turn to be quiet. She could almost hear the wheels in his head clunking around this new development. "So, that's a yes, right? You do want me to come over? To just talk?"

"I think that would be a good start. And we can see where it goes."

"Where it goes...huh. Well, that could be promising." His optimism returned full force, his smile beaming through 5G. Neoma liberated her distressed hair and let her forehead fall into her palm, not releasing the phone. This conversation was going to be tricky.

"Great, thanks Nae! Oh, I've missed being with you. I'll see you soon." The line clicked off before she could respond.

Neoma looked at Tugman swimming lazy circles in his bowl. "What did I just do?" Tugman blew bubbles. Clearly the fish was out of answers. Neoma sighed.

<hr />

THE SOUND OF CALEB'S BIG DIESEL TRUCK DIED IN THE driveway, the rushing silence announcing his arrival. Neoma exhaled and steadied herself. The previous conversations with her mom and Meg were playing in her head on constant repeat. They were right, if this feeling of impending disinterest was any indication, it was time to let Caleb go. The realization didn't make the bitter taste on the back of her tongue go away;

it clung like lichen to a storm-pounded rock, unmoving and impossible to scrape off.

"Hey sexy," Caleb called out as he opened the door. "I'm so glad I could come over. I've been thinking about you all day."

Neoma cringed inwardly, maybe tonight wasn't the night to call off this tryst? Doubt nibbled at her as she sat on the edge of the bed, her hands balled in her lap. Reluctance and determination warred inside her. Caleb was at least company, a way to scratch her itch for human contact, even if the contact was purely physical. Sure, he was pretty to look at, but she wanted someone who made her hormones do a happy dance, not just whistle and think "nice." She wanted to be moved, in body and mind, and to invoke the same response in another person. The physical piece was no longer enough, had never been enough. Finally admitting that was a sweet sort of pain.

"Hey Caleb."

His eyes raked over her, never meeting her gaze. "There is something about you that I need." He blushed before he found the will to wrestle his contemplation from her body to acknowledge her. "Are you ready?" he asked as he toed off his boots and sloughed his jacket onto the chair by the door.

What am I supposed to say to that? She flashed back to their last encounter, his hands roaming her body with abandon, his touch rough and gentle in equal measure, selfishly hungry, devouring what she was, but not who she was. Taking his pleasure from her skin until he needed to be deeper, even as she still floated on the surface.

"Caleb," but words failed her. She thought of all the nights he shuddered above her before rolling over, sighing, and telling her thank you. Manners were great and all, but with how they interacted, she really could be anyone lying underneath him. Yet time and again, she attempted to wring her own enjoyment from the brief interludes, telling herself he was a good man, and that was enough. Why did she continue to put herself into a situation where she felt...purely functional? She needed to be a participant, not a prop. They both deserved more than this.

The big man moved across the room as her head spun; a bull in a China shop with her needs the fragile vessels. They shattered as he tromped towards her, a dopey smile springing from him as he tugged off his shirt and started to unzip his pants.

"Wait, stop." Neoma held up her hand. "I didn't mean to imply we were jumping into something here."

"But, Nae, please, I've been thinking about you all day. I know you said you wanted to talk, but can we talk afterwards? I've missed you." He stepped closer, resting his hands gently on her shoulders, rubbing her arms. His bare chest rippled with muscles honed from hard labor. Neoma's libido took interest, and she shoved it away, hard.

He fell to his knees before her, taking his groin out of her face. Slowly, he leaned forward, levering himself up from the bed to reach her neck. His lips brushed her skin, whispering in her ear between kisses, "I want to see you stretched out on the bed, all of you, it's like heaven for me. Please Nae."

She had to give him this, he was very persuasive. *Yeah, the first five minutes are so promising, and he's built like a sexy brick wall, but this is really not meeting my needs on any level.* Neoma sighed, reminding herself she wanted more in bed than one-sided satisfaction. *This is going to suck.*

"Caleb," Neoma hesitated before carefully tugging his hands from around her, guiding him to sit beside her. The bed wasn't the best choice for this conversation, but her small space afforded little else in the way of furniture.

Caleb smiled and flopped onto it backwards. "Yeah?" He put his hands behind his head, looking up like he was stargazing, instead of peering at popcorn plaster. When she didn't join him, he rose up on one elbow, his expression puzzled.

She turned slowly, sitting stiffly on the very edge of the mattress and trying to keep her eyes on him and her voice neutral. She would not be apologetic, she would simply state the facts.

"I think I need to stop seeing you like this."

"Like what? After work?" His literal translation made her wince.

"Well, yes, but no. Caleb, what I mean is I'm ready to let this fuck buddy relationship go. This isn't working for me anymore, and I think I'm keeping you from finding someone really special."

"What? Neoma, no, you're really special. Why would I need to find someone else? You're everything I've been looking for." Heartbreak cracked his voice. Her mom had been right, Caleb was in love with her. Or at least he thought he was. Damn, she had let this linger for too long.

Neoma steeled her resolve, looking down at Caleb's big round face. His eyes were clear pools of hope as he gazed back at her, a small piece of straw from the farm caught in his hair. She picked it away with compassionate fingers.

"Caleb," her voice sweet and low, "you want kids, don't you?"

"Yes," he breathed, hope igniting.

"I don't."

"But…" he floundered.

"No buts. I know you want someone to run the farm with you. Even if my RA magically disappeared tomorrow, that would never be me. Come on, you know this." She cupped his face.

"But we've been so good together, Nae, we could make it work. I'll try harder. Do you want to do doggie style? Reverse cowgirl? I'll try anything, I'm sorry I haven't been more creative, but that can change right now." His eyes darted around her small room, looking for something that might change her mind.

"Caleb, a relationship is about more than sex. At least it should be. Don't you want someone who will be your partner? Who would at least want to go to football games with you?"

He moved away from her, sitting up, his big shoulders drooping. She heard him sniff as he wiped at his nose, replacing his shirt and zipping his jeans. "I know you're right. You would never even go to a game in high school. But I hoped maybe you would go with me sometime." His voice was empty, she placed her arms around him, resting her head on his shoulder.

"Caleb, I hate football." He scowled.

"Yeah, I know." He looked at her. "Neoma, what do you want?" The question was sharp and caught her by surprise. She fumbled.

"Honestly, I don't know anymore. But I will figure it out." Her spirits sparked as the words rang true. She would figure this out, and this was the first part to getting to where she wanted to be.

"Paris was right," he grumbled under his breath.

"Excuse me?"

"Nothing." His look sullied. "I better go." He heaved himself off the bed, brushing her arm away.

"Caleb, wait."

He roughly shoved his feet into his boots. "Wait for what, Nae? You just told me you don't want to do this anymore. That you don't want me. What am I waiting for?"

She didn't know, and his wounded expression cut her. "Caleb, I'm sorry, I just thought this could be a bit of fun between us. That's all, I didn't mean for you to get hurt."

"Well, I'm sorry that I was hoping it could be more. Guess we're both disappointed." He grabbed his coat and paused at the open door. "Sorry I couldn't be a monster for you, I guess I'm too nice."

"Monster?" her voice trembled despite herself.

"Yeah, I've seen the books you read," he indicated the nightstand where her latest to be read pile rested. "Why read it if you don't want it? Especially if I'm right here." His emotional blow landed like a slap, a sting of loneliness hot in its wake.

Maybe he's right? I'm always reaching for the impossible. But her own cold rage started to uncoil within her. *He thinks he's a nice guy? Nice guys don't sulk and aim for tender spots when they're told no.* But before she could say anything in response, Caleb gave her another damaged glare.

"I hope you find your monster Nae. See how happy that makes you."

Neoma winced as Caleb slammed the door, his words feeling like a curse as his footsteps crunched violently down the gravel path. She continued to sit in the dark long after his truck had snarled away, wondering if loneliness is what freedom felt like.

CHAPTER 12

Danger in the Roots

Matrix

Trees whispered around Matrix, a morning prayer of gratitude to the light. Their voices were the rustle of leaves and needles, the clacking and clicking of branches, and the groan of trunks as the wind stretched them tall. If he listened close enough, he could almost hear their roots reaching underground, thirsting for a sip of water filtered through the loam.

The morning would be calm except for the bickering voices around him. Their slowly rising pitch was taking him away from the waking woods. It made him itch like fleas in his coat, his brother's perceived problems an annoyance he just couldn't be rid of. If only he could somehow communicate more clearly. But he couldn't, doggie charades lacked the nuances needed to tell Tobin how daft he was being. Matrix sighed.

"He wasn't a werewolf," Tobin repeated, jaw clenched.

A.B. Herron

"Pity, that would have been so easy for you." The dryad quipped. Matrix got the impression she was mocking Tobin. "So what will you do now?"

"Is it possible that Nora isn't a werewolf? I mean, there must be other creatures out there that can shift into wolves, right?" Tobin demanded.

"Possibly. With magic, there are always other options."

"Stop being coy with me, Fey. I'm doing my part and studying every old book I can get my hands on, but there's no mythos out there that matches exactly what I've seen so far. It's as if your kind can't be captured accurately in books. I'm sick of it. You offered to help me, so help."

"To what gain, man-wolf? What do you tender me in tribute for my assistance?" She tucked a trailing leaf behind her ear, the green a bright spot in her dark tresses. She looked very prim sitting on the low branch of an ancient big leaf maple. Today, her dress was made of fern fronds and cat's ear flowers, rustling around her in a slight breeze.

"You expect me to give you something for what you've already freely offered? That's going back on your word, and from what I've read, your word binds you. Unless that detail is also inaccurate." Tobin glared at her, his bare chest heaving with frustration. Matrix made himself comfortable on the soft duff. This would take a while.

"What answers do you seek, man-wolf? Are you even aware of what you really want? You come out here day after day, running, doing little else. Your black beast has more of a plan than you do. He is at least learning while you continue to whine about being alone."

Tobin glanced at Matrix, and the dog quickly averted his eyes, attempting to look uninterested. Inside, he cursed the dryad for bringing him into this. Was she talking about his hunting activities? He supposed where there were trees, there were eyes and ears, and she seemed to oversee the goings on in these woods. Did she mind him eating the creatures he found? The small Fey? He'd only wanted to help the sprites. And they were more than willing to identify the predators around their nest. With each taste of bitter green magic, the fog of his canine brain dissipated, leaving human logic exposed like rocks at low tide.

"What I want," Tobin's eyes flashed, "is to go back to Portland. But that cursed faun made it very clear I wasn't welcome. He called me weak." Tobin paused, and Matrix could see his brother replaying the confrontation with the faun. "He called me packless. That, that is what I need to fix. I need a pack."

"Well, what about this Nora person?" The dryad lazily plucked petals off a small flower, only to reattach them with a touch of her finger before eating the whole thing in one bite.

"You sound like Matrix," Tobin bristled.

"I was not aware the dog could talk." She leaned forward with real interest in her light pink eyes. Matrix lifted a lip but didn't bother to move past the flash of fang. "Oh," she pouted, "you were doing that human thing and lying."

"I'm not lying, and you have no room to talk. I've been reading up on Fey. For all your blustering about telling the truth, Fey are the worst liars in these woods."

"If you lie with the truth, is it still lying?" She mused. "Are you going to reach out to this wolf or not?" She picked another flower from her dress, her legs swinging as she studied the plant.

"No, I'm not. I..." Tobin faltered, embarrassment and regret leaking into his scent. Matrix lifted his head from his paws and looked at Tobin's back. This was a new emotion from his brother. "I couldn't get her to see reason the first time, why would she be willing to listen now? Besides, I hurt her, and I can't imagine she'd want anything to do with me. I wouldn't be surprised if she wanted to hurt me back." His head and shoulders dropped, and he scuffed the dirt with his toe.

"You want her to respect you." The dryad leaned forward, calculating, but Tobin didn't notice. "You want her to see you as an equal."

Tobin's head shot up, and he spun to face the Fey. "I need a pack of my own. Tell me, how do I make one?"

"Ah, now we are getting somewhere," she purred. "I will tell you what to do, but you must figure out how to do it. And when you succeed, you will promise your pack as guardians of these woods. This will be your new territory, where you can lead your wolves in safety. There is no other pack in these parts, and a forest needs wolves after all." Her smile was teeth and temptation.

"I will not be chained to another," Tobin growled at her, his hand rubbing at the red lines of scar tissue under the tattoo of a fiddlehead fern. The burn from enchanted silver was a constant reminder never to trust a Fey.

"I see," the dryad mused, hopping off her branch to walk a slow circle around him. "Then I have no reason to help you. I spoke in haste, thinking we wanted the same things." Her hand trailed over Tobin's scarred ribs, and he jumped away from her.

Matrix lunged to his feet and moved between them before things could get ugly. He growled at the dryad, seeing green and red energy move around her like a mirage. Then he swiveled and huffed at Tobin, giving a doggy shrug and pointing his head toward the house. If this creature wasn't going to help Tobin, then they were wasting their time, and Matrix was getting tired of his brother's self-serving agenda.

Tobin glared at the Fey and went to follow Matrix's suggestion.

"Wait." The word froze them both.

"What?" Tobin glared over his shoulder. The dryad looked like a young girl standing in an enchanted forest, rays of light from the afternoon sun dusting her dark skin with gold.

"To turn a human, you have to do what was done to you."

Tobin stiffened. "I will not torture another person."

"Are you so sure?" The dryad seemed to speak these words to herself. "To get what you want, I wonder at your limits."

Matrix bristled, his hackles rising. This creature was dangerous, tripping all his protective urges. The need to attack her built like a storm behind a mountain. He fought for restraint even as he licked his lips remembering—her blood was sweet.

"Peace, I seek no quarrel with you."

Matrix dropped his head and showed his fangs. He could not allow this dryad to toy with his brother any longer. He wasn't sure what he could do, but some instinct was telling him this game she was playing was a wicked one, with thorns hidden among the tempting fruit.

"Fine, I will give what I offered," she spat at Matrix. He stopped growling, surprised at her acquiescence. Annoyance flitted across her features as she restored her attention to Tobin. "Listen close, man-wolf. I will not repeat myself. To give magic to the immune, you are required to strip away their armor of ignorance. Make them believe. Give them faith in the impossible, the unprovable. When they wholeheartedly trust that magic is real, then your bite will have power, and magic can have its way with them. Otherwise, their brain will continue to shield them, and magic will slide off them like rain from a leaf." And with that, she leaned against a tree and was gone.

A chill rose every hair on Matrix's body. What had she just planted? He examined his brother as a thoughtful look kindled deep in Tobin's hazel eyes, the bright spark of an idea already taking root. Matrix's head drooped, tail hanging low as they returned through the trees. How could he protect his brother from things so far out of his control? He didn't know, and each day, the idea of regaining his human form seemed to slip further from him. He'd resigned himself to life as a dog, and that scared him. But would being human even help at this point? Matrix gave a soft whine and moved into a trot to hunt. Maybe eating a bogey would make him feel better; it couldn't hurt.

CHAPTER 13

Mr. Tasty

Neoma

Neoma ignored her lunch on the bookstore's counter. Leaning forward, she took slow measured inhales, attempting to get her pain under control. Another arthritis flair was sinking its claws in deep, the cursed disease attacking her upper back and elbows. Why the three vertebrae right between her shoulder blades? It was anyone's guess. Rheumatoid arthritis mostly went after the hands and feet but seemed willing to take on other joints just for fun. And each time it did, Neoma felt like her body no longer fit, like the burn and the ache and the throbbing was just a transitory sensation leading her towards...towards what?

Neoma winced as she adjusted herself on her stool, attempting to find a more comfortable position to wallow in. *But the pain never transmutes into anything. It just builds, then recedes, then builds again! And why the hell did my RA decide to hate me today? It's not like I changed my routine or even cheated on my diet. What gives? I keep trying to do everything right, every damn day.* Her anger sparkled with frustration because things had been better recently, and for long enough that she had dared to imagine she'd made some progress.

But no, I couldn't even get a full week of relief. My fucking disease woke up and chose revenge. Neoma despaired, sinking lower onto the counter with a sigh as she flailed for a positive thought, something bright to cling to. *Okay, upside, I can hold a glass of water because my hands aren't swollen. And, well, the Hunchback of Notre Dame thing I've got going is sorta literary.* She rolled her eyes as her back throbbed, making her crumple further. *Maybe tomorrow will be better.* She sighed.

But her attempted optimism faltered. Depression, potent and bleak, glided down nerve endings along with her pain. The uncomfortable cocktail slipped into her brain like silky venom, dimming her hope with each burning throb. She fought the demoralizing darkness and cranked up Enya on her phone, pretending she was floating, weightless, painless, in an ocean where nothing could touch her except her own thoughts.

Neoma's eyes desperately tracked the traffic outside as she attempted to numb her pain further. A welcomed distraction came into view dressed in tight jeans, walking what looked like a black bear on a leash. The man stopped to tether the enormous beast to a spindly tree, his toned arms flexing as he secured the knot. Now Neoma sighed for a different reason, enjoying the play of his shoulder blades under his tight t-shirt as he moved, his back towards her. She allowed herself to envision this man removing his shirt, imagining the rest of his skin as tan as his arms. She slid a hand across the smooth wood of the counter, pretending it was the playground of his physique, warm hills and valleys for her fingers to roam.

Neoma shook herself, looking down at her hand. *This is quickly becoming a low moment, I'm fondling a counter,* she grumped, stilling her tactile travels across the space. Yet her eyes returned to the stranger, there was something about him.

It's the line of his shoulders I think, they seem so familiar, like I've seen him before, but not in town, so where? she mused. *Turn around, come on, you can do it, just a little pivot, I mean your back is pretty, but who are you?*

Much to her growing frustration, he continued to face away while having a small conversation with the sasquatch he'd just bound to a tree. Abruptly, the man straightened and walked out of view. *Oh come on! Would it have killed you to walk the other way?* Neoma drummed her fingers on the counter while she studied the beast that she grudgingly admitted must be a dog. *Well, at least I still have something to look at, even if it isn't a fantastical creature.* The aforementioned canine perked up, looking through the glass, a dopey expression on their sweet face as a big, plumed tail began to wave gently.

"So big black and furry, you like books?" she asked then wondered if the dog could hear here from where she sat inside. "Or is it my lunch that you're drooling over? Because you might smell roast beef, but you're not getting roast beef. However, if you decide to purchase a thirteen-book series, in hardback, I'm happy to open negotiations on the beef." A small grin tugged at her mouth as she tucked her lunch back into its container, stashing it under the counter for dinner later.

"Can you hear me?" The dog wagged their tail faster, and her smile grew. "In that case, let's start bargaining, because I'm hard up for someone to talk to. So what genre would you read if you could? Or are you a non-fiction kind of canine? Let me guess, historical crime novels?"

The dog sneezed and glanced to the side just as her front door opened, causing the bell to chime and Neoma to startle out of her one-sided conversation.

She scrambled to turn down her music and force herself into a straighter posture, schooling her face into a mask of pain-free friendliness. Miranda had been right; book sales were down. It was hard to compete when a reader could get their bookish fix with one click and never have to leave their house. Instant gratification without getting off the couch, the new name of the game. But damned if Neoma was going to admit to that. Personal touch and loyalty still meant something. She hoped. Yet things were getting tighter each year and if it wasn't for the rabid following of bibliophiles that supported local, Neoma would already be out of business. She gave thanks for her community, but new customers were sorely needed.

The primary owner of Rainy Day Books, her mom, insisted on diversifying as much as possible. As a result, the small store had floor to ceiling shelving, ladders to reach those out of the way spaces, and an atmosphere that made Neoma think the shop would fit right into a fantasy story. She smiled despite the pain in her back and breathed in the smell of books, ink, paper, and dust—always dust. She was right at home as she faced her potential customer.

"Anything I can help you with?" she called out. The person had taken a sharp right into the stacks, bypassing her counter space. Now they were lingering in the far back where the game section made its home. Neoma glanced at her security cameras, but the tiny man on the screen was just browsing, one hand touching a game here, a title there while he held a stack of papers in his other hand.

Neoma squinted at the screen, it was the dog's owner. He pulled out a book, glanced at the back, then replaced it on the shelf before gliding up the aisle towards her. Neoma tore her eyes from the monitor to face him and did a double take. That glide, she knew that glide. *No way, is this really Mr. Tasty?*

The book dragon from Portland was in her store, walking towards her. Well, he didn't walk, shuffle, or amble, something she had noticed immediately at the book fair, this man moved as if made of water, gracefully stepping around piles of books without even looking at them. A small pang shot through her chest. She missed that freedom of movement, and it was well out of her reach today. But the regret didn't linger as he stopped in front of her counter, his hazel eyes behind the dark rimmed glasses were as intense as she remembered.

"Hi. Neoma, right?" He smiled at her, his jawline strong, voice low and smooth. Neoma shook herself, nodding affirmatively. Yep, he was as pretty as she remembered him. Her gaze flicked over the well-defined forearms and biceps as he fiddled with a stack of papers in his hands. "I'd assumed you lived in Portland. It was a pleasant surprise to see Kelso on your business card when I got home."

"Why? Don't you live in Portland?" she asked. *Well, that was witty.* Neoma collected her thoughts and attempted to appear more professional.

"I used to," his face got hard for a second, then relaxed. "Anyway, I live in Kelso now. I've only been here a couple months. Honestly, work has been keeping me busy, and I haven't really been out to explore, so your card gave me a good excuse. That and I wanted to let you know our conversation inspired me." He handed her a flyer with little tear-off email addresses at the bottom. "I was wondering if your store would be willing to post this?"

Neoma slid her eyes off the arm candy and actually looked at the sheet. A huge werewolf lunged out of the paper at her, red lettering plastered over its gaping maw. *Ever dreamed of being a werewolf? Like to game? I'm looking for a group of people to join my pack for a Werewolf: The Apocalypse live gaming group. Interested? Please send me an email and let's Rage together.*

Neoma raised one sculpted eyebrow, something fluttering in her belly. She put the flyer down, giving herself a chance to think. She wondered if this was a second opportunity while slowly gathering her tight curls at the nape of her neck, securing them into a messy bun with two pencils.

"Sounds like you're using *my* book to build your own world."

"You're book?" He raised one brow in return.

"I had my hand on it first, and I gallantly let you take it home on loan."

"Funny, I remember paying for it." He leaned in a little, his nose flaring, eye contact unblinking. "Well, I'm going to hold onto it a little longer, it's been a helpful part of my research, invaluable actually."

"Fascinating. I wasn't aware that werewolves tangled with ancient European Fey."

"It would seem that magical creatures are no longer limited by borders. It's a small world after all." He grinned as if he knew she would now have that song stuck in her head for the rest of the day. "Besides, werewolves also originated in Europe."

Oh, touché, he knows his monsters. Point to him. Neoma grinned.

"Well played sir. So I was right. You do like live action role-playing games, don't you?" She studied him. *Don't judge a book by its cover indeed! This man looks like he should be scaling a rock wall somewhere, not RPG-ing.* She shrugged internally. *Everyone has a hobby, and now I've uncovered why he wanted that book so badly, my instincts aren't too rusty.*

"Actually, truth be told, I'm a bit addicted to them. I mean, usually I game online, but since I just moved here, I figured making some in-person connections, and I don't know, friends, might be good. I realize it's a novel concept." He shrugged, his tight shirt moving over pecs and shoulders. That shrug looked good on him. Neoma tried not to bite her lip.

"This is pretty old school, you know, handing out flyers. But I appreciate the proactive spirit." Neoma was impressed, and slightly jealous. She'd been watching her little brother involve himself in the mural painting on the outside of the store. The older kids had enthusiastically folded Lukas into their activities, teaching him about perspective and painting. The ease with which her little brother was making new friends had been tugging on Neoma, inciting a sense of isolation that she resolutely ignored. "I know how hard it can be to meet people when you're new in town. I understand now why you mugged me for that book. It was an act of desperation."

"Oh, so now I've mugged you? I see." He chuffed in amusement before his excitement in RPG dimmed, the teasing draining away. "No, that book…that's for a slightly different project, although I suppose the two are more related now that I think about it. Anyway," he seemed to reset himself, "you're the one who let go of the book first. It's not my fault you didn't have the gumption to hang on." He gave a small smile, and she decided he was trying to be funny. "When I'm done with it, I'll give you a chance to buy it from me."

"Really? Well that's very generous of you, magnanimous even," she said, and he smiled wider. "Or would be *if* it was actually *your* book. Yet as I've already stated, I had it first," she said dryly, a small twist quirking her lips before tapping her chin with a finger. "Although perhaps I should consider charging you for hanging your flyer?"

"What?" He startled, then collected himself, "Oh, um, yeah, sorry, um, you win, please no. I've been told my humor needs work, case in point." He toyed with the papers in his hands. Somehow, Neoma wasn't surprised at this guy's awkward side. "And my people skills could use a tune-up as well. I suppose being on a computer all day isn't doing me any favors." He raised his eyebrows, as if hoping she might contradict him and tell him he was charming.

Neoma chuckled and tossed him a conversional bone instead. "So you chose gaming to meet people, in lieu of, oh I don't know," she waved a hand in the air, "a running club, or hiking, or mountaineering? There's a Mazamas outfit that would probably be happy to accommodate you, if you wanted more social outlets." *Am I trying to drive this guy away?*

He squinted at her, as if thinking the same thing.

"Sorry," *now I'm apologizing, why am I apologizing?* But she continued unheeded with her unfiltered dialogue. "I shouldn't question your hobbies. You just seem more outdoorsy than indoorsy. Ya know, and RPGs tend to be strictly an indoor sport." She shrugged, feeling frustration color her cheeks. *Come on brain, let's get back to the flirting, stop giving unasked for character critiques.*

"Oh, no, that's a fair assumption." He glanced down at himself, as if seeing his athletic physique for the first time. "I mean, I try to stay active. That's my brother's fault. He forced me into the outside world. I kept trying to hide in my computer after our parents died, but Max wouldn't have it; he continued dragging me out and making me participate." The man dropped his head, his cheeks reddening slightly. "Sorry, sometimes I overshare without thinking." His hands slid into his pockets, and he seemed to become shy for a moment before visibly steadying himself. Neoma was struck by his transparency. Even his body was oversharing, telegraphing his feelings with each posture. Was he even aware he was doing it?

"Oh, it's okay." She gave him the easy out, at least she wasn't the only one making this conversation awkward. "People overshare with me all the time. I'm what you might call a 'captive audience'." She indicated the desk and shop with a wave. The man chuckled.

"I'm Tobin by the way." He held out a hand, she hesitated and then slowly took it. His grip was warm and firm when he squeezed, and she winced slightly. "Oh!" He snatched his hand back. "I'm so sorry, did I hurt you?"

"Just a little, but it's not your fault." She held up her hand so he could clearly see her twisted knuckles. "I have rheumatoid arthritis, it just makes things a little more sensitive sometimes." She waited to see pity fill his face, to hear him say 'oh you poor thing, but you look so young.' He didn't, instead, a pensive expression creased his brow, and he gave a little nod to himself as if a question had been answered.

"That's why you smell like eucalyptus and mint then. A sore muscle rub?" He asked.

"Yeah." She blinked. "You can still smell that? I thought it would've faded by now."

He shrugged. "I have a nose for it. Hey," he put his papers down and reached out his hands indicating he wanted her hand again, "may I?" His question was tentative.

Neoma pulled back slightly, quizzically considering him. He seemed harmless so she relinquished her hand. Tobin's finger pads were callused as he cradled her hand in his, holding her carefully. His skin was hot, the heat soaking quickly into her, soothing her sore joints.

"Is that better?" He asked.

"Yes, how did you know to do that?" She felt weird. His touch was platonic yet intimate as he simply supported her hand between his. The instant relief from his body heat was welcomed, yet the proximity of this stranger was unsettling. She wasn't sure if she was grateful or freaked out.

"Magic." Tobin winked at her, and she fought the urge to glower at him.

"No, seriously." She pulled away, and he let her go. She found she missed his heat as she picked up his flyer.

"I had grandparents that helped raise me. My grandmother had arthritis. Heat always seemed to help her, and I run warm..." He shrugged, looking slightly bashful as he rocked back on his heels. "So, is it ok if I post that in here?" He signaled the flyer that draped limply in her grip, the snarling werewolf between them.

"Oh, of course." She handed the flyer back and pointed to the corkboard next to the door. "Help yourself, there should be plenty of tacks."

"Thanks." Tobin shifted to go, then hesitated. "You wouldn't by any chance be interested, would you?"

"In playing werewolves with you?" Neoma chuckled.

"Sure, why not?" Tobin's eyes were serious, that edge he'd had in Portland was back. Calculating.

Neoma tilted her head to the side and stopped her reflex of flat out refusing. She embraced solitude for a reason, it kept her safe, kept her from being a burden on other people. Yet she couldn't banish Megan's voice in her head encouraging her to put herself out there and try something new. "You're not a burden, Nae, you just have some physical challenges. You, as you are, are more than enough wonderful for someone. Trust me, anyone would be lucky to have you in their lives, I know I am. So stop hiding and live it up."

This would be that 'something new' Megan keeps griping about. Neoma sighed inwardly. *I could do this. Gaming with people, in...person. Ugg, why is this so hard?* She could hear Megan and her mom cheering her on. With work as her only social outlet apart from her online support groups, some real human connection would probably do her some good. After all, Tobin was here trying to reach beyond the digital, perhaps he was on to something? Besides, he was cute. She glanced at his arms again, noticing that pattern of scars that looked like shooting stars ringing his right forearm. The urge to trace them with her finger made her cheeks flush.

"I'll think about it," she answered carefully, feeling the first stirring of interest in a social activity prickle to life like a limb regaining circulation.

"That's all I ask."

⁘

"MR. TASTY LIVES IN KELSO!" MEGAN CROWED, AND NEOMA pulled the phone away from her ear to scowl at it. She could practically hear Megan's feet doing a happy dance.

"If you don't tone down your triumphant gloating, I'm going to end this call right now," Neoma groused.

"You wouldn't dare! This is the best entertainment I've had in weeks. Unless you count balancing things on Steve when he sleeps because that's just priceless."

"I'm really starting to worry about you."

"Yeah, well that would be the kettle addressing the pot."

"Ha ha, Meg."

"Seriously, Nae. So was he as hot the second time around?"

"Yes," the word escaped her before she could stop it, and she gave in. "He was so hot, rocking this kind of bad boy with a halo vibe almost. He kept slipping from confident into super shy with this slightly crooked smile. Which was an improvement over the edgy focus he'd had in Portland. And his arms, Meg, his arms." Neoma sat back in her overstuffed chair and gazed out the window allowing her mind to play over Tobin's biceps in slow motion.

"Am I interrupting? Want to talk later?"

"Oh, shut up, you started it."

Megan barked a laugh. "Fine. So are you going to join his group?"

"Yeah, I think actually I am. I mean, why not?" So many reasons shot through her head, but she slammed them down before she could talk herself out of this.

"Ok, then, I have an idea. How about using the store to game at? You'll be in your comfort zone, but it'll be more neutral ground for everyone else. And maybe if you mention it on your website, you can get some more late-night activities going on."

"That's not a bad idea. I would have to get Stewart to man the counter if we're going to be legitimately open, but I don't think he would mind. However, if this all goes to hell, I'm blaming you."

"Deal." Megan sounded way too proud of herself. "Oh, Nae, I'm sorry I gotta go. Talk later this week?"

"Sure thing, love you."

"Love you too." The conversation ended. Neoma staired at her computer, tapping a finger against her lips in contemplation.

Well, why not? She glanced at Tugman. The Betta fish seemed to bob up and down with enthusiastic agreement. Neoma nodded and with slow keystrokes she typed out the words, *Becoming a Werewolf, a Journey into the Unknown.* Then studied the screen. She'd been contemplating a new project, why not write a satirical piece about RPG-ing? There would probably be gaming magazines that would be interested. She shrugged and resumed typing.

An hour later, she looked up from creating her werewolf character, surprised at how much fun she'd been having. Digging through her bag, she unearthed Tobin's email address from the flyer and started typing. *Hi Tobin, it's Neoma from the bookstore. I've decided to give your group a shot. I looked up the details of the game and it sounds like it might be a fun experience. If you haven't found a place to meet, may I offer up the bookstore? It's pretty central for most people, and we have room in the gaming section which I'm sure you saw. Just let me know. Thanks, Nae.*

Her cursor hovered over the send button for about three heartbeats. *Once I do this, there's no going back.* She laughed at herself, what was she afraid of? She clicked send and shut her laptop.

Tugman bobbed at the surface of his bowl, asking for attention. "There's no reason to worry, right Tugman?"

Flashes of Tobin's well-defined arms floated through her mind, blotting out her reservations about adding new people to her social circle. Tobin hadn't treated her with any pity, maybe the rest of this group would follow his lead? She fed her fish and crawled into bed. "After all, how bad could it be?" she whispered as she flipped off the light. "It's just a game."

CHAPTER 14

Promises, Prey, Price

Tobin

"Full moon tonight," Tobin said while bouncing on his toes and punching the air as if boxing. Matrix merely huffed and rolled over onto his back in the giant dog bed dominating the floor.

"You're coming with me, aren't you?" Tobin grabbed a bowl of hot dogs off the counter and stopped to look down at his brother. Was Matrix bigger? He blinked, but the dog continued to sprawl across the memory foam and spill onto the floor, limbs akimbo. Maybe the bed shrunk in the wash? Internally, Tobin shrugged and went back to his bouncing. He could feel the energy cresting inside him, a hum just beyond his hearing, and it made him restless.

"Tonight's going to be different, there's no fucking faun up here to sling rocks, and I'm not sticking close to the house again like last month. No, tonight we're going hunting. We will own these woods." His confidence soared. He'd been training these last six weeks, running, working out, learning to box with a heavy bag in the garage. He challenged what his new body could do and found those physical limits, then went beyond them, getting stronger, faster, more adapted to being wild. At the same time, he studied everything he could get his hands on about Fey and other mythical creatures. Now he was ready for whatever might be out there. The mistakes of being unprepared for this new life would not be repeated. The Portland wilderness had been a learning moment, and Tobin had always been an exceptional student. Besides, after weeks of running in these woods, the dryad was the only large magical creature he'd encountered. The forest seemed deserted.

Night fell like a silken sheet over the fields behind the run-down mobile home, softening the ragged appearance of the dwelling. Tobin didn't care about aesthetics, the electricity functioned, he had Wi-Fi for his job, and there was plumbing. He really couldn't be happier out here far from neighbors. Especially tonight. He didn't need to drive to find isolation for his shift, he simply walked out the back door.

Which is what he did now, the grass cool and damp on his bare feet, his body naked except for a pair of super stretchy boxer briefs. No reason to let his man bits dangle. Matrix padded out behind him, still yawning as if bored with the whole thing. Tobin wondered at his brother's attitude as he set down the bowl of hot dogs. The dog had become increasingly disinterested with Tobin's activities, choosing to go out into the woods for hours alone. What was he doing by himself?

But his musing melted with the moonlight as it touched his skin. Sweat began to pour off Tobin's body as the change took him. He could feel his metabolic system rev into high gear as bones broke down and regrew, fur sprouted, and new teeth cut through his gums. The pain was blinding, taking him to his hands and knees, but he breathed through the experience, welcoming the shift, begging for more, willing more strength, more brawn into his muscles, more everything. Beyond the pain, power simmered, a river of magic rerouted by the moon into Tobin, filling him until his body burst apart and remade itself.

He loved every fucking minute of it.

Stars danced in his vision, little pinpricks in the fabric of his visual reality. Carefully, he came up onto his knees, keeping his breathing even and deep. His enhanced night vision gave the field a patina of grays, darkening to charcoal at the tree line. Matrix sat like a midnight monolith, looming in the empty expanse of grass, watching everything.

Tobin tilted his muzzle towards the moon, relishing the burn of energy coursing through him. It washed away the pain to leave him surging with power. He flexed his clawed hands and rolled his shoulders. Yes, this body was what he had been waiting for his whole life; the strength and potential in it made him giddy. He savored the moment for another breath and let his attention expand back out to the world around him.

The sound of slow clapping met his ears, and he jerked his head to the trees. The dryad stood leisurely applauding with a condescending expression.

"Well done, man-wolf, you did not scream like a dying rabbit this month. Perhaps you can be taught."

"Try having your body rebuilt, and we'll see how you scream," he spat at her as he gobbled the hot dogs waiting for him, his mind filling with the moon's call, distracting him and dulling his reason.

"I know pain on a level you could never imagine," she whispered, her voice gone smoky, pink eyes gleaming like embers in his night vision. "Of course, there are probably many things that escape your limited perspective."

Tobin growled and lunged to his feet, spittle flying. He now towered over the Fey and savored the change in status. "Don't taunt me tonight Fey, I'm more than willing to taste you under this moon."

"Well, I have not had an offer that enticing in ages." She giggled and sauntered forward. "You are not bad looking in this shape, I could do worse." Her eyes raked down him, a suggestion twisting her mouth.

"What?" Tobin blinked, losing his bluster, suddenly very glad he was wearing underwear.

"Dense, like an oak. Pity. And enough of this 'Fey' nonsense, I have a name."

Tobin recovered and went back to looming. "You've never bothered to share it, Fey."

She narrowed her eyes at him. "Fine, that is fair." Petulance wormed across her face then was gone, her features smoothing. "You may call me Aithne."

"Anna?" Tobin's werewolf features knotted in confusion.

"Close enough for a man-wolf, I suppose." Tobin glowered, Aithne ignored him. "I have a quest for you this night, if you have the stones for it." Her eyes drifted down to his groin and Tobin's hackles rose as he resisted the urge to cover himself further.

"I don't bow to you."

"Who said anything about bowing? I could do with a good grovel, it has been a while. But let us face it, your heart is not in it. No, think of this as a job interview. If you pass, perhaps we can discuss a partnership."

Tobin was slow to respond, turning her words around in his mind, looking for the trap as his body itched to run. "What do you want?"

"I am offering you a hunt. There is a creature in my territory that is running amuck. I need you to kill it, and soon, before it destroys any more of my trees. Will you do this?"

"What's my reward?"

"Reward?" Aithne laughed and the night became a little colder. "I have just given you permission to hunt a magical creature in my domain without repercussions." Her gaze narrowed and slid to Matrix for a moment. "Is that not reward enough?"

Tobin stood up a little straighter, forcing his mind to work, his thoughts muzzy as he fought the hypnotic pull of the moon. He wanted to hunt, wanted to taste blood and let his wild instincts loose, but the scar of enslavement burned on his side, and he wouldn't make that mistake again. He held on harder to his reason as he spoke. "I came here because no one rules here. Now you claim this is your territory, and I need your permission to hunt? That doesn't smell right to me." Matrix backed him up with a soft growl, moving slowly to flank the dryad.

"Maybe you are only as dense as hickory." Aithne mused. "My domain is the trees, but you are correct, I do not command total sovereignty, yet. Unfortunately, there are a few pesky predators adapted to hunt me, which you, dear man-wolf, I believe, have the skills to eliminate. Why be only strong, when together, we could domineer? That is what I keep trying to get through that wolfish skull of yours. You want territory to make a pack. You want to rule, to build an alliance. Go kill this creature, think about what you could gain, then come back to me."

She tossed a chunk of something that splattered when it hit the ground, causing Tobin to take a step back. Matrix approached and sniffed it, a small growl building in his throat. Tobin joined him. The piece of flesh was ragged as if torn free of something. Blood still oozed from the skin, making small trails of red that looked black in the moonlight. It smelled like decaying leaves and sharp magic.

"What is this?" Tobin sniffed it again, and his belly rolled with hunger from the change, making bile creep up his throat. He would not eat meat she tossed at his feet as if he were her dog. He would not. He licked his lips.

"It is from a creature that feeds on the very magic of living things. No matter how much it consumes, its appetite is never sated. Fair warning, do not let the mouth touch you. Happy hunting." And she was gone, a shadow in the dark.

Tobin looked longingly at the fresh meat, denying his urges as anger seized him. Hunger, he'd use it to motivate the hunt. "Let's go," he growled and leapt into the woods, the tentative hold on the man dissolving, releasing the wolf fully to the moon's call.

⸻

MATRIX KEPT PACE WITH THE WEREWOLF, WATCHING HOW Tobin easily navigated the dark as if born to it. Something about Tobin's quick acclimation to his new life made Matrix uneasy, but he couldn't put his paw on why.

The scent trail they were following was wide. Whatever this creature was, it moved with stealth. Not many branches were broken or disturbed, but the area seemed saturated with odor, as if the thing was large.

A river cut their path, the scent stopping. The brothers split, each running the length of the river in opposite directions for about a hundred yards, then sprinting back before finding and fording the shallows. They'd discovered

Tobin didn't swim well in this shape, he was too heavy, and Matrix didn't have a Newfoundland's skills for water rescue. Deeper water had become a barrier.

The far bank revealed the creature's scent trail heading north into thicker woods. Matrix wanted to run this beast to ground. Needed to. That itch of "threat" budded in his hindbrain, growing into a tangle of compulsion and desire. Whereas Tobin seemed to think he was defending territory, Matrix was protecting it. Whatever this thing was, it was draining the life out of the trees as it passed them as evident in the dark patches on trunks and the wilted and shriveled understory plants. Each affected organism looked shrouded in wounded gray light that stung Matrix's eyes. This creature's consumption didn't encourage the ecosystem to flourish, but annihilated everything it touched. No wonder the dryad feared it. Whatever this was, it was not native, and it was scarring the very ground it walked over.

Also, its smell was not improving.

A branch snapped and the brothers froze, each one scenting the air, ears swiveling. Something was moving up ahead, they'd found it.

The creature weighed somewhere between a moose and a small elephant. Long sinuous legs allowed it to progress through the brush with ease. The body fluttered as if covered with leaves, making a soft sound like the wind blowing through foliage. It blended so well into the dark forest that Matrix wouldn't have seen it without movement. Its head was crowned with spiral horns, the tips looking like sharpened sticks. Its mouth was long and fleshy, protruding like a fly's proboscis, darting out and sucking the energy of one tree, before traveling to another. It ambled like a grazing animal, taking a little bit here, a little there. However, it paused at one tree, beady eyes darting up into the limbs as its snout snaked forward and plucked something as if it were harvesting an apple from a branch.

The turkey barely fluttered before going limp, the life sucked from it like someone would drain the last drops of a milkshake. The creature discarded the deflated body, the husk turning to dust as it fell, and grabbed another sleeping turkey from its roost.

Matrix watched in horror as the act was repeated five times before the rest of the flock awoke to the danger just below them, their alarm calls piercing the sleeping woods as the canopy exploded in a frantic rush of feathers.

"It's a Drainer." The small voice in Matrix's ear almost made him bolt. Pure instinct kept him from shaking his head to dislodge the tiny sprite that was now sitting on his brow. How had she done that? "Hush now, Guardian, allow me to tell you how to destroy it because it will keep feeding until there is nothing left. It samples the plants, but it kills whatever animals it can sneak up on. When the animals are gone, it will turn to the trees and devastate them all. It is a blight on life." Anger and rage rolled through the little voice, making her bark-covered body hum.

Matrix gave the tiniest growl to show he understood.

"Good. The danger lies in the harvesting mouth. If its opening touches you, it will drain you dry. But that appendage is also its greatest weakness. Be careful, its hooves are like claws, and it has a mighty kick. I cannot aid you, it is immune to my poisons." And with that dire warning, the sprite leapt from his head onto the back of a swooping screech owl and was gone.

Matrix had no way of communicating this to Tobin, he only hoped his brother would be smart enough to stay out of harm's way. Up ahead, Tobin crouched down within the sword ferns, studying the drainer as it snuffled through the underbrush looking for something, the long snout undulating like a vacuum hose.

"I'm going to move around to that big maple and see if I can get above it. If I can drop and sever the spinal cord, we can end this quickly. Distract it." Tobin didn't wait to see if Matrix agreed before sprinting off into the dark. The dog huffed and started to stalk forward, head low, tail flat behind him.

Five feet from his target, the drainer froze, its beady eyes locking onto Matrix's location. This close, the creature was massive, the long legs like house stilts holding up a body that was so bloated under the strange leafy covering that it could have been a balloon in a parade. A ragged hole could be seen in its side, a chunk of flesh missing, still dripping viscous blood onto the ground like red rain.

A.B. Herron

Matrix didn't hesitate, he charged forward, then dashed to the side at the last minute as the drainer swung its body to try and swipe at him with its front claws. The blow left gashes in the duff, but Matrix was already dashing back around to its other side, barking and snarling, all need for stealth gone.

Another long leg lashed out, a kick that flicked past faster than the dog expected, nicking Matrix's ear and sending hot pain through the side of his head as he ducked and rolled just as the hoof came down to trample him. Dirt and ferns flew, and the creature trumpeted a battle cry, twisting in the night, trying to find its target.

Matrix harried it like a herding dog, snapping at its hocks, nipping at its sides, each time dancing out of the way at the last moment only to try for its head again. The drainer kept its snout out of reach, only snaking it after Matrix when he was in retreat. The creature was well aware of its vulnerable spot and wouldn't allow the dog to get near it.

With a desperate lunge, Matrix dodged underneath the body, and jumped upwards, aiming for the wound. Teeth made contact with flesh, jaws clamped closed, and Matrix let his momentum and body weight do the rest.

The flesh tore free with a wet rip that flipped Matrix upside down and into a log, the impact stunning him as the creature screamed in pain.

Matrix thrashed, trying to regain his feet as the sound of hooves pounded towards him, shaking the ground. He wasn't going to make it, the world was still upside down, his legs not working right. The drainer suddenly shrieked, its charge derailed as it bucked and spun away in panic. Tobin was perched on its back. Matrix could see the werewolf rip and slice with his claws, trying to penetrate the thick leafy material that made a ruff around the creature's neck.

His efforts looked futile, the drainer was too well protected as it continued to heave, attempting to dislodge Tobin. Matrix wrenched upwards and dashed forward once more, timing his approach for when the drainer's head came down and its back feet went up in an attempt to throw Tobin from its back. His timing was flawless.

Matrix wrapped his jaws around the creature's snout, forcing his teeth through the tough material. The drainer tried to scream again, but no sound escaped, Matrix had closed off its air.

Now the drainer thrashed in desperation, slamming into trees, trying to scrape or claw the brothers off its body. Matrix put everything he had into holding on, closing his eyes and ignoring the slash of claws down his ribs, the impact of his body into trees. He knew, with the taste of the blood on his tongue, that this thing needed to die, or nothing in this forest would be safe. His fate didn't matter, only its death. The image of the little sprite, her body encased in fluffy down, floated through his head. She was worth saving, he could hang on a little longer.

CHAPTER 15

Freaked Out Feline

Neoma

"Good morning, Neoma," Kristin greeted as she entered the downstairs, absorbed in her cell phone. "My kitchen seems to be quite popular with you lately." She kissed her daughter on the temple, then paused with her one hand outstretched for the coffee, her brow furling. "Kjære, didn't you say the man who's starting the gaming group has a giant black dog?"

"Yeah, why?" Neoma turned away from the stove, leaving her eggs to sputter in the frying pan like angry cats.

"Carol just texted me, says Doctor Jenson is going into emergency surgery with a huge black dog who was attacked by a bear." She looked up from her phone. "They're putting the word out to see if anyone knows the owner because the poor young man looks almost as beat up as his dog and is refusing care for himself."

The magic and madness of small towns. People cared, to the point of meddling sometimes, but nothing moved faster than gossip to get the word out when help was needed. Carol, the office manager at the local vet clinic, and one of Kristin's closest friends, had put out the call. This news was coming from the source. It was still fresh and firsthand, not crusty and caked with day old rumors and supposition.

"Do you have a description?" Neoma asked, fear and certainty crawling through her on needle feet. She clutched the spatula as if brandishing a weapon to battle the inevitable. How many new strangers in town would own a giant black dog? Tobin had already told her where he lived, and it was pretty remote. A bear attack wouldn't be unheard of.

"Tall, sandy brown hair, well built, in his thirties. Drives a charcoal gray truck. Apparently came in wearing only basketball shorts and flip-flops, covered in blood and dirt." Kristin looked up to see if the description rang true.

"Shit, that sounds like Tobin." Neoma smelled burning eggs and rescued them from the stove, clicking it off. Should she do something? She bit her lip. If this was Tugman in trouble she would be an emotional mess. Sure, Tugman was a fish, but she really loved her fish. Tobin was probably beside himself with worry seeing as that dog seemed to go everywhere he did. And now Tobin was all alone in the vet clinic afraid his dog was going to die. Sympathy washed over Neoma. In his shoes, she would appreciate someone showing up to sit with her. Waiting for bad news should never be shouldered alone, this was a core family value that Neoma took to heart. Her decision made, she straightened.

"Mom, can you cover the store this morning please? I need to go help a friend." She grabbed the burned eggs, quickly shoveling them into her mouth. "And do we have any day-old pastries lying around here?"

"A friend?" Kristin's voice rose with a cloying question.

"Sure, well, we just met, but I think he could use a friend, and I want to help. Don't get too excited." She narrowed her eyes. Kristin held up her hands in defeat.

"I was just teasing. Go, help, I'll take care of the store." She smiled warmly at her daughter.

"Mom, you're the best." Neoma put her plate in the sink, kissed her mom on the cheek and turned to go.

"Don't forget these," Kristin thrust a bag of day-olds into her hands and a thermos of coffee. "Good coffee and a bit of sweet never hurts."

"I wanna go!" Lukas squeaked as he dashed into the kitchen on stocking feet.

"You don't even know where I'm going." Neoma said, grabbing her purse from the kitchen table.

"You're taking the Danishes, I want to come." Lukas put his hands on his hips as if she were stealing the family jewels.

"No." Both Neoma and Kristin said together, then laughed.

"Fine, then I want pancakes." He pouted at his mother.

"I think that can be arranged." Kristin tussled his hair. "Kjære, please keep me updated."

"Will do, thanks for telling me." Neoma smiled at her mom and hurried towards the door.

⸻ •◦◆◦• ⸻

WHAT AM I DOING? NEOMA THOUGHT FOR THE HUNDREDTH time as she pulled her little car into the parking lot at the veterinarian's office. Doubt at her actions had started to creep in like an insidious fog, dulling the bright certainty that her presence would be welcomed. *I don't really know Tobin, we've just exchanged a few emails about this gaming group. It's not like he called me and asked for me to swing by.* She slowly banged her forehead against the steering wheel as indecision seeped deeper, weighing her down. *This is crazy.* Yet she pried herself from the car and shuffled towards the door with a strange sense of purpose.

Neoma entered the small front office. Comfortable vinyl seats lined each wall on both sides with a clear "cat" and "dog" waiting area and a walkway leading up to reception. Frazzled faces greeted her from behind computer screens. On a high shelf above them perched a tabby cat with every hair standing on end. The cat glared murder at the man pacing back and forth in front of the counter, lips twitching to flash needle fangs.

His steps faltered as the door closed, and his head snapped up to look at her. Hazel eyes, naked without their glasses, blazed and there was blood across one cheek. Someone had given him a faded green scrub top two sizes too big, and it fluttered around him as he moved. His gray basketball shorts were smeared with blood and his muddy feet were indeed in flip-flops, streaks of rust matting his leg hair. More blood.

"Nae?" Tobin's voice was ragged and rough as if his vocal cords had been abraded with sandpaper. "What are you doing here?" His confusion was etched in every line of his body.

"I heard your dog got attacked by a bear, and thought maybe you didn't want to be alone." She held her head high and met his eyes. He looked unfocused and almost strung out. "Are you ok?"

Tobin blinked at her in confusion.

"I brought food." Neoma held up the bag and coffee. Maybe this had been a bad idea?

"Coffee?" Tobin shook his head, rubbing his eyes vigorously. "How did you even know I was here?"

"Oh you poor man, this is what small-town living's all about, community. You'll get used to it." She smiled in a comforting, nonchalant way. "No pressure, I can just leave these and go." *Oh this was a stupid idea.* Neoma berated herself and turned to leave. The cat on the high shelves hissed, making her turn back, straight into Tobin's chest. She hadn't heard him move.

"No, please," he carefully caught her shoulders to keep her from tipping over as she tried to put some space between them. "I'm sorry, I'm not used to this…" He waved a hand vaguely between them. "I'm a bit rusty with friendships." His smile was tremulous as he dragged his hand through his disheveled hair, fidgeting, his biceps flexing.

"It's okay, we all need a friend sometimes. How's your dog doing?" Neoma asked carefully and watched Tobin's face fall, guilt, anger and fear chased themselves over his blood-streaked features.

"You know what, don't answer that, you look like you've been up all night cage fighting." She handed him the thermos and grabbed his arm, leading him to a chair. "Sit, drink this, and breathe for a moment. Let me get some towels and water and we can clean you up." To her surprise, Tobin did exactly as she bade him, almost crumpling onto one of the vinyl chairs and unscrewing the lid on the coffee. *Okay, one small crisis handled, let's see what else I can do.*

Neoma approached the front desk. "Hi, do you ladies have some things I could use to get the blood off him? And if it's dog blood, do I need to wear gloves?"

"We'll get you what you need," said the young woman, Patty, according to her nametag. "And thank you, I wasn't sure how much more pacing I could handle," she whispered and ducked out to get supplies.

Within a moment, she was back with a bowl of hot water, some clean towels and exam gloves. Neoma nodded and took the offerings. "Any updates?"

"Matrix is still in surgery. That bear really knocked him around, I'm surprised he's still alive." Her voice was soft, but Neoma could see Tobin stiffen in her periphery.

"Thanks. Please let us know if anything changes." She went over to Tobin who sat like a man beaten. He clutched the thermos cup, his knuckles whitening. Neoma didn't say anything, simply put on the gloves and slowly cleaned the blood off Tobin's face with careful strokes. He had a nice face, strong jaw, a little stubble that snagged on the soft terry cloth. Neoma let herself fall into her task, moving down his arms, noting the well-defined muscles under her care. As she began to dab at the dried mud and muck of his forearms, Tobin stirred.

"It's ok, I can do this," he said softly. His fingers brushed hers as he handed her the coffee, distractedly taking the towel from her grip. Neoma noticed the cloth was rusty and damp with diluted blood. Tobin scrubbed vigorously at the crusty mess, his actions efficient. But the sludge was tenacious, and he finally excused himself to finish with some soap from the restroom.

Neoma resisted fidgeting. Instead, she watched the cat who wouldn't stop tracking Tobin. The poor animal was rigid, its tail flicking through the air with menacing agitation. When Tobin passed the counter on his return, the cat hissed, a low growl followed, making Neoma's hair stand on end. That was one freaky cat.

"Better?" she asked as he sat down, accepting the coffee.

"Much, thank you." His eyes were still haunted as he sipped. "I don't know what I'll do if he dies. I can't go through that again."

"Again?" Neoma lifted an eyebrow.

Tobin dropped his head and hunched further over his lap; she could see that his eyes were screwed shut. "Sorry, this is just bringing up a lot. I lost my brother four years ago to a work accident. I got Matrix shortly after that. I know he's a dog, but he kind of filled the space that my brother left. I can't lose him too." He shook slightly, the coffee sloshing in his cup.

Neoma didn't know what to do with that much raw loss. Should she pat his shoulder? Hand him a tissue? Pretend not to notice that his heart was bleeding in full view for everyone to see? She knew what it was to lose a piece of oneself. There was still an aching void where her ability to dance once lived. So she'd avoided comfort from others, feeling like it would make her weak. Yet in this moment, she didn't believe Tobin was being weak, he was being honest. With a stranger. How much courage did that take?

"Mr. Baxter?" Patty called from the front desk. "Dr. Jensen will see you now."

Tobin leapt up so fast the cat screamed and launched off the shelf through the door to the back office while coffee splattered across the floor. He put the cup on the counter and bolted into the exam room that was held open for him.

"What the...?" Patty gasped. "Why is Mabel so on edge today?" No one answered her as she shut the door, returning to the desk. Neoma watched as a person in surgical scrubs came out of the back and entered the exam room, a clipboard in hand.

The awkward feeling came back full force as Neoma rescued the cup and helped the receptionist clean the floor. Some emotion was percolating in her deep brain, something that was urging her to act upon it. "Is the dog okay?" she whispered to Patty, struggling to untangle her insistent feelings.

Patty leaned forward. "It looks like the surgery was successful, but that's all I know."

"Okay, thanks." Neoma stood slowly and retrieved the untouched paper bag. Should she stay? The murky emotions suddenly crystallized in her thoughts, making her take in a sharp breath. She needed to talk to her mom, now, before she lost this moment of clarity.

"Crap, I need to go. Can you please let Tobin know I had to return to work?" Neoma looked at Patty as if begging the young woman to understand why she was abandoning her new friend.

"Oh, of course, that was so sweet of you to come in the first place. We really appreciated it." Patty gave her a grateful smile. Apparently, the cat wasn't the only one stressed out by Tobin's presence.

"Here, feel free to split the Danishes amongst yourselves." Neoma handed over the bag. "I think you've earned them." She shared a look of camaraderie, grabbed the thermos and left, forcing herself to walk unhurriedly back to the car.

"So how'd it go? Were you able to help your friend?" Kristin asked as Neoma stalked up to her and wrapped her in a hug, burying her face in her mom's shirt. Kristin smelled like clean laundry, coffee, and caramelized sugar.

"I've been a fool." Neoma mumbled into her mom's shoulder.

"Kjære," Kristin cooed and put down the book she'd been shelving, before placing a comforting hand on her daughter's head, her touch light and careful. "Whatever happened, I don't think you made a fool of yourself by showing up to support someone. Kindness is rarely foolish or seen in such light."

Something inside Neoma started to give, cracks spreading through the armor she'd donned since her diagnosis. She'd cut herself off from everyone, even her mom, determined to be self-sufficient, to be strong, to not be a burden. The first tear that escaped was hot on her cheek, leaving a trail that burned as it descended, shame and fear following.

"Mom, I'm sorry."

"Oh, Kjære, no dear one, what do you have to be sorry about?" Neoma raised her head. Kristin's blue eyes, like mountain lakes, clear and calm, were filled with deep compassion. It freed another tear.

"I've been so stupid; I keep shutting you out. Shutting everyone out. I didn't understand what I was doing to you." Another treacherous tear escaped, slipping past her control, revealing her need.

Kristin moved her daughter back so she could see her face. "Kjære, daughter, I know you've been hurting, I know you're trying to be strong in the face of all this, and you are strong, you're amazing. But you don't have to be strong all the time. You don't have to do this alone. We're here for you, to help when you need it. And it's okay to need a little help sometimes."

"You never seem to need help." A compressed sob escaped with her words. Neoma was a small child in her mother's arms, trying to be what her mother was and failing.

Kristin barked out a laugh. "What do you think your grandparents were?" Neoma twisted in her mother's embrace and Kristin let her go, handing her a tissue from the nearby counter.

"What do you mean?" Neoma asked as she dabbed her face, not even trying to stop her falling tears, letting the emotions spill out of her, she was so tired of trying to hold them back. Her body sagged onto the short stepladder her mom had been using.

"Do you think they moved all the way out here because they wanted more rain in their lives? They left their community in Minnesota to be here for me. To help me. Because I was too stubborn, proud, and pregnant to move back home after your father died. I was determined that I could do it all on my own." Kristin's smile was small, stretching through self-deprecation until the emotion dissolved. "You're headstrong, like me. It's a trait that will take you many places, but it can be isolating if you're not careful. I knew you would figure it out eventually if I just gave you the space. My parents did the same with me. We're patient people, Kjære, thankfully more patient than our pride…most of the time."

"Is that your mothering way of telling me I've been a stubborn fool?"

"Perhaps," her mom's smile was all love and warmth as she tucked a stray curl behind her daughter's ear. Neoma leaned forward again, melting into her mom's arms, letting herself feel supported for the first time in what seemed like years. And with that, her words came tumbling forth, telling Kristin everything that had happened at the clinic.

"I just stood there, staring at the spilled coffee and feeling…weird. Like it had been a good thing for me to be there. That I'd supported him when things were falling apart by giving him this moment to put down his worry and his burden because I was there to hold space for it. Giving him a chance to take care of himself. Then the vet returned, and Tobin leapt back into his worry again, and I was looking at the fallout, wanting to do more, but unable to."

Neoma glanced away from the tissue she'd been shredding into confetti as she spoke. Her eyes flickered across Kristin's face but there was only understanding mirrored there. "Something got bumped loose then." Neoma gave an ashamed shrug. "I realized that must be how I've been treating you, and Megan, I suppose. You guys show up when I need you, and then I walk away as if your efforts don't matter, leaving you with a mess. Mom, I'm really sorry, I'll do better."

"I know you will. Kjære, when people are hurting, they're not thinking rationally, especially if we're dealing with new pain. Your kindness gave him room to breathe. That is all I've ever wanted to give you, *room*, when your loss was overwhelming." Kristin reached out and touched her daughter's tear-stained cheek with tender care. "I'm grateful this helped you see the people around you again. The ones that love you. Remember, it's okay to grieve, but you don't have to do it alone. We're here if you need us."

"Thanks, Mom," Neoma straightened up. "But I think that's all the understanding wisdom I can handle for one day or I'm going to drown over here." Neoma was surprised by the sincere grin that crept through her tears.

Kristin laughed even as her eyes glittered. "Okay, message received. Now, do you want me to cover the store so you can go home, maybe take a day off?"

"Nah, I've got it. You've done more than enough."

"All right." Kristin gave her daughter a kiss on the forehead and patted her cheek. "I'm proud of you, Kjære, for being brave enough to be vulnerable again. Keep it up."

"Mom, enough!" Neoma laughed and made a shooing motion.

"Fine, fine, mother wisdom is leaving. Have a good day. Love you."

"Love you too Mom."

CHAPTER 16

Wooden Consequences

Tobin

Tobin's shadow lay over Matrix like a shroud, casting the black dog in even deeper darkness as he bent to pull Matrix from the truck. Putting him in the cab hadn't been an option, so Tobin had layered the truck bed with every blanket in the house to insulate his brother's wounded body for the ride home. But Matrix was disinclined to move. The dog opened one bloodshot eye and growled a warning, showing a single long canine that gleamed white in the moonlight.

"Oh...kay," Tobin drew out the word, pulling back, his eyebrows pinching together in confusion. The swollen moon above bathed the surrounding night in sharp grays and silvers. Night birds sang in the distance, their notes tripping over Tobin's already taut nerves.

"Max, I can't leave you outside. It won't be safe. I can smell the blood and damage on you from here and it screams midnight snack." Matrix growled at him again. "Oh come on, at least let me get you inside. Then, if you want to continue to be mad at me, go right ahead. At least you'll be mad and *safe*." The last word slipped out prickly with stress. Tobin put his trembling hands on his hips to hide their shaking, eyes locked with Matrix who was still warning him away with his wrinkled lip. The almost full moon was not helping. It called Tobin, and despite his best efforts to ignore it, the urge to answer was making him irritable. Today had been hard enough; he didn't need werewolf urges adding pressure. He tried reaching for Matrix again, only to have that flash of fang tell him to back off.

"Fine!" Tobin threw his hands up and stormed inside, batting away the moisture that had crept down his cheeks. Opening the fridge, he pulled out half a dozen steaks that had been swimming in marinade since yesterday. He started the grill, and went through the mindless task of shucking corn, grilling food, and cleaning the kitchen.

Despite the fuzzy memories that seemed to always follow a shift, there were some that had stayed crystal clear. Those were the ones Tobin was trying to leave buried. Trying to pretend that he didn't know why his brother was mad at him. Trying not to hear the wet crunch of bone as the drainer had fallen on top of Matrix, crushing the big dog beneath its massive body.

There had been no screaming, no yelp of pain to punctuate the disaster. Tobin hadn't realized what had happened, so deep in his own hunting song and blood lust. He'd continued to rip at the drainer's neck until the vertebrae inside all that meat and muscle was unearthed. The spinal cord had tasted sweet.

That memory still lingered.

And Tobin would have continued to feed if something small hadn't fluttered into his face, slicing deep into his sensitive nose. Hot pain had exploded, poison racing into the wound, burning through his nerves like a lit fuse until his face sizzled. The first sneeze had pitched him up and back, spraying blood everywhere. The second sneeze had sent him flailing backwards off the drainer's corpse. Hitting the ground hard, Tobin had driven his face into the dirt, trying to smother the fire in his muzzle when he'd heard the smallest whine. Looking up, tears matting his fur, he'd seen his brother's body pinned underneath the shoulder and head of the dead drainer. That whisper of sound had been Matrix's last breath while he held firm, teeth still clamped around the creature's snout.

Tobin remembered all that. But the hunt? The conversation he had with the Fey? How he'd gotten Matrix back to the house? It was blurred and fading fast. Like some bad dream that left behind only the gore like a sadistic aftertaste.

That moment bore down on Tobin again, a memory set on replay, inescapable. How had he been so thoughtless? How had he forgotten about his own brother? Guilt ate at his guts until he felt hollow. He stared at his human hands holding the tongs, seeing only his torn and bloody claws, the nails cracked and ripped away from his struggle to exhume Matrix from that creature's carcass. Tobin was completely healed, not a scratch on him. But Matrix? The vet said she'd never seen such injuries on something that was still alive.

Tobin loaded the steaks onto two plates and added the corn cobs and tater tots from the oven. The meal seemed lacking, but the food was hot, plentiful, and ready to eat. His hands shook as he picked up the dishes and walked outside.

"Here," Tobin pushed a plate towards Matrix's prostrate form, then backed off to sit in the grass, his back resting on a huge tree. He now understood the feeling of pressure that came from unwelcome proximity to a predator. He could tell Matrix was experiencing this, and he didn't want to make his brother any more uncomfortable than he already was.

The food tasted like ash.

"Family spat?" Aithne's mocking voice drifted out of the dark a moment before her scent hit him. Tobin ignored her, shoving more food into his mouth, and chewing aggressively.

"Drainer got your tongue?" Her words bit at Tobin, stinging his guilty conscience.

"Leave me be." He mumbled through his food.

"Tsk tsk, is that any way to treat the Fey that has granted you hunting rights to her land?" A strange thrill of magic skittered across the back of Tobin's neck. "I only wished to congratulate you, man-wolf. I wondered if you were up for such a task, and you proved with blood and bone that you were."

"And if I hadn't?" Tobin's voice was devoid of emotions.

She stepped out of the tree next to him and shrugged. Tonight, she was shrouded in a dress of shadows and spider silk that draped her body in seductive ways, showing her hickory brown skin to full advantage. He noted that the pattern of vines twirling over her flesh had gained green buds, some unfurled into pale flowers that glowed in the moonlight.

"You were the least destructive way of dealing with that cursed creature. Had you failed, stronger measures were at my fingertips." Her pink eyes seemed to burn in the darkness and for a moment there was heat on Tobin's skin, like summer sunshine. He blinked and it was gone.

"Go away, Aithne, I'm not in the mood for your games." Tobin returned to his meal, stuffing his mouth robotically. Lack of appetite didn't appease his body's need for calories.

"Games? Oh, man-wolf, we are far from playing games." Her smile was cruel as she shook hair away from her face, the small leaves nestled at her hairline rustled with the movement. "Come now, what brings you so low?" She sat next to him, her body warm as she lay her head on his shoulder. Tobin went rigid, but she only snuggled closer.

Anger erupted. "Matrix almost died last night because of your 'quest'." He shook her off him. "And now you inform me you had other ways of dealing with that thing? You didn't even tell me how to kill it! Matrix figured that out on his own and it almost ended him while I was wasting fucking time!"

"It would not be a quest, as you say, if I had given you all the answers, now would it?" Her eyes flashed. "Besides, you enjoyed every moment of that kill. I saw you." She gained her feet and crouched behind him, her voice whispering into his ear. The shiver of breath and proximity had all the small hairs on his body up in alarm.

"You were beautiful in the moonlight, digging deeper and deeper into the hot meat of its neck until you tasted bone. I saw you eat your fill as your dog lay pinned underneath, slowly being crushed while you sated your hunger for the kill."

Tobin lunged, spinning around, his fist slamming into the trunk of the tree, knuckles splitting open, splashing the rind with crimson. He struck the tree again and again until the bark pulverized into a gooey mass of sap and blood. He howled as electricity buzzed up his arm as if he'd touched a live wire.

"Damn you!" Tobin snarled. He scoured the dark for some glimpse of her. But she was gone, only her laughter lingered in the needles of the Douglas fir until words unfurled in the night, blooming like moonflowers.

Of bark and bone,
The heart in kind
I've tasted yours, you've tasted mine.
Our blood-sap power, ripe on the vine
Now harvest that which blocks your mind
Shove off the chain, accept the pine.
Deep in the forest, your power bind
A slip in time
Outside the moon
I grant, my wooden wolf.

Tobin watched the mutilated tree bark heal itself in a flash of amber light, his knuckles doing the same. "Feel free to hunt at your leisure, man-wolf, you have earned the right, and I enjoy the sight." Then her presence faded from the forest, and Tobin was truly alone.

He slumped back against the tree, his head cradled in his hands, his breathing anguished pants while his body shuddered as if transformed. A wet nose poked up under his arm, and then Matrix was there, his big head pushed up against Tobin's chest.

He clutched the dog to him like a kid would grasp a teddy bear. Matrix didn't fight it, allowing Tobin to mumble all his apologies and promises into his shaggy coat. At last the storm passed and the brothers pulled apart, magnets unwilling to let go.

"I'm so sorry Max, I don't...I don't know what's happening to me. I won't let the moon take me like that again. I would die if I lost you. Please, please forgive me?"

The big dog tilted his head to the side, then huffed out a huge sigh, rolling his eyes. He took Tobin's hand in his mouth and walked backwards, pulling him to his feet before letting go. Slowly he swung his battered body around and limped towards the house. Tobin followed, collecting the dishes and closing the truck bed. He'd come back for the blankets.

After tucking Matrix into bed, Tobin lay still, staring at the ceiling. Images of the day flashed through his mind until he caught and held one. It was Neoma, and her surprising appearance at the clinic today. How had he forgotten? He blinked and remembered her commanding tone as she took charge and made him stop pacing and clean himself up. She had been kind, and a little pushy. The soft feeling surrounding those memories pulled his eyelids closed, sleep sucking him deep before he could decipher it.

Matrix waited restlessly, worry tight in his chest, until Tobin's breathing evened out before dragging himself off his dog bed.

A whimper of pain choked him as his body protested the movement, but he refused to make a sound. Limping carefully across the vinyl floors, Matrix pulled the front door open by the rope Tobin had installed for his brother's convenience, the dog door in the kitchen only gave him access to the enclosed yard, and he knew he couldn't jump the fence in this condition. Once outside, the big dog carefully pulled the door closed until it almost shut, leaving a small gap to prevent the catch from clicking. Tobin usually slept like a dead thing after a shift, but Matrix didn't want to chance it.

The night was clear and clean, no odors lingered from the dryad, and Matrix couldn't tell if that Fey had spies, or if she just used the trees. Deciding it didn't really matter, he hobbled across the road into the shadows of the forest, heading for the nearby creek that wanted to be a river. He needed to know what had happened, to make sure they were safe, to assure himself that the drainer was dead.

The sprites found him before he was more than ten paces into the trees.

"No, you must stop, go back. Rest." The small voice chastised him from the back of a fluttering bat. Matrix smiled a doggy smile, waving his tail gently and laid down, feeling the last of his tension ease. As soon as his head was on the ground, a small collection of puffballs tumbled out of the ferns to dance around his nose like animated dust bunnies.

His eyes lit with delight, the youngest sprite he'd saved had brought her two brothers, and they played a game of tag over and around him, being mindful of the newly stitched wounds. Matrix let his eyes drift closed, feeling comforted by the tiny bird-like sounds the kids made, feeling safe in this moment, knowing that the adults were near and would not allow danger to sneak up on their family.

A large downdraft of air shocked him out of his doze, and his eyes flew open, ready to act. Registering that the kids were all perched on his head, he went still so as not to disturb them. A huge great horned owl regarded him from two feet away, eyes round and glossy in the dim light. It bobbed its head back and forth, opened its wings and leapt into the air, leaving something on the ground where it had landed.

Matrix sniffed, the object smelled of wilted green magic, blood, and it glowed slightly. He wrinkled his nose, even as drool started to pool in his jowls.

"Our gift to you, Guardian." A little voice trilled as an adult sprite stepped out of the shadows and pointed at the glowing glob.

Matrix wrinkled his brow in clear question.

"Your slaying of the drainer was altruistic, and you suffered for your actions. This stolen magic cannot be restored to those that are now dust, only repurposed. Our belief is that you are worthy of this power. We apologize for this was all that Horas could carry, but it should be enough."

Matrix tilted his head to the side, making the children squeal and tumble sideways until they all hung from his floppy ear. They gripped his fur with tiny hands, giggling, pushing off his face as if they were playing on a rope-swing.

"It should help heal you. Eat it quickly before she realizes we have taken it." The sprite's tiny face implored him, seemingly nervous of the repercussions if discovered. Why would they risk taking such a treasure from the dryad, for him?

"She will claim it for herself if she finds it. But she did not earn it. You have the right to it; you slayed the beast and saved our home. Kindness, heart, it propels you. Defines you. Allow us to show our gratitude." The sprite held a fist to its chest and bowed its head, pale hair floating around its face. "My name is Wrennen, and these are my children." Her smile was indulgent as she raised her face back to his. "Although I am not sure they will remain so much longer if they cannot treat our guests with more respect."

Wrennen inclined her head, and the fluffy kids let go and flocked to her. She embraced each one and laid a small kiss on their brows. Their cottony bodies made the adult look as if she had gotten stuck in thistledown.

"We must go. Eat, return home, and sleep until your body tells you the healing is done. Blessing to you, Guardian." They all held a fist to their chest and the kids grabbed onto their mother just as the owl returned and picked them up in his sharp talons. In a flash they were gone back into the night.

Matrix was sad to see them go, yet warmed by their gratitude, a satisfied sense of purpose settling into his battered body. Finally content, he did what he was told and ate the gelatinous mass of green goo. It tasted of crushed grass and bitter rosemary but left a clean tang on his tongue as he swallowed the last of it, heat beginning to kindle in his belly. With an effort he limped home and made it back to his bed before fatigue flooded his senses. He dropped into unconsciousness like a stone into a black well. Somewhere, he heard the echoes of the little sprite's laughter, her tiny fingers still warm on his ear.

CHAPTER 17

Brownies for Werewolves

Neoma

N eoma paced back and forth from the counter to the table setting up for tonight's first gaming group. She kept tweaking things, adding pens, getting more scrap paper, moving the chairs around.

"Neoma, it looks great." Stewart assured her as he glanced over the rim of his glasses when she passed him for the fifth time muttering to herself.

"Are you sure I don't need more napkins?" She looked back down the stacks, wondering if it was crazy to allow food and drink near the books. "Was food a bad idea?"

Stewart took a big bite of the brownie she'd placed in front of him and groaned. "Judging by the moistness of this confection," he paused to swallow. Clearly, he'd been watching too much *Great British Bake Off.* "I would say no, food was definitely not a bad idea. If you want to make people stay and play, these treats should do the trick. What did you put in these?"

"Oh, it's my mom's recipe, there's some dark roast coffee in there and then you swirl a marshmallow cream cheese mixture through the brownie batter then bake."

"I might have to marry your mother." Stewart said under his breath. Neoma yanked her head around.

"What did you just say?" But the door opened, and a gust of wind and noise blew in between them and snuffed out the conversation like a candle flame.

"Hello and welcome to Rainy Day Books!" Stewart said way too loudly, his cheeks reddening, then shoved another mass of chocolate into his mouth and fled the front, Neoma narrowing her eyes after him.

"Stewart, we're not done!" Neoma hollered to his retreating back.

"Yes we are." Came the muffled reply.

"Did I interrupt something?" Tobin asked mildly. "We did say six thirty, right?"

Neoma turned back and bit the inside of her cheek. Tobin stood there in jeans and a tight black t-shirt, holding a box of supplies that made his arms flex in distracting ways. The shadow behind him suddenly moved and shocked her out of her adoration.

"Is that your dog?" Neoma did a double take to make sure a black bear hadn't just wandered into the store. She didn't remember his dog being that big, but the one time she'd seen him, he was outside tied to a tree.

"Yes. Nae meet Matrix, Matrix, Neoma. And you better be on your best behavior, or she won't let you come back," he warned the dog. Neoma swore the dog rolled his eyes.

"Hi Matrix," Neoma said, holding out her hand, uncertain. Normally she bent down to say hi to dogs, but if she did, her head would be lower than his. That was uncomfortable.

The black beast gave her a very polite inspection, then flopped down on her feet, almost knocking her over. He rolled so she could rub his chest, and she couldn't tell if it was an invitation or a demand. She shrugged and bent over to acquiesce to the huge canine's wishes—it seemed like the safer option. There were shaved areas where his wounds had been stitched up, but the gashes looked more like scars than fresh injuries, white hairs starting to grow from the shiny new skin. Maybe dogs healed faster than she knew?

"Weird," Tobin muttered.

"What?" Neoma asked as she scratched the dog under his armpits and watched his feet flop back and forth with doggy joy.

"Nothing, he just rarely does that for people."

"Oh, well, this is outside my normal too, but it seemed like an offer I shouldn't refuse." Neoma shrugged and spent another moment rubbing the big dog before standing carefully. "He's really a handsome devil. I've never seen a dog quite like him." Matrix got to his feet and shook himself briskly before giving her a doggy grin, his one upright ear at a jaunty angle.

"That being said, Mr. Handsome, you pee on one book, and your hide will make an excellent rug for my bedroom." Neoma frowned at the beast in mock threat. He actually dropped his head and nosed her hand gently, giving her a tiny lick as if in some solemn promise.

"Oh, don't worry, he loves books, he would never hurt them." Tobin assured her.

"He loves books?" Neoma gave Tobin a curious glance and watched as his cheeks colored slightly. *Is everyone saying weird stuff tonight just to mess with me?*

"I mean, um, where can I put this stuff down?" Tobin asked, looking around.

"Table is back there. I pulled out a couple folding chairs. How many people do you think are coming?" Neoma ducked back behind the counter and fussed with some receipts. Tobin made his way down the stacks, and she watched his butt flex as he walked. Oh, he had a nice ass. Tonight he once again had on the dark-framed glasses, they made him look right at home surrounded by all the books, and yet she could see him stepping out of a photo shoot for Abercrombie & Fitch. Where *had* this man come from?

"There should be two other guys joining us. Seems like a good start for this game, and we can always fold in others if people show interest." His voice sounded disappointed as he unloaded books from his box.

A.B. Herron

"Hey, having four people starting off an RPG is not bad, especially since you just moved here."

"I know, I was just hoping for more."

"Well, my little brother was kind of interested," Neoma supplied.

"Is he over eighteen?"

"Nope, twelve."

"Thanks, but no, I'm looking for an adult group, no minors." His voice firm, the dog looking up at him with a small whine.

Neoma squinted at him. "Hey, simply trying to pad your numbers." She raised her eyebrows and finished shuffling receipts.

"I'm sorry, I'm sure your little brother is cool, I just want to get to know people my age, that's all." His hazel gaze implored her to understand.

"Fair."

"Mind if I start setting up? I brought a few snacks if you're ok with food in the store?" He eyed the brownies as he spoke.

"As long as people keep food away from the books, I'm fine." Neoma waved her hand

The door chimed and a skinny guy with a big smile came in. His blond hair was mussed, and he kept running his hands through it. "Hi, I'm here for the werewolf game?" He looked around like he'd never been in a bookstore, brown eyes taking in every angle. "Cool books! I didn't know you guys were here. I always head into Powell's for my books."

Neoma resisted the urge to cover her face and scream in frustration. *We are on Main Street, we can't get much more visible, come on people, look around your own town.* But she held back and reached for civility. "Well, thanks for coming in." She gave him her best smile and brightened her voice to chipper. "The game is being held in the back, Tobin's already setting up." She pointed and the guy bobbed his head, not really listening as his eyes scanned the spines around him. Well, maybe he would start coming here instead of making the drive to Portland.

The door rang again before she had a chance to do more than blink. The face that greeted her was a lost memory from high school. Shadowed eyes watched the world from under a dark baseball cap embroidered with a single pine tree. His hair was jet black, long enough to peek out from under his hat, skin a light tan. His wide shoulders made him look even shorter than he was, his head a bit below hers. She scrambled for his name, but it was covered with too much disuse for her to unearth it. "Hi," she said lamely.

"Hi Nae, it's Martín," he said softly, his Spanish peeking out as he said his name. He held out a wide palm for her to shake. "It's been awhile since math class. It's okay, I didn't expect you to remember me." They shook and Neoma could feel heat rising into her cheeks, his grip was callused, but kind.

"Sorry, Martín, I do remember you."

"Your mom give you updates?"

"From time to time." She smiled, the mom hotline didn't degrade with years.

He gave a small smile in understanding and looked around. "Well, bookstore is where you landed?" He was being kind and skipping over her recent past just as memories of his surfaced. Martín's dad, Devon, had lost his job and started working for a long-haul trucking company when Martín had entered his freshman year in high school. Martín's mom, Camila, was suddenly saddled with raising all the kids by herself, while working and pregnant, her family in Mexico and too far to lend a hand. So Martín had stepped up working part-time while he finished high school, then helped his mom with the rest of the kids while his dad came and went as the road demanded. As gossip reported, not a lot had changed since high school.

Neoma remembered these details because Camila had worked at the bakery for a short time with her mom until she'd been able to find steady employment. Kristin always tried to help those in the community when she could. Besides, Neoma and Martín were some of the few bi-racial students in their school, an aspect they tended to be sensitive to. But she hadn't thought of him in years, and could only scrounge up a few recent details, like he did some kind of computer work, but that was it. The man had been a shy boy, and it seemed like not much had changed, but he was known because of his family's struggles. Well, his family, and the rumors he was gay. It was a small town.

"Yep, this whole place is half mine, what do you do nowadays to stave off boredom?"

He smiled at her from under his hat brim, not quite meeting her eyes. "I work for the forest service, IT mostly, filled in with playing ranger for the rest. When called upon, I do search and rescue. You know, just trying to pass the time, fill up the hours, find a hobby." His serious downplay of what he did was not lost on Neoma.

"I see. So knitting was too extreme of a sport for you?"

He coughed on a laugh, seeming to reevaluate her and grinned. "I hadn't considered it, but now that you mentioned it, have you seen the size of those needles? Thanks, but no. I'll stick with S.A.R. and being in the outdoors where it's safe." His grin warmed into a smile as he considered the shelves. "You could find worse places to idle your time away. Nice store. Do you guys carry any Joe Nesbø? I love his mysteries."

"Of course, what kind of book store do you take me for?" They both grinned. "I can show you later, or feel free to look around if you want, but I think Tobin might be waiting on us." *Did I just make a friend?* Neoma wondered as she ushered him back. Stewart returned, taking over the front desk, not meeting Neoma's eyes. That's ok, she would grill him later.

"Hi everyone, thanks for coming," Tobin started once they were all seated and had introduced themselves. Turns out, the smiling guy was named Robin, he worked in the local Walmart and wanted to try something new. Apparently, Tobin had plastered flyers all over town trying to draw people in, and Robin had found one at the bus stop.

"So tonight I'm going to go over how the game is played, we'll talk about your characters, address questions, and go from there. Any questions to start?" Tobin glanced around the group, but everyone stayed quiet, Martín eating his second brownie and chewing with a look of reserved anticipation.

"Well, let's begin."

· • ◈ • ·

"BUT I DON'T THINK WE SHOULD GO THAT WAY!" ROBIN ALMOST screeched, pulling on his messy hair for the umpteenth time.

"Why not?" Neoma asked, trying not to lose her patience. Every time she'd made a decision, this guy had second-guessed her. Every. Damn. Time.

"Weren't you listening? He said there was a skittering sound down the left hallway. Clearly it's a trap!"

"Yeah, but Rob—"

Robin cut Martín off with a hand gesture and a hiss.

"I'm sorry, Horn Hound," Martín corrected to Robin's werewolf name, "if we go right that leads back into the chemical plant where the extremely foul odor is coming from. I think we need to cut our losses. I can't handle another shift right now and if we get stuck in a tight space, I'm toast."

"Well, no one asked you to shift to your warrior form when we met up with the toxic waste rabbits, there were only three of them, I could have handled it," Robin spat out.

"I was saving Ylva Moon! She was checking the astral plane to see if we could escape that way. If I hadn't shifted, they would have killed us all." Martín had really come out of his shell and was arguing quite passionately with Robin. Neoma hated to admit it, but she was thoroughly entertained by this interaction.

"Well," Robin paused for dramatic effect and enunciated Martín's chosen moniker, "*Mack Torn*, I'm not going that way." He sat back and crossed his arms over his chest, daring Martín to budge him.

"The sound of a small engine grows closer, and in the distance, you can faintly hear the screaming of more toxic rabbits. The air around you is starting to fog, the smell of chemicals getting so dense your group starts to cough, eyes watering," Tobin intoned, narrating their impending doom.

"Mack Torn," Neoma said with clear command, "will you allow me to take your guns and cover my back while I go forward? I'm a smaller target, if something is waiting to ambush us, they might not expect me to still be human. I can shoot, and you can rip them apart with your claws if we need to, but we gotta move."

"Yes, Ylva Moon, I'll guard your back."

"So Mack Torn and Ylva Moon move forward down into the dark hallway, leaving Horn Hound behind—" Tobin was cut off this time.

"No, wait, I'm coming! I mean, jeez, if you guys are going *that* way I better come so you don't get killed." Robin huffed magnanimously.

"So, the three warriors move together into the thickening blackness while the noxious odors from the chemical plant fade into the background. With one more turn they emerge from the toxic mines and once again see the clear and open sky, Gaia singing them home."

"Yay!" Neoma actually clapped her hands while Martín grinned at her in triumph. But her elation was cut short by Robin.

"That's it? Are you kidding me, what about the skittering noise?" Robin sat back in his chair, crossing his arms over his chest. "Man, and we were just getting warmed up."

"Warmed up?" Stewart's voice broke from behind them. "You guys have been at this for hours. Neoma, I'm heading home unless you need something more? There were actually some late-night people who came through; I took care of closing down the register."

"Thanks Stewart, would you be willing to do this again? That is if everyone..." Neoma cast around the group to check their interest. Seeing nods of excitement she barreled on, "Next week? Same time?" She was shocked at how much she wanted to play again. She actually had a great time, and all the worries of daily life had faded away while they played.

"Sure, for a price." Stewart gave her a look, she knew exactly what he was referring to and pursed her lips, frowning.

"Fine, deal."

"And you don't speak of it to your mother, either."

"Okay, mums the word to mum, I promise." She mimed turning a key at her lips.

"Great, see you crowd next week. Night!" And Stewart spun jauntily on his heel, another brownie in hand, and whistled as he went out the back.

"What was that about?" Martín asked.

"I don't think we're allowed to inquire," Tobin replied, putting things away in his box. "But I think Stewart has the hots for Nae's mom."

The guys laughed, and Neoma sent Tobin a withering look. "I promised my silence for this group's continued leisure, let's not pursue this further."

"Okay, so how did you all like being werewolves for an evening?" Tobin asked, his eyes sweeping the group with veiled curiosity.

"That was awesome!" Robin chimed in first. "I always wanted to be a werewolf." His smile was wistful.

"Why?" Neoma asked, surprised.

"What? What do you mean why? How could you not? Oh, wait, let me guess, you're a vampire chick aren't you? Team Edward for the win, am I right?" Robin gave her a disapproving look.

Neoma saw Martín move uncomfortably in his chair, and she put up a hand to forestall whatever he was about to say. "I can fight my own battles here, thank you," she said softly before spearing Robin with a look. "Robin, if you are incapable of answering a simple question without turning it around and insulting me, when you only just met me, then I'd say you are done here. Feel free to keep driving to Portland to buy your books." Neoma finished and glared at him.

"What?" Robin looked like he had been hit in the face with a board. "What did I say?"

"I think it was calling her a chick," Tobin offered.

"Or insulting her taste in men and monsters." Martín shrugged, toying with the corner of his character sheet. "But you have a lot of options to choose from."

Robin looked around at the table, his mouth a little ajar, then dropped his eyes, shoulders hunching. "Please don't ask me to leave, Neoma. I'm sorry, I'm just, really really bad at this." He mumbled and motioned around the room.

"Bad at what?" Neoma asked, her back still rigid, her voice unyielding.

"Being social." Robin seemed to shrink in on himself. "Please don't ask me to leave, please? I've been looking for an RPG group for a while, I miss this. And, well, I'm shit with talking to women, I thought you were mocking me."

Neoma eyebrows inched towards her hairline.

"Did you really mean it? You want to know why I wanna be a werewolf?"

"Yeah, I did."

"Oh," Robin looked up nervously, then seemed to regain some of his gusto. Neoma had to give him that, he was like a Labrador retriever with his enthusiasm. "Well, I mean wow, to be able to change shape. You know, be stronger, faster, heightened senses and all that. Not to mention never getting sick or injured. How cool would that be? And you don't have to be dead to be powerful." His smile was a hundred watts of geeky fantasy driven fervor.

"Huh," Neoma hadn't considered the perks of never getting sick as she rubbed her sore elbows. They were protesting being leaned on for the last hour.

"I've always wondered about the animal instincts part." Martín softly mused. "Like would you be able to tell when danger was nearby? Could you feel someone following you? And would it give you a deeper connection with the forest?"

"Yeah, that would be so awesome. I mean you walk into the woods and could be like, I feel you nature, and I'm here for it, let me put on some fur." Robin laughed, and Neoma chuckled with him.

"But what about being chained to the moon?" Tobin asked, cutting through their chuckles. "Would that bother you?"

"You mean only being able to shift when the moon is full?" Robin asked and Tobin nodded.

"Depends on the lore you read," Martín said. "I mean, which legends and stories do you want to adhere to? Personally, I'm willing to believe all magic has to have a price, right? Nothing in this world can happen without a give and take. You want the powers of a wolf? Well, you have to accept the price to gain those powers. Life is consequence, I don't see how magic could be immune to that basic universal law."

"I never thought of it that way," Tobin sat back in his chair. "But would you be willing to pay that price?"

"Depends," Martín started as Robin jumped right on top of him.

"Hell yes! In a hot minute, sign me up."

"It's not going to make you any smoother with women, Robin," Neoma said dryly.

"Oh come on. Animal magnetism, women would dig me!" he said with a shy wink and a hopeful expression on his face. "I could roll over and they would have to rub my belly."

At that, Matrix popped his head up and barked, a disgruntled rumble following his announcement. He had been lying under the table between Neoma and Tobin and the other guys hadn't seen much of him. They stared, Robin looking ready to bolt, but Martín remained calm and curious.

Matrix hooded his eyes and put his head on the table next to Neoma, she dutifully started petting him, playing with his floppy, velvet-soft ear.

"Tobin, dude, you said you had a dog. That's not a dog," Robin whispered loudly.

"Nope, this is my brother, the weredog." Tobin gave Matrix a rough thump on the shoulder. "He can't transform, so don't ask him to bite you, it won't help. Martín, I was curious, what were your stipulations to becoming a werewolf?"

"What? Oh," He blinked and looked up from Matrix. "Well, it would depend on if I turned into an animal, or if I had a humanoid form and whether or not I was in control. I have no interest in becoming a beast bent on killing for killing's sake. Our characters would be a prime example of what I'd be willing to become. I want control over who I am. I'm not willing to lose myself to a monster, that's too high a price."

"Even if you were stronger and better looking?" Robin asked.

"Not at the risk of waking up with my hands bloody and my family dead, no." Martín was very resolute with his conviction.

"Wow, you guys have all given this some thought." Neoma was surprised.

"You never dreamed of being something more than you are?" Tobin asked.

"Well, sure…" Neoma went silent as she thought. What had she daydreamed about? As a kid she'd imagined being a dancer, nonstop. Had there ever been another dream? Snippets from books billowed up in her mind. But in these fantasies, she was always the beauty commanding the beasts, never the person being transformed. Perhaps her holding the control was her dreaming about being different? Powerful? Heat rushed through her, and she fought it back. "Yeah, I guess I did dream of being something more, but then I got heavy into dance and invested in that future. Only RA, the arthritis eating my joints, spoiled those plans, and I've been too busy dealing with the fallout." Her words fell like weighty stones as she watched her hand play with Matrix's ear, the joints slightly swollen and achy.

The table hushed, the sound of the store clock rushing in to fill the stillness. It ticked sharply with a dusty rhythm that spoke of time and old books. Suddenly, Neoma seemed exposed, her life laid bare by a few sentences about broken dreams. She cleared her throat, but no words followed.

"It's okay," Tobin said quietly. "You can dream about being werewolves with us." His voice was a comforting blanket, an invitation. "If you want to." His eyes were filled with the knowledge of wrecked promises and rerouted dreams. Yet something lurked deeper, darker.

Matrix nudged her hand, breaking the spell. She looked around; Martín gave a supporting smile. He was intimately familiar with life malfunctioning. Well, if Martín was willing to let go and indulge in the fantastic with his tattered past, why not her?

"Thanks Tobin, I think I'd like that."

CHAPTER 18

Selfish Bait

Tobin

T he feeling of success buoyed Tobin through the following two weeks. Each subsequent game night fed his feeling of achievement, making crafting adventures effortless. Now, with the weekend in full swing, he pondered the next quest, tweaking it to ensure the pack would learn to work together, to rely on each other. There were things he could be happier about, sure, the number of people had been a letdown, but who they had would be a great test group. Tobin tumbled all the details around in his brain as they ran through the dappled woods, looking at different angles for approaching each individual.

"Honestly," he told Matrix as they stopped at a hidden falls to take a drink and a quick dip, the mid-August heat clinging like flypaper, "I think if more people had shown up, I wouldn't be able to manage everyone. With only three people, I should be able to tease out what it will take to break their natural aversion to magic."

Matrix looked up at him from his semi-submerged position in the pool at the fall's base. The dog resembled a strange land seal, his fur floating in the water making him appear twice his size. Matrix tipped his head to the side and narrowed his eyes.

"You're judging the morality of my decisions here, aren't you?" Anger rushed through Tobin, tempered by something else. Was that shame? Sure, he was lying to the group, but ultimately, they would have the chance to choose, just like he had. He would not force his bite on anyone. He pushed the annoying prickle of emotion to the side. "I'm not poisoning their Kool-Aid here, if anything, I'm slowly educating them about the real world they live in. I'm helping them see behind the curtain."

Matrix gave a low grunt and blew bubbles into the water with his nose, clearly dissatisfied with Tobin's reasoning.

"You have a better suggestion? I'm doing this for us, and for them. Are you going to lay there and tell me there isn't a single person whose life wouldn't be improved if they became a werewolf?" Matrix sighed and blew more bubbles.

"What if it helped Martín better support his family? Hell, Robin could use all the help he can get." Matrix chuffed. "And Neoma, what if it's the cure she needs? What if she could live a normal life again? Do you think there's anything they wouldn't give for those opportunities?"

Matrix's eyes slid to the side, he whined, radiating some emotion that twisted into Tobin's guts like hookworms. "You still think this is wrong, don't you? Well how am I going to fix you if I can't protect us? If the rest of the magical community sees me as a joke? I don't know another way! Power is privilege. It's the ability to do what needs to be done, that's all I'm trying to do here. Build us a home so we can survive."

Matrix sneezed and lifted his lip.

"There isn't a better way. Don't you think I've tried? We talked to Shawn, but he was a dead end. I don't know who made Nora, and I'm not willing to risk both our skins by trying to approach her. What if she takes back the magic? What if she refuses to help you? Then where would we be?" Tobin beseeched his brother, willing Matrix to understand. But Matrix gave his head a hard shake and snapped his teeth.

"I'm not you Max! This is the best idea I have!" Tobin clenched his fists feeling like an incapable child. "You always followed the rules, even when the rules were wrong, and look where it landed you." As soon as the words hit the air, Tobin tasted their cruel impact.

Matrix leapt up, water flying in a cascade of broken rainbows. His growl rattled the gravel in the stream bed, and his bark rang from the stones with the clear tones of a gong.

Selfish.

The word sliced into Tobin's brain. He crumpled and clutched his head trying to protect his sensitive ears, but the word was a feeling, not a sound, and he couldn't escape it.

Resonance continued to bounce over river rocks, at last giving way to the hums of water and wind. When Tobin finally uncurled, his brother was gone, soggy pawprints leading deep into the dusty undergrowth.

"Matrix?" Tobin's voice shook.

"Max!" Only silence echoed back. Had Matrix spoken? Was that word real? Fear and confusion tangled inside Tobin, jerking him to his feet.

"Fine! Run away then." Tobin spun and sprinted home, but the miles he devoured didn't sate the hollow feeling widening inside him. *Selfish*, his brother thought he was selfish. He stumbled into the house, slamming the door. *How did he do that? Why did he leave? He could have stayed, he could have actually talked to me.* Tobin became a child again, powerless, useless, unwanted…selfish. *Why doesn't he understand?*

He fumbled into the shower, body shaking, turning the tap to cold. The water did nothing to cleanse the word from his skin, the hurt. He emerged into the silence of the small house. Empty, alone, abandoned. Somehow, it made the word louder.

• • ◉ • •

THE DRIVE TO TOWN WAS SHORT, TOBIN'S GOAL AIMLESS AS HE spied signs for the Cowlitz Farmer's Market and followed. He'd refused to stay in a crappy shack alone, waiting like a jilted lover. Let Matrix come home to an empty house, see how he liked it.

As he pulled into the parking lot, people bustled towards the popup tents like bees towards a hive. The farmers' market was a flurry of activity despite the heat, half the booths under a permanent, open-air structure, the rest of the vendors jostling for space and shade.

Tobin meandered through the noise, using the swarming activity to fill up the echoing space inside him. The overabundance of stimuli assaulted his senses, from the smell of hot asphalt to the stench of unwashed bodies, diapers that needed changing, and fresh produce and flowers all floating atop the damp green scent of river three blocks away. It was an odd miasma of odors, and he practiced isolating each one, identifying the source. He couldn't believe how much information humans were blind to. His enhanced sense of smell gave the world textures and flavors that made him giddy. The sensation was akin to getting glasses for the first time. Suddenly, the world had come into focus, trees no longer amorphous blobs of color, but multi-layered giants with individual leaves. He hadn't been this tuned in at the Portland book fair, he really was still changing, adapting to his senses, honing them; it was fascinating.

A tree sheltered him as he reclined on a bench, taking a needed break to sip homemade lemonade while indulging in fresh pastries. He studied the movements of the masses with idle fascination, noticing the patterns people fell into as they functioned in a group.

"Tobin?" The voice almost made him jump.

"Nae?" Sure enough, she was standing there in a loose cotton dress, small white flowers blowing across the yellow fabric. A large sun hat shaded her face, her dense curls in a tight bun at her neck. She pulled her sunglasses off and let them fall into her woven grass basket slung over one arm.

"I didn't take you for a farmers' market kind of guy." She smirked. "Too much brooding."

He shrugged, the corner of his lip twitching. "I needed to get out, be around people. Seemed like a good way to get to know the local color."

She snorted. "Well, since you're here, want an insider's deep dive? Assuming of course, you don't have better things to do?" She raised her eyebrow at him, a challenge and a question, taunting him to act.

"And if I do?" Tobin was accustomed to being dismissed by women, yet he'd noticed Neoma got…barbed when it was just the two of them. But it didn't smell like dismissal, maybe a self-defense mechanism? Tobin was intrigued, drawn in by her, lured by this behavior that seemed to dare him to get to know her.

She called his bluff. "Then I'll leave you to soak in the local…color." A family chose that moment to park under the tree to organize their squirming chaos, the baby screaming as if someone had detached its fingers.

"I would love a tour of the market," Tobin flinched and leapt to his feet, offering to take her basket.

"Excellent choice." Neoma grinned, ignored his hand, and led them deeper into the swirling humanity.

They browsed the booths, Neoma picking out different items and tucking them away. She seemed to know all the vendors and spent a moment talking to some, introducing Tobin, and helping him feel welcome. Before long, Tobin had his own collection of bags filled with fresh produce, bread, more homemade pastries, and jerky. He even had homemade dog cookies for Matrix, but only because Neoma insisted. He hoped his brother wouldn't be insulted.

"Thanks for the company," Neoma said as they stopped at a quieter bench, this time further away from the bustling masses. They both sat and Neoma slipped out of her sandals.

"You're welcome. Thanks for the tour. Do you come here often?"

"Please tell me that's not a pickup line." She rolled her eyes, letting her toes play with the grass.

"What?" Tobin paused. "I mean, if you want, I could go with, did it hurt when you fell from heaven?"

Neoma blinked at him before giving him a real, full-throated laugh. "Oh that was cheese, but I needed it, wow. I didn't know you had that in you. Well played, sir."

"I aim to impress." Tobin gave a small bow. The joy in her laughter did strange things to him.

"Well, I wouldn't call that impressive..." The sentence dangled between them as she studied him.

"Okay, hard to please, I can respect that. So what do I need to do to be memorable?"

"You could give me my book back."

"You mean my book?" *Are we flirting?* Tobin was uncertain.

"Debatable."

A genuine smile tugged at Tobin's mouth, and he relaxed back into the bench feeling some of the morning's stress start to slough off him.

Neoma fanned herself with her hat. "How about you share some deep dark secrets?"

"Such as?"

"Why the werewolf passion?" she blurted.

Tobin straightened, then leaned back, putting space between them. How did he want to play this?

Selfish.

The word slammed into his machinations, making him flinch.

"Tobin?" He'd never noticed that her eyes were the color of green sea glass. Brown flecks, like fall leaves, swirled in their interior, giving her gaze movement. "Are you okay?"

What do I tell her? His heart rate sped up and he glanced away, his fingers picking at the flaking paint on the bench.

What if he'd been able to make different choices back in March? Could he have fought the pull of the Bone Wraith and approached Nora with the truth? Rather than trying to get Nora to trust him and spill her secrets, would the use of brutal honesty have been more effective than dropping hints? Would that have prevented the need to drug her, to manipulate her into biting him? Would she have instead agreed to help him, undertaking the ritual to awaken her power of her own volition?

Selfish.

Would she have helped restore Max, and change Tobin into what he was now, if he had simply asked instead of trapping her? Instead of letting the Wraith torment and use them both?

Selfish.

His stomach clenched.

"Hey, what's wrong?" Neoma leaned forward, placing a careful hand over his.

Tobin smelled vanilla as the heat in her fingertips fluttered against his skin. There was an open expression on her face, the bluster and teasing gone, replaced by something tentative and new…and vulnerable.

Fuck, does she care? About me? He blinked and saw his opening.

CHAPTER 19

Improbable Conversations

Neoma

"Do you really want to know?" Tobin's voice was a whisper filled with hope and warning.

A cool draft moved over Neoma's body as if a storm brooded on the horizon. Neoma started to sit up, but Tobin flipped his hand over, so her fingers were resting in his palm. He didn't move to grab her or stop her from pulling away. His fingertips now curved into hers, warm little circles pressing carefully against her skin.

"Know?" Neoma's throat was dry.

"Why I'm all about werewolves. Why I picked the game."

"Yeah, I kind of do."

One fingertip moved slowly along her palm, sending gooseflesh shivering over her arms despite the heat of the afternoon.

"Do you believe in magic, Nae?" The way he asked her, in all seriousness, stilled her reflexive response, her flat-out wounded refusal. How could there be magic, or miracles in this world, when she had wished so hard, for so long, for something good to happen? Magic meant wishes had a chance, right?

"I have yet to see evidence of its existence," her answer was bitter, stilling his finger against her hand.

"Ahh, so you're someone who has to see to believe." His face went thoughtful.

"Don't most people?"

Tobin removed his hand, pulling away from her almost reluctantly. She missed the contact, curious at his retreat. His appearance twisted, as if he wrestled against something.

"I'm not sure." Tobin watched a kid run by with an ice cream cone wobbling precariously, a father chasing after while a pregnant mother moved ponderously in their wake. His expression changed to pained. "I've never thought like most people." He clarified, "I've always been willing to believe in what I haven't seen."

"How many miracle cures have you purchased off the internet?" Neoma's attempt to tease fell flat.

Tobin shrugged. "That's not what I meant."

"Explain it to me, then."

"Why?"

She leaned back, putting space between them. Why did she want to know this? Why was Tobin's fascination with werewolves making her defensively pick at him? Something about this topic, about him, drew and repelled her. Tobin had these little moments of being vulnerable with her, like at the vet clinic. But then he went back to being too smooth…too deliberate? He was friendly, nice to look at, companionable with the group, but he seemed to set himself apart, almost above them. Yet today he was back to feeling more like a reachable person.

Maybe the problem was her? Was her general defensive stance on life putting up barriers between them that weren't real? Megan was always encouraging her to give people a chance before she dismissed them as 'unworthy.' "Nae, that wonderful imagination of yours creates narratives for people before you ever get to know them. Get to know them first, then you can build up fictional reasons not to connect with them." Meg said it with gentleness, but it had hit home. Neoma had become prickly since her diagnosis, and her attitude kept people at arm's reach. Here she was now, afraid to let him get too close, using nonchalance like a shield, sarcasm like a sword.

"I can be a hard person to talk to." Neoma said. Tobin raised an eyebrow. "I mean, I'll listen to customers, be friendly, interact with all the right social cues, but when it comes to real conversations with people—well, I'm a bit…rusty." She waved her hand in the air helplessly.

"Rusty?"

"Fine." She huffed. "I'm aggressive, and somewhat irritating, according to my best friend." She glowered. Tobin laughed, his posture losing some of its tension.

"So, allow me to try this again. Tobin, why do you believe in werewolves? I would honestly like to know." She kept herself from crossing her arms over her chest. Instead, she shifted on the bench and tucked one leg up under her, letting her long skirt drape like a blanket. And waited.

"Why don't you believe in magic?"

"You're avoiding my question. That's irritating, and I'm working on being real here."

But Tobin was no longer looking at her, rather past her, his nose up like he was scenting the air. "Is there a reason a man might be glaring at you?" He asked.

"Huh?" Neoma followed his attention, her gaze slamming right into Caleb. He actually looked like a scowling brick wall, and standing next to him was Mark, with Miranda and Paris shopping with the kids a few booths away. "Oh, fuck," she muttered under her breath.

"Problem?" Tobin didn't stiffen, but he shifted somehow, his posture reading as ready whereas before it was attentive. Relaxed.

"Possibly, I'm just trying to decide how much of a shit show I'm willing to indulge in today." Neoma sighed, dropping her eyes. Maybe if she ignored him, he wouldn't come over.

"He's coming over." Tobin muttered, a bland expression in place.

Oh, for fuck's sake, Caleb just walk away.

"Hi Nae." Caleb's baritone rumbled between them. "Who's your friend?"

"Caleb," Neoma turned as if surprised, her smile bright. "What brings you to the market today?"

Caleb's eyebrows scrunched, "Oh, um, I came with Mark. We're going to go catch the little league game with his nephews afterwards."

"Well, that sounds like fun. You guys have a nice time. Thanks for saying hi." Neoma smiled again and turned away. She could feel Caleb's heavy presence at her back, like a brooding volcano.

"Nae," he laid a hand on her shoulder. "Can we talk? Please? I miss you."

Neoma squared her shoulders, and Caleb dropped his hand. She took a breath and called for composure. Paris and Miranda were now watching, she just knew it. She was not going to give them the satisfaction of gossip if she could help it.

Tobin's distant gaze confirmed her suspicions. He refocused on her, tipping his head to the side in a question, but what he was asking eluded her. *Why does this have to be a thing? We aren't in high school anymore, not even in the same social circles. I leave them alone, you'd think they could extend me the same gratitude.* Cold anger breached inside her like a calving glacier, her senses sharpening. *I will not be cornered out here in public, in the sunshine, on a beautiful fucking day.*

"Caleb, we've said all we needed to." Neoma uncurled from the bench and threaded her feet back into her sandals before standing. "Now, I better get home before my produce wilts any further. Tobin, you said you'd give me a lift?" She quirked an eyebrow at him.

Tobin rose smoothly and grabbed her basket along with his bags. He behaved as if Caleb wasn't balling his hands into fists. Instead, he stood off to the side, giving her plenty of space to maneuver, his expression contemplative. She was happy he didn't posture or interfere at all. This was her problem, and he wasn't going to take it from her. He was letting her lead, so she led.

"Nae, I could give you a ride home." Caleb tried again to make contact, but she stepped past his reach, stopped him with a look, then turned and gave a little wave at the watching women like they were old friends.

"You don't have to be like this. Please Nae, I want to talk to you." Caleb shuffled his large body into her path, not attempting to touch her.

"You want to talk to me right here? Right now?"

"Well…" His eyes slid to Tobin. "Sure, if that's what it takes. I'm willing to fight for us."

Neoma took the barest step closer, dropping her voice. "There is no 'us'. That was the arrangement. You know this, and I don't appreciate whatever this is that you're trying to do. Make this kinder on both of us and *move*." She tasted frost on her tongue.

Caleb quickly stepped out of her way. "Wait," his gaze was confused, "can I call you later?"

"Nope, I've got plans. You have fun at your game, Caleb." She didn't make eye contact as she put on her sun hat. "I hope you find someone who can share that with you. I'm not it." She nodded and walked towards the parking lot, Tobin a taciturn shadow at her side.

"I'm going to have to give you a ride home now, aren't I?" Tobin asked her quietly when they hit the asphalt.

"Apparently." Neoma grumbled, her cold anger melting. "I'm just glad I'm parked behind the bookstore, at least he won't see my car when he leaves."

Tobin chuckled.

• • ◉ • •

"MOM, DO YOU BELIEVE IN MAGIC?" NEOMA PUT DOWN THE cold drink and plate of fresh veggies with dip on the outdoor table before taking her seat in the shade. The ride to her house had been filled by the rumble of the truck engine and the wind blowing through the windows. Neoma hadn't been inclined to talk, her emotions needed to thaw. Tobin seemed wrapped in his own personal struggles. Letting Caleb go had made room for Neoma to ruminate further about werewolves, magic, and the man who seemed to embrace them both. Now she needed to talk about it, and Megan wasn't answering her phone.

Kristin stopped digging out weeds and mopped her brow, smearing dirt across her forehead. "Where did this come from?" Kristin asked, moving over to join her daughter under the large striped umbrella.

"Why is everyone answering my questions with a question?" Neoma grumbled, sipping her drink, the condensation dripping onto her dress.

"Oh, one of those days. Okay, Kjære, I'll take you seriously. Magic? Do I believe?" Kristin sipped her own iced tea, face thoughtful. She smelled of crushed herbs, dirt, and Mom. The tight space inside Neoma began to relax. Hummingbirds buzzed back and forth from the feeder, their squeaky song filling up the contemplative silence.

"Did I ever tell you much about your great-great-grandmother?"

"No, not really."

"Aha, well Mormor was unique. Mom said she used to talk to spirits, would argue with the gods, and when it was her time to go, she wandered into the woods and vanished." Kristin made a 'poof' motion with her hands.

"Mom, be serious," Neoma laughed.

Kristin chuckled. "Okay, there was no cloud of smoke, but the rest is true. I was still very little when she went missing. Morfar had passed away by that point, but I remember that Mormor never looked as old as Morfar. I recall braiding her hair, it was thick and heavy, colored like golden silk. She would guide my hands with hers, and they were wrinkled but strong. And even in winter there was this deep warmth to her. We would snuggle under blankets when it snowed outside, and she would sing old songs and tell me stories." Kristin paused, wistful. "I asked my mother once why we never looked for Mormor, and you know what she said?"

"What?" Neoma couldn't help herself; she was engrossed in the story, her mom had never talked about her great-great-grandmother before.

"She said Mormor went home, to live out her last days in the wild, as she was meant to be." Kristin's sky-blue eyes glimmered, and a cool breeze blew through Neoma's soul, ruffling something lonely and forgotten. "I still miss her. For years after, I would wander the Minnesota woods behind my parents' house looking for her. Sometimes it felt like she was right there, so close, and if I closed my eyes, I could catch a faint whiff of scent, a ghost of memory that was all her."

"What did she smell like?" Neoma whispered.

"Blueberries and loam." Kristin's face was peaceful, her voice soft. "I feel connected to her when I'm in the garden, with my hands in the earth. It brings me back to home." She shook herself out of her repose and took her daughter's hand.

"Kjære, I know life has given you many reasons not to hope. But hold on to this. There is something wonderous in your blood, both from my Mormor and your father, may his spirit be peaceful. He would not want you to become hard to this world, he saw possibilities everywhere, especially in you. And that my dear daughter, is magic."

CHAPTER 20

To Catch a Bird

Tobin

"Ready to play?" Tobin asked as he shuffled through notes on their next adventure. Nerves fluttered under his breastbone. Tonight was important, the first tumbler of his plan needed to drop, like a perfect key sliding into place. This had to line up right to unlock their magic.

Neoma sat down, placing a plate of butterscotch oatmeal bars in the center of the table and Tobin inhaled deeply, the sweet aroma tempting his boundless appetite. He could hear Stewart up front mumbling about buttery textures and flaky perfection, making his own mouth water in anticipation.

"Are these really for the group, or are you bribing Stewart for his continued cooperation?"

"Can't they be both?" Neoma asked, raising an eyebrow, her lip quirking. An unfamiliar emotion taunted Tobin as he stared back without responding. Neoma continued, undaunted. "The problem I keep running into is that I can't eat what I'm baking." She gave the oatmeal bars a sour look.

"Why not?" Tobin was grateful there didn't seem to be any walls between them after their werewolf conversation was interrupted over the weekend. Things felt normal again, including the return of Matrix. The big dog was still giving him the cold shoulder, but at least he'd finally come home later that night.

"I have to follow a strict diet." Neoma sighed and folded herself carefully into a chair, her hands graceful as she fiddled with the plate, pulling it towards her and pushing it away, her finger flexing smoothly, making her clear nail polish catch the light in flashes. "It's annoying really. Sugar's an inflammatory food, so if I don't indulge, I don't hurt as much. Same with alcohol, dairy, wheat. You know, all the good stuff that our bodies like to get addicted to." She gave a huff and sat back, glaring at the treats.

"You seem to be moving well today."

"Sure, yeah, today. But who knows about tomorrow?"

"Psychics?" Tobin offered.

"You are actually funny sometimes." Her words created a warm spot in his chest, and he frowned. "Anyway, people keep telling me that I'll adapt to my new diet, that I won't crave sugar anymore. But they don't live with my mother."

"You're telling me that sugar is a drug?"

Neoma laughed. "Yes, my drug of choice."

"So, your mom is the local drug dealer, you are her apprentice with an addiction, and you're drugging us all?"

A wry grin flirted with Tobin's lips. Neoma's sarcasm beckoned him closer. Her general edgy attitude and sardonic nature soothed him because he didn't have to guess where he stood with her, she told him.

"Well, when you put it that way…"

"What way are we putting things?" Martín asked as he dropped his pack by another chair and flopped down, reaching for an oat bar.

"Nae is aspiring to be a drug kingpin," Tobin told him with a straight face.

"Seems like a reasonable goal." Martín shrugged and took a bite.

"Also, the treats are filled with addictive poisons and will slowly kill you." Tobin added.

"I'm going to die so happy," Martín mumbled around a second mouthful. "Besides, your puny human poisons don't work on werewolves." He gave Neoma a wink. "Will you make these for my wedding?"

"You planning on getting hitched sometime soon?" Neoma asked.

"Just got to find the right man." Martín's eyes darted up from under his baseball cap, this one sporting a small forest of trees in a rainbow of colors.

Tobin smelled the spike of stress in his scent and softened his body language. Neoma's expression remained curious, waiting for more. Martín stopped chewing, his eyes dropping to the crumbs now littering the table. Even his breathing stilled as he poked at oat flakes, as if trying to organize their very existence on the clean surface would help him.

Neoma reached forward, her fingers wrapping around his hand, smoothing out his jerky movements. "Martín, I'd be more than happy to bake for your wedding," her eyes slid to Tobin, and he nodded. "And Tobin will be there to move any heavy things that need moving to make your day perfect. Do you have someone in mind, or do we get to start the match-making process?"

Martín flushed scarlet, then almost choked trying to get the rest of his bite swallowed. Relief seeped out of his pores like peppermint, a shy smile spreading across his face. "I'm not sure you know enough people to set me up. I have standards."

"Well," Neoma hedged, tapping her finger on her lip, "I didn't see a ring on Robin's finger last week, so he's definitely a contender."

Martín paused mid bite, his mouth hanging open. Neoma smiled sweetly at him.

"Wow, Nae, I thought you liked Martín," Tobin murmured.

"I'd rather date Matrix," Martín bemoaned. Matrix popped his head up on the table, and made very direct eye contact with him, his nose twitching.

"That might be a yes to your proposal," Neoma said, watching the dog. "Or he might just want your bar as a bribe for his loving." She scratched the big dog's floppy ear, and he sighed.

"Last I knew, Matrix didn't swing your direction Martín, no offense." Tobin offered.

"He could be bi." Neoma countered. "I mean, it's not like he's hiding under the table. I think he's considering his options."

"I'm trying to decide if I should be offended here." Martín licked his fingers and sat back, glaring at them, his wide shoulders flexing as he rapped the table with his knuckles. "I just came out to you guys, and this is the response I get?"

"What were you expecting?" Tobin asked.

"Not dog dating."

"Hey, you just told me you didn't think I knew enough people. So allow me to prove you right, because this group here is all I really have to work with." Neoma looked around the room. "And poor Matrix is even more limited in his dating options. There's you, Robin, and Stewart. And we all know Stewart's heart belongs to another." Neoma made a face.

"This is my dating pool?" Martín looked horrified. "I knew I couldn't trust you! Wait a minute, what about Tobin? He's single."

"No, eww, Matrix is Tobin's weredog brother."

"I was talking about for *me!*" Martín frantically gestured at himself. "Come on Nae, stay focused here or I will never get my wedding."

"Oops, sorry, Matrix is so cute, and I didn't want him to be left out, so I started to consider his options and went down a mental rabbit hole."

"Clearly, I see where the humans rank." Tobin said dryly.

"Yeah, so, can you blame me?"

"Not really," Martín and Tobin said in tandem.

Neoma snorted and continued. "Okay, Martín, if you're attracted to Tobin, I guess *you* can date him?" Neoma slid her eyes to Tobin, and he caught how her gaze brushed his arms before touching on his face and away. She was still interested in him. Tobin quickly schooled his features to attention, flexing his arms over his chest, that curious feeling back. Her cheeks flushed and a scent close to vanilla crept into the air. A sense of triumph flooded Tobin like a drug.

Martín sighed dramatically. "Nope, I'll take the weredog. No offense Tobin, but I like my men hairy."

"None...taken?"

Neoma laughed, and Matrix bounded over to Martín, licking his face as the man made kissing noises and growled playfully into the big dog's neck. A stirring of connection fluttered in Tobin's chest, and he joined in the revelry and bad pickup lines that Neoma and Martín began to exchange while trading affections with Matrix. The dog bounced between them like a puppy, tail smacking Tobin in the face and making them all laugh harder.

The moment shattered.

"Did I miss something?" Robin's nasally voice broke in, the group going silent as if they'd been caught in the beam of a police flashlight.

"Nothing to see here." Martín brushed the dog hair off his

shirt, voice deep, as Matrix crawled back under the table.

"Were you making out with the dog?" Robin huffed indignantly as he placed his drink and notebook down.

"Well, it was you or the weredog." Neoma said, sweeping a curl from her face. "Turns out, Martín has high standards."

The last couple weeks of play had seen continued tension between Neoma and Robin. Tobin was concerned. He needed them to get along, or he needed to find someone else to join this group. He still sensed that Robin's immunity would be the easiest to break, the man practically salivated when they talked about real werewolves. But if the two of them continued to nip at each other like disgruntled children, this little pack he was trying to build wouldn't hold.

"Hey Robin, thanks for being here." Tobin said as Robin glared at Neoma, clearly not understanding what she was talking about, but knowing it was something demeaning. "How about we start? I have a great adventure for your pack tonight."

• ◦ ◉ ◦ •

I MIGHT HAVE TO KILL THEM ALL. TOBIN SAT BACK IN HIS CHAIR and pinched the bridge of his nose, guessing that if he still got headaches, he'd have one now.

"But if we do that, the rope might slip, and he will end up just as dead!" Robin practically screeched at Neoma from across the table.

"Yet if we sit here any longer discussing this, we die too.

And then Mack Torn will perish from starvation as he hangs up there in that cage." Neoma's voice was ice, her arms crossed over her chest as her eyes blazed green fire.

Tobin was a little taken aback by her intensity when the games got underway. He hadn't expected her to bring this amount of passion to the table—he enjoyed it. The bickering, not so much.

"The toxic waste fumes might kill me first." Martín deadpanned as he reached for the last oat square.

"Or that." Neoma ground out and glared at Robin some more.

Really, if Tobin thought about it, and he'd been thinking about it, this was all his fault. He'd written this adventure to trap Martín so that Robin and Neoma would have to work together, proving to themselves that it could be done. He'd thought it a brilliant plan— "delusional" might have been the better descriptor. He wondered if he had given his DM migraines back when he'd played D&D.

"You're right," Robin ground out. "This is getting us nowhere."

The whole table fell silent and stared at Robin. Had he really just capitulated?

"I am?" Neoma's expression of shock almost made Tobin laugh.

"Sadly, yes, you are." Robin looked back at his notes, eyebrows scrunched together, messy hair over his left eye. "I misjudged my calculations, and I think if we tried it my way, I run a greater risk of dying. So let's do it your way. Go ahead, roll."

Neoma didn't argue, even though her character was now at risk. The dice roll favored her, the rope held, no one died, and Mack Torn was pulled to safety. Martín thanked his rescuers, and they began to pack up for the night.

"Same time next week?" Martín asked as he gazed longingly at the empty plate.

"Hell yeah!" Robin cried. "I need to kick some more toxic chimp ass and flex Horn Hound's muscles." He flexed his own arms and Neoma rolled her eyes.

"I can't next week," Tobin said without looking up. "Full moon." The table went silent.

Neoma laughed. "Seriously? Wouldn't that be a perfect time to play?"

Tobin shrugged. "It's also the perfect time to be in the woods at night. Sorry. But the following week for sure." He smiled at everyone, reading their faces. Robin looked pissed, Martín curious, and Neoma suspicious.

"Okay," Neoma squinted at him now, he could almost hear the wheels turning in her head. "Well, with Books After Dark a current success, maybe I'll do a special full moon sale and see if I can drive in a little more business. We can't all go play werewolves in the woods."

"The offer's always open if you want to give it a try." Tobin stood, hoisting his pack, and started to walk out of the store,

Matrix at his heels. He could hear them murmuring behind him.

"Do you think he's serious?" Neoma whispered to Martín.

"Well, it would explain why he's in such good shape."

"Martín!" Neoma huffed a chuckle. "Behave."

"A boy can look."

"Look at what?" Robin asked.

Tobin walked out of the store, the door closing. "Matrix," he said softly, "can you stall at the tree and give it a long sniff?"

Matrix sighed and went to work inspecting the bike rack and tree as if he were a drug dog on duty. Tobin continued to eavesdrop through the glass, his head down as if he were watching Matrix's progress.

Robin's exit interrupted Tobin's concentration, and he lost the thread of conversation between Neoma and Martín. They'd been talking about dating in a small town, and he'd been curious if his name would come up.

"Hey Tobin, you're still here?"

"Yep, I can only move as fast as Matrix lets me." Tobin indicated the continued examination of the tree.

"Huh, well hey, do you really think there are werewolves?" Robin's expression was stuck somewhere between serious and guarded, making his face look young and vulnerable.

"Yeah Robin, I actually do. Why?"

"Really? You do?" His eyes rounded at Tobin's humorless expression. Tobin nodded. "Wow, I just, well wow. You know my roommate keeps telling me I'm ridiculous because I believe in things like Bigfoot and UFOs. But I just can't accept that this," he gestured around at the dark streets with a car driving by, "is all that there is."

"I agree." Tobin waited to see what Robin was going to do next.

"Are you, I mean, this sounds crazy," Robin shuffled his feet. "Are you…a werewolf?"

Tobin laughed. "That sounds like a personal question, Robin. I don't know you that well."

"Oh, yeah. I guess you're right. Sorry. I mean, yeah, why would you just tell me? But you canceled the game next week because of a full moon, and that, well that seemed like you opened the door for the question, so I thought I might as well ask…" He trailed off, blushed, and dropped his gaze.

"You could always come to the woods and find out," Tobin offered.

"Is that an invitation to come hang out at your place?" Robin looked a little giddy. Tobin wasn't sure this was going the way he'd hoped.

"How about this, you want to see a real werewolf?"

"Oh hell yeah I do!" Robin was bouncing on his toes.

"Okay, here." Tobin took a piece of paper out of his bag and scribbled some geo-tracking coordinates and a time on it. "I'll give you this on one condition." Robin looked like he was going to spontaneously combust, and Tobin wondered if he was nuts for entertaining this experiment. What if Robin didn't show? Or what if he recorded him? Or what if he couldn't break Robin's immunity? Tobin grimaced. He needed a guinea pig, and he was willing to sacrifice Robin in this pursuit. "If you bring another person, or try to film in any way, you will see nothing. Got it?"

"Promise!" Robin grabbed the paper. "Wait a minute, you're not going to pull some stupid prank on me are you? Try and scare the hell out of me and film it or something?" He took a half step back.

"No Robin, I wouldn't do that." Tobin said. "I know what it feels like to have people make fun of you for things you're passionate about. I promise you, I'll never do that." He put his hand on Robin's shoulder, gave him a squeeze. He remembered his brother doing the same thing with him after Tobin got bullied at school for talking about magic.

Robin took the paper slowly and backed away. "Yeah, okay, I'll think about it."

"I'll understand if you don't show. But I'll leave my truck there, so you know you're in the right place."

"You won't be there?"

"Not in the truck. No."

Robin nodded and turned away, walking to his car. Looking back, he gave a hesitant wave and left. The bittersweet smell of contemplation heavy in the air.

"What have I done?" Tobin asked Matrix. The dog ignored him, lifted his leg, and peed.

CHAPTER 21

Dark Roasted Drama

Neoma

*I*s *coffee really worth this?* Neoma asked herself, feeling Paris's glare boring into her back. She was surprised her dress wasn't on fire.

After being up late for the gaming group the previous evening, and having to get restocking done tonight, Neoma was running on fumes. She didn't quite share her mom's obsession with coffee, but there were some days when she had to join the dark side of the roasted bean. Neoma couldn't stomach the thought of drinking the swill Stewart kept at the store, so off to the coffee shop she'd trotted. Good thing Darkly Roasted Slightly Sweet was right down the street.

And apparently, Paris and company all had the same idea. They appeared to be fresh from a little league game, all adorned in ball caps, jerseys, and frowning at her. *I just wanted a good coffee. Why can't I lower my standards? It would make my life less stressful.*

As if the universe listened to her inner dialogue, Caleb and Mark walked in with a few other kids and dads, and Caleb's eyes drew to her like a magnet. *Kill me now.*

"Hi Neoma," the young voice yanked Neoma back towards the coffee counter. "Working late tonight?"

Neoma gratefully faced forward. Committed, she was now committed to coffee. "Hey Bren, yeah the delivery truck was running slow so I'm stuck restocking. But if you swing by tomorrow, I'll have those books you were waiting for."

Bren squealed and did a little happy dance. "Awesome! I can't wait. And the author is really coming next month for a signing?"

"Yep, I promise, he's coming."

"Fantastic, you just made my day. Okay, what can I get you to keep you conscious?"

Neoma gave her order and melted towards the back wall, pulling out her phone and attempting to look busy. A text from Tobin gave her something to focus on.

Hi, did I leave my notebook at the store? I can't find it.

I didn't notice, but you're welcome to come look. I'm working late. Or I can just text you if I stumble across it.

I'll come look, I gotta get dinner anyways. Thx.

Some instinct made Neoma raise her head. She noticed Paris tugging on Caleb's arm, her glare now focused on her cousin. Caleb raised his huge hands as if in surrender and backed up like he was going to join the mass of chaos that the baseball team was creating on the other side of the store. But as soon as Paris began to manage the kids, Caleb slipped past her and beelined for Neoma.

I don't have the energy for this again. Neoma sighed and steeled herself. She had no idea that Caleb would be so persistent. Why couldn't he text her like a normal person? Each time she saw him, he seemed unable to simply wave, nope, he had to come over and talk. Maybe he was just being friendly, and it wasn't anything more? *It's a small town, Nae,* she griped at herself, *learn to navigate this and move on.* Neoma mentally crossed her fingers and hoped her coffee would hurry up.

"Hey Nae," he rumbled, blocking her view of the counter.

"Hi Caleb." Neoma tried to look past him, but he didn't take the hint.

"Late night? You only ever get coffee when you're really tired."

"Yep." Neoma glanced back at her phone.

"Oh, um, how've you been?" Caleb began to fidget, shuffling his feet.

"Good. Yourself?" Neoma didn't raise her eyes, fingers swiping the screen.

"Keeping busy. I'm helping coach little league. It's been a blast." At the enthusiasm in his voice, Neoma looked up. Caleb beamed at her.

"That's great," she said, meaning it. "I'm glad you're enjoying it."

"So um," he stuffed his hands in his pockets, "are you dating that guy we saw you with at the market the other week? Who is he?"

Neoma gave him a cool stare, her blip of interest in the conversation evaporating. "Are *you* dating anyone, Caleb?"

"No, I mean I'd like to, but geez, Nae, I can't stop thinking about us. And if you're not dating that guy, maybe we could go out? You know, let me take you on a real date, since we never did that. I've been thinking maybe that was the problem, ya know, we never did anything together. Maybe if we do some couple stuff, you'd see how much fun it is to be a couple. Would you like that?"

"Coffee for Neoma!" Bren's voice rang out.

"Caleb, I gotta get my coffee." Neoma tried to move past him, but he wouldn't budge. "Caleb," she could taste frost on her tongue, "look, I've tried to be civil, I've tried to be clear, I don't know another way I can tell you…"

But she didn't get a chance to finish her thought. Paris grabbed Caleb's meaty arm and tugged, forcing the big man to step back. Her eyes were dark fire, the usual enmity that Neoma dealt with was now aimed at Caleb.

"Caleb, *so help me…*" Paris pointed a finger at the man's face, her back now to Neoma. "We talked about being a role model for my little girl! Starla will not witness this behavior from you. Neoma said no. She has said no to you multiple times. Knock this shit off and leave her alone. She might be a self-centered martyr, but you are being an asshole, and I won't stand for that behavior from my family. Be a better man Caleb, I will not tolerate less from someone who's hanging around my little girl."

Caleb's face turned purple, went white, then settled on red as he sputtered, then hung his head and stalked back to the group.

Neoma was left floundering. *Did Paris just call her beloved cousin an asshole? She can't actually be, what? Defending me?* She cast around the store looking for flying pigs, snowballs in hell…then her brain caught up to the insult.

"Self-centered martyr?" Neoma asked, blinking in confusion. Paris returned her glare to Neoma.

"It's more explicit than simply 'bitch'." Paris spat. "I like to be clear."

"Color me confused."

"Color yourself whatever emotional shade you want, I don't care, and clearly it doesn't matter to you what any of us think." Paris hissed low and turned to go.

"What does that mean?" Neoma couldn't help but ask, feeling attacked for no reason other than existing.

Paris whirled around, keeping her voice low and her back to the kids. "Seriously? Are you that self-absorbed?"

"You know what, I didn't ask for this conversation. All I wanted was coffee." Neoma held up her hands, her shock at the confrontation mutating into unease. Her hind brain did not want to linger in this space.

"Look," Paris grumbled, pinching the bridge of her nose as a sense of resolve seemed to settle over her features, "let me break this down for you because this shit needs to stop."

"Don't bother on my account." Neoma cut in, wishing she was still talking to Caleb.

"Oh trust me, I'm not." Pairs crossed her arms. "I'll make this really simple for you. Have you even seen Trisha's new baby? Called her? Texted congrats with little pink flowers or something? Spared a thought about her since the baby shower?"

Neoma flinched, guilt drenching her.

"Yeah, that's what I thought." Paris said, seemingly exhausted as she continued to engage in their muted conversation. "You sit in your bookstore mad at the world because your dreams didn't pan out. Well, welcome to real life. You think the rest of us haven't had the same problem? Do we look like we're living our dreams? I'm not dancing on Broadway, Miranda isn't styling hair for Hollywood elites, and Mark isn't coaching the NFL. Near as I can tell, you mentally left this town, didn't look back, and now that you're back, you're still gone!" Paris seemed to wrestle with keeping her words hushed. "I don't care if you wither away in there with the books, but for some fucked up reason, you mean something to my cousin and my friends. You're hurting them, acting stuck in the past as if we're all still in high school. Standing apart and judging us for making a life together."

"You can't be serious! As if you haven't continuously judged me for breathing," Neoma wanted to scream, but kept the words soft and biting, cold anger rising in her.

"It was never the breathing, it was the attitude." Paris shot back with venom. "You waltzed into high school acting as if you were better than everyone there. And we had all fucking grown up together."

"I remember things a little differently."

"Narcissists usually do."

"Fuck you, Paris," Neoma fought to keep her voice low, but could tell people were starting to be curious, necks craning to look at them. Her cheeks burned with the unwanted attention, yet she continued, her anger spiking. "You and your friends started acting like my mom was the town slut when she got pregnant. Meg was the only one who didn't. And then what happened senior year? You found yourself pregnant, in the same state you'd denigrated my mom over." Neoma knew she'd crossed a line as soon as the words slipped past her lips.

Paris's eyes bulged. "This, this right here is why I told Caleb to get lost."

"What are you talking about?" Neoma shied back, suddenly realizing she didn't want the answer to her question.

"Whenever you feel wronged, you lash out with that self-righteous attitude of yours," Paris hissed, Neoma could almost taste the anger coming off the other woman.

"Paris, *Caleb* chose to come over here and talk with me. To push an issue that I've been very clear on. Then *you* came over here and told him to leave, as if defending me for reasons I can't fathom. What the hell? All I wanted was coffee and…" Paris jerked her finger up into Neoma's face like she was disciplining a dog, cutting Neoma's protest off.

"You're confused? You think I was helping you?" Paris actually laughed, dropping her hand. "Allow me to enlighten you. It's true, Caleb has no right to keep pushing at clear boundaries that you've laid down. It's his failing, and I won't tolerate a man in my family being a dick, making women feel unsafe. And I will pound that into him, even for your benefit. Yet you were about to damage him, and I don't have time to clean up your mess."

"What?" Shock paralyzed Neoma.

Paris looked like she was breathing hard, a sneer across her face. "Oh don't give me that, you know exactly how to verbally castrate people. You seem to know where their weak spots are, and you don't care about the fallout of your words. All you seem to want is to be left alone and miserable. I wasn't defending you Neoma, I was protecting Caleb *from* you."

Neoma shook, something in her core cracking. Confusion and anger were making her vision waver. She wanted to get away from Paris with a desperation she'd never experienced before.

"As if you were any better during high school. Every day, you painted a target on my back each time I turned around. The whole dance team hated me by the time we graduated, Paris! And why? Because of my mom? Or because I danced a little better than you under pressure? It never made any sense. You couldn't have the scholarship so you burned me in effigy. I had nothing to come back to. My life here was gone!" Neoma's voice shook.

"Oh get over it! That was ten years ago, we were teenagers for fucks sake. You had everything going for you, including an escape route. So yeah, I was jealous. But you know what? I picked myself up and made something of what I had left. If you had nothing to come back to, that was because of your choices, not mine. And it's not like you're unable to grow up now, so stop being stuck and blaming it on other people."

Paris swiveled, picked up Neoma's coffee and handed it to her. "There, you got what you wanted. Now leave," she said with a snarl, then turned, her long black hair sliding like a curtain between them, ending the conversation.

"Paris," Neoma reached out, guilt, anger, and uncertainty propelling her to…*to what? To attempt to make amends? Have I lost my mind?* But the verbal cuts that Paris had made in her sense of self began to weep memories of the past, betrayals that had never been addressed, never given a chance to heal. *I can't do this now.* Neoma thought, dropping her arm before she could touch the other woman. "Never mind."

"Whatever."

CHAPTER 22

Shelves of Emotion

Neoma & Tobin

W hat just happened? Neoma clutched her coffee as she re-entered the bookstore, her head spinning. Someone had just flipped the script on her. Paris thought she was self-centered? A martyr? A narcissist? Each word was a remembered slap, her emotions stinging with the impact.

The chime of her cell phone pulled her out. It was Tobin again.

I'll be there in 20, gotta get something from the store.

Sure, no problem. Neoma's fingers trembled as she typed those few words.

By the time Tobin showed up, Neoma had shoved her turbulent emotions into the back of her mind. Sipping her coffee, she'd forced herself to get lost in the smell of books, the dulcet sounds of Norah Jones, and the comforting creak of the wheeled cart as she made her way down the bookshelves. One book at a time. That was all she needed to focus on.

The soft rapping on the glass brought her out of her sensory distractions. Moving around the cart, she shuffled her way to the door and let Tobin in. A soft rain had started, and he carefully took off his jacket, mindful not to shake water towards the books. *No wonder my joints are aching, even the weather is against me.* She grimaced, losing a bit of her calm. However, the sight of Tobin in a slightly damp, skin tight, t-shirt was really helpful.

"Hey, thanks for letting me intrude." He lingered in the entry, a nervous energy buzzing from him as he stuffed his hands into his pockets. The action drew her gaze to his flexed forearms, her eyes tracing the white ring of scars that seemed to shimmer in the soft lights. She yanked her attention back to his face.

"No problem, it's nice to have company." Neoma flushed slightly, then frowned at herself. "Go ahead and look around. I just went right to work since I knew you were coming. If you find my lost sanity along with your notebook, let me know."

He gave her an odd look before walking away, and she wanted to knock her head against a shelf. *Come on Nae, this is your chance to get to know him better, be friendly!* But Paris's words had undercut her self-confidence, so she continued her restocking, humming along with Nora Jones to "Come Away with Me." She shelved a couple more books before Tobin returned. Without saying a word, he began to help her. They worked together in silence, the music filling the space between them.

Tobin wasn't sure why he'd come, and why he'd made up the ridiculous lie of having left his notebook. Besides, had he left it, he could have picked it up next week. Or tomorrow. But tomorrow wouldn't cut it. Some restless energy had infected him after the sun went down. He'd tried to catch up with work, but his pulse kept pounding, making his hands tremble on the keyboard and turning his focus to shit. Going for a run hadn't helped, working out hadn't helped, and his mind kept spinning back to gaming the other night, to Neoma.

He rubbed the back of his neck, that odd, warm feeling rising. The memory of her vanilla scent teased some new part of him, unacknowledged until now. Until Neoma. He wanted answers. He also wanted to replicate whatever action he'd taken to make her smell that way. But right now, she just smelled like bitterness and cracked feelings, a sharp scent that was almost more sensation than odor.

What do people do with these feelings? Jokes? Confessions? Small talk? Tobin tussled with the idea as he shelved another book. But what did he hope to gain from coming over here? Gritting his teeth, he rerouted his thoughts away from tactics and tried to simply be present.

"Nae," Tobin ventured. She stopped frowning at the shelves and looked up.

"Yeah?"

"Did something happen today? You seem…off." *There, that was empathic, right?* Tobin considered just walking out of the store, it might be easier.

Neoma's expression hardened, and she turned away. "I'm not up to discussing my bad mood. I'm sorry if it's leaking through. But thanks for asking."

"No problem." Tobin went back to work. *Now what? Should I make an excuse and go?* Yet that tug in his emotions wouldn't let him leave. No, it wouldn't let him leave *her*.

• ◦ ◉ ◦ •

"SO WHY DID YOU MOVE TO KELSO?" NEOMA FINALLY ASKED after she had flattened Tobin's attempt at conversation. *Why do I do this? I wanted a distraction, here he is!* She shook herself and engaged her curiosity. "This isn't the bustling mill town it once was. And you don't do forestry stuff. So why relocate here?"

The emotional upheaval from Paris could be dealt with later, now she'd focus on enjoying the quiet moment with a handsome man in a bookstore. While it rained. *I'm living a cliche right now, I should be happy.* But as she searched for the right shelf to place the next book, a nagging irritation bloomed anew. Had Stewart gone on one of his reorganization campaigns again? He had, hadn't he? *I'm going to poison his coffee with…laxatives! I told that man to ask me before rearranging the store!*

"I think that goes here," Tobin pointed to a shelf to her left, his eyes casually watching her irritated movements. "Are you plotting Stewart's murder?" he asked while idly glancing at the blurb on a book before returning it to its exact spot. She appreciated his attention to detail.

"No, not murder, simple revenge. The man has got to learn to communicate when he goes on an organizational bender."

"I don't think bodily harm will help with that."

"It's only dietary distress, and he'll learn. Now answer my question." Neoma found the new location for military thrillers and shoved her book home. Yes, the rearrangement made more sense in the flow of the shelves, but she wasn't about to admit it. Being irritated was better than feeling depressed, and, if she was being honest, was closer to her normal baseline these days. *Maybe Paris had a point?* She slapped that thought down hard.

"Kelso? It wasn't really a choice, more of a last-minute need coupled with divine intervention. The rent was cheap and not too far from Portland." Tobin shrugged and handed her another book.

It was kind of him to help her restock. *I'd have thought he'd have better things to do on a Thursday night than hang out in a closed bookstore. With me. Unless...* she shoved that notion away. Every time she thought he might be interested in more than friendship, he pulled back, and Neoma was starting to find that frustrating too. *Why is life one continuous irritant?*

"Vancouver would have been even closer."

"Yeah, but it didn't feel…right."

She looked at him, and he handed her three books. Her RA groaned in protest. "I need more than a vague summary please."

"Need a distraction from plotting Stewart's demise?"

"Possibly."

"I'm not sure what else I can share without sounding more obtuse." Tobin's eyes avoided hers, flitting over the books as if afraid she might read some secret lurking there.

"Good word, Shawshank."

"I'm trying. Nice movie reference."

A smile threatened to creep across Neoma's lips, but she kept her focus on the books in hopes he'd keep talking.

"Honestly, I can't explain it. It was just this feeling, this instinct. I had to leave Portland unexpectedly and something kind of tugged my attention this way. And when I looked for somewhere to live, everything fell into place so fast. I wanted a house in the remote woods, and there it was. I needed to be able to work from home, and suddenly had all the online temp jobs I could ever want. Plus there was nothing in Vancouver that had rent and land that I could afford. Kelso did."

"I'm sorry."

"I'm not."

Neoma sighed and reached for another book. "You haven't lived here long enough." Her hand came up empty. They'd already finished?

Outside, the rain increased, a persistent drumming that blended with the soft music and subtle throb in her joints. She clutched the handle of the cart, making it creak. The bookstore seemed to be enveloping them, wrapping them together in a paper cocoon, slowly shifting the idle feel of the conversation into something charged. Or maybe Neoma was imagining things. She glanced up at Tobin, meeting those penetrating eyes.

"I'm happy to live here longer. How about I give you a full report in a few months?"

"For research purposes?"

"Sure, we can go with that."

"Hmmm, sounds like your excuse from the book fair."

Tobin rested his hands lightly on the empty cart, his eyes never leaving her. "I would hate to change my story now."

"Well, the rewriting would be a bitch."

"Yeah, that." They both chuckled awkwardly, the empty cart seeming to stretch between them.

"I have a couple more tasks to attend to in the back before I leave. You don't have to stay if you have other things to do."

"Do you want me to go?" Tobin looked unsure. His hand drifted to a shelf, running his fingers over book spines. His gaze leaving her allowed her to breathe again. She watched his muscles flex under summer-tanned skin, and caught a whiff of his scent that reminded her of crushed pine needles.

"No." Honest. She would be honest.

"Okay. I've got no place to be. Matrix can take care of himself for a while."

"You could have brought him, he's always welcome here." Yet even as she said it, Neoma could feel a sense of relief that the big dog wasn't present, that she got this unguarded moment with Tobin. Her fingers slipped free of the handle. Something about the dog changed the dynamic between them, but she couldn't pinpoint how.

"I didn't want to." Tobin said softly, still tracing book spines, his glasses going opaque in the reflected light.

Neoma stepped around the cart and into the aura of his body heat, leaving a book's width between them. Now she could see his eyes as they returned to her, dilated, his nostrils fluttering, and he gulped, making his Adam's apple bob up and down in a distracting way. Their height difference demanded a slight lift of her chin to meet those hazel depths. His intensity seemed to regard her like a dangerous fish in a tank; safely seen but untouchable behind his glass barrier. She was going to change that.

"What do you want, Tobin?"

"I don't know," he whispered.

"Why are you here?"

"Because..." his breath caught, "I needed to see you."

She took his hand from the books, tugging him gently towards the back of the store. He didn't resist her.

<hr />

WHAT AM I DOING? TOBIN DIDN'T KNOW, BUT HE FOLLOWED her willingly into the back room, his mind spinning, heart thumping. Was this part of his plan? Is this how he was going to break her immunity, through seduction?

Or is this how someone starts dating? That random thought sent fear spiking through him, and he almost pulled free of her grip. Tobin didn't do romantic relationships. He could never figure out what there was to be gained. Yet everyone else seemed so infatuated with the idea that he'd given dating a try, only to discover how bad he was at it. Feeling confused and uncomfortable while someone across a random dinner table was expecting something from him never worked. They left annoyed, and he remained awkward and embarrassed but not understanding why. The dating experience didn't benefit him.

Still, there'd been the physical component to consider. So he'd given sex a try. More than one attempt actually. But each experiment had been an utter failure. A confused flailing of limbs and body parts until his partner had left angry and disappointed. Tobin always remained behind, humiliated and befuddled, seemingly unable to muster whatever that need was that drove other people into bed together. He'd written off relationships as a mystery, an illogical connection between humans. Clearly, he wasn't built to seek out that type of attachment because it only ever caused pain. So he wouldn't. And yet, a hollowness had endured.

And then he'd met Nora and been surprised as emotion stirred within that echoing space inside him, derailing some of his logical existence, affecting the plans he'd had for her. Nora was the first woman he'd garnered genuine interest for. Sure, he'd needed to get to know her, but he'd found he'd also *wanted* to know her. To befriend her, to unlock her secrets, and not just because he'd been instructed to do so. But he hadn't navigated that well. Hell, he'd burned that bridge to ash because he'd been unable to get her to trust him. To confide in him. That was behind him now.

But with Neoma...with Neoma, he was starting to feel similar things, starting to want things he didn't have words for. It scared him. Was it the werewolf in him that was changing him?

Her tug urged him forward, and he couldn't hold on to the analytical thoughts swarming his brain. He needed to experience what this deep instinct was insisting he be present for. Letting go of his control the tiniest bit, he breathed in her sweet smell and tried to make sure he wasn't misreading her intentions. Was this what she wanted?

"Nae, I..." he trailed off, not sure what to say as she stopped them in the office space that doubled as her rare book storage. The room was surprisingly spacious, with papered over windows nestled high up against the roofline, exposed beams in the two-story ceiling, and an area where an old couch rested near the overburdened bookshelves and reading light. Stacks of books made columns in random corners, and a garishly colored plush Turkish rug spread out under the couch and small expanse of clear floor. It was a clean yet unapologetically cluttered space, spontaneously adorned with art, a lot like Neoma herself. The room just fit her.

"This is my collection." She released his hand. She had maneuvered them onto the rug in front of the couch. He wasn't sure what her home was like, but he felt this space held her heart. He swallowed. She had invited him in, demanded it, really. Suddenly, he couldn't look away from her.

"I guess I do owe you a book." His hands fidgeted, empty, unmoored.

"I guess you do." She stepped up to him again. She smelled like vanilla and parchment. He licked his lips.

"I'm going to be blunt, Tobin, mostly because it's my strong suit, but are you interested in me?"

"Interested?" his voice wobbled.

"Attracted?"

What did that mean exactly? Did he think her face had a nice shape? That her hair was appealing? That the sight of her made him want to write poetry? Tobin wasn't sure. He was at a complete loss for all his choices this evening. *What's happening to me?* Logically, he knew the answer she wanted was "yes," yet he wanted to understand why he'd say yes. But he didn't. He didn't understand the elements that went together to create what people called attraction.

All he knew was that right now, he wanted to be closer to her. He wanted her to take his hand again. He wanted to bury his nose in her hair and breathe her in until he found that next layer of scent that snuggled against her skin. He wanted her to…to what?

"I…Nae, I…" words left him. Reason left him. He watched the brown flecks in her sea-glass eyes swirl and all he could think was he was ready. He was here. With her. But he needed her to help him, to release him from his ignorance about what to do next, of how to interpret these new feelings building within him. It felt as if the full moon was rising, and he was pushing at the borders of his human skin, but he couldn't break out of this form. He didn't know how!

"I don't know what I'm doing," he whispered.

Neoma studied him then asked gently, "Have you dated much?"

"Not really."

"Have you had sex before?"

Tobin shrugged. "Sure, I mean, sort of, but it never turned out well."

Neoma blinked. "Okay…I was attempting a seduction here, but I don't want to do something you're not interested in, or ready for. There's no pressure, no wrong answers. Do you want to be here with me now?"

"Yes."

"You sure?"

"Yes."

"We can just continue to talk, hang out."

Tobin shook his head.

"You want me to continue?"

Tobin nodded.

"Do you want to have sex?"

"Yes?" He could taste the question and saw her wince. He thought for sure she was going to demand that he leave. He knew this was not going well. Something was off. There had to be a way to fix it. He cast around but no answers jumped out of the shadows to save him.

"Tobin."

His eyes shot back to her. "Yes?"

"You're always so controlled, wound so tight." Her words were careful, measured, as if trying to calm a panicked animal. "Can I try something with you? You can stop this at any time, but you'd need to give over a little control."

Tobin balked, panic tried to flood him. But the curious need to stay with her, to be closer to her won out.

"I'll trust you," he said, voice rough.

"Tobin," she commanded him. "Get on your knees."

Something wonderful broke inside him, and he dropped to the ground with a muffled thump. Yes, oh yes, this was what he needed. Looking up, he sucked in the scent of rain and vanilla and whispered, "Yes…"

CHAPTER 23

Delicious Desire

Neoma & Tobin

Neoma gazed down at Tobin as he kneeled before her, a thrill running over her skin, through her blood. She grabbed a fistful of his hair, using it as an anchor to pull herself one step closer to him, and watched as his eyes rolled back slightly in his head. Tobin moaned. He needed her to be in control. This measured, restrained, disciplined man needed her to take the lead here, to tell him what to do, and she was more than ready to explore this.

She gave his hair another firm yank, then lifted his glasses off his face, folding them carefully as he watched her, his eyes glued to her every movement. She placed them on the desk, just out of reach. He whimpered.

"Take off your shirt."

His breathing increased, and he did as she bid, stripping the soft fabric over his head and letting it land in a heap at his side. His eyes looked black; pupils fully blown open. She could see his pulse pounding just under the soft skin of his throat. She trailed her hand down his cheek, feeling his rough scruff scratch her palm before resting over his speeding pulse.

Neoma cradled his throat, watching his eyes close, his body shudder. She allowed her gaze to linger on his bare shoulders, his chest, his arms. On his side, she glimpsed a green tattoo of a fiddle head fern, red scars stretching from the curled head to the stalk. She would need to explore that.

For now, she simply admired the man kneeling before her. He was stunning, toned, athletic, a body sculpted by movement. A "T" of soft brown hair whispered over his chest and down past rippling abs to dip beneath his pants. She wanted to follow that trail, see what waited at the end of it.

"You're going to obey me?"

"Yes," he groaned.

"You will stop me if there's something you don't want to do. Understand?"

"Yes."

"Yes what?"

His eyes fluttered open. "Yes, Neoma."

Her body clenched in response, heat pooling in her lower belly, erupting upwards, spreading under her skin like warm water. "Good boy, Tobin." He shuddered under her hand. "Now undress me."

He reached forward, and she dropped her grip on his neck. All his motions were careful, slow. His dark eyes seemed to watch her as if noticing every nuance in her expression. Her sultry grin stretched across her face like a satisfied cat as he found the hem of her long dress and began to lift it hesitantly upwards.

"Touch me as you undress me."

He immediately complied. His hands found her lower legs, gliding along the skin, seeking upwards, his big palms surrounding her thighs, her hips. Slipping over her silken thong, he continued his ascent. He guided her dress up her torso, tracing bra-less ribs, fingers lingering for a moment in the soft places between bones. Neoma drew her arms over her head, caressing his shoulders as she did so. Tobin deftly gained his feet, sliding the fabric further, brushing it over her tight nipples, making her gasp and shudder. Her response froze him.

"Keep going, Tobin. I want to be naked."

He kept going until the dress was free. He paused, stretching away from her and draping the garment over the back of the desk chair as if it were a precious thing. Returning to her, his hands found her skin again. His fingers fit into the grooves of her ribs as if they belonged there, holding each of her breaths, feeling them catch at his touch. His expression was that of wonder as he licked his lips, and she sighed at the heat in his encompassing hands.

Draping her arms around his shoulders, she captured his hair again, and he shivered. "You're not done. I'm not naked." She gave his head a gentle shake, her joints protesting slightly.

Tobin's eyes locked with hers as he slowly descended to his knees, reversing the path that his hands had just traveled until his fingers snagged on her thong. She nodded, and he continued, letting the wisp of silky material flow down her thighs. When the fabric encircled her feet, she lifted first one, and then the other, using his shoulders for balance. His skin was as firm as it looked. She sighed as the muscles beneath her flexed and moved, skillfully removing the last vestiges of clothing.

He started to bend his head towards her then stopped, eyes darting up. His back bent, showing her the muscles that framed his spine. Neoma wanted to run her nails down those defined ridges of flesh.

"Go ahead Tobin, follow your instincts, touch me. Now." Neoma was gloriously nude, standing in her bookstore, her special space. Before her was a handsome man following her every direction, willingly, wantonly, giving her what she desired. The control was as much of an aphrodisiac as his hot hands.

Tobin bowed his head against the skin of her thighs as she tickled the nape of his neck where his hairline stopped. Goosebumps danced away from her nails. She could feel a similar tingle kindling where he touched her, nuzzling where her leg and hip joined, licking down towards her inner thigh, his groans of pleasure building. She parted her stance, and Tobin seemed to whimper, crouching lower. His lips kissed up her inner thigh, trying to go deeper, but the angle wouldn't allow it.

He tipped his head up, his tongue darting between her lower lips, his eyes searching hers, face buried in her. His eyes were wild, almost desperate.

"Your scent," he breathed into her skin, "I want more, please."

"You better lay me down somewhere comfortable then." Tobin didn't hesitate, scooping her up as if she weighed nothing and startling a gasping laugh from her as his strong arms pinned her against his chest.

"Did I hurt you?" His eyes widened as if panicked. She could almost see his thoughts as he seemed to remember her RA, remembering that she was a wounded thing. She refused to be wounded tonight.

"No, I'm good, just achy all over, but you can help with that." She wrapped her legs around his waist with a little effort, joints complaining softly, but she ignored them. There were much better sensations to focus on. Like the feel of his hard body against hers. Her voice husky with need, she gently commanded him. "Lay me down Tobin. Somewhere soft."

Her verbal nudge propelled him forward, and he carried her the three steps to the couch before laying her down like something breakable. Her clit brushed against his abs, sparking lightning through her thighs. She fought the urge to buck against him, to grind into that chiseled stomach and take her pleasure. But she resisted as he continued to hover over her, face to face, breathing each other's breath. He waited for her to unlock her legs from around him, to give him permission for more.

Neoma chuckled low in her throat, enjoying the delicious dynamic building between them. Unwinding her legs, she released him, and his knees slowly sank towards the floor, his torso beginning to slide down her body.

Tobin paused at her chest, his nose sliding over her skin with little puffs of air that made her arch up into him. A soft whine escaped him as he began nuzzling her chest, tasting her nipples. His mouth and hands seemed to be everywhere, firm yet careful. His scruff was a satisfying friction against her skin as he passed his face side to side over her breasts, her ribs, her belly. His fingers gripped her hips like a lifeline. He moved down to cup her ass, bringing her mound up to rub against his stomach. Each touch fueled that ball of warmth in her lower belly. The sensation spread, building the heat, subduing the ache from her RA until she was almost begging him to move lower.

But she wouldn't beg. That was his job.

Again, she seized his hair, fingers sinking into his thick strands. It almost felt like fur. For a moment, she gloried in the silky soft texture sliding between the sensitive spaces of her fingers. Tobin groaned, his hips bucking against the couch, hands grabbing her ass and sliding her tighter to him. She reached one hand down his back and raked her nails up that tempting ridge of muscle to the side of his spine. Tobin growled, literally growled.

That was so hot! Neoma thought and did it again, feeling her nails indenting his flesh, leaving red marks in their wake. Tobin carefully nipped her nipple in response, another growl muffled in her chest. She arched her back, pushing her breast deeper into his mouth, moaning long and low and hungry.

"Tobin, I want your mouth on my clit, now. And lose your clothes." Tobin hesitated, body going still above her.

"Nae…" he trailed off, she could almost feel something twisting inside him, uncertainty warring with desire.

She untangled her fingers from his hair and smoothed the ruffled strands off his face. "It's okay Tobin, you don't have to do anything you're not comfortable with. I promise. This doesn't need to be anything more than it is. And it's supposed to be fun for both of us."

She waited a heartbeat, then two, her heat starting to bank to coals inside her. But she wouldn't push him into something he wasn't ready for. She continued to stroke his head, a gentle smile reaching her eyes. *I care for him, damnit, when did that happen?* But she did, and she wasn't about to tank this friendship over sex. Even if this sex was exactly what she'd been searching for. *Stupid, hot, mind-blowing, dominance play!* She took a deep breath and let her body relax back into the couch. Continuing to stroke his hair, she let her nails play over his scalp in secret patterns.

"Nae, I'm not ready to be fully naked." Tobin confessed, his cheeks heating. "But I don't want to stop either." His hands squeezed her hips, his need shining bright as he moved his head to nuzzle her palm.

"That's okay. Really. You don't need to be naked to play."

"You sure?"

"Absolutely. Do you want to continue?"

"Yes, please, Neoma." The way he said her name, all breathless desire, had the heat in her belly reigniting. It flared through her, a hot wet flood as her inner moisture began to drip.

"Then taste me Tobin, I want to feel your tongue deep inside me."

Tobin complied.

• ○ ◉ ○ •

HER SCENT! IT WAS DRIVING HIM TO MADNESS. AND NOW HER flavor…he stopped thinking, he couldn't think, all his tactile senses were dialed up to maximum intensity and all he could do was feel. And he didn't want it to stop.

Burying his nose between her thighs, he followed her alluring scent, hair tickling his cheeks, until his tongue could reach that inner wetness now coating his lips. She tasted like vanilla, and pleasure, and something wild all rolled up into a sensation he couldn't label so he just kept licking, nuzzling. She grabbed his hair, urging him deeper, words spilling from her lips that he wasn't sure he could understand.

"Good boy."

"That's it."

"Yes, yes, yes…"

He tilted her up further into his mouth, his hands supporting her low back and hips, shivers running through him like a river as she clawed his shoulders, dug into his forearms, and demanded more. All he wanted to give her was more. And he was so fucking hard!

He could feel his erection straining his jeans, a glorious, almost painful pressure that continued to build with each noise she made, each swipe of his tongue deeper into her velvet folds. Tobin thrust against the couch, rocking them both, as his nose encountered something firm in Naoma's softness. She moaned, deeply, breathlessly, bucking against his face.

"YES."

It was one word, but it was the only word he needed.

Focusing all his attention on that little pearl, Tobin alternated between sucking, flicking his tongue, and lavishing the area with firm swipes, paying attention to how her body responded. She shuddered, moaned while her breath hitched, and squeezed her thighs tighter around his head.

He almost couldn't breathe.

He didn't care.

Working his tongue faster, harder, as she heaved against him, crying out, clutching his hair again, her body convulsing. He moved lower, thrusting his tongue in and out between her lips as she shook, then kept shaking. His body started to shudder along with her until she gave a final cry. He couldn't stop. He exploded! Pulsing in utter ecstasy, he ground into the couch, soaking his jeans, feeling heat move through him like wildfire.

He had come. They both had.

Arms trembling, Tobin lowered her body gently to the cushions, disengaging until he was untangled from her legs. He slipped the rest of the way to the floor, back resting on the couch, hands on his knees, his body alight with pleasure he'd never fully experienced. He blinked dumbly at the garish carpet. *What does this mean?*

Neoma made contented noises behind him. Rolling to her side, she placed a soft hand on his shoulder.

"Tobin, that was delicious." She hesitated when he didn't respond, shifting behind him to creep into his peripheral vision. He could feel the weight of her gaze caress his features. "Hey there, are you okay?"

He grabbed his shirt, swiping her wetness off his face, feeling...*awkward?* Yet he wanted to never wash this shirt again so he could smell her forever. *What am I doing?*

"I'm not sure." Tobin whispered, turning his head to partially meet her regard. Neoma's hair was a wild cloud around her head, her eyes looking satiated yet careful.

"Did I hurt you?" she asked, tracing a small scratch down his shoulder.

"No, not at all. I wanted this," his voice was rough, strangled as he tried to reassure her. Yet her touch pulled heat in its wake as it traveled over him. He wanted more. He could feel the need to keep touching her renewing with each breath he took. He couldn't...he couldn't stay. He needed to understand this, not be blinded by his body's emotions. How had he let himself get consumed like this?

"Tobin." His name in her mouth made him tremble, and he hunched forward, hugging his knees. *How can I feel so good, and so fucking terrified at the same time?*

Neoma moved away from him, the couch creaking, her body heat leaving made him feel exposed. Fabric swished over skin, a sliding sound that echoed the passages of his hands over her flesh. He bit his cheek, chasing back the desire, concentrating on the uncomfortable wetness of his jeans before her presence returned to envelop him. Neoma knelt before him, her dress covering that skin that he still wanted to explore with his tongue. She didn't touch him as he continued to tremble.

"Tobin," she whispered, and he looked up. Breathless, he was breathless. "I need you to talk to me, please, because I'm starting to worry about where your head's at." She gave him a small, encouraging smile. "Please."

"Nae, I...I think I need to leave." Her eyes widened, and he tripped all over his tongue trying to find words that wouldn't hurt her. "I'm sorry, you did everything right. I'm...somewhere I've never been before, and I'm overwhelmed. I can't think right now, I can't process this. I need, I need…" But he didn't know what he needed, couldn't find the words. *Why can't I hold it together?*

Tobin bolted to his feet, almost falling backwards over the couch as he struggled into his shirt that smelled like her. She continued to sit on the floor, watching him, a concerned expression on her face. A wave of embarrassment swamped him as her eyes flicked to his pants. He ducked away, casting around for his shoes and socks. Finding them, he turned sideways, but he couldn't meet her questioning gaze.

"I'm sorry," he whispered and began to leave.

He heard her sigh under her breath, a defeated whisper. "That's a first. I've never had a guy run from me before."

Tobin stopped at the door, partially turning towards her as insight flooded his mind. He couldn't leave her thinking she'd chased him off.

"I'm not running from you, Neoma, I'm running from me."

Her scent spiked with stress, the burnt vanilla odor pursuing him through the dark storefront and into the rain.

CHAPTER 24

Letting Go of Gravity

Neoma

*H*ey *Nae, want to go out this afternoon?*
Neoma squinted at her phone, double checking who was sending the text. Huh, well that was unexpected.

Martín, I didn't think I was your type. She wrote back. His quick response littered her screen with laughing emojis.

You're not. He continued. *But I know you have your little brother for movies today, and I have my two sisters that are about Lukas's age. We could tag team, talk boys, eat popcorn...*

Let me guess, you want company because you've seen the movie already? She smiled as she typed it.

So. Many. Times. Neoma could almost feel Martín's stress in each word and laughed, taking pity on him.

Sure, let's play chaperones. I'll bring the treats.

I love you.

You better, see you at 2:30.

"I thought you said we were going to the new Disney movie?" Neoma asked as Martín attempted to sink further into the worn-out theater seat. How had he gotten his compact frame even shorter? Neoma attempted to keep a straight face as the man shielded his eyes with his broad hands.

"They tricked me," he muttered, then cursed in Spanish. "They say they love me, then they *lie*. They lie like flea-bitten Chihuahuas on the mangled remains of my sanity!" His voice squeaked.

Carla wiggled around and hushed her brother. "Hermano, stop whining. You work with the dead all the time."

"Yes, the dead. Not reanimated corpses trying to eat my brains." On the screen, a head blew apart, splattering brains and goo everywhere. Martín gagged and sunk lower, Carla rolled her eyes and went back to the movie as Lukas cheered. The youngest, Sofía, continued to stuff her face with popcorn as she giggled.

He works with the dead? Neoma wondered what that was about, but she was too busy chuckling at her friend to quiz him. She nudged Martín with her elbow as the movie ended. "You can take your hands off your eyes now," she stage whispered.

"Do I have to? There might still be killing."

"All the killing is done, now there's simply dying and picking the bones clean while the credits roll."

"You understand how twisted you are, right?" Martín took his hands off his eyes, only to slap them back in place as gore splattered the camera lens. "I thought you said they were done." He moaned.

"You know, for someone who wants to be a werewolf, you're pretty squeamish," Neoma observed.

"Hombre-lobo, sí. Zombie, no." He descended into more Spanish as the kids in front of them all swiveled and spoke in unison.

"Ice cream!" They crowed, making faces like the movie zombies. Lukas attempted to drool on Carla who shrieked, slapping him. Sofía continued to giggle and made puppy eyes at Lukas while chanting "zombie, more zombie" under her breath. That kid had a dark side, Neoma approved.

"No, we need to get you home for real food. I have some work errands to run before it gets dark," Martín said, inciting a chorus of boos and hisses from the pre-teens.

Neoma raised one eyebrow, and they all stopped, mumbling apologies.

"Can you always come with us?" Martín asked. "I'll pay you."

"You must learn to control your own hooligans," Neoma told him firmly. "And you can't afford me."

"Probably not, but we'd make a good team. You know, I'm the muscle to your brains."

"Says the honor roll student." Neoma rolled her eyes. "I remember that about you in high school. You destroyed the curve for the rest of us." Martín shrugged.

"Ice cream please?" Lukas tried in his best grown-up voice. "Carla and I both love waffle cones with butterscotch, and it's Saturday, you said weekends were for breaking rules."

"You break rules?" Martín looked aghast.

"I will bury your body where no one will find it." Neoma poked his shoulder. "And I will take the ungrateful pre-teens home for you if you succumb to their demands."

"A threat with benefits?" He debated as he tugged on his hat brim. "Well, in that case, I might as well have ice cream before dinner. Let's go." The kids cheered.

———— ✦ ————

SMALL MANIACS CAPERED BEFORE THEM, THEIR SHADOWS gruesome stick figures in the long rays of the late August sun.

Neoma watched them laughing, feeling wistful as they ran at full tilt before dodging and weaving between the picnic benches playing tag. The minor discomfort in the joints of her feet and knees slowed her down but wasn't making her shuffle. Martín walked at her side, sedate as he finished the last of his banana split waffle cone.

"Do you think Tobin believes he's a werewolf?" she asked.

"What?" Martín chuckled through his ice cream. "Why? Because he canceled this week's game?"

Neoma nodded, feeling unsettled about blurting the question. *But that growl the other night.* A bit of pleasure slipped through her at the memory.

Martín swallowed and popped the end of the cone in his mouth. Crunching loudly, he wiped his fingers on a paper napkin while he took in her serious expression. With a shrug, he answered, "Seems like a stretch, but the guy leans towards dark, brooding, and mysterious. So maybe he's trying to cultivate that image? After all, it's a supermoon this month, perfect opportunity to lean into that persona. I mean, there have been a lot of weirdos in the woods predicting all sorts of strange events. I suppose it brings out the eccentric in everyone. So maybe Tobin is just playing up his brand."

"You think Tobin's a weirdo?" Neoma paused, facing Martín.

"I didn't say that." Martín scratched his wide jaw, contemplative. "I haven't put my finger on Tobin yet. On the surface, this is all a game we play every week, but the way he watches us…there's an intensity there that's out of place for a game." His meaty shoulders rose and fell, his hands facing palm up. "The whole thing with Matrix is a little odd though. I've never seen a dog behave like he does. And the way he interacts with us, I'd almost be willing to believe he's a weredog."

"That you made out with." Neoma laughed as Martín blushed.

"I don't see you hooking up with anyone. Why is that, Nae? Even in high school you never seemed to date much."

It was her turn to shrug. "I was too busy dancing. It was my ticket out; I wasn't going to let a guy get in the way of that."

"And now?" Martín's brown eyes were almost russet in the evening sunlight before he used his ever-present hat to hide them. "I've seen the way you look at Tobin."

"Excuse me?" Her stomach dropped and heat flooded her cheeks. She glanced at the kids as they sat like birds on a bench, checking out something on a cell phone. "And how would that be?"

"Like he's a fine piece of art that you're considering taking home, but you're not sure about the price tag."

Neoma looked back at him. "That was a shockingly accurate statement." She worried a stray curl. *Do I tell him?* She hesitated. "I didn't take you for a psychoanalyst Martín, you might have missed your calling."

"I haven't missed anything yet, life's still young. Besides, when I'm working search and rescue, it helps to understand what makes people tick so we can predict what they might do when lost or injured. I read a lot and work on analyzing people when I'm in groups."

"So that's why Carla said you work with the dead. And here I thought you moonlighted as an undertaker." She nudged him playfully. "I'd forgotten you worked search and rescue. I meant to ask, is it part of your forest service training? Or did you volunteer for it?"

"We're all volunteers, but my work as a ranger does overlap."

"What made you want to do more?"

He paused as though considering her question. "Honestly, I'm always feeling pulled into wild spaces. I feel this connection to, well, let's call it nature, I suppose." His ear tips reddened slightly. "And hiking is great and all, but I wanted something more. Search and rescue seemed like a good way to scratch my itch for being outside, giving my wanderings purpose while helping those who really need it. It's a rare thing to be able to do, you know? To really help someone."

He paused, and Neoma's chest tightened as he continued.

"S.A.R. gives me that, and work is extremely accommodating when I get called out. I think they like having me doubly trained." He shrugged and met her eyes for a moment. "And Nae, please don't say I 'work with the dead,' that's pretty macabre. We work hard to find the missing, and some days we don't get there in time. When that happens, I always remember that the body belongs to someone who loved it, and to treat them with respect, even in death." He bowed his head slightly.

Still waters are deep indeed. Neoma thought, impressed with Martín's compassion. "Forgive me, my dad went missing after a tour van dove into a ravine. It was S.A.R that found his body. I know you guys are all volunteers, thanks for treating your work with this much reverence."

"Oh, Nae, I didn't know." His brows wrinkled.

She patted his arm pushing away the ach in her chest. "It's okay, it's not a loss I ever really experienced. My mom was pregnant at the time." It was her turn to shrug and navigate the memory back into the past. "Hard to miss what I never had."

Martín gave her a sideways glance, as if he didn't believe her nonchalant reaction. Neoma ignored him, and the prick of pain announcing thoughts about her father. Instead, she lapsed into silence, feeling the warm air around her, focusing on enjoying this rare feeling of companionship and peace.

"Did I get too personal?" Martín asked, breaking her reprieve.

"Huh? Oh, no, I just need more practice opening up to people." She looped her arm through his. "You're the first local friend I've had in ages. I just get lost in my own head. I don't mind questions, so no need to edit yourself." Neoma smiled, and Martín's posture changed as he stood up, escorting her around the playground like a renaissance gentleman. There was a shyness to Martín that Neoma was only beginning to appreciate. He really participated one on one, but out in public, he tended to hang back. He'd deferred to his younger, louder sisters as they'd purchased the movie tickets, popcorn, and then ice cream. At first, Neoma thought he was letting them be independent, but she soon realized by the rolling of his shoulders that he wasn't fully comfortable with strangers.

Martín paused their walk. "Do you think Tobin is playing games with us?"

"I'm not sure. I agree that Tobin seems to have an agenda sometimes, but…" She trailed off thinking of the man, damp with rain, and completely unsure of how to ask her for what he wanted. Tobin hadn't had an agenda the other night, only emotions. She shook herself. "I think I need to approach this another way. Do you believe in the impossible? Like, you know, werewolves, zombies, fairies, Loch Ness, magic."

"Loch Ness the lake is totally real, it's the monster I question." She glared at him. "Ok-ay," he dragged out the syllables, "what's impossible look like to you?" His question was open, kind, curious, or she would have pulled away from him. She hated when people fielded her questions with questions. But she appreciated Martín making her think.

"You're going to tell me that impossible just hasn't been discovered yet, or some such thing."

He laughed. "Yep."

Neoma stewed, counted to ten, took three deep breaths, but he didn't continue. "Don't make me get out the crowbar here Martín, expound."

"Sorry, just thinking." His eyes were far away, and he kept…just…thinking.

Neoma stopped walking, taking her arm back and crossing her arms over her chest while tapping her toe.

"Oh you want an answer now?" He looked taken aback.

She dragged her hand down her face and moaned, "Martín!"

"But," he looked flustered, "you're rushing my process."

"I don't care," she snapped.

He sighed but continued, "Fine, if you're talking about a man turning into a monster, well then," he paused, lips pursed, "we would have to define what a monster is."

"This sounds like semantics."

Martín surged forward at her expression. "Yet a person turning into another creature? Well, caterpillars turn into butterflies, so is that impossible? Or do you consider that magic?"

"That's their life cycle, it's established." Her tone was dry. "And it seems to be an insect thing, to transform, not a skill mammals possess."

"That we know of!" Martín said.

Neoma sighed, rubbing her head.

"Okay chica, okay, I'll take this seriously. I mean, I'm a big nerd who just loves to pull this stuff apart, and you just introduced magic to this equation. Let me think." He looked down, toeing the line in the cement. Neoma took his arm back, squeezing for him to continue. He gave a small grin and carried on in a hushed voice. "I believe in the impossible because I've seen things in nature that boggled my brain. So if the impossible is magic, then sí, I believe in magic." A considering expression lingered on his face before he spoke again. "But do I believe that Tobin thinks he's a werewolf? Because, sure, I'm willing to concede that the man thinks he's a werewolf. He has been playing right into that role. But you seem to want to consider something more outside our everyday box."

Neoma nodded her head, her breath held.

"Then I will go down this rabbit hole with you." He seemed to steel himself, as if preparing to let go of gravity. "My logical mind says no. How could a werewolf endure without discovery? The lack of proof gives credit to the impossibility of their existence. So many years, so many full moons, so many people checking shadows hoping to catch a glimpse of a monster. Yet we have nothing to show for it. There's more proof that sasquatch exists than werewolves. And I can't cobble together an evolutionary reason that would predispose a human to turn into a wolf because of moonlight." He mused, watching the kids. Something inside Neoma deflated, and she wasn't sure why.

"But," the word loitered between them, building momentum, "my heart wants werewolves to be real. The hair that lifts on the back of my neck when I'm alone in the woods wants werewolves to be real. And when the night sky shows us the universe is endless, I look up and believe in magic."

"And werewolves?"

"And werewolves."

"But Tobin?"

Martín shrugged. "I can't say I've seen him do anything like smell someone before they come into a room or lift a car."

That growl, Neoma thought, *that effortless way he lifted me, so gentle, so controlled. And he'd heard me whisper...*but

Martín's evolutionary logic held weight. Maybe Tobin was just really strong and had good hearing. An odd disappointment crept forward again.

"However, there is an animal magnetism to him. The man moves like a cat, no effort, all flow." He watched her expression. "Who knows what secrets we all keep behind our eyes? He might just be really kinky."

Neoma laughed, feeling blood rush into her cheeks. Martín's eyes widened.

"Nae, what do you know?"

"Oh gosh, nothing, I know nothing." Her face flamed. She wasn't ready to share what had happened between her and Tobin. It was too fragile. A surreal moment. Giving it weight could shatter the future possibilities. *Do I want something in the future?* She wasn't sure, and she didn't need to have those answers yet. "I refuse to indulge in a conversation about kink right now. Martín, think of the children."

He laughed like she hoped he would. "Besides," she continued, "you have responsibilities, and so do I. Thanks for the ice cream, movie date, and entertaining my weird questions."

Martín squinted at her but acquiesced, and they resumed their walk to round up the kids, both thoughtful.

"Neoma, whatever happens with the group, I'm glad you and I reconnected."

"Well that sounds ominous." Neoma shivered. Yet his words soothed something inside her that Paris's insights had cracked. She hugged his arm tighter, not willing to lose this rediscovered connection.

"Sorry," Martín seemed to glance at the long shadows, the August heat around them pressing in. "There's just something…happening. Some edgy feeling of anticipation." He shrugged and gave a weak laugh. "It could just be my overactive imagination coupled with this conversation. Anyways, you never told me, do you believe in magic?"

"I think, my friend," she paused as warmth blossomed in her chest. *This is what it is to care about someone outside myself again.* She became giddy with the simple joy of it. "I'm beginning to."

CHAPTER 25

Chasing Vanilla

Tobin

The phone sat on the table, a hunk of technology and glass. An unresponsive masterpiece of human ingenuity that could just as easily be a paperweight for all the good it was doing him. Tobin sighed and removed his glasses, running his hand through his hair before getting up to walk around the room. Should he call her? Text? Email? Send flowers?

Oh what a stupid thought! He paced another loop in the small family room, fingers laced behind his head, trying to think clearly.

It was Saturday, Neoma wasn't working this weekend, and Tobin couldn't seem to discard that detail from his mind. Would it be too forward for him to invite her out? He was itching to finish their conversation from the Farmer's Market...*the market?* Who was he kidding? The image of Naoma, stretched out before him on the couch, in the back of the bookstore, flooded his senses. He could smell her vanilla and parchment scent, taste her skin on his tongue. He could feel her soft thighs pressed against his cheeks as he lifted a hand to his own face, closing his eyes. But what he saw was her sea glass gaze, brown flecks swirling within those iridescent pools, pulling him towards her.

"Why can't I stop thinking about you?" he said out loud.

Matrix rolled over on his dog pillow and cocked his head to the side.

"Never mind, I'm just thinking," Tobin grumbled, pivoting to finish another lap.

The big dog lumbered to his feet, stretched, and yawned. The exposed teeth made Matrix look feral. Then his lips fell, and the illusion of dopey dog was restored. Tobin blinked, sometimes forgetting that Matrix had the equipment to be dangerous.

The dog sat, demanding Tobin enunciate further on his verbal outburst.

"Fine. I want to call Neoma and see if she'd like to go out to dinner. You know, something casual, friendly…" *A date.* His traitorous mind supplied. Stupidly, Tobin scrambled for a logical reason, he had to stick to his plans! "I think her immunity is going to be hard to break and getting some more insight into how she thinks could be helpful," he finished and looked away.

The dog squinted his eyes, then sneezed. Shaking his head, he "woofed" repeatedly before falling to the ground and rolling over on his back. With his tail wagging furiously, he proceeded to paw at the air while snapping his teeth at nothing as if laughing at his little brother.

"You are absolutely no help!" Tobin fumbled as he grabbed his phone and wallet and stormed towards the door. He paused at the mirror on the wall to check his hair and embarrassment flushed his face. Cursing, he shoved his glasses into place. In the family room, his brother kept up his sneezing 'woofs,' causing Tobin's ears to burn. He glared back at the dog who was still rolling around on his back, tongue lolling in a goofy grin.

"You're useless!" Tobin yelled and slammed the door.

• • ◆ • •

"WHY DIDN'T YOU BRING MATRIX?" NEOMA ASKED AS SHE MET Tobin at the front of the parking lot. The sun loitered, leisurely stretching the evening towards twilight. This time of year, people were never in a rush to get indoors, and businesses capitalize on these lingering days.

Food trucks made a horseshoe shape around a small live stage celebrating summer. Lights were strung from trees and patrons milled around laughing and drinking while a folk band filled up the additional space with catchy music.

"I wasn't sure this place would accept dogs." Tobin mumbled, watching more than one well-behaved canine walk sedately by their owner's side. Guilt nibbled at him, but then remembered the mirth drunk mongrel and decided Matrix could hunt for his own dinner. "I'll bring him some leftovers."

Tobin placated Neoma's concerned look. Why was Matrix always so popular? His confidence slipped, and he straightened, resuming his self-possessed posture. He'd called her, the least he could do was act like he knew what he was doing. *What am I doing?*

"I'm guessing he's not terribly picky." Neoma chuckled, surveying the options.

"You'd be surprised." Tobin sighed. He wanted to step closer to her, to make casual contact, but he stopped himself. With the crowds and moving wind currents, he was just able to scent the floral soap she used, but not her. It was maddening.

"Anyway," he shook himself, "what are you in the mood for?"

"Anything not in my fridge is going to make me happy. But I'm leaning towards pizza actually. I'd offer to share, but I have to do gluten-free, and I have strange topping tastes. However, don't let that limit you, honestly, I've heard you can't go wrong here." Neoma smoothed her dress, a dark blue with tiny diamond patterns. Her hair was loose, bobbing around her head like a springy cloud. She fiddled with her small backpack straps.

Is she nervous? Tobin breathed in her scent, she had a mix of excitement that tickled his nose and made him want to sneeze, but underneath was a cold that seemed to speak to determination.

"So, divide and conquer?"

She laughed. "Funny you should mention conquering. I have a bone to pick with you about the last gaming campaign you sent us on." Neoma rolled her eyes, softening the flash of irritation with a small smile. He loved that she picked an easy topic to talk about.

"Whatever it was, I'm not culpable. I only write the framework, you guys choose where to go and what to do." Tobin put up his hands in mock defense.

"And yet somehow, I refuse to believe it's that simple. You set me up to work with Robin. What I haven't figured out is why." She studied him as the band finished their first set and announced a break. Tobin flushed under her gaze, wanting to step closer to her and yet stare her down, all at the same time. He caught the whiff of vanilla as his mind whirled, tension building inside him. He needed to make some space before he tried to hold her hand, or some other physical gesture that would probably go horribly wrong.

"I'm going to go jump in line before everyone else swarms the trucks. First one to finish ordering grabs a table?" He jerked his thumb over his shoulder, eyebrows raised.

"Awe, deflection then retreat. Smooth move. Maybe I should try food as a bargaining chip next time you have me cornered." He flinched. She narrowed her eyes, then laughed at his apparent discomfort. "Huh, I must have guessed right. Don't worry, I'm not mad, just hungry. Food will fix my overabundance of snark. Carry on and conquer you who pulls the strings on werewolves." She waved her hands at him in dismissal, still chuckling.

Tobin nearly tripped over his feet as he turned and backed up in tandem. What was wrong with him? He pondered his reaction as he stood in line at a burger truck that promised the best burgers north of the Columbia River.

There was a connection there, he decided at last. An awareness, something that called to his wolfish side and made his animal instincts more pronounced around her. If he focused, he could feel his wildness creep forward trying to fill up his senses. It was odd, and he didn't know what it meant, yet closing his eyes, he could almost feel where she sat at the edge of the bustle and noise, and it was…comforting. Tobin mentally backed away from the feeling and the wash of confusion it brought.

Grabbing his initial order, he stalked through the crowd, trying to leave those feelings behind. People instinctively moved away from him. He paused, took a deep breath and reined in his chaotic emotions. Calmer, Tobin joined Neoma, depositing a basket of truffle fries between them while sliding onto the bench seat. She was studying him again.

"What?" he asked around a sip of his pale ale. "I brought you offerings to apprise your snark."

"And my snark thanks you." She fingered a fry. "Did you know you move like a dancer sometimes?"

"A dancer?" *Or a predator.* But he kept the latter thought to himself, resolving to pay closer attention to his movement in the future. And yet, he wanted her to guess. Didn't he? To wonder about him? To draw a little closer and ask the question: What are you? His belly fluttered, and he let words escape, "Dancers are not the only ones out there that can move fluidly." He hoped he smiled mysteriously as he grabbed some fries, feeling very clumsy under her scrutiny.

"True, but you don't strike me as a martial arts type." She popped the fry in her mouth and leaned her elbows on the table.

Tobin gave a small chuckle, the fries feeling dry in his throat. "No, I'm not into karate. I was always the one getting beat up, not doing the beating."

Neoma blinked and sat back up. "Really? Why?"

"I was a big nerd in school." He shrugged, the memories of who he was seemed to belong to another person. Even as he dredged them up to share, they no longer needled him like they used to. He wondered distractedly if that was because he'd gone through this metamorphosis to werewolf, the frumpy human pupa stage utterly discarded. "I was the kid whose parents were dead, living with my grandparents and older brother. I was quiet, wore thick glasses, and lived in my head most of the time. And I rarely spoke to anyone. I was a very easy target."

"Wow, that's a truth bomb and a half." Neoma snagged another fry before giving him a wry smile. "So what you're telling me is that your people skills suck."

Tobin couldn't help himself, he laughed. "You tell me. After all, you said yes to coming out this evening."

"Touché. However, my people skills definitely suck, which is why I suspect we're getting along. We're like two peas in our own fucked up pod." She paused, "Wait, should I say pack?"

A strange tingle of warmth infused Tobin when she said pack. It imbued the thing inside him that longed for connection. He squished it and took another drink, shrugging.

"Only say pack if you mean it."

Their eyes met as her number lit up on the table making them both jump. She moved to grab it and winced slightly. He could smell caustic pain on her.

"Is your RA bugging you?"

"When isn't it?" She rolled her eyes. "Sorry, I think it's making me a little crabby, but yeah, it's flaring, probably should have avoided pre-dinner ice cream." She rose to get her food.

"Allow me, Neoma?" Tobin held his breath, he'd used her full name. Immediately, the intimate evening from the bookstore erupted between them. Neoma froze, about to swing her leg over the bench, hands braced on the table. She closed her eyes, seeming to shudder. Suddenly, a sweet cloud of vanilla wafted from her. He trembled. "Please?"

Why did this small act of service suddenly feel weighty? *And why the hell did I offer?*

His question broke whatever emotion she was in. Neoma shook herself and finished exiting from the table.

"Is this a date, Tobin?" she asked softly, smoothing down her dress.

"I don't know." Why did he lose all reason around her?

"That's okay then, I don't know either. How about we just keep the evening friendly? Get to know each other more, see how that works?"

She's giving me an out. He realized. The insight was not a relief.

"Does that mean you don't want me to get your food?" Tobin tried for levity but could tell it didn't land. Neoma was gracious anyway.

"Thanks, but no," her voice was rough, "I'll move until this disease leaves me no other options. I appreciate the thought though." She gave him a measured glance and walked away, leaving him to twist in his tangled emotions. Yet he couldn't help but watch her controlled pace through the crowd, a saunter that was almost a ballet. His stomach clenched, he was probably the only one who knew what that grace cost her.

CHAPTER 26

※ ● ◉ ● ※

Past, Pride, Personal

Neoma

N eoma retrieved her pizza in a daze. Tobin had used her full name, and her hormones had done a happy dance worthy of a half-time show. If there hadn't been a table between them, she would have reached for him and demanded he say her name again, then carry her to the car where she would insist that he—Neoma reeled back from that thought. *No, no, no just no! This is not a date, he's clearly not ready for a date. Give the man some time. This is just two people hanging out. For crying out loud, Robin calls you Neoma all the time, and you never think twice about it. Why the hell is Tobin's casual use of it making butterflies come out your nose?*

But it wasn't casual, the man was too careful for that. He'd said Neoma, not Nae, not hey you, Neoma. He'd shown her deference, offering to do her bidding, not simply using her name to get her attention for something mundane. This unusual man had deliberately proffered himself up to her whims, in public. Did he realize the effect that had on her?

She wanted to fan her face as heat threatened in her lower belly. Neoma focused on the pizza she was carrying, breathing in the savory odor of pear, prosciutto, goat cheese, and basil. Heaven on a cauliflower crust. *Yes, lead with your appetite.* She thought as she sat back down at the table. Her libido poked her, reminding her she had other hungers. She reprimanded it by stuffing a piece of too hot pizza into her mouth and burning her pallet.

"Fuuuuck!" she moaned, spitting out the blistering cheese and scrambling for her drink. Tobin pushed it into her grabbing fingers, his eyebrows raised in alarm. She fished out an ice cube and held it to the burn using her tongue. "Oh, that was graceful," she muttered between her teeth.

"Well, when I rip into a deer, I'm not very graceful either." Tobin said, his expression deadpan as he took a huge bite of his burger, causing ketchup to spurt and run down his fingers. He smiled around his bulging cheeks. "There, even." He forced past his food.

"Ha, so you are a werewolf." Neoma's momentary embarrassment lifted slightly as Tobin nodded, chewing vigorously. She appreciated his use of whimsy to distract her from her pain. At least her libido was fully banished. However, if he licked that ketchup off his fingers, she knew she was done for. Handing him a napkin, she explored the burn with her tongue. It wasn't too bad; she could still eat.

"So what you're telling me is werewolves don't have table manners?"

"Exactly," he leaned in close, "but surprisingly, we do floss."

"Really?"

"Yep, gristle is hell when it gets stuck between molars." Tobin bared his teeth. "Dental health is important."

"I learn so much from you," Neoma intoned.

Across the crowd of people, she glimpsed a raven head of hair. Paris. *You have to be fucking kidding me. Seriously? Again?* She swung her focus off the woman lest she trip her bitch radar. Tobin saw and casually looked around as if watching the band. She could tell when he spotted her. At least Caleb wasn't with her, just Mark and Miranda. Apparently, the universe wasn't that cruel twice.

"What's the history between you two?" Tobin asked nonchalantly as he mauled his burger further. How the man could make such short work of a double decker meaty madness, Neoma had no idea.

"I'm not sure I know you well enough to go into details," she answered him honestly. Neoma could have focused on the more recent interaction between them, but high school reared up to take center stage in her mind's eye. Paris's tear-streaked face glared at her, full of broken hopes. The locker room, the sobs coming from the bathroom stall, discarded dance shoes with blood from popped blisters. And those whispered words Neoma was never supposed to have heard, "I'm bleeding, oh

God, I'm losing the baby too." The memories abraded Neoma's insides like splintered bone. She didn't want to relive this. Turning to her food, she nibbled the pizza, letting the hot cheese sear her tongue in an attempt to burn away the past.

"That sounds layered." Tobin said, not pushing or prying, but his silence was a vacuum that drew answers forward.

Neoma fidgeted, *to share or not to share?* She didn't like the idea of airing all her darkness right as she was getting to know someone. Yet there was a freedom there if she did. A small unburdening that came with being vulnerable. Of course that accompanied the heavy risk of rejection, or confirmation that her past decisions were really as terrible as she suspected. *I suppose I'm just masochistic enough to entertain this conversation.* Neoma sighed.

"Yeah, but if you were in my position, how would you feel if I asked you what the worst thing you've ever done was? Would you want to answer me?" The flirty mood had fled the scene, and she wondered if she should follow it. *Is this really what I want to talk about tonight? Seriously?* She internally rolled her eyes at her behavior. *This must be self-sabotage at its finest.* She wanted to hit reset on this conversation.

"That bad, really?" He regarded her, chewing. "I don't think I want to tell you my fuck-ups yet. Besides, do you think there would be anything productive to be gained from sharing these answers?"

"Good question." She liked that he was allowing curiosity to propel the conversation. "Perhaps airing out our worst moments will give us a clearer picture on how we proceed with this…friendship. This way, we won't waste each other's time if we discover there are unforgivable mistakes lurking in our pasts. If I can accept your flaws, and you can accept mine, then we're golden."

"Huh, interesting hypothesis. Are you this practical about everything?"

Neoma thought about it. Thought about high school, rules, fairness. She again saw Paris looking gutted, hiding in the locker room, sobbing and holding her stomach. "Yes, sadly, I believe I am." She embraced her newfound self-awareness. "Since my diagnosis, I keep feeling like I don't have any more time to waste on the games people play. They annoy me. Life has given me too many short straws to be frivolous with my emotional output."

Tobin cocked his head to the side, dark thoughts seemed to pass behind his gaze. "So you want to just cut through the bullshit and what? Have a deep in-depth look into each other's souls? What happens if I tell you my secrets, and you decide I'm damaged beyond salvage? I'll lose the bookstore, and how will I build my werewolf empire?"

Neoma snorted at his satire but pivoted back to serious. "People are allowed to be damaged. The question is whether you make decisions from a place of damage, or a place of cruelty. It's the difference between being an asshole and being a sociopath. And you just lost a point for monetizing our relationship because of a convenient gaming location."

"Hey, I have goals," Tobin smiled.

"Your goals are weird." Neoma quirked her lip. Razzing Tobin was swiftly becoming her favorite pastime. He never seemed to take offense to her bossy demeanor, actually leaning into her jibes. Heat started to spread from her middle, and she mentally punched it back down. *Stay*, she thought.

"So," Tobin prompted, "are you going to tell me about your high school drama? Or should we switch topics?"

The choice was hers. Did she really want to admit to him how she'd intentionally sabotaged someone else for her own gain? *Why is this a weekend of Paris? Wasn't Thursday night enough?* Yet somehow, this part of her past had been haunting her for weeks now, a persistent reminder of her regrets. *I was a stupid, ignorant child trying to escape this town at any cost. I just didn't grasp that the cost wasn't mine.* Neoma felt sick, and the pizza she'd been picking at lost all its flavor.

"Hey, it's okay." Tobin said before shoving the end of his burger into his mouth. He swallowed it down quickly and cleaned his fingers on a droopy napkin. His expression was grim, as if some internal scales were struggling to balance. He reached out tentatively and laid his warm hand awkwardly on top of her's. "I was just following your lead, we really don't need to discuss this."

She grimaced. "Sometimes I wonder if my RA is the result of karma in action. You know, like I did something that completely screwed Paris, so life decided to tip the scales, let me experience what she must have endured."

"What, you gave Paris an incurable autoimmune disease?"

She glared at him. Tobin put his hands in the air. "Perspective, that's all I'm saying since I don't know what you're talking about."

He had a point, yet Neoma couldn't let go of her guilt that easily. Nor did she deserve to. Sure, Paris had never been a friend, but the enmity remained civil enough in high school until people's dreams were on the line. The New York Dance Academy had been the catalyst. They arrived with one scholarship and five dancers frantic for a chance at a new life. The resulting pressures agitated animosities into a frothing boil. Turns out, desperation brought out the worst in Neoma, much to her shame.

"Paris was my biggest rival in high school, the only person with enough talent to really make me sweat. I think the two of us actually made each other better. Nothing like competition to inflame the work ethic."

Tobin nodded.

"When Juilliard showed up, well, it wasn't pretty. Paris was my only obstacle to freedom, to leaving this little town under my own power. And I knew her Achilles' heel."

Neoma stopped, her throat dry, her vision wobbly as she cast a glance towards the far table where her nemesis had settled. Paris hadn't been her enemy all those years ago, she'd simply been a teenage girl, newly pregnant, scared, and wanting out of this town as much as Neoma. A baby hadn't been anyone's plan. New York had been the only plan. The only goal, and it had drowned out everything else, even morals.

It had been so easy to slip a note to the scouts, to make them aware of Paris's condition, introducing an unexpected roadblock that Paris couldn't outperform.

"It shouldn't be so easy to betray someone," Neoma whispered. "Even when you don't like them." It didn't matter that Paris had always resented her, it hadn't given Neoma the right to vandalize a fair fight.

Tobin's face was ashen when she dared to look. His hand extended across the worn wood of the table, fingertips resting against hers. His touch was so gentle, so warm. *Careful,* she thought. *He's acting like I might break.* She studied his face again. *No,* she corrected herself, *he's afraid he might break. But why?*

Neoma could almost feel something within Tobin that was an echo to her own guilt. But she was so invested in her memories that the words kept coming. "The day of the audition, we danced like our lives depended on it. In some ways, I think they did. We both left everything we had out on the floor, and I still couldn't tell you whose performance was better. Yet the judges had been told by an 'anonymous source'," Neoma was air quoting, she hated air quotes, "that Paris was pregnant. Did that tip the scales? I'll never know. But in the end, Paris lost the scholarship, and the baby shortly after. Her future was in ruins while I got on a plane heading towards everything I'd ever wanted, only to have life yank it away a few years later."

And here I am, back where I started, wondering if Paris lost her shot because of me. If I hadn't interfered, would she have been the one in New York right now? Would she be signed to some big company as the new principal dancer?" Neoma's eyes were bone dry, but she quivered under the weight of regret and unanswerable questions. Shame burned inside her, another layer of pain that she couldn't remedy, couldn't cure.

Tobin's eyes hadn't left her face, his fingertips four hot circles against her skin. She searched for horror, rejection, pity, some negative emotion that surely must lurk within the curves and concaves of his features. Yet she discovered only lines of tension, regret, and understanding. *Am I reading him right? Is he commiserating with me? What personal ghosts have I summoned from his past with the howling of my regrettable demons?* Neoma took a deep breath.

"What's the worst thing you've ever done?"

Tobin's skin looked sallow as he swallowed hard. He seemed to pry his words from his mouth as if they were burrs that wouldn't leave his tongue.

"The same as you." His expression had never looked so dark and lost. "Betrayed someone. Only…it was someone I cared for."

"Would you do it again?"

His eyes met hers, a reflective sheen to them beyond the glasses. His voice when he spoke was all growl and determination, "If I can help it, nothing like that will ever happen again...You?"

Neoma glanced back towards where Paris sat laughing with Miranda.

"Never, and if I could take it back, I would."

Tobin paused, as if to agree. Yet he hesitated and pulled his hand away.

"I'm sorry Nae, but I need to go." He shook his head, his eyes scrunching shut. "I think I'm getting a migraine." He bowed forward, rubbing his temples, his hands trembling.

"What can I do? Want me to take you home?"

She saw the pain etching deep grooves in his face as he stumbled to his feet and swayed. "I'm sorry..." he beseeched her, his eyes bright behind his glasses. She blinked, but before she could move, he'd fled into the gathering dark leaving Neoma alone, surrounded by humanity, and emotionally spent.

CHAPTER 27

────── • ◦ ● ◦ • ──────

Forced to Change

Tobin

What the fuck is wrong with me? Tobin pulled the truck over into a secluded turnout. The emotional turmoil from his impromptu soul searching with Neoma seemed to be morphing into some sort of physical rebellion. He rolled down the window for fresh air and the smell of rancid beer and used condoms assaulted his nose. He scrambled to put the glass up, choking back vomit, and peeled out onto the road. But he didn't get far as his body mutinied.

The next trailhead he parked at was blessedly deserted. Tobin scrambled to get the truck turned off and reached for his go-bag. He sprinted into the woods towards the sound of water. There was no time to strip, his skin was on fire, twitching, itching, and feeling like it was going to tear itself off his back and slither under a cool rock. Tobin just about belly flopped into the river as his body convulsed, spasms running through his muscles like electric eels. He came up panting and howling, thrashing, his limbs locking and unlocking with random abandon.

"FUUUUUUUUCK!" The trees clattered in the hot August wind, the blushing evening light painting them the color of diluted blood. "Help," Tobin sobbed into the water, his body feeling like it wanted to change, but so. Much. Worse!

The moon is still a day away. A day away. Away. No, can't. Can't. CAN'T. Tobin's thoughts pounded with his heart.

His vision dimmed.

A bark rang over the water, causing his very cells to chime. A furry body brushed him, making him scream from the contact of too much raw sensation.

Let go. The command whuffed through his mind.

"I can't. Can't. Moon not full." Tobin choked out, his hands clutching Matrix's ruff to keep his head above water.

Can. Try.

"It hurts," Tobin whimpered and bit into his cheek, blood flooding his mouth with bright copper. The precise pain cleared his head, the taste of blood bringing his animal side to heel. And he felt it, felt that swelling like his skin was too tight, his bones aching like loose teeth. So close. Pain swamped him again. He didn't fight it this time, because on the other side of it was freedom.

Tobin curled into himself in the water. Matrix had his back, keeping his body stable against the current. He let himself go. He grabbed for the pain, pushing it along his abused nerve endings, begging his human body to give up.

Pain was the catalyst, his will, the fuel. Nails scored deep gouges in his skin, trying to tear it off. He bit through his lip and heard a toe crack as his foot spasmed so hard it broke bone.

Matrix's teeth slid into the flesh of his neck, sweet surgical knives, clamping down and shaking him like a puppy as he dragged Tobin from the water. Stones abraded his bare legs, slammed into kneecaps, hips, elbows. Yet his human body still held.

"NO!" A shriek, followed by sound. An explosion. Pain lanced through Tobin's shoulder.

It was enough.

The world went white, and the wolf came free.

⸳⸳◈⸳⸳

BLOOD.

It was everywhere, soaking his fur, coating his brother in a rich sticky veneer of midnight red. What had happened?

Matrix's ears rang from the shot at close range, somehow the bullet had missed him, plunging into Tobin's shoulder with a wet, meaty thud. Who had fired the gun?

"Back off!" The voice radiated authority, yet fear scented the air. Matrix crouched low over Tobin, shielding him, his head pivoted towards the intruder.

"What the hell?" The man's hands shook, the steel barrel of the pistol vibrated, but the aim appeared steady enough.

Matrix was not willing to chance sudden movement, that only spooked people into firing. "You're not a bear."

Matrix gave the smallest of whines, sounding like a distressed dog.

"Matrix?" Martín dropped his gun and straightened, blinking in the dim light.

Matrix could smell Tobin coming back to consciousness, his body tranquil, his breathing starting to even out. The transformation was complete. The dog prayed he wouldn't come awake fighting.

He wagged his tail sympathetically at Martín and gave a soft woof.

"Oh holy cows in hell, did I just shoot Tobin?" Martín started to rush forward, but Matrix growled deep. The man stopped dead, took a half step back, turning his body to the side and crouching down. He dropped his voice and started speaking melodiously in Spanish, calm, careful. He was talking too fast for Matrix to glean the meaning, his own Spanish a ghost from his dead past. But the rush of words became an assuasive rhythm, and despite himself, Matrix was soothed.

Martín crept closer, holding out a hand, fingers curled, palm down, eyes averted. Tobin flinched under Matrix, then jerked and started to push at the dog's chest, the prick of sharp claws threatening. Matrix growled, then barked at Tobin.

Lie. Still.

Martín stopped moving. "Tobin?" Tobin went motionless, taking big breaths, trying to scent the air from under Matrix.

"Martín?" Tobin's voice was thick, the name slurred around fangs and through fur.

"Yeah, it's me. Are you okay? Matrix won't let me get closer, and I'm afraid I might have shot you." To Martín's great credit, he kept his voice calm, but Matrix could smell the fear sweat soaking the man's shirt. Flashes of yellow moved around Martín's head like agitated spirits, yet his body was cocooned in mystic blues and purples. This man was deeply grounded despite things.

"Oh...yeah, so that's what happened." Tobin slurred. Fur rose along Matrix's back as unease gripped him. A moon drunk werewolf was an unpredictable creature.

Focus! Matrix barked but could feel the authority ebbing. He didn't have many words left tonight. This new ability had limits.

"Don't. Do. That. Again." Tobin ground out from beneath him, his claws punctuating each word. "Headache, bad."

"Hombre, you okay?" Martín had crept even closer while Matrix was distracted. The dog stood slowly, giving Tobin room to scoot out from under him. Matrix kept low, the shield between werewolf and man.

"Yes, I'll be fine. Scratched from wrestling with Matrix, that's all. Sorry to scare you."

"You were screaming. I heard you from the parking lot. And what I saw wasn't wrestling. Come on, let me check you, I have a first aid kit in the truck. Please tell Matrix to move."

"Martín, you don't want to see this. You're not ready. Go, please. I'm fine, I just need to be alone."

"Not ready? What'cha talking about? I've worked search and rescue for years, you don't have anything wrong with you I haven't seen. Now please, Tobin, I gotta help you before you go into shock or something. Bullet wounds are serious business."

"I'm not wounded," Tobin growled softly, his frustration from hunger was bitter and stretched on the evening air. Matrix whined for real, begging Martín to leave, for Tobin to keep it together.

"Tobin, I can smell blood, which means there's a hell of a lot of it. Tell Matrix to stand down, let me help you. Or I'm going to have to go get my taser here when you pass out. Please, amigo." Martín's voice was still even, persistent, with an edge of worry fraying the calm. "Why won't you let me help you?"

"Because I don't need it," Tobin snapped. "Why are you even here, Martín?" He was slinking backwards towards the tree line, scuttering like a crab on all fours. Daylight had finally surrendered its hold on the sky and the river now moved through an exceedingly ravenous darkness. But the moon was near. Matrix could almost feel it gliding behind the trees, ready to ascend and bathe them all in silver light.

"I always check the trailheads on my way home. Especially when there are full moons coming. We make sure kids aren't starting trouble, hikers aren't lost, you know that sort of stuff.

I saw your truck and didn't realize it was yours until I parked. When I got out, there was a flicker of fire deep in the trees. Fires this time of year are bad news. I came to chew you out, but then I heard you screaming." Martín shrugged, still down in his nonthreatening crouch. He tried to inch closer, but Matrix warned him off.

"There was no fire," Tobin chuffed. Martín shrugged again.

"It's what I saw."

Show him, the voice whispered from the trees like a breeze. The brothers went rigid.

"No," Tobin growled back, snapping his teeth at the air. "He's not ready."

"Ready for what?" Martín cast a glance around, as if he'd heard something. His scent changed, a trickle of unease seeping into the gathering gloom.

This, right here, is how you get him ready, the whisper continued. *Do not squander this moment man-wolf.*

"Fuck you, Aithne." Tobin spat and lunged for the trees just as the moon hit the sky.

Matrix jumped upwards, drawing Martín's eyes, but he was too late. The young man's face was blank with disbelief and uncertainty. The dog ran forwards, bumped him gently with his nose in apology before sprinting after his brother. Martín's silence pursued them into the forest.

CHAPTER 28

Moon Shadows

Neoma

"Mom, I'll be in the backyard talking to Meg if you need me," Neoma announced as she wandered through the kitchen, her mother sitting at the table drinking coffee.

"Oh Kjære, your date's over already?" Kristin got up and captured her daughter, hugging her tight. "If you need to talk about something…" She let the sentence hang.

"Thanks, but it's okay, I think I need to run this by Meg first. And I need to be outside." Neoma frowned at her mom's wistful expression as Kristin tucked an errant curl behind her

"You just remind me of Moma sometimes." Kristin summoned a small smile. "She always had the need to be outside when things weighed heavy on her. You have the same habits and I'm feeling nostalgic since we talked about her. Full moons tend to have that effect on me, bringing memories forward. But enough, off you go, tell Megan hello for me."

"Sure, Mom." Neoma puzzled at her mother's expression as she ducked out the door. The August night greeted her with a warm embrace and a choir of frogs. The moon hung in the sky, looking like a circle that someone had tried to erase along one edge. If it was bigger than normal, Neoma couldn't tell, but she imagined a stronger pull tonight. One more day, and it would be fat perfection up there in the dark. The first supermoon of the year, so close to the earth she might be able to brush it with her fingers.

"Why are you laughing?" Megan asked as Neoma nestled into the hammock, phone to her ear.

"Oh, I was thinking about touching the supermoon and how I'd need a really big ladder to even try." She laughed again. "Can you see me up on a ladder now? Disaster waiting to strike."

"Maybe, but worth the risk?"

"Perhaps. However, the fall would be killer."

"I'd hold the ladder," Megan replied.

"I know you would." Neoma sighed. "Meg, I miss you."

"I miss you too." The stillness filled with chirps and peeps.

"Mom says hi."

"Please tell her 'hi' back. Now, I've been waiting for an update. How's the gaming group going? Making any new friends?" Megan was not one to let awkwardness grow.

"Actually yes, remember Martín Flint?" Megan made affirmative noises. "Well, we went to a movie with the kids this afternoon. He's a pretty deep guy, I've enjoyed getting to know him. But he can't stand horror movies."

"I don't blame him. So, what's his take on werewolves?"

"Well, he wants to be one. But it seems like that's the aspiration of everyone in the group," Neoma sighed.

"You told me about Robin," Megan laughed. "Where does that leave you? You were writing that blog about becoming a werewolf, so is there a conclusion to your story?"

"Have you been reading it?"

"When I can. The internet up here is really hit or miss most days. Now, answer my question because you appear to be stalling."

Neoma sat up further in the hammock so she could watch the edge of woods where the backyard ended, and BLM land began. *If only we had fireflies like the Midwest,* she mused before answering. "I've been taking a poll recently."

Megan cut her off. "Nae, really? A poll? Come on, you do realize you are doing the very thing you hate. *You* are dodging my question with a question."

Neoma sighed, Megan was right, she was. "I'm sorry, the entire day has been odd. I think I'm dodging the whole day and focusing on frivolous fantasy."

"Okay, I'm willing to indulge your imaginative thinking a little longer, but we are going to circle back to the hard stuff. Fair?"

"This is why I love you."

"I know. Now tell me where you've landed on becoming a werewolf. I'm dying to know."

"This feels like I'm giving you a book spoiler or something." Neoma laughed at the enthusiasm in her friend's voice.

"Oh you totally are, and I couldn't be happier. Remember, these are the important questions in life. Does my best friend want to be a hairy monster? And why or why not? Now please, satisfy my curiosity, I can't take it anymore." Megan was keeping her voice light, but there was something just under the surface that Neoma couldn't tease out. Was Megan tired? Stressed? Was something keeping her from sharing what was wrong? Neoma chalked it up to communal living and too many people potentially listening in. Trusting her friend would share if the chance presented itself, she continued.

"Wow, okay, I guess I better tell all." Neoma laughed but it was weak. For some reason, this answer held weight. Maybe it was the full moon? Too many horror movies? Was she letting her fantasy world take up too much space in her conscious thoughts? *Why can't I just brush this all away as silly ponderings? Too much time listening to the guys debate this unrealistic premise?* Neoma didn't know, so she gave up and answered her friend.

"I've never wanted to be a monster, Meg. Even as I listen to the guys expound on all the benefits I still sit back and think, nope, not for me."

"I guessed as much. But you're still worrying at the topic, why?"

"Because," Neoma held her breath. But if she couldn't admit this to Megan, who could she confess to? "Because the idea of monsters...is attractive?" Her voice broke with her embarrassment. "They..." But she couldn't finish her thought, her cheeks heating.

"Turn you on?" Megan finished carefully. She knew about Neoma's love of paranormal romance. They had talked about it at length when Neoma was trying to figure out her deep attraction to the books. She craved the idea of an out-of-control monster being gentled. All that raw wildness being overcome by the desire to be what their partner needed, submitting to love and taming their inner beast. All that power surrendering to Neoma, just because she was asking. The thought was intoxicating, and the reality impossible. There were no men turning into mythical creatures, yet she shivered at the scenario all the same.

They had discussed this before, but tonight the admission seemed real, plausible. Maybe it was the open air, the huge moon, the dark woods? They weren't inside under blankets, sharing secrets. This conversation was exposed. "But you want them to be real, don't you?" Meg whispered.

"Yeah, I still do." Neoma chewed her lip. "How odd is that?"

"Not odd. We all have our things that get our motors running. Due to this preference of yours, I would have thought you'd want to turn, given the chance. Join the monsters."

Neoma chuckled, letting her embarrassment go and leaning into the topic. "You misunderstand, I don't want to be the monster. It's the human monster dynamic that I find thrilling. You know, dangerous beast being subdued by love. It might be corny, but, well, it works for me."

"That and you like telling people what to do and having them do it."

"I'm never telling you anything again," Neoma laughed. "You know me too well."

"Hey, Mistress Neoma has a good ring to it." Megan continued.

"Stop, please stop, I'm going to pull something."

"Seriously though, I'd have thought you would be down for the whole healing aspect of the werewolf mythos. You know, get rid of your pain, jump small buildings in a single bound, that sort of thing."

Neoma wiped her eyes, still giggling. "You're mixing your fantasy with superheroes. But you're right, that stuff would be cool. Not sure what I think about turning fuzzy, so I'm still going with no thanks. But fangs could be kinda fun."

"You're still hung up on vampires aren't you?" Meg accused.

"Truth. I have standards." Something in the shadowed tree line moved.

"What is it? You just got super quiet." Megan's voice was soft in her ear as she shifted slightly, trying to make out more.

"There's a shape in the trees. I'm guessing a deer, but there have been some bear sightings lately, and someone caught footage of a cougar on their security camera. I'm just making sure I'm not about to get ambushed."

"You could yell or trip the motion lights." Megan's voice was matter of fact.

"I could, but where's the fun in that? I don't want to scare it off until I know what it is." Neoma's curiosity mounted, but the woods refused to divulge their mysteries. "Huh, maybe I just imagined it."

"Well, we are talking about werewolves and things that go bump in the night. Speaking of night bumping, anything to tell about Tobin? You said he was hot."

"You're terrible." Neoma chuckled even as her body shivered with thoughts of Tobin.

"No, I'm lonely and need to scratch an itch somehow, so give me something, woman, I'm desperate." Megan whined, pulling a wider smile from her friend.

"Oh, something has happened, but it's been eclipsed by the weird date tonight." Neoma played with a curl as she watched the dark. How much to tell?

"Hold on, you know you're killing me, right?" Megan's energy buzzed across the connection. "Let me do a recap. You had the market with the Caleb debacle where you guys didn't talk afterwards."

"Uh-huh."

"And then weren't you planning on restarting that conversation this last week after gaming?"

"Yes, but Martín and I started gossiping about dating and Tobin slipped out."

"Nae!"

"Meg!"

"Oh for the love of! Fine! Then what? You've had a weird date? Why didn't you lead with this?" Megan sounded hard-up for entertainment. Neoma decided to gloss over the bookstore moment, it was…hers.

"Meg, it was weird." Neoma's tone dampened her friend's enthusiasm.

"You said that already, what precisely do you mean?" Megan asked.

"I ended up talking to him about Paris, and what went down in high school." Neoma kept watching the dark trees, was there movement again?

The low whistle from her friend brought her back to the conversation. "Nae, that's some heavy emotion for a first date. How did he respond?"

"I didn't bring it up intentionally," she said, her tone dry as she organized her thoughts. "Paris was there at the food trucks, and we'd had an argument a few days before at the coffee shop. It's like I can't escape her. Anyway, he asked, and I just…kinda answered."

"And?" Even the crickets seem to have stilled.

"Apparently, I'm not the only one who has done stupid things to get what they wanted." Neoma could feel her shame rise for the second time tonight, not as strong, but still as bitter. She wanted to spit.

"He said that?" Megan sounded shocked.

"No, I'm paraphrasing." Her friend took a relieved breath. "He actually looked like I'd triggered him. Whatever it was, the memory was so intense it seemed to cause a migraine. He went pale and started shaking. Then jumped up, apologized, and left."

Flustered at the retelling, Neoma pulled her eyes from the dark woods to watch the moon over the trees, trying to take some peace from its visage. The phone line buzzed, and the crickets serenade restarted.

"None of us are perfect people, Nae," Megan said softly. "That being said, do you think that's a giant red flag? Do you feel like you should walk away from whatever is building between the two of you?"

"Why, because whatever he did apparently caused him that much stress?" Neoma turned that idea around, looking at it from different angles. "As you just said, nobody's perfect. He listened without moralizing me for my past mistakes. He could have judged me and walked away. He didn't. The least I can do is give him the same opportunity to share if he wants to, then decide from there."

"Well that's progress. You've dismissed people before for less. Way to give someone a second chance Nae, I'm so proud."

Megan said with snark and good humor. "I'm not trying to push you into something toxic. If you think he's a bad egg, now's the chance to get out."

"No, I don't think he's a creep. Even after this weird conversation, there's still something about him that pulls me in, then pushes me away." And she flashed back to the couch, his scruff between her thighs, her hand knotted in his hair. She shook herself. "Anyway, I can't tell if it's him or me. I mean, he's easy as all hell on the eyes, and his forearms Meg—" she sighed.

"I know, you've mentioned them. And if we're going to downshift into physical attributes," she said with warm humor, "then I want to hear more about his chest. In detail. Arms are your thing." Megan mock salivated.

"You would not be disappointed if he's wearing a tight T," Neoma said, appreciating the conversation's tangent. *And you should see him without a shirt,* she thought, biting her tongue.

"Thank you, that's all I ask." Megan sounded like she needed a cigarette.

"Are you that hard-up?"

"Don't throw stones, woman. You're as needy as me, and don't try to deny it." They both laughed.

A tree trunk moved. Neoma didn't jump, but let her eyes go soft, watching out of her periphery. There. It moved again. A twig snapped and the spring peepers went silent along with the crickets.

"It's still here," Neoma whispered, straining her eyes and ears. A creepy feeling itched at the back of her skull. One heartbeat, two…

"Do you see it?" Megan's voice almost made Neoma squeal.

"Woman, you're gonna give me a heart attack!"

"Sorry," her friend was contrite. "But seriously, what is it?"

"Not sure, but you know, I keep pondering the legends claiming werewolves can only change during a full moon. And yet, there are other mythos where they can change whenever they want. As a wildlife biologist, what do you think would make the most sense?" Neoma tried to keep her voice normal, as if she hadn't noticed the suddenly silent wildlife.

"I've wondered that too." Megan paused. "I think for them to have a fighting chance at surviving and making more little werewolves, they would have to be able to control their change. If the moon is the catalyst, then I'd think there would have to be an inhibitor to contend for that. I mean, nothing exists in nature without an opposite, opposing force, right?"

"Yep, I'm with you." There was a large stretch of mowed lawn between her and the trees, anything that wanted to get closer would have to cross a wide expanse of silver light.

"So what if it's human pheromones? Humans are the biggest threat to their existence, right? What if the presence of humans inhibits the chemical rush of whatever the moon incites? I mean, I'm assuming that a transformation would be precipitated by a cascading chemical reaction inducing the body into changing."

"You've given this a lot of thought." The tree frogs had started up a staccato rhythm once more. Whatever was there seemed to be biding its time. Predator? Little hairs began to rise on the back of her neck. Neoma licked her lips. "But what about changing without a full moon?"

"Oh, well I'm assuming that a person would simply have to find a way of triggering that catalyst. Sometimes, there's more than one way to get our bodies to react. You can get a burst of adrenaline because you're afraid, or because you get really angry, but it's the same hormone getting spit out into your system." Megan was in full science mode now.

At the base of a big pine, light flashed, then winked out. Only to flash again.

"Meg, we don't have fireflies out here right?" Neoma was dead sure, but sometimes species migrated, or got introduced by well-meaning humans. The flashes came again, about two feet off the ground and moving through the brushes. Eyes.

"No, not in Washington. Why do you ask?"

"Because something just twinkled silver in the trees, in sets of two. I was really hoping you were going to say fireflies." Neoma held her breath, waiting for them to wink again. Excitement laced with caution trickled through her.

"Nae, did you say sliver? No natural animal has silver eyes. Trigger those lights Nae, do it now. Talking about werewolves is fun and all, but let's not push this. Please." Concern crawled through Megan's words, she was spooked. Meg didn't get spooked by the wilderness.

"I'm not afraid, Meg. It's probably a stray dog." Neoma swung her legs out of the hammock and sat up, seeing silver flash in the trees again. Only now a green set of eyes joined them. "Hello?" Neoma called, then whistled as if summoning a dog.

"Nae, please, please just get in the house. This feels wrong, really wrong. I've seen some strange stuff lately, and these eyes would fall into that category. Don't pursue this, trust me." Megan was pleading.

"What?" But Megan's words didn't make any sense, and the silver eyes had stopped. Two bright spots slowly floated upwards until they hovered about six feet off the ground. "Megan, do deer stand on their hind legs?" Neoma was on her feet, heart beating rapidly in her chest as she clutched the phone to her ear. But she couldn't look away.

A sound flooded the empty field. It started soft and gained volume, deep and resonant until it enfolded Neoma, vibrating the hair on her skin, the blood in her veins. Her heart leapt and cold filled her, chasing away the lingering heat and her initial fear. She took two steps forward, head high, eyes trying to peel back the obscurity and see what had growled.

"That's not a coyote!" Megan shrilled over the phone. "Neoma, *RUN!*"

"But I don't want to." Neoma wasn't sure the words were hers. Her fingers went numb, and she let the phone fall. "Show yourself," she commanded the dark.

And the dark obeyed.

CHAPTER 29

All in the Fluff

Tobin

White noise. The world was filled with it.

Tobin stopped at the edge of the shadows. Everything was different, and he couldn't put his claw on what was happening. Every time he tried, he would catch a glimpse of the moon, and his head would fill with soundless resonance again, like someone had stuffed it full of cotton balls and lit it on fire. The not noise burned, it hummed, it blotted out the world, and he couldn't think, he could only move.

Movement made it better. It made everything better.

So, he ran faster, following a flickering light. But a shape kept getting in his way, knocking him down, trying to herd him away from his goal.

He had a goal.

But what was it?

Oh yeah, *her*.

MATRIX QUIVERED. WHAT DID HE DO NOW? ACROSS THE LAWN, Neoma sat talking on the phone. The word "werewolf" floated over the grass, but Matrix didn't have the focus to spare. Tobin had gotten away from him multiple times!

The big dog wanted to sink into the earth and melt. His tongue was a thick sponge soaked in old dishwater. He'd never seen Tobin move so fast, and every time Matrix had gotten close, trees would smack him in the face, or vines tangled around his legs. His lips were torn and bleeding where he had taken on blackberry thorns in a desperate attempt to free himself.

Now they were here. And Neoma knew she was being watched. His entire scruff lifted as power breathed out of the trees, the grass, the moon. Something waited at the edge of awareness, as if on a sharp knife, curious to see if the blade would cut.

Brother. Stop. Matrix tried to form the words, but he had nothing left, they blew away like dandelion fluff on the breeze of emotions. He made one last desperate lunge for Tobin's tail, but a branch from a nearby bush smacked him so hard he saw stars.

Tobin stood up. So did Neoma.

Matrix changed his tactics and bolted into the open grass ahead of Tobin just as Neoma spoke.

With one last surge of strength, he found his way to her side and placed his body between her and the shadowed forest.

He couldn't protect Tobin, so he would guard Neoma from his brother and shield them both.

⋯ • ◦ ◉ ◦ • ⋯

WHO WAS HE? IT DIDN'T MATTER.

The woman ahead of him stood tall, moonlight trailing off her like spider silk. He could almost see her green eyes washed clear in the illumination, see the dark spots in her irises float to the surface of sterling pools, enigmas waiting to be fished out. The scent of her on the breeze fanned the fever inside him, she smelled of ordinary old paper and ink mingled with rosemary. But there was a faint aroma that was her, not the things she brushed against, not the smell of desire, or emotion, but her. He breathed in deep again, taking a step closer.

There, yes there. So faint it smelled like a memory of vanilla. But there was more now, something sweet and earthy. Her true scent, held trapped beneath her skin.

"Matrix!" Her voice smacked the air with surprise. Tobin growled, pinning his ears.

The werewolf watched as if he were an observer and this was a movie. The huge dog whipped around and placed himself between the woman and the woods. The beast lowered his head and raised his lip, huge fangs slicing the light into white splinters.

"What is it?" The woman's voice was not afraid, her scent curious on the wind. She reached down and stroked the dog's ruff, soothing him with murmurs. Jealousy lanced through

Tobin as he observed her gentle touch. His lip curled and saliva dripped from a canine.

"Tobin, is that you?" Neoma, her name was Neoma. And she knew him. His ears swiveled forward as he rose from a crouch he hadn't meant to take, teeth covered once more.

He didn't want…didn't want what? He shook his head, but the moon fog wouldn't clear.

You want her to see you. The voice whispered from the trees.

Did he?

That seemed reasonable, and yet…

He looked down at his hands, or were they claws? What should they be? The words chased around in his head, refusing to resolve into meanings. But there was something wrong, and not wrong about his appearance. He wasn't wearing a shirt, or pants. Why wasn't he wearing pants?

Show her. The voice insisted.

At least he still had underwear on. Sure it was hot, but did he want Neoma to see him near to naked? Part of him recoiled, insecurity bubbling to the surface in cold bursts.

"Neoma?" His voice was a rumble. Why was he here? He didn't remember coming over. What did he remember?

"Tobin?" Uncertainty now as the scent of doubt grew stronger. "If this is a game, I'm not amused. Get out of the shadows."

The big dog whined.

"Why am I here?" he dared to ask.

Stop talking, take another step. The whisper bit at him, feeling like blackberry thorns in his ass. He jumped and whirled, and a vine let go of his tail trailing blood. A tree behind him revealed two glowing coals embedded in its bark. The coals blinked.

"Aithne!" he snapped, and the moon fog cleared. Martín, that's right, he'd been in the creek when Martín had…had shot him! "What the fuck am I doing here?"

"Not listening to me," she spat, and a wave of focused heat slammed into him, pushing him out into the moonlight, his arms flailing.

Neoma gasped, Matrix lunged. Tobin scrambled to get back into the shadows, his chest feeling like it had been seared by a hot poker, the moonlight a physical weight on his fur.

"Tobin, wait." Neoma's words cooled the heat on his chest, he paused, too surprised to think. "Come. Back."

The command tugged at him. He wanted to…answer it? *Really? What the hell?* His mind again muzzy with moon shine, his logic tangling like he was drunk. What was the worst that would happen if he did? She had just seen him right? She hadn't run screaming. But maybe she hadn't really seen him? He still couldn't think clearly, why couldn't he think clearly?

Matrix shoved his head into Tobin's hip, trying to push him towards the trees. The shove derailed his thoughts, yet Tobin stood rooted in place, eyes locked with Neoma's.

He scented the air. Her emotions were bubbly? Bright? Excitement? The odor tickled his nose. She was *happy*? The smell of mundane human sloughed away, leaving something fresh and tingling, and precious. Her hidden scent, blueberries and stardust.

Her immunity had just broken.

She smelled delicious.

Oh shit, what have I done?

CHAPTER 30

———— • ◦ ◉ ◦ • ————

A Fractured Reality

Neoma

N eoma stood in her apartment watching Tugman swim in circles as she fed him pellets. Her mind was numb, icy. She'd tried to call Megan back, tried to call Tobin. No one was answering their phones. The calls kept going to voicemail, and she wasn't about to leave a message. Texting produced the same results, which was none. She considered panicking.

What had just happened?

That couldn't have been real.

This must be a dream.

Neoma moved to the bed to sit. She gazed out her window until the pewter light faded, replaced by the peach of morning. And still, she doubted her senses, her sanity.

• ◦ ◉ ◦ •

"THANK YOU LADIES FOR COMING IN, ENJOY THE REST OF YOUR weekend." Neoma said on auto pilot, waving at the trio of

White Haired Wonders that had stopped in to peruse the romance section. They were some of her best customers, always leaving with arm loads of books and showering her with advice on dating. Gladys, the ringleader, liked to wink and encourage Neoma to read the Kamasutra before bed. Neoma wondered if Gladys was going to give some poor man a heart attack one of these nights.

Idle thoughts drifted like clouds across the surface of Neoma's mind as she went through the motions of closing down the store for the night. Some part of her recognized she was in shock. Another part kept telling her to call Tobin again. Text him again. Demand that he confirm or deny what had happened. Yet she didn't want to stop the drift. If she did, her feet might touch ground, and she would have to come face to face with the impossible.

Did I really see a werewolf? Is Tobin actually a werewolf?

She jolted back from the register as the door chimed. Martín was standing there. He didn't move. His clothes were rumpled, scruff dusting his cheeks, and his ever-present hat was clutched in his hands as if it were an anchor line. Dark eyes wide, he swallowed and continued to stare, his stout body shaking.

"Martín, are you okay?" The hair rose on the back of Neoma's neck as his eyes focused on her.

"I-I'm not sure." His voice was so calm it freaked her out. Something inside her knew, with unwavering clarity, that his previous night had been as strange as hers.

I don't want to know this. An inner voice wailed. *But don't you?* A deeper part asked.

Neoma held up a hand to forestall more words. She shuffled to the door, flipped the sign to "closed" while looking up and down the street. The sun lingered, the street was simi filled with summer evening traffic as people wandered in the late heat, window shopping or heading to the bar for a bite.

The deadbolt sounded like the lock on a cage as she slid it home. Taking Martín's hand, she led him back into the stacks, the books muffling the sounds from outside, creating a fictional oasis for, what she assumed, would be an improbable conversation.

She sat Martín down in his usual chair, before fetching water and some leftover cookies that Stewart had stashed away for later.

"Chocolate will help," she said in her best fake British accent.

"Your accent is terrible."

Neoma shrugged. "I have other talents, and that's not why you're here. You saw something last night, didn't you?" She leaned forward. "Tell me."

Martín looked slightly surprised, sighed, and shoved a cookie in his mouth before speaking. "You're not going to believe me."

"Clearly you think I might, or you wouldn't be here. And Martín, my night last night, was not…normal."

His dark eyes rounded, and beads of sweat gathered on his forehead like morning dew. "You saw him." His voice choked, and he paled under his dusky complexion. "I was hoping I was wrong, I was hoping I could write it off as too much ice cream, like a sugar induced hallucination coupled with that movie. This can't be real." He was actually babbling, his voice imploring her to lie to him. To tell him something pretty and simple. Something that would put the werewolf back in the illusory box. Did she want to?

Neoma untangled his hands with careful fingers, laying his rumpled hat aside. She marveled at the way her body was moving, as if every joint had been oiled, every ball bearing replaced with new ones. A giddy laugh tried to break free of her chest. Magic, there was real magic in this world, and that knowledge seemed to have changed her somehow. She felt...different.

"Martín, he came to my house. He stood in the trees, in the dark, and his eyes glowed silver. Then Matrix was there, putting himself between us. Protecting me, I think. But I'm not sure. I didn't feel like I was in danger, but there was something so strange happening." She grew quiet.

"What was it?" Martín whispered.

"It was like I could see the shadow. I could see him standing there, but my mind kept telling me it was something else. It wasn't until he spoke that I could really focus. But I'm still not a hundred percent sure what I saw. It was Tobin, and yet..." Helplessness welled inside her. It had been so dark,

Tobin had only been out of the shadows for a second, he had looked misshapen, his voice rough like coarse cloth. His whole body had been dark, ill defined, and when the moonlight touched him, she would swear he had been covered in fur, claws on his hands, pointed ears. His eyes had glowed silver, no animals had silver reflective eyes. They had been drops of brightest chrome, like mercury swimming in between the trees.

She gripped his hands harder. "Tell me," it was her turn to whisper. "Tell me what you saw."

"I'm not sure," Martín moaned. "I heard terrible screaming in the woods, and I thought Tobin was being attacked by a bear. I-I shot at the mass of blackness and the night broke!"

Neoma didn't know what to make of what Martín was saying, and yet it somehow made sense.

"And then Matrix was there, it was like I could see clearly whereas before there had just been shadows. But I could see this black dog, standing in the black woods, and could hear Tobin. Matrix wouldn't let me get near him, but then Tobin wouldn't call him off. He was saying such weird things, he didn't sound right. But it was him!" Martín began breathing harder as he continued. "And then the moonlight slipped through the branches, and Tobin jumped from behind Matrix, but, but, he didn't look right, he looked oversized, like he was wearing a fur coat, and he moved so fast I doubted what I saw. Yet there was something just THERE." He freed a hand and cut through the air.

The tension in the room built like a tsunami, a wave about to crash down on their heads with his next words. Neoma held her breath, willing Martín to continue, praying he wouldn't.

"The problem," his words fell like dust motes, so slow was their journey from his lips to her ears, "is that I don't want to unsee this."

"I don't either."

They shivered together as if a cold wind had just blown through them, forever changing the landscape of their reality.

CHAPTER 31

So Fucked

Tobin

Death would be preferable to this pain, Tobin thought as he cracked his eyes open. Sunlight stabbed a heated knitting needle into his frontal lobe. He winced as his brain sizzled and moaned, burying his face further into the dirt. But that hurt too, his skin overly sensitive to every point of contact. He felt like he'd been flayed.

Without opening his eyes, he pulled himself to his feet, leaving his soles screaming about the weight he was forcing them to bear. He could feel sunlight on his tender skin. A breeze moved over bare flesh and left it aching. *Why am I naked? Why do I hurt so much? And where the fuck am I?*

"Matrix?" The word seemed to rip away scabs in his throat, and he choked. But a soft whine came from the left. "Am I safe?" He was blind, the world hurt, and he had never been more exposed. Fear threatened to smother him with the unknown, but he held on to reason. Until there was a problem, he refused to panic.

Matrix gave two heavy pants indicating safety. Tobin scented the air. He smelled aluminum, crushed gravel, and roofing tar. He was at the house. He dared to crack his eyes again. He saw a blur of a structure before his head tried to split in two, flashing the world with black.

Somehow, he made it inside, into the bed, and let the darkness take him. Hours later, a knock echoed through the house like a gunshot. Tobin bounded to his feet, the world spun, and he steadied himself with the wall, shaking his head. The pain had receded to a dull hangover, and he was starving.

Fumbling, he slipped into a t-shirt and shorts and glanced in the mirror. There were dark circles under his eyes as if he'd been drinking. Dirt was smeared on the side of his face. No blood, that was good. He finger combed his hair as he stumbled forward.

"We have guests?" Tobin asked Matrix who stood at the threshold, hackles up. Tobin opened the door, bright sunlight making him hiss and hold up his arm.

"You refused to be commanded; it was disappointing." Aithne said from the tree line. She stood in shadow, a dress of wildflowers draping from her collarbone to her knees. Her expression pouted at him, squinting as she twirled a daisy between her fingers.

Tobin rubbed his ass, remembering the bite of blackberry thorns forcing him out of the shadows. Without thinking, he leapt from the doorway, clearing the drive and landing in front of her reaching for her neck.

"Do not." Her word froze him. "Kneel." He dropped. "Good boy."

Terror swamped him, but he clawed through it with righteous anger. "You did this to me! Last night, how? How did you make me change?" He snarled and spit flew as sweat broke out over his body, fear pumping through his veins.

"You resented being chained to the moon. I freed you from her bonds, mostly. But do you really think a werewolf can exist unfettered? That is not the nature of the creature you have become dear man-wolf. You cannot be this," she waved her hands at all of him, "without a mistress. I promise you, I will give you more freedom than the moon will." Her smile was pitying as she stroked his cheek. Tobin smacked her hand away, showing his teeth.

"Oh," she stepped back, "is someone feeling beastly today?"

"Fuck you, Aithne." Tobin pushed against his mental restraints, feeling them soften, and regained his feet.

"You say that a lot, and yet never offer to comply. I do not think you really wish to couple with me, man-wolf. I think you only wish to tease." She touched the flower to his chest, tracing down to his waist as color burned bright in his cheeks.

"We had an agreement, you broke it."

"And what deal was that?"

"I killed the drainer, you gave me hunting rights to this land. You don't own me, or mine."

"Tsk tsk. You have become my wooden wolf. You mingled your blood with my sap and accepted the power to change without the full moon. Where do you think that power came from? No magic is free, man-wolf. There is always a price. And now you need to make your pack so we can rule this territory, bow to no one."

"You have me bowing to you!" Tobin snarled.

"You have a long leash, it will not chafe," she huffed.

Tobin growled and paced, his mind working furiously as fear nibbled at the edges. He was chained to a Fey, again! How had he allowed this to happen? Terror streaked through him, and insight flashed. He rounded on her.

"And what shackles are you trying to escape from Aithne? Why do this? Who is it you fear?" Tobin loomed over the diminutive Fey.

Her spine went straight and for a moment, he would have sworn he saw fire dance in her pink eyes. "That is not for you to know now, Tobin." She took a step forward, and he retreated as her anger wafted over him, sharp with the scent of charcoal and ashes.

"Tonight, you will go change your pack. You will bring them to me, and we will unite them all with the trees, tying them to the land. So mote it be. Now go." Her command rang like a gong and before he knew it, Tobin found himself back in the house, making food, preparing for another shift this evening.

His hands trembled as he reached for the phone. He couldn't pick it up. What was he going to do? This was not the plan. He slid down the counter and puddled on the floor, shivering. He could already feel the moon on the far horizon, calling his wildness to the surface. Neoma's scent memory filled him, blueberries and stardust.

"Oh Max," he moaned. "What have I done?"

* • ● • *

MATRIX WATCHED WITH DETACHED SPECULATION AS AITHNE torched his brother. The dog knew the Fey had deeper plans for Tobin that Matrix hadn't uncovered yet. But as he observed the game, he could see more of the moving parts.

Green lines of energy wrapped around Tobin like vines, pulling him into submission. Yet they were not connected to him in a way that Matrix had come to associate with bonds that entangled the soul. Tobin had a soul bond to the moon that allowed the wolf to be torn from his skin each month. What Aithne had done was somehow create an opening into Tobin. She'd wound her power in and around him. If Tobin's wolf was a moth that was attracted to the full moon, Aithne had opened the blinds that kept the moth from seeing the moon every night.

Yet the price for allowing the wolf to surface was obedience. Matrix suspected Tobin's desire to change at will was the opening the Fey had needed to shackle his brother to her whims. What would happen long-term each time Tobin chose to change outside the moon's invitation?

A shudder ran through the big dog, dread weighing him down. He watched as Tobin marched back into the house and started to make food; he moved like an automaton, his eyes wide with panic as his body functioned without his input.

"Oh Max," Tobin moaned. "What have I done?"

Matrix went to him. Carefully taking a pulsing vine of green energy in his teeth, he tried to sever it. It fought him, searing his tongue, and wiggling away. He selected the smallest one, focusing hard to hold the slithering energy between his molars and nipped it cleanly in half. Tobin slumped to the floor sobbing, clutching at Matrix's thick fur as the green energy fizzled out of the house like a lit fuse.

"I promised I'd meet Robin tonight. I can feel the compulsion in my gut like a hot splinter. It stabs deeper each time I resist. I have to go, don't I?" Tobin asked.

Matrix solemnly nodded. Something stirred, something beyond Aithne and her petty games. The woods around here wanted wolves, wanted a pack like Aithne claimed, but not for whatever reasons she held close. The realization clicked in Matrix's head, settled into his bones as if all his joints just realigned into perfect harmony. He vibrated with his insight, perceiving the rightness of it.

"No matter what happens tonight, Max, don't let me turn anyone who doesn't want it." Tobin's hazel gaze swirled with conflict and moon-madness, but his determination was a clean blaze of empathy. Matrix nodded once, he would protect his brother and their friends.

CHAPTER 32

Down the Rabbit Hole

Neoma

"Hello?" Robin answered his phone as if afraid of who was calling. Neoma gritted her teeth and reminded herself again that Robin wasn't a bad guy. Just annoying. Somehow that didn't help much.

"Hey Robin, it's Neoma. What are you doing tonight?" she asked.

"Why?" Suspicion sizzled across the phone.

Neoma looked at Martín, tilting her head to the side, puzzled over Robin's response.

"We were wondering if you wanted to…" her voice trailed off, and she grimaced as if tasting something sour before spitting out her words. "Wondered if you wanted to go look for werewolves with us." She hit the mute button and scowled at Martín. "I sound stupid." She griped.

Martín shrugged. "Give him a minute, you probably just gave him a woody."

"You are not funny and now I need to sterilize my brain."
Martín's grin was evil.

"You pretend to be a nice man. You are not a nice man."

"Call it gallows humor." Martín replied as Robin sputtered
into the silence. Neoma took her phone off mute.

"Are you with Martín?" Robin asked.

"Yes, actually, and now you're on speaker."

"Hey Martín," Robin sounded giddy. "I don't want to talk
about this over the phone, can I come meet you guys?" The
whine in Robin's voice made Neoma's scalp twitch.

"Sure, fine, whatever. We're at the bookstore."

"Sweet, be there in ten." The connection went dead.
Neoma put down her phone, rubbing her sore joints. "Remind
me why we're doing this again?"

"World peace," Martín said with a straight face.

"Now you're just trying to make me hate you." Martín gave
a small smile and shrugged. "Keep it up and no more cookies
for you." Neoma said, sliding another cookie towards him. She
stormed off to recheck the supplies before he could see her
grin.

ROBIN ARRIVED TEN MINUTES LATER, DRESSED IN ALL BLACK,
with a camo bandana tied around his head. He sported a bulky
backpack and skittered in the door as if he were being
followed. He glanced around, hit the interior lights, and
plunged them all into darkness.

"What's wrong with you?" Neoma asked, flicking on the light by the register. The fear from last night, coupled with what Martín had shared, brought her too close to the edge of her coping abilities. "Do you think the FBI is after you or something?"

"Sorry," Robin mumbled, but immediately launched into over-caffeinated squirrel mode with a rush of words so tangled Neoma put her hands over her ears.

"Robin," Martín laid a thick hand on Robin's shoulder and shook him gently. "Breathe and try that again. You're safe." The stocky man's stoic energy seemed to help Robin regain his sanity, and Neoma lowered her hands, leaning forward on the desk.

"Sorry, sorry. It's just, well, did Tobin invite you guys too?"

"Maybe." Neoma cut Martín off with a look. "But he said to talk to you first before we did anything."

"Oh yeah? Really? Wow, that's great. So, he does trust me?" Robin squeaked. "I was afraid this was all a set up, but if he told you guys, this has got to be legit."

"Yes. Now spill." Neoma felt a little bad lying to Robin, but it seemed like the quickest route to clarity.

"Okay, well, Tobin gave me the coordinates of where to meet him tonight if I wanted to see a real werewolf." Robin looked back and forth between them as if waiting to be booed off stage. Her stomach fluttered as adrenaline pumped into her system. Martín appeared nonplussed, but the tightening of his lips belied his calm.

Neoma shook her head. That meant last night had been real. "Go on," she whispered.

Robin didn't need the encouragement in the face of their apparent acceptance. "Tobin promised this wasn't a joke. He was actually pretty sincere, so I was willing to go anyway, but you guys coming too makes this so much cooler." He beamed. "He was really firm on one point. No filming and no extra people or he wasn't going to show. So, wait, when did he talk to you guys?"

"Last night." Martín answered.

"Really?" Robin sounded unsure.

"Trust me, Robin, we had a real show-and-tell moment with Tobin, minus the tell. We were hoping tonight would shine some more light on what we experienced yesterday." Neoma tried to look reassuring.

"Oh! Wow! What did you see?"

"That's the problem, Robin. We aren't sure, but it involved Tobin, the moon, and possibly fur."

Robin did a nervous little happy dance. Neoma grew concerned that he might have peed on the floor.

"Okay, okay, everyone be cool. This is really happening!" Robin suddenly went serious. "Okay, this is what we're going to do. I'm driving because he's expecting my car. I have everything we need loaded up: first aid, food, weapons, extra clothes. Sorry Neoma, I didn't think about underwear for you."

Neoma blinked. "Uh, that's fine, Robin."

"If we leave right now, we'll be there a little before the moon is due to rise. It's late tonight so I have flashlights and headlamps if we need them. I'm sure once it's up we'll be able to see just fine. I'm hoping Tobin will meet us there and actually show us a change. But it might be deeply personal, I didn't want to pry. You never know." His face was grave.

"That's," Neoma paused, "surprisingly considerate of you, Robin."

"Well," he looked away embarrassed, "this is a big deal. He's inviting us into his world. I've been waiting my whole life for this. I don't want to screw it up."

Cold washed through her. Neoma saw her fear reflected in Martín's face as she grabbed her keys and followed Robin out to his car. Martín made a quick detour to his truck and dashed back.

"Is this a good idea?" she whispered as he held the door of the car open for her. She eyed the pile of sporting goods that roamed freely inside the tiny Geo Metro.

"What have we got to lose?" Martín asked, tipping the brim of his hat back with one finger.

Neoma sighed, *what indeed.*

CHAPTER 33

Regretful Moon

Tobin

T obin quit fighting Aithne's compulsion and drove straight to the coordinates he'd given Robin. Without resistance, that splinter in his gut vanished, yet each time he thought about going in a different direction, the nagging pain would resurface until he refocused on the road ahead.

"What am I going to do?" Tobin asked for the umpteenth time. Matrix shrugged and gave a small whine, bumping Tobin gently with his head. Tobin maneuvered off the winding gravel road into an obscure turnout overlooking an older clear-cut.

The land was ravaged. Blunted stumps poked out from under hillocks of grass, shrubbery, and blackberry. Loggers had planted seedlings, but the spindly trees had a long way to go before someone might call them a forest. Around the edges of the open space, straight trunks stood like an army gazing upon a field of their fallen comrades, darkness shrouding their grief as the sun set. Stars poked holes in the fading light, distant candles ignited in memory of the departed.

Tobin wondered if now would be a good time to start praying, or if the gods would only laugh at his last-minute attempts to absolve his sins. He shook his head and exited the truck, at least he would only have to contend with Robin tonight. That was something to be grateful for.

Stooping, he began to gather wood, heaping it into the makeshift fire pit left by some long-ago teenagers. The site was no longer visited, and no human scent or garbage lingered. The logging roads made this forsaken place perfect for Tobin's needs. He'd discovered it weeks ago while running and had appreciated the sweeping view to the east. Moonlight would flood this clearing like an unfettered tide into a cove. Tobin shivered and cast around at his feet. The abandoned ring of stones huddled on rocky ground, clear of vegetation. This time of year, it was not worth risking a spark, yet Tobin needed light, as if it might keep the monsters at bay a little longer.

"Oh shit, M, how in the hell am I going to do this?" Tobin knelt and stuffed tinder under the dry wood and lit it. "This was supposed to be me making my pack. Not conscripting toy soldiers for an unstable Fey." He blew on the tiny spark, heat rising in his voice.

"Hell, Robin didn't ask for this, he just wants to be a werewolf." Tobin snapped his little stick into confetti, feeding it into the tinder with violent thrusts. "I don't even know what it takes to make a werewolf," he admitted, sitting back on his heels, clutching his head. The weight of what he had initiated was finally becoming clear. He was messing with people's lives, and they didn't have all the information. Just like the Bone Wraith, he was preying upon their ignorance to achieve his own goals. How had he been so callous?

Boxes of memories that he kept on a distant shelf in his mind opened unbidden. The image of Nora splattered across his mental canvas. Nora, drugged and terrified, fighting with everything she had to escape the Bone Wraith's agenda. Tobin had never asked her what she wanted, he'd just assumed she would covet the power the Wraith was unlocking. He never even asked the creature about what it would mean for him to be affected by her magic. Like a genie offering a wish, Tobin's greed had agreed, never considering the consequences. And magic always had consequences.

How had he missed that? Yet would his choices be different if he'd possessed all the information? The wildness under his skin howled for release, and Tobin flinched. The addiction to his new life tugged at him while the chains that bound him tightened. Nausea rolled up his throat, could he really do this to someone else without their consent? Did he even know how?

"Transformation could take only a scratch," he muttered to himself, thoughts tangled. "Or I might have to maul him to within an inch of his life. What if I kill him?" Tobin sat down on the ground to watch the flame grow, eating the dry grass with hissing bites as the orange and yellow light swelled, lapping at the wood until the bark began to char and smoke.

Matrix sat down and leaned against Tobin's side, his head higher than his brother's. Tobin brought up an arm and clasped the giant dog to him, wondering when he'd hugged him last.

He watched the fire as Matrix gazed at the surrounding woods and sky. The moon was still well beyond the horizon, but Tobin could feel the slight itch under his skin, the tug of the wildness testing its barriers, waiting for them to thin. Was the wolf really him? The lucidity of the change dulled in the light of the next day. All that strength, power, and connection got wrapped in thick dreamlike layers of memory until he sometimes doubted his experiences. Even the injuries he sustained while changed were wiped away like Halloween makeup.

But last night had been different, vivid, outlined in pain. He remembered it, mostly. Clear shards of memory came to him when called, but they didn't all fit together to complete the puzzle. He saw and smelled Martín crouched in the dark holding a gun. He was pulled towards Neoma as he hid in the shadows of the trees. The images were surfacing in his mind's eye, when earlier they had been a blur. Yet he didn't remember how and why he went from the creek to Neoma's house. The holes bothered him. What had changed?

I've changed. The thought chimed through him. *I now have a say in my transformation, I'm no longer a blind slave to the moon.* He shuddered. *Only a slave to a Fey.* Somehow that new

A.B. Herron

collar chafed more even as it gave him a level of autonomy. What had she coerced him to do?

He didn't know, so he focused on what he was aware of. He could feel the moon as the catalyst, waking the wolf, sharpening his own senses. His skin itched and the restless feeling intensified. He held it at bay.

The wolf paced, caged behind his human flesh. An anxious animal in a trap. Tobin hadn't felt that before, but now the awareness burned bright. Now there was only a thin barrier between his two forms. Last night had taught him to push against that barrier with everything he had. But it had been the bullet slamming into his chest, shattering his human casing that allowed the wolf to boil free.

And Tobin wanted to feel the wolf, he couldn't help himself. It was a need that roiled inside him. A hunger for the powerful body wrapped in corded muscle and sharp teeth. He ran mental fingers along that line between them. It was like stroking water, but he couldn't break the surface tension. The yearning to change climbed up his throat until he choked. With effort, he yanked his mental hand back. Not now. He had to keep his head clear. He shoved the wild urges away and leaned heavier into his brother's furry side, poking at the fire.

"She's watching us, isn't she?" Tobin whispered. Matrix nodded, not taking his eyes off the surrounding trees. Despite the warm night, Tobin shivered. A pull, like a thread thin tap root, tugged his awareness to the south. She was there, waiting. He could almost taste her.

"M, I have a confession. I'm not always in control when I shift." The big dog harrumphed. "You've guessed that, haven't you?" Matrix nodded again. "Well, there are some holes in my memory that are bothering me. Last night, I...I didn't hurt anyone, did I?" Tobin was suddenly a small child again, hoping his brother could make all the scary things better. Hoping the remembered smell of broken things was some olfactory illusion because he didn't recall anything breaking.

<hr />

MATRIX LET OUT A SIGH, MAKING THE FIRE DANCE. HE SWIVELED his head to regard his brother. How could he answer that? Tobin hadn't technically hurt anyone, but he had damaged something inside both Martín and Neoma. Would it bring them pain? He didn't know, but he understood that the Fey wanted that piece to break, wanted these humans to lose their magical immunity. To what end? Did she really want them all to become werewolves? Did they want to take that plunge?

Under his paws, Matrix could feel the pulse of the earth. If he focused, he could pinpoint which tree Aithne rested in, watching them. If he concentrated harder, he could start to pick out the different magical creatures that moved around the forest, see the golden threads of their existence in the tapestry of life that flowed over and through this country like a river. There were snags of inequality in that fabric, snarls where the flow of balance tipped too far into chaos, or too far into harmony. He used that vision now to try and glean some answers.

Ultimately, when he studied the flow, there wasn't a good or bad force at work. It had taken months of practice to arrive at this conclusion, and Matrix had been startled by the revelation. However, he understood there were good and bad outcomes that would result if the balance was not maintained. So where did Aithne and Tobin land in this web?

Using this insight on such a broad expanse was mentally exhausting, and just now he sat in the middle of these threads. He couldn't parse them out. The dog shut it down, overwhelmed by the grandeur of the experience. He had tied himself to this land somehow. Like Tobin was tied to the moon, and Aithne was tied to the trees. Matrix didn't understand what that meant for him yet, but he swelled with the need to keep balance in these territories, coupled with a purpose to protect those he cared about.

He loved his brother, despite the chaos that lived inside him, but Matrix could see balance taking root in Tobin's soul. There was still hope that his brother could be more than selfish.

Matrix touched his wet nose to Tobin's head, *Be you.* The words whispered between them just as they heard a distant car making its dogged way towards them. Whatever happened tonight, Matrix was ready to do what he must to restore the balance this land so desperately craved.

CHAPTER 34

"No Howl?"

Neoma

"Is that actually a fire?" Martín was incredulous as Robin pulled into place next to Tobin's truck and cut the engine. "Cabrón, werewolf or no, you and I are going to have a strict talk about fire season and what it fully means." His words altered to unintelligible mutterings as he undid his seatbelt.

"Rethinking your choice to come?" Neoma asked. "Or are you redirecting?" She rubbed her elbows that had started up a dull complaint on the way over.

Martín muttered more Spanish under his breath, his thick shoulders almost touching his earlobes as he slumped lower in the seat. "This feels like a peaceful scene from a horror movie right before the killing starts. I hate the killing."

"Oh I love that part!" Robin trilled before bouncing out of the car.

Neoma gave Martín a small, brave smile in the rearview mirror. "No more Red Bull for Robin."

"Agreed." Martín blew out a breath and pulled himself from the car, forcing the seat forward and offering his hand to Neoma so she didn't have to flounder her way out of the short Geo Metro and its clutter within.

"Robin is also never driving us again." Neoma grunted, rubbing her back, her annoyance at the subcompact and its supplies covered up the butterflies behind her breastbone.

"Agreed."

Tobin launched to his feet as Neoma and Martín got out of the car. He was shirtless, in dark boxer briefs, and barefoot. The almost nudity confused her. After last week, she intimately understood this man's shyness and wanted to hand him a jacket. Yet Tobin was anything but body conscious as he glared at Robin as if he were about to attack him. Adrenaline flushed her system causing sweat to prickle along her spine.

"Robin, what the hell! I told you to come alone." He gestured in their direction, his voice barely above a growl, and Neoma took a step back before she recovered. She studied Tobin, every toned line of him was brushed by shadow, and though he looked pissed, he was still just Tobin. No fangs or fur to be seen. Neoma straightened her spine and marched over. Robin was sputtering like a landed fish, his face turning red in the firelight as she stepped between them.

"After last night's performance, do you think we'd let him come alone?" She had the satisfaction of Tobin taking a small step back. His eyes locked with hers, and she saw a battle within them.

"I need you to leave," he ground out. "Now."

"Tobin…" She was attempting to be soft, to nurture that tie that had been building between them.

"Neoma," Martín warned as he approached from behind. Her skin prickled, but she waved a dismissive hand at him, not moving away from Tobin.

Tobin's posture wilted for just a second. "Please, Nae, please just leave."

"Why?"

"Because if you don't go, I can't promise you'll stay safe." His hazel gaze seemed to burn ochre in the flickering light. "And I have no wish to hurt you, Nae."

"Then don't, Tobin." She pushed closer into his personal space.

"Is this really what you want?" His hand lifted slowly, and he brushed a wayward curl off her forehead. It was the most intimate touch he had yet indulged. She shivered.

"How can I answer that? I don't know what the question is." Martín's hand was warm on her shoulder, but she shrugged him off, her attention locked on Tobin.

When had they gotten so close? The heat of Tobin's body brushed the length of hers, the thin fabric of her summer dress no hindrance. She gulped. The planes of his face hardened and softened as the fire danced. But his eyes seemed to burn with fever while the muscles in his neck and shoulders twitched like a horse rousting flies.

"What's wrong with you?"

"You have to know. That's why you're here, isn't it?" The wilt in his posture was gone. His voice was now gravel and dark things, making the hair rise along her arms. "I can't hold this back any longer, the moon is touching the horizon. *Neoma, run!*"

Tobin yanked his body back and around. He tripped, going down on hands and knees groaning, scrabbling at the earth with his fingers. Neoma tried to rush towards him, but Matrix blocked her, and she slammed into his ribs, almost going down. She felt Martín's hands on her shoulders again, keeping her upright.

"I think we should run." Martín gasped, pulling her backwards as Tobin screamed. His back arched off the ground, lines of black appearing in his skin like fractures. On the horizon, the supermoon sliced the sky, the barest edge skimming the horizon like a leviathan breaching.

"Oh my god," Robin shrieked, "this is happening!"

Martín tugged Neoma again, but it was weak, both of them rooted in the spot with terror and fascination as Tobin's body contorted, stretched, and remade itself. Skin blistered in the moon's light, bubbling and breaking as fur sprouted and muscles swelled. Tobin's screams muffled to a high pitch whine as his face pulled like taffy into a muzzle, nose blackening and flaring, ears moving up his head into points, his features filling in with dark brown fur.

Neoma gawked as Tobin's thighs expanded. They stretched the seams of his boxer briefs, as a tail sprouted through the fabric, thrusting behind him, thick and fur covered. His feet elongated, toes spreading, solid black nails digging into the dirt while his hands grew claws, fingers thickening, arms and chest bulging, back arching, head ducking out of sight.

Then there was silence except for a high-pitched keening coming from Robin, but even that stopped as Tobin began to rise. He unfurled like a seedling reaching for the light. His huge body stretched outwards and up, silhouetted by the bloated moon peeking halfway over the distant hills. Neoma lurched back, knocking into Martín, and tumbling them both into the dirt on their butts, making Tobin look even bigger.

The werewolf slowly turned his head toward them, eyes gleaming silver with reflected fire. Neoma's breath caught. Her mind shivered with the sight; he was impossible, dangerous, gorgeous.

Gorgeous? What the hell is wrong with me? Cold flooded her, a river of ice moved down her spine, breaking apart her fear like brittle rock, and her head cleared. *This is my monster.*

"What," she snapped as she got to her feet and dusted herself off, "no howl?"

CHAPTER 35

$\cdot\ \bullet\ \textbf{\textbullet}\ \bullet\ \cdot$

Dissociation

Tobin

There was yelling in his head. Yet somehow it was drowned out by the absurdity of the question the woman had just asked him. What had she asked him? It no longer mattered. She mattered. Her voice was some kind of tether. It focused him despite the singing of the giant moon. Despite the insistent urging of the Fey to bite everyone before they had a chance to recover. Despite his need to glory in what he had just become. Despite not knowing who he was.

Her eyes held him.

He stepped toward her only to have his bones rattled by the huge dog's growl. He showed his teeth to the creature and slunk down into a crouch, starting to circle the humans and the little fire. He didn't like the fire, it singed his eyes, stole the night's lucidity. But it painted his prey in unmistakable hues of heat and life.

And *she* kept watching him.

The small one made a squeaking noise and scurried closer to the other two, putting the fire between them. A bird. The little man was like a bird. The fear smell coming off that one was tainted with longing and cowardice. It stabbed his nose until he sneezed.

The Bird might be worth experimenting on.

Movement drew him back to the group. The other male, he was interesting. Square shoulders, sturdy. Stopping his stalking, he breathed deep, pulling the clean smell of controlled fear and curiosity through his nose like a sommelier sniffing wine. Strong body, deep notes of courage, hint of yearning.

Yes, he would be an excellent addition. The words moved through his head like a news feed. They were not his. He restarted his slow turn around the fire, hugging the edge where the light and the dark did battle. He knew their eyes couldn't fully see him. He was the shadow following in the wake of the flame, never to be obliterated. His tail swished, and he growled a soft love song to the night and the glory of the moon while his powerful form moved with effortless grace. The humans before him shuffled like ducklings attempting to stay under a mother's safe wing, in awe of the fearsome predator creeping ever closer.

"Tobin," the woman's voice was a cold hiss that splashed him with the memory of words, "you still in there?"

He shook himself and paused again, one claw lifted. Words. They could be another tool if wielded properly, a way to get what he needed. His brain whirled, why was he here? What did he need? Why were they here?

Oh, now he remembered.

"I thought this was what you wanted," he ground the words out past his beastly appetites. "And yet you shudder and shy away from me like prey."

The square man frowned and planted his feet, while the woman considered him. The Bird stayed tucked in their shadows, but his eyes never left the wolf. Need shown in that hungry gaze. The black dog stood firm, a breakwater prepared to meet the coming storm. He chuffed at the dog, expressing his amusement at the futile display. He was the wilderness given reason, a werewolf no hound could overcome. And yet why was the black dog in his way? They were pack. They were supposed to hunt together, not oppose one another. He inhaled deeply, trying to sniff out causation.

Stay away from him my pet, he seeks to unmake you. The wishes of the Fey were unimportant, and yet were all he could obey.

"I have no desire to become a mindless monster." The woman's voice was soft. "You once told me I had nothing to fear from you. I'm not sure I believe you anymore."

Somehow, the words hurt. How did words hurt? He pinned his ears, he did not like this. Shaking his head, he backed further into the dark, out of the flame.

"I can leave, if that's what you want," he snarled.

"No!" The Bird burst out, jumping into the firelight. "No, Tobin, please," he whined. "I want to be a werewolf!"

"Robin!" The woman snapped. "Are you insane? Look at him, he doesn't know who he is right now. He doesn't know us. What's the point of suffering through that change if you don't remember what you experience on the other side of it?"

"But he's talking! He knows us. Don't you, Tobin? You know me, you asked me to come here tonight. I'm here to be part of your pack. Remember?" But the Bird's voice wavered, and he hesitated to take another step.

Just bite him! The words seared his thoughts. *He wants to join you and worship the moon in the dark.*

Above, the swollen goddess hovered, and he took a moment to revel in her song. Her light caressed him but no longer bound him. He could enjoy her without losing himself. But he had lost himself. There was something he needed to remember. Opening his eyes, he stared at the Bird.

"If you want this," he crept closer into the firelight standing tall again on two paws. "I will give you this…Robin." Yes, that's what this Bird was called.

The Bird, no, Robin, surged forward but the black dog knocked him over. The small man tumbled to the ground, scrambling to get past the surging canine as the dog attempted to pin him. But there was more fight in Robin than the werewolf would have expected. The small man wiggled and squirmed, twisting like a crocodile under the black mass of fur while the other two humans yelled. Suddenly, Robin scraped the ground and flung a handful of dirt and grit in the dog's face. Bellowing, the black dog tossed his head, pawing his eyes and thrashing while Robin wiggled out past furry legs.

Robin scrambled up to him, dropped to his knees, and held out his arm yelling, "I would be honored to be part of your pack Tobin. Bite me, please. *Hurry!*"

He didn't hesitate this time. Whatever block had made him pause didn't rise as he opened his jaws and bit down. Teeth punctured through flesh with little pops like bubble wrap, sinking deep into the soft forearm as blood welled up. The taste was...odd. It didn't call to him like the tang of deer, or the buzz of the drainer, and instead of taking something from this bite, he gave. Magic trickled from him, cool as the caress of moonlight. It oozed into the human with reluctance, then gained momentum until it rushed like spring thaw into a new river system.

Robin screamed.

He snarled back. His mouth was full as a body thudded into him, ripping his teeth free of flesh as the screaming got higher. What had impacted him? Who? The body on top of him scrambled for a hold on his throat, its grip relentless. The scent of the square man covered him in clouds of protective desperation. The attacker's will was so strong he almost bowed to it. But no, he was the alpha here, this was his night under the moon. No human would take that from him.

With a lunge, he flipped the fight, taking the other man to the ground beneath him just as hands found his furry throat.

Snarling, he snapped at the man's face. *Martín*, his name was Martín. The label bubbled up in his reasoning. Yet the affable memories that came with the name didn't slow his actions as the grip around his throat tightened. Raking claws down Martín's arms made the square man gasp, but his grip didn't lessen. He dug in again until he hit bone, sliced tendon, and the arms buckled. Suddenly he was falling onto Martín, his mouth open and roaring.

His teeth stopped as they touched flesh and everything in him recoiled. He tried to back away, but his body was frozen. Aithne's binding built until the pressure seemed about to obliterate him if he didn't capitulate. Yet he resisted, pulling barbed words from his throat.

"Do. You. Want. This." Drool ran in rivulets down Martín's shoulder and neck, his mouth stuck open as he pinned the bleeding man. Their heads were close enough that they were breathing each other's breath. Pain, blood, and magic exhaling around them in a fog of helplessness.

"Damn you, Cabrón," Martín wheezed in agony, his life leaking out of his shredded arms with each beat of his heart, "you've given me no choice. Yes, I want to live."

Guilt saturated him as he let go, he hadn't meant to hurt him. But it didn't matter, he couldn't stop. Invited, his teeth sunk into Martín's shoulder instinctively.

Blood bathed his tongue for the second time, clean, rich, ready. Magic burned with moonlight, hot with possibilities as it pooled into Martín. Flowing as if made of molten wax, coating every inch, each cell. Coaxing forward a wildness that was already natural, somehow stifled by Martín's humanity. But that limiting birthright had been broken, and magic was free to remake the vessel.

Horror penetrated his awareness. Ripping away from Martín, the man crumpled, eyes fogging over, face going slack. He scrambled away, dropping into the shadows, panting heavily, wiping his bloody muzzle on the backs of his forearms. This blood was not sweet, but it was clean, scrubbed free of the human's natural immunity to magic.

It tastes like potential, my little man-wolf. So many powerful prospects. And you have been the key to unlocking the gates, granting me access to humans who were once untouchable. Thank you for that. Now, you have one more.

He looked unbidden across the fire at the woman and the big dog. She was his last hope.

CHAPTER 36

Unwilling Witness

Neoma

Silver eyes gleamed at her out of the darkness, the only piece of Tobin she could still see. Rooted in place, she didn't dare move, and each time she tried, Matrix wound himself around her. His entire coat was standing on end. He looked so big she was debating throwing a leg over him and telling him to run for the hills. They might actually make it.

Robin was no longer screaming, but weeping softly, huddled around his bleeding forearm. Martín lay like a felled tree, right on the edge of the firelight, and she couldn't tell if he was breathing, or if the flames were toying with her emotions as shadows danced. She was starting to hate fire.

"Matrix, I can't stay here, they need help," she said for the tenth time, but the dog wouldn't move. He kept glancing around, his nose in the air, growling uncontrollably with every breath he took. Neoma was beyond scared now. She had left scared behind in Robin's crappy car and probably should have stayed back there with it. Now it was too late, she was in this nightmare with no way of waking up. Yet despite everything, there was a weird thrill of exhilaration, and with it a chill that calmed her.

"Meg, why can't you be here right now?" she muttered. "I could really use some advice, like what would you tell me about dealing with werewolves? Scream and run like a little kid? Show him who's boss? Assume the fetal position and kiss my ass goodbye?" Giddy panic bubbled in her chest as she beheld the silver eyes moving in the darkness. Her whole being buzzed with muddled excitement and terror, her joints aching with each tiny movement as she tracked the predator stalking her.

"SHIT!" Robin screamed, arching backwards. Inarticulate sounds tore from his throat, his body beginning to boil and thrash.

"No," Neoma gasped in disbelief. This couldn't be happening. But as she watched Robin writhe on the ground, she braced herself for this second horror show, unwilling, and unable, to flee.

Skin blistered and broke into spots of fur, peppering the small man's flesh with mutant freckles. Robin rolled to his side, heaving like he was going to puke. A muzzle forced its way out of his face while blood gushed from his mouth to trickle down his chin. His limbs stuttered like a stop motion film as they lengthened past human norms. A shoe went flying, fabric ripping to the sounds of distressed denim as Robin's cries muted and garbled with fleshy snaps and plops. Neoma wanted to look away. She wanted to run. But she couldn't leave him, even when fingernails popped off like firecrackers, claws erupting through nail beds. Neoma gagged, the smell of blood and ozone filled the night as Robin started to seize.

"Robin!" her voice cracked in her throat. She was powerless. Neoma wanted to hide her head. She wanted to scream. Robin's transformation was far worse than Tobin's. The panicked sounds of his breathing etched in her brain will fuel her nightmares for life. Never did she want to hear a creature struggle like that again. Never.

She'd gone to her knees, clutching Matrix, ensnared by Robin's suffering, and useless in the presence of magic. "What am I going to do?" She also felt torn in two. Something was ripping free from her own bones, gaining momentum. Some inevitable transformation of self, irreversible and unstoppable. Unless she fled now.

A dull gleam of metal caught her eye. Robin's keys lay on the ground two feet away, pulling her from the monstrous event unfolding under an insensitive moon.

She could do it. She could grab them and run. The Metro might be a shit car, but it had to be good enough to outrun a werewolf. Besides, Matrix would slow Tobin down, she could feel it.

But she couldn't get her damn feet to move. Couldn't coerce her stubborn fingers to release their grip on the black dog. And she couldn't get her breaking heart to forsake their friends.

I won't leave them. She gripped her courage in both hands and on shaky legs, she stood. The pain in her joints flared, then faded. Neoma straightened to her full height, *pain be damned!* She shook her wayward curls from her face.

"Matrix, move." She tasted frost and the big dog got out of her way. With two strides, she swiped the keys and went to Martín's side, watching Tobin circle. Matrix kept pace with her. She had to know if he was still alive. She glanced back at Robin. He lay in a furry heap, panting and whining, seemingly unconscious. He was beyond her meager help.

"Martín," she knelt at his side, trusting the dog to keep the wolf at bay. A fine tremor ran through him, he twitched and shuddered. But he was breathing. And human. She laid her hand on his shoulder and shook him gently. "Martín!"

His head lolled towards her, and she saw his neck. Blood flowed from angry punctures in his flesh, a sluggish river of black bleeding into the gloom. His body was burning up and when his eyes cracked open, they shone yellow. "Oh what the ever-loving fuck! This is not happening!"

A twig snapped. Neoma turned.

"And yet, I believe it is." The voice emerged from the dark to twine around the little horror show like a noxious weed. "And you my dear, are the next in line." The laugh sounded like flowers blooming and wood burning. Neoma scanned the gloom and saw a small woman step into the feeble light. She was bathed in silver until the fire anointed her in gold. Her skin seemed to cling to the dark yet was festooned with tattoos of white moon flowers. She swished into the ring of light barefoot and wearing a dress made of layers of magnolia petals that shone like opals. She was unearthly. Delicate vines were entwined in her hair, holding the russet mass so that it cascaded down her back in a waterfall of waves and blossoms. Tiny heart-shaped leaves grew at her hairline.

Neoma was struck by her wild beauty. "You're about to be a big pain in my ass, aren't you?"

The Fey laughed.

Matrix had never been a violent person before his death. Even as a cop, carrying a gun, he had been cool, level-headed, and compassionate with the suspects they'd had to apprehend. But right now, watching the people he cared about be used like puppets in this mad Fey's experiment, he was ready to bring the killing.

The only problem was he wasn't sure who he should be killing.

Tobin was under Fey compulsion. He wasn't fully acting of his own free will. Robin hadn't done anything bad yet, but

Matrix could feel dark threads of chaos knotting around the newly fleshed werewolf like swarming piranha. He shivered.

Martín was still shrouded in mystery. A pivotal thread in the tapestry that overlay these lands, but what he would mean was still undecided. Neoma needed to be protected at all costs. She shone with promise, with balance. He backed up closer to her, trying to shield her from Tobin and the Fey. He was not enough to defend them on open ground.

And then there was Aithne. He growled, lifting a lip, feeling his shoulders stretch as he tried to make himself bigger. The Fey paused, a finger to her lips as she studied him. Energies pulsed around her. Vibrant colors that muted and shimmered as if the aurora borealis condensed around the dryad. In her wake, she trailed chaos as if it were a bridal veil, but wore harmony in bands of gold on her fingers. She had the potential to weave the future of the forest, and her death would harm the lands in ways Matrix could not unravel. He couldn't kill her. But he wanted to, with every last fiber of his doggy body.

"You want to eat me, do you not, Guardian?" Her smile was wicked. "But you can see it, can you not? You have evolved that far. Impressive. Most mortals are ill-equipped to bear the mantle of responsibility demanded by a wild territory. And yet you are taking to it like a birthright." She cocked her head. "You still have a way to go before you can oppose me. At least, tonight, we can stay friends."

Aithne sashayed over to Robin's still form. As she squatted down, her pearl white dress billowed out, making her look as if she sat in the heart of the moon. Her dark hand extended to caress the new werewolf's head. "Oh you poor thing," she cooed. "You really were completely mortal, were you not?"

Robin whimpered, his limbs twitching, his muzzle opening and closing as drool pooled on the gravel. "Hurts," he croaked, the word raw.

"I know, Little Bird, your body was not made for this." Aithne oozed sympathy like tree sap as she stroked his ruff. She leaned forward. Matrix could see her breath move the fur in Robin's ear as she whispered dark hopes like a lover's promise. "Would you like me to make it better?"

NO! Matrix barked, his entire will going into the word. But the command fragmented around the Fey, her power dismantling his. She never took her eyes off Robin as Matrix leapt, aiming for her neck. But he was caught midair by Tobin's tackle. They slammed into the ground in a tumble of limbs and claws.

Matrix scrambled. With his paws under him, he heaved Tobin off his back. But his brother grabbed his tail, yanking hard. Pain shot up Matrix's spine, numbing his brain for a heartbeat, but it was long enough. Tobin wrestled him flat, pinning him with an arm across his neck, restraining Matrix's front leg in a vise-like grip. Pressed under two hundred and fifty pounds of werewolf, Matrix couldn't move.

"Please," Robin wheezed, "please make the pain stop."

"Tell. Him." Matrix froze at his brother's voice above him. He whined in surprise and tried to see Tobin's face but could only glimpse teeth as Tobin spoke again. "No. Tricks."

"You are no fun," Aithne pouted. Her hand played softly with Robin's whiskers, moving his lip to gaze at his new fangs. "These are quite pretty. Little Bird, the moon holds you now, that is her pain you are feeling. My magic is much kinder, would you prefer it?"

Matrix could see Robin's face as he glanced at Tobin. "Tobin?" His question was all fear and uncertainty, begging for guidance.

"Silence!" Aithne snapped at Tobin, and the werewolf's mouth clamped shut. "He will make this decision on his own."

Matrix struggled again, but despite Tobin's apparent objections, his grip remained true. He looked for Neoma. She had not been idle. Using the distraction, she'd been dragging Martín slowly towards the car. Could he buy her more time?

Robin was whining again, looking back and forth between Tobin and the Fey. Water wept from his yellow eyes. "Please, please make the pain stop."

"Are you sure, Little Bird?" Aithne asked, her finger running up and down his canine.

"Yes! Please, yes!"

Aithne jabbed her finger into the end of his tooth. Blood the color of amber spilled forth, and she ran her finger over his gums, his tongue lapping at the liquid like it was ambrosia. Matrix's mouth watered, even as dread filled him. He had tasted her, uninvited, and that blood had tingled with power, and sang with all the flavors of the forest. He knew part of what Robin experienced as his eye went wide and he began to sit up, the far side of his face crusted with gravel and dirt.

"Mistress," he said, his voice free of pain, his eyes now flashing silver in the firelight. "Thank you."

"Robin, you idiot." Neoma's voice rang true as she swung her arms. A baseball bat whistled through the air, colliding with a firm thunk to the side of Tobin's skull. He crumpled to the ground, and Matrix wiggled out from under him. "You should never thank a Fey."

CHAPTER 37

Waking Up to a Nightmare

Tobin

L ight flashed in his skull with the intensity of a nuclear bomb. There was no pain, no sound, no smell. One moment he was holding the black dog down, fighting a battle within and out. The next…white light.

Something felt different.

Smell. He could smell the dirt, a mix of ashes, oil, and earth. He could even taste it. He was lying on his side, snout in the ground, one lip rolled back and his canine tooth scraping on rock. His head hurt. His ears rang like it was the only sound in the world. Then static. A noise skittering, crumpling, moving as if down a long hallway trying to reach him.

He tried to reach back.

A fire crackled nearby. He could smell the wood charring, flames feasting. And then noise pummeled him as if someone had taken the TV off mute.

"Back the fuck up, we're leaving." The voice was cold and hard, yet it slipped through his brain with a refreshing sweetness.

Laughter bubbled through the air next, stealing the relief from the first voice. "Leave? Where will you go? You think there is a healer that can help you? You would put his life in danger taking him back to the humans. I am his only chance now."

"Somehow I doubt that." That was Neoma's voice again.

He coughed, dirt rough on his parched tongue. Blood, he tasted blood.

"Little Bird, restrain her."

"Robin, no! Matrix!"

Little Bird? He didn't get to puzzle out the thought as a dog fight erupted, the snarling ripping his eyes open. He was on the ground. He was wolf. There was a full moon, Aithne…Neoma. He was Tobin. *Fuck, what did she do to me?*

Tobin struggled to his feet, shaking off the last of his head pain as if it were water. Robin, *Little Bird,* was tearing after Matrix as if he were going to eat him, claws flashing obsidian in the moonlight. But Matrix was fast, and this wasn't his first fight. He dodged around Robin's reaching arms, shouldering aside the new werewolf, and sunk his teeth deep into Robin's ass. Tobin winced and the werewolf made a sound like a strangled cat. The big dog locked his jaws and shook Robin as if he were a squeaky toy. He thrashed the man-wolf against the ground and then tossed him sideways with a rough jerk. Flesh gave and tore free, leaving a bloody hunk the size of a pot roast twitching in Matrix's jaws.

Robin screeched with new pain as he rolled across the unforgiving ground before coming to a ghastly stop. His body shook as he wailed in agony, clawing his belly while he struggled to get his arms under him. Firelight gleamed against white sinew and red meat; a wet outline of bone glistened where his left butt cheek had been. He whimpered and tried to stand, but his missing muscles defeated the effort, and the werewolf crumpled to the ground, sniveling and crawling towards Aithne. The Fey's face was a mask of temper, eyes burning, her small fists clenched at her side.

Matrix held his head low, dropping his jaws open in a doggy grin of triumph. The meat that used to belong to Robin made a sickening splatter as it hit the ground leaving blood dripping from Matrix's muzzle. He barked, and it rolled over them in a thunderous wave, no words, just warnings.

"You think that is a neat trick, do you?" Aithne sneered. "He will heal. Eventually." She cast her gaze at the sniveling werewolf before turning to Tobin. "I see you are finally awake. Go, bite her."

Tobin felt compelled by her words. They forced him to move forward. Yet this prodding now came from a distance. He knew who he was this time; she didn't have him, not completely. But even as he thought to deviate from her instructions, that splinter in his guts twisted and forced him forward. It seemed like it didn't matter if he was aware or not. He would do her bidding through persuasion or pain. Aithne didn't care which.

"Tobin, stop, please." Neoma was bent over Martín. She had bound his shredded arms, stopping the arterial bleeding. Somehow, she had dragged him within range of the Geo, but she couldn't get his limp body into the subcompact. She grunted and swore under her breath as she tugged on the stout man from under his arms. His head lolled from side to side with each heave, her efforts to inch him into the car futile. Tobin could smell the tears of frustration as they leaked down her cheeks, even as her voice remained controlled.

"You don't have to listen to her." Neoma's statement was so matter of fact, she could have been telling him the sky was blue, or that water ran downhill. "She's done something to you, but I don't think it was your choice. You don't strike me as someone who'd hand over your autonomy."

He wasn't, he wouldn't. She knew him.

Matrix hovered between them, his red maw warning enough for his brother. Yet it wasn't a warning that Tobin could accede to. As he fought the compulsion driving him forward, Martín suddenly went rigid, his back arching off the ground in Neoma's grip.

"Martín, no, no no no no no!" Neoma wailed and collapsed to the ground, pillowing Martín's head in her lap.

"Wait," Aithne whispered, and Tobin's guts untwisted, allowing him to breathe again, the stabbing pressure ebbing. He took a small step back, giving Matrix more space. The dog spared him the slightest nod and turned to Martín, grabbing his ankle to drag him away from Neoma.

"Don't you dare, Matrix!" she spat at him, the crisp texture of her words giving Tobin chills as Matrix let go, his ears and tail drooping.

"Nae, don't." Tobin spoke low. "Let him go."

Her head whipped towards him, eyes going wide. He could see the specks of brown dancing in her green irises as if moved by the hot wind from the fire. Was that relief? Something squirmed through him, a helpless hope that he could protect her, that he *wanted* to protect her.

"And give him to her?" Neoma stared daggers at Aithne as Martín spasmed onto his side, curling into a ball. "Not a chance. I trust him. He—won't hurt me." Her hands didn't leave Martín's shuddering body.

Shame blistered through Tobin at her words, the weight of his bonds dragging him into despair.

CHAPTER 38

Consent in the Blood

Neoma

Neoma couldn't keep her attention on Tobin. Martín's body was on fire under her touch. His face twisted in pain, jaw muscles flexing until she thought his teeth would crack. He was fighting, fighting the inevitable change.

"Oh Martín," Neoma chest caught. Somehow she knew he battled on her behalf. She looked down his body, seeing the bandaged forearms soaked with blood still actively dripping while the wounds in his neck continued their steady seeping. How much blood had he lost? How much longer could he resist the magic trying to remake him? And would struggling gain him anything? She glanced up at the moon and the pain in her joints seemed to pulse in time with Martín's ragged breathing as she beseeched the ethereal orb. "If he comes to you, will he still be my friend?" she whispered.

The answer didn't matter.

Neoma gathered her courage and bent over Martín, feeling the cold command inside her freeze out her fear. "Martín, you're safe. I've got you." Frost filled her mouth, tasting like snow and peppermint. "Remember how you wanted to be a part of the woods? Here's your chance. Let go, feel the moon, embrace the wildness inside. It's already a part of you."

A tear dripped onto Martín's skin, and he went still. Neoma moved a strand of dark hair off his brow, stroking his damp head. He'd lost his hat. "It's okay, my friend. I'm here, I won't let go. But you need to."

Martín pulled air into his body like a bellows, and he kept distending with the breath. His head began to shift in her lap, his build stretching under her hands. Where Robin's transformation had been monstrous, Martín's was natural.

"I've got you, keep going," her voice was a compassionate command. Urging, supporting. She encouraged him to accept what was happening. He stayed limp, surrendering to the magic as the wounds in his neck closed and covered with gray fur. She watched his ears broaden and migrate up his head to perch like sails from a mast while his nose morphed into a short muzzle.

"You've got this," she stroked his face, around his ears. The thick fur on his head was like dense gray velvet, tipped in black.

He continued to shift as fabric tore and seams ripped. The makeshift bandages fell away from his shredded arms, revealing whole skin before fur sprouted and engulfed the flesh. Neoma caught a sob in her throat to see him healed, but she didn't let it break her flow of words.

"I'm here. This is what you wanted, accept this gift, this change. Imagine how fast you will run through the trees. Imagine the adventures you will have." She was babbling now, and she knew it, but she couldn't stop. "I won't let you lose yourself. You're my friend. Even in your new fur coat you're still Martín. You will always be Martín. I won't let you forget yourself."

The night went quiet, and Neoma fell silent. Whatever energy had been at work ebbed away. Nothing moved except the fire, its tireless dance animating the stillness surrounding them. They all watched the new werewolf. Even Robin had stopped whimpering.

When Martín moved, Neoma jumped, her hands left his head as he pulled himself up into a half sit. His shoulders were massive, thick muscles ran down his neck, filling out his chest, and rippling down his arms. He turned his wolfish head and looked at Neoma. His eyes were a deep amber, darkening to chestnut. He opened his mouth, running a pink tongue over sharpened teeth.

"I heard you," he growled out in a volume that sounded like canyon echoes, sonorous and expansive. "I hear the moon too." He shifted his gaze upward, eyes rolling closed as he basked in the moonlight. The fur on his throat and chest was pale under the illumination.

"She wants me," Martín whispered. Then opened his eyes and looked at the Fey. "And so does that one." His snout wrinkled, and he showed his new fangs. "But I get to choose." Martín rose to a crouch and moved himself further between Neoma and the Fey in white. His back was a dark wall of muscle as Neoma scrambled to her feet, noticing his tail as she stepped around to his shoulder.

"Oh," Aithne murmured, swishing her magnolia petal dress back and forth. "You are perfection."

Matrix came up on Neoma's other side, and she sank her fingers into his thick ruff.

"I think we're at a stalemate," Neoma said.

"Hardly," the Fey snapped and raised her hands. Roots erupted from the ground, twining around Martín and Matrix, tangling them in writhing brown cords. "Get her!" Aithne screamed at Tobin who sprang forward. Neoma flinched backwards, tripping over a root and fell—into Tobin.

Time seemed to slow while Neoma descended into Tobin's embrace. His arms encircled her, scooping her against his chest, cradling her against one shoulder like a dance partner. His eyes floated above her, yellow ringed in silver light. In the background, her friends fought the roots, snarling and tearing. The noise of plants ripping and snapping filled the air, but it didn't seem to touch Neoma.

Tobin knelt on the earth, still holding her gently.

"Do you want this?" he asked. She could feel the tremble of his body, guessing he battled the Fey's orders. He was fighting to give her a chance, a choice. Her heart fluttered. Did she want this? She looked at his canine features, his strong and furred body. The thoughts of a pain-free existence flashed through her. *No more RA, no more watching what I eat, no more agony when I move.*

But I never wanted to be a monster. She reached up and caressed his cheek, letting her fingers glide down to the whiskers around his muzzle. He was beautiful and strange, fully him now more than ever, but did she want to join him? Did she want to be a werewolf?

"No," Neoma said without regret. She could feel it now, something deep in her hummed, but it wasn't the need to become what he was. No, it was something more. Something that had always been hers. Her bones ached, joints complaining, her body flaring with pain as something deep struggled to be realized.

Tobin closed his eyes. "I'm not sure how to stop this." His body shook violently, but he didn't let her fall.

"Fight her, Tobin. Release me," she spoke softly while she caressed his furry cheek, ignoring the pain that screamed at her for moving, for even breathing. She didn't care, she needed to reach Tobin if she could. "Please, Tobin."

Tobin slid her slowly to the ground, her hand falling down his face to pause on his chest as if physically holding him back. He trembled and wheezed, starting to double over. She tried to scoot away from him, but he captured her arm in his grip, falling to the earth and curling in on himself, shaking harder.

"Tobin, let me go." Her breath crystallized in the warm night air as she commanded him. She willed cold power into him, willing him to be free, to free her. The pain in her joints intensified.

"I...can't," he panted, looking stricken.

Neoma wasn't sure what to do. His eyes were locked on hers, the yellow covered with a patina of iridescent silver. But she could see Tobin looking out at her, pleading somehow, still aware despite his obvious fight for control. But what did he want? What could she do?

"Neoma, forgive me." Tobin drove a claw into her palm, so sharp the pain didn't register. Blood puddled in her hand as she watched in shock, then he tipped it, allowing it to fall onto his tongue.

"What are you doing?!" Aithne screeched from behind them.

"It's okay, Nae," he slurred up at her. "Blood is usually the answer."

• ◦ ◉ ◦ •

MATRIX JOLTED AS IF STRUCK, HIS HEAD WHIPPING AROUND TO where Neoma lay cradled in Tobin's arms. She bled. Panic and power filled him as a root twined around his muzzle. He thrashed violently, but thorns extended like cat's claws, digging into his flesh. He froze, and the thorns backed off. To his right he could see Martín coming to the same inescapable conclusion. They could not prevail. The new werewolf was flat on his belly, blood oozing from multiple points where thorns the size of meat hooks had slipped beneath his skin. Martín's eyes glowed with rage, thin roots studded with prickles encircling his muzzle.

Matrix was no better. Hobbled and gagged, the two of them looked like hogs prepared for the spit. All they needed was barbeque sauce. He simmered in his helpless frustration, casting around for some means of escape.

Aithne dashed past his nose. Her bare foot so tantalizingly close Matrix could taste her in the air, drool pooling on his tongue. But he was powerless to grab her. She paused for a beat, looking down at Martín as he continued to thrash, a frustrated pinch to her features. "You are powerful, but a slow learner," she spat. "Stay put, I will return to make you mine." She extended her hand and more roots erupted. She clenched her fist, and they heaped atop Martín, winding over him until he seemed to be buried under a woodpile, only his face peeking out.

Aithne swayed on her feet for a moment, but Robin was right there, his body a dark smudge against her white dress. "Thank you, my pet," she cooed, regaining her balance to continue towards Tobin and Neoma.

Robin limped in Aithne's wake, partially dragging his damaged leg as he crept by on all fours. Matrix glared at the man-wolf, his bones vibrating from Martín's growl now resonating through the very ground. The light brown man-wolf shied away from Martín and avoided Matrix's outraged stare. Instead, he snapped and snarled as he passed well out of range, following his mistress.

"Time to give her to me," Aithne demanded.

CHAPTER 39

· ◦ ● ◦ ·

Atonement

Tobin

T obin heard the Fey's words. They moved through him searching for the binding that would twist and rip at his guts if he did not comply. But her words were not specific enough, and so he was able to release Neoma from his grip under the guise of "giving her" to the Fey. An act, that a moment before, should have been beyond him.

Fury bloomed in his chest as he shuffled back on his knees. Neoma held her injured hand while pain and confusion warred over her features. But he could see the spark of her anger. He could smell it like sulfur on the end of a matchstick right as friction is applied. Carefully, he licked her blood off his claw. The taste of it froze more of the Fey's power. Immobilizing the invasive flora that twisted through his system. Neoma's eyes narrowed, thinking, and she clutched her injury closer.

A.B. Herron

"What did you hope to accomplish?" Aithne hissed, grabbing Tobin's scruff and jerking his neck back with surprising strength. Her hand was hot as a branding iron, and Tobin could not help the wince at her touch. She held his head still, trying to peer into his eyes. "Did you think a human's blood could free you from me? You and I are bound, through blood, sap, and this land. It is my master, and I am yours. Now stop all this foolishness. We are needed. Finish your task and bite her, or I will have him do it." She indicated Robin, who panted at her side, the ever-loyal hound. Tobin sneered, his lips peeling back to show all his front teeth.

"You will not touch her," he snarled at Robin despite being restrained by the Fey.

Robin slid his eyes up to Tobin and then away, gaze finding Neoma with a feral glow. "I shall do as my mistress commands. You are not in charge anymore, Tobin. Get used to it."

Tobin went to lunge, but Aithne shook him, heat searing his skin. "Leave my bird alone." Her words made him go limp in her grasp as he fumbled to pull air into his lungs through the weight of her command. But it did not twist his guts this time, and other than the power flooding him through her touch, his mind was more his own.

"Good boy," she loosened her grip while pushing him down until he was on his hands and knees. He peered up at Neoma, begging her to run, knowing there was no escape. He wanted to weep at his helplessness. He had not meant for her to be here. It was just supposed to be Robin. Only Robin. Now the young man seemed to be relishing his new role as the Fey's lackey.

Please, he silently begged Neoma. *Please forgive me. I didn't intend for you to be here.* Her look was hard as she met his eyes, her lips a firm line. He could see the sweat trickling down her skin like tears. He could smell pain coming off her in waves as she shuddered where she stood. He was sure that her hand hurt, but it wasn't that grievous of an injury. Was it? He perked his ears forward in concern, but his attention fractured as Aithne started to smooth her hands over him, fondling him like a pet.

"You are mine, and somehow you keep forgetting this, man-wolf." Tendrils of her power rooted into him, spreading through his skin.

"Don't touch me," he snarled, trying to shake her off, but he couldn't move. Terror lanced through him. Trapped, he was trapped!

"You will do as I say, or I will do as I wish with you while she watches. Now obey me." Her hands slid over his ribs, smoothing down his sides toward his hips. A mindless panic grew inside Tobin as she played around the elastic of his boxer briefs and chuckling deep in her throat. "This can all stop, man-wolf. All you need to do is bite her." Aithne's tone dipped lower, like her fingers around his waist.

"Stop." Neoma's voice was a clear bell as she gained her feet.

Aithne snapped her attention back up. "If you submit yourself to his bite, all this can end."

"No, I won't do it. She said no," Tobin ground out around his revulsion. He would not force her. He wanted to be better than this. He had told Neoma he was better than this. His skin crawled in tandem with the touch moving back and forth over his hips as magic attempted to burrow deeper. Yet a wall of cold inside him kept the power from penetrating, kept him within his own body.

"I'll do it, mistress," Robin said, eagerness fresh like new leaves.

"Like hell you will," Neoma spat. Tobin watched in disbelief as Neoma took two confident steps towards the injured man-wolf, and Robin scuttered backwards to hide behind Aithne's skirts.

"That's what I thought," Neoma muttered. But now she was closer to them, too close. "Let him go, Fey," Neoma demanded. She was shaking now, hunched over, as if she were folding in on herself. The pungent scent of suffering clung to everything. Tobin was surprised Aithne couldn't smell it. But the pain didn't show on Neoma's face. The confusion that had been there was replaced with steely determination, the green in her eyes shining brightly.

"You want me to consider this? Get your hands the fuck off him."

"As you wish." Aithne withdrew, and Tobin's panic was replaced with a new fear.

CHAPTER 40

A Flurry of Blue Fur and Frost

Neoma

*T*hey considered each other in silence, the woman and the werewolf. Neoma thought to herself. *Man I wish I could write this story and not live it.* But she had no pen, paper, or time. What was she going to do? How did she save her friends and herself? And could anyone be saved?

Agony and despair pushed her to the ground, her knees buckling. *What is happening to me?* She reached for that cold place inside, that icy strength that froze her fear and kept her fighting.

"Interesting," the Fey mused, walking a tight circle around them. Tobin was back on his hands and knees, so close to Neoma she could count his whiskers in the moonlight. "You are not fully mortal either. Man-wolf, you chose well. Or were simply lucky."

"What do you mean?" Neoma wheezed, light flickering at the edges of her vision, every fiber of her body seemed to have caught flame.

"Can you not feel it? Something inside you laboring to be free? It has been dormant your whole life. Caged by your human immunity. Bound into silence but still fighting. Now you know more than what you have been bred to believe. You can finally see behind the lies. Acknowledge what your body has been trying to tell you all this time. Your magic wants out." Her grin was feral, gleeful as she rubbed her hands together. "So what will it be, human? A continued life of suffering, or are you ready to embrace your heritage?"

"My what?"

"You heard me. Now choose."

Is she serious? Neoma thought about the last few months. The conversations with her mother, her pull towards nature, even her choice in reading material. Her whole life she'd pursued something that was lacking, and only when dancing had it seemed within reach. Yet even then, it hadn't been enough. Hadn't filled that hollow void inside her. *But I'm not a monster. I've never felt like a monster. And I refuse to let her make me one.*

Neoma glanced at the full moon. Glanced at her friends restrained under thorns, Robin cowering behind the strange Fey, and at last Tobin. His yellow eyes were no longer silver. He pushed at the Fey's compulsion, to his own detriment. He was absorbing this suffering to let her make her own decision.

Giving her what her disease never had. A choice in her future, her destiny. *Monsters don't give people choices.* Something clicked inside her.

"Let's do this," Neoma whispered, offering up her arm. Tobin's breathing stirred the small hairs as he panted in clear panic. He had dog breath. Neoma fixated on that silly detail while red pain filled every joint and threatened to swamp her consciousness, but she refused to succumb. *I will not abandon my friends to fainting, come on body, we are in this together this time. If there is really magic within my bones, I'm going to make her regret this transformation.*

"Tobin, please. We're backed into a corner here. She will keep hurting all of you until someone cracks. I can't live with that. If there's magic inside me, I want it. It can be a gift if I let it. If she forces this, it will be a curse."

"Why do you have to be so practical all the time?" Tobin asked, his body trembling with his own pain.

"Because it annoys people." She gave him the tiniest smile.

"But Nae," he started to object, she shushed him.

"Tobin, please. I'm so tired of hurting." A tear escaped with the truth, and he needed to hear it, or he would keep resisting. She wasn't willing to watch him suffer further. Besides, her body flared like a dying star, every joint inflamed and getting worse by the moment. Was magic why her disease had suddenly decided to go nuclear? If she didn't allow this bite, would this be life moving forward? *I won't live like this.* She thought, her resolve strengthening. Two birds, one bite, and maybe she could smash this Fey with a stone before she got enslaved. Besides, fuzzy had to be better than agony. Anything was better than agony.

The thought made her vision swim, and she steeled herself for more pain. Black motes of not-light seemed to pull towards her. Like dandelion fluff made of the night itself, these spots in her vision detached from the very world and began to waft in her direction. She blinked but they didn't clear.

Tobin's teeth sank into her arm. She saw them enter but the pain didn't register. It was too small compared to what roiled in her joints. *I can do this. I will do this. I want this…gift.* Neoma reached for the ice inside her, pulling it forward, focusing all her will on what she wanted. *I'm going to rip this Fey apart like I'm deadheading daisies.* She thought as cold began spreading, a flash flood of arctic chill through every aspect of her inflamed flesh, quenching the pain and opening her further.

The black motes in her vision rushed faster, and she welcomed them, each one a soothing touch, soft as a snowflake. She closed her eyes with a sigh and slumped back on her heels as Tobin released her, whining deep in his throat as she went blessedly numb.

"It's okay," she thought she'd whispered while fabric tore. Only sound registered as her body awareness diminished. But the sounds, the sensations rapidly engulfing her, were so much *more*. Neoma felt the night awaken. Smell swamped her brain, giving the auditory world textures. Emotions suddenly had a language of odor that she was abruptly wired to understand. Neoma was lost to the new sensations inundating her, too in awe of the abundance of fantastical information to do much more than savor the experience.

Anger and disbelief had a scent! They wafted from the Fey tangled with the odor of forest and fire. Robin was a weak, oily, wolfish musk with bitter undertones that wove through the Fey's dominant fragrance, the two married together. Tobin, he smelled like…she didn't know and took another huge lungful of air trying to separate out the feelings that filled up the aroma. She never knew there was so much information missing before. Never guessed that smells and feelings and identity could be one thing made of so many. She reached for more information, opening her eyes. The whole forest around them was now alive, sentient, as if at any moment it would breathe and speak to her in a voice that would sound like home.

"NO!" Aithne shrieked.

Neoma jumped and blinked. The black motes were gone. Had she changed? She looked down and could feel that she was seated, but the light chill of the summer air was muffled. And her palms were on the ground, but again there was this insulating feeling. And her arms were…blueish?

"Gggurrff?" she asked, searching for Tobin. A long nose followed in her visual field, distracting her further. She tried again to make words, a whuffling cry spilling forth. *What the fuck? Why can't I speak?* Panic started to make her tremble.

The guys could all speak! She picked up her hands and looked. They were paws, really huge, five-digited paws with one-inch-long black claws. These were not hands, not even close.

Her eyes found Tobin. He was now shorter than her, both of them still sitting on the ground. His mouth was hanging open, the look of shock on his wolfish face comical. Neoma snorted, then jumped at the deep sound that came out.

"Neoma?" Tobin asked. She nodded her head, the movement ungainly. "Nae, you...you're a bear."

A thrill went through her. *I'm not a werewolf! How? Why?* But those answers could come later. Right now, her body was buzzing with strength, the pain had all been washed away by those black not-lights. And the Fey stood off to the side, losing her shit.

Excellent.

Neoma lumbered to her feet and charged.

• • ◆ • •

MATRIX WANTED TO LAUGH. HE WANTED TO HOWL IN DELIGHT at the sight of Neoma in blue-black and gray fur. That potential he'd seen in her, it had boiled to the surface and erupted in wildness. His brother's bite had opened the last lock that kept it contained. Whatever magic Tobin carried that compelled a person to change, it didn't seem to have firm rules. It was mutable, chaos with some small direction. And it had been the key to something Neoma already had buried inside.

Neoma charged towards the Fey, her silver-colored bulk shining like mist in the moonlight.

"Wait!" Aithne screamed, holding out her hand. "We can talk about this." Robin stuck to her side as the two moved backwards from the stampeding bear. Neoma slowed, opened her mouth and bellowed. She swung one massive paw at the ground, gouging up dirt and rock to shower the pair in grime.

Aithne shrieked at the onslaught, covering her face. Dropping her arms, she snarled back, her eyes blazing and took a step towards Martín and Matrix, twisting her hand in the air. Matrix gasped as the roots tightened around them further, digging in their thorns. Neoma rumbled at Matrix's distress while barbs wiggled deeper into his soft nose. Robin darted forward growling, but Neoma went up on her hind legs. She towered at almost seven feet and swatted at the man-wolf, clipping his shoulder and sending him tumbling.

Dropping to all fours, she rushed Matrix, swiping at his muzzle. Her aim was true as she shredded the plants encircling his nose, lacerating him in the process. He didn't care as he pulled in a huge breath of air and barked!

ENOUGH!

With a tremendous shudder, the roots and vines rustled and convulsed, slithering away like spooked snakes until even the holes in the ground had filled in. They were free. Matrix heaved himself up and shook, leaves, dirt, and blood flying. Martín mirrored him, the wounds in his gray coat slowly closing.

Aithne had dropped to her knees. The power she had expended to keep them trapped seemed to have drained her. Yet her eyes still burned as she watched the boys move towards Neoma, flanking her as Tobin joined them.

Aithne pointed at Tobin. "He is mine. You cannot have him. Tobin, come."

Tobin twitched but didn't lift a foot. Matrix concentrated and saw the shimmer of a new soul bond stretching from his brother towards Neoma. It was as brittle as frost on a spider's web. Yet where the new connection overlapped the Fey's green tether, blackness spread, coldness killing the uninvited bond. He leaned towards the blackening thing and severed it with one snap. The magic tasted like rotting vegetation, and it parted with ease, leaving a nasty film on his tongue. As soon as it dissolved, the shimmering bond between Neoma and Tobin flashed an arctic blue and crystallized between them. They both jumped and looked at each other, confusion plain on their animal faces.

"No," Aithne moaned. "No, you do not even know what it is you are doing! This is not your pack. It is mine!" Her anger was withering to despair, only to bloom again with vehemence. "Do you really think you can give this land what it demands? What it needs to survive? You are binding yourself to a purpose that is beyond your ken."

The Fey seemed to shrink into herself. Her hands fluttered around her petal dress, the white flowers blooming on her skin were wilting. Matrix could see a petal had already fallen from one, frozen in its tumble down her flesh. Her eyes rose, focusing on Martín and her hand raised to point. "Give him to me. He has yet to be claimed. He still serves the moon and that is a chain I can snap."

Neoma shook her huge head, eyes narrowing and huffed a warning. She turned and put her nose on Martín's furry thigh, a question in her glossy eyes.

Martín gave a guttural bark. "You think I'd choose her? I trust you Nae, go ahead and claim me." The gray werewolf flinched slightly as her teeth sank in, barely stopping himself from stepping away, but suddenly, his amber eyes went wide, and he nodded.

"I accept," he growled low, and it meandered across the clearing, silencing the crickets. "I will join this pack." Matrix saw another ice blue soul-bond form between the bear and the werewolf, but it tied to each like embracing a friend, not binding a supplicant.

Neoma let go and turned to Matrix. Blood still flowed freely from the gashes in his nose where her claws had nicked him. She held her head to the side in question, and he stepped forward. She licked his nose and chilled magic rushed through him, soothing the wounds while asking permission. Did he want to accept?

Matrix explored the offered connection, allowing it to twine with the bond he had with the forest. They melded perfectly.

A huge sigh escaped him as he accepted the bond, bowing his head to push into Neoma's fuzzy forehead. They stood like this, breathing in each other's breath, a silent promise floating out between them to the land. They would accept this mantle together, learn together, be its caretakers.

Words were hard, so Matrix stepped away and nodded his head and wagged his tail, joy flooding between them. They could feel the emotions floating down the pack ties, a communication beyond words.

Neoma's eyes met Matrix's and flicked to the Fey, the question clear. What to do indeed. Matrix considered, seeing the swirl of the world and how Aithne was still a powerful force for both harmony and chaos. They needed her, and the forest needed her, but for what he didn't know.

Emotions churned with the abundance of things he could not say, could not understand enough to form words for. He released his vision, stepping away from Neoma, and walked slowly to the Fey until they were eye level. Robin paced a circle around them, a threatening shadow with teeth. Matrix ignored him.

Her pink gaze flickered with internal flame. "This is not over, Guardian."

He bowed his head to her. *Leave, peace.* He barked.

"For now, if I must." Dirt smeared her petal dress as she tried to wipe it away, her hand trembling. "Have you ever seen a root fire?"

The question was so random, Matrix snorted, scrunching his eyebrows together, confusion plain.

She continued, "They are rare. When fire penetrates the ground, burrowing into the very roots of the forest, they can burn for months undetected in the loam. They torture the trees, eating them from below and within, with very little sign that they are there. It is agony to die by internal fire. There is not much oxygen, so the flames are banked, leisurely nibbling, drawing out the destruction. Your heartwood is devoured in lazy embers while the rest of your flesh tries to flee. A tree would do anything to make it stop."

He tilted his head, her meaning beyond him.

"Think on this, and balance, and what we all need to walk that line. To be what we are meant to be. For containment breeds resentment and chaos, and that poisons the land as sure as any human plundering." She looked sad and wild as she nodded to him, then rose and walked back towards the trees until her hand rested firmly on the bark of a huge Douglas fir. She paused and looked back. "Little Bird, come to me." Her hand extended. A monarch awaiting the kiss of fidelity.

They all watched Robin make his way towards her. His limp was better as his flesh filled in the missing muscle. He hesitated, looking back at them. Neoma made a sad cry in her throat, and Martín held out a clawed hand.

"Robin, you don't have to go with her." Again, the deep baritone rumbled, almost unintelligible with its depth. "You can stay with us."

Robin looked back and forth, one claw raised, trembling.

"You are mine, Little Bird. My wooden wolf. But if you wish to be weak," she shrugged, speaking as if in dismissal, uncaring at what he would decide. "Go to them and their bastard pack of misfits."

She turned to go, and Robin leapt to follow her. He scrambled across the duff with a whine in his throat until he gained her feet. Her smile of victory flashed in the darkness as she caressed his head. "Good boy," she cooed before grasping his scruff and melting them both into the tree trunk with a sigh.

CHAPTER 41

Fighting Forgiveness

Tobin

"What do we do with Robin's car?" Martín asked, scratching his new fur coat. The night had come back to life around them. Moonlight stretched shadows into ponderous shapes now that the fire had gone out.

"We leave it," Tobin said. He carefully inserted his claws into the handle on his truck, popping the door open. All his clothes and keys were right where he'd left them.

"What do we do with ourselves?" Tobin didn't have an easy answer to that question.

"I'm not sure." Tobin looked around to Neoma. She sat with Matrix leaning up against her, the two watching the night, their noses twitching. She looked like a large, mottled rock, and the dog her shadow. He wondered how she was doing with this new body she found herself in, but he was hesitant to approach her. Instead, he pulled packages of hot dogs from the truck and tossed one to Martín who caught it and deftly dissected the meat from the plastic.

"Will we turn back when the moon sets?" Martín asked. The volume of his question rattled Tobin's bones so that he pinned his ears. "Sorry," Martín said, noting his expression, "this is the only volume I seem to have." The bulky werewolf shrugged and looked down at his paw-like hands before shoving a hot dog in his mouth. "Damn, these are good."

"I'm not sure we're linked to the moon," Tobin said, his mind whirling. He looked up at the ghostly orb floating towards the west and didn't feel that ethereal pull that he once had. The addiction had been replaced by a deep sense of joy. He could get used to this change.

He slowly made his way over and sat next to Matrix, offering him a hot dog. His brother swallowed it down in one bite. Neoma watched him, her ears forward, a little drool starting to slip from her jowls.

Tobin offered the processed meat. Neoma took the frank gently with her lips before sitting back to hold it with both paws. A delicate bite followed. Tobin chuckled at her as her eyes sprang wide and the rest of the meat disappeared in one chomp. She reached her paws forward for another. Tobin complied, wishing she could speak, and somehow grateful she couldn't.

"What do you mean you don't think we're linked to the moon?" Martín asked, taking a seat next to Neoma. She carefully accepted some of his food before tipping her huge head onto his shoulder with a sigh. Martín reached up and scratched her ears with his claws. She rumbled contentedly and returned to watching the moon. Tobin could feel satisfaction radiating down their bond—it was weird.

"Can't you feel it? The difference, I mean. The moon, it pulled like a magnet before, like a hunger that I couldn't sate. When I shifted, I was never able to think straight. I was like an addict with a fix, and Matrix had to keep on top of me so I wouldn't do something impulsive. But now? Now I feel the pull, the attraction, but I'm..." Tobin searched for the right word.

"Grounded?" Martín supplied. "To her." He turned his wolfish head into Neoma's, and they rubbed foreheads and grumbled at each other. Matrix wagged his tail and panted at all of them with hot dog breath.

"Yes," Tobin said. He was pulled to touch the bear, rub his fur on her like Martín was doing. Yet he held back, unsure, his ears flattening. "Aithne apparently broke my bond to the moon and tied me to her. Which is why I was able to shift the other night. But now I feel a bond to Neoma, and to you, and Matrix. I'm guessing this is what a pack bond is? And because of that, I don't think the moon can hold us in these forms."

Martín raised his amber eyes to Tobin. "You think I could change back now?" Neoma swiveled her head, her dark eyes bright with interest. She gave a curious grunt, looked at her paws and back up.

A.B. Herron

"I think you could, maybe. I don't know, this is new to me. But Nae, bears don't seem to be limited by the moon. I think that's just a wolf thing. I'm not sure, I don't know a lot about bear shifters, I…I'm sorry." Tobin hung his head. He'd never felt so out of control before. He was used to having the answers, for being responsible for himself and Matrix. This feeling of having more people to care for was as foreign as flying, and twice as terrifying.

"How do you change back?" Martín's question held tension. "I mean, this is pretty awesome, and I'd like to explore it more, but I get the feeling we would all feel a little better if we were in skin right now. Maybe with some brownies and a good hamburger."

Neoma nodded vigorously.

Tobin's spirits sunk further. He'd never tried to change back. He usually went to sleep at the end of the night and woke up human. He looked away from them, the thought of disappointing them a tender feeling in his chest. *What's wrong with me?*

"I've never changed back on my own," he mumbled, not meeting their gazes. "And I've never wanted to. I'm usually so drunk on being a wolf that I can't think about anything else except being lost in the moment. This is the most…human I've ever been during a shift." He looked around, feeling the night pull at him, the desire to run and hunt and howl itched under his fur. But he also wanted to be here, with them, and he didn't want to run alone.

Neoma nimbly gained her paws, her movements effortless despite her size. He wondered what she'd looked like when she danced. Had she held the same wild grace she did now? Her strange colored fur flashed blue in the moonlight, like a Burmese cat. Glacier bear, that was the color. The memory of a random nature documentary popped into his mind's eye. Black bears had several different color types, and this was the rarest, the blue bear.

You're beautiful, he thought, but his tongue froze in his mouth, guilt rising again. She had asked him to bite her, but only after they'd all been backed into a trap with no escape. What if she hated being a bear? Was that why they both wanted to get out of their fur so fast? Were they angry with what they had become?

A strange panic rose in Tobin's chest. He'd failed them. These people who had trusted him, that he had befriended with selfish intent, and now their lives would never be the same and it was all. His. Fault. His eyes stung with the acid of his betrayal, his throat tightening as he tried to swallow. He wanted to run, to flee, to put distance between them and his mistakes.

A huge paw snagged his torso, furry limbs encircling him, pulling him tightly backwards and holding him in place against a warm body. Sympathetic crooning rumbled up from Neoma's chest as she sat him further back into her nest of blue fur.

"Breathe, cabrón," Martín whispered, his clawed hands holding Tobin's lower legs. "We've got you, you're okay." His deep words held him as tightly as his grip. He was surrounded, even Matrix was pushing against Tobin's thigh, everyone touching him, holding him, keeping him here. Didn't they understand? He was a danger to them, look what he'd already done!

His panic swelled, and he tried to struggle, but the bear just squeezed harder, muttering unintelligibly in his ears, snorting, and growling. He could feel her concern harden to irritation in the background of his mind. Water ran from his eyes as he feebly tried again to tear himself away, his head tipping back, keening his distress and guilt to the moon in great sobs.

His first howl as a werewolf, and it was pathetic. He wilted.

Cold blackness erupted around them, a cloud of charcoal snowflakes that melted as soon as his eyes brought them into focus. The grip on his body eased, the fuzzy arms gone, replaced by slender human limbs that barely reached around him. He stopped struggling lest he hurt her.

"Enough of this shit!" Neoma spat into the fur on his shoulder, her chin stretching to reach high enough to breathe. "Tobin, we chose this! Both of us. And we choose you. Get over yourself. Yes, you screwed up! But you fought that bitch every step of the way. You fought for us. And we don't always win when we fight, but it means something that we give it all we've got. Sure, that Fey backed us all into corners we wouldn't have wandered into without your help. But that's not the point now. Now is all we have, and in the end, I don't think we're unhappy with the results. Martín?" she asked the hulking werewolf.

His smile was all teeth. "Can't say I'm disappointed."

Tobin could feel Neoma narrow her eyes at the other man. Martín shrugged. "This is new to me, give me time."

"Fair enough. Look, Tobin, my point is we have to make peace with the situation we're faced with. We're a pack. We're bound to each other, and I don't know how you feel about that, but I won't give this up. You, Martín, Matrix, you're all worth fighting for. So don't you dare leave us. Don't you dare leave me. I'm not sure how to be this, this—well whatever I am now. Anyway, we're going to need your help to have a fighting chance against that crazy tree woman. Do you hear me? You are needed. You are wanted. And you are forgiven." Dampness soaked his furry shoulder as she stopped speaking, breathing hard.

Neoma let go of her embrace, placing her hands gently on the backs of his shoulders. "I'm not good at leaning on people either," she whispered. "We can learn how to do this together."

Her body folded over his as he crumpled forward. One of Martín's clawed hands reached out, tenderly rested on the back of Tobin's furry neck, while Matrix snuggled closer. Tobin clutched his knees, hiding his face in his arms. His sobs were quieter now, but coming from a new place as his pack held him. A place of hope.

CHAPTER 42

⋅ ◦ ● ◦ ⋅

Scars of Change

Neoma

Tobin's truck pulled into her driveway, and he cut the engine. They were a mess. All covered with dirt, dried blood, and smelling like hot dogs. The last part surprised Neoma. Actually, if she focused, she could smell the blood, and who the blood belonged to. *Nope!* She pulled that thought back, *I can't think about that, or my head might pop.* Yet a smile flirted with her lips. She was a little kid who'd just discovered the impossible existed and didn't want to let it go. *There is real magic. Real fricking, body altering, magic.*

Someone moved beside her, and she jumped. She'd been staring out the windshield at the setting moon. When she glanced at Tobin, he was doing the same thing, hands still on the steering wheel. Matrix and Martín had ridden in the truck bed, and the dog had elected to stay back there after they'd dropped Martín home. Now the truck cab filled with the sound of crickets and anticipation.

Neoma reached out, placing one finger on Tobin's scarred forearm. She traced the white flesh, a shooting star burned into his being.

"Is this the bite that changed you?"

He simply nodded.

"Did you want it?" she asked, her finger tracing another smooth mark.

"More than you can imagine. I…" he ran out of words. She waited. There was a distinct echo of emotion in the new bond, but it wasn't as clear now that they weren't in fur. That was good, she didn't want to know everything he was feeling at every moment. *And I sure as hell don't want him to be able to feel everything going on in me second to second. That would drive anyone nuts.*

"I started out trying to save my brother. And at some point, all I could see was what I would get out of it. And the things I did to make this happen." He gestured at himself. "It's not a happy story of underdogs fighting the good fight." He glanced at her and away. "I'm no hero Nae, you need to know that."

Her finger made another pass across a scar. No, it was a wish. These marks were a wish that had branded him, burned him with their terrible price for being granted. She knew the cost of selfish wishes. The hair along his forearm rose as her finger continued to explore the narrative on his skin.

"Why did you want this?" She took off her seatbelt and pulled one leg up under her so she was facing him on the bench seat. Vinyl stretched between them, an unimpeded expanse.

Tobin bridged it, removing his hand from the wheel and into her grip. She continued following his scars.

With a long breath, Tobin let himself sink backwards into the seat, surrendering to her exploration.

"Somewhere in the midst of my childhood, while losing everyone I loved, one by one, I decided that being a werewolf would solve my problems." He bit his lip, his body staying loose. "The idea of pack, wolves, and family is lodged in my head. That being stronger and faster would solve things. That being powerful and hard to kill would solve things. And building a pack would mean I wouldn't be lonely anymore."

He cracked open an eye and watched her. Neoma kept her face neutral, her fingers moving over the firm ridges in his flesh.

"I know," he whispered. "It's selfish, childish. A wish made in the dark without thoughts to consequences. Another way to avoid doing the real work of building relationships or processing grief."

"You've given this some hard thought."

"You have no idea," amusement flickered across his features. "Max called me out for being selfish. And you." He opened his eyes and rolled his body sideways so he was looking at her, his forearm still in her grip. His other hand went up to make a pillow under his cheek as he gazed at her with hazel intensity. "You became real to me, Nae. And that changed everything. See, I have this terrible way of looking at people as separate from myself. Like another species, beneath me. When

I changed, that personality trait didn't improve. I became more separate, and all I could see were my goals. I was willfully ignorant of how those goals would alter others' lives."

"Self-centered. Got it."

"I think that's an understatement."

"Probably, but do you need me to mentally flog you further? Seems like you've done a pretty good job so far." She ran her nails down his arm and his breath caught. "Keep talking Tobin."

He blinked but continued. "I wanted the power to keep from being out of control. I never wanted someone to be able to oppose me again, to make me feel small or weak. I wanted friends who wouldn't be fragile, who couldn't be taken from me because of a car accident or a bullet." Dampness filled his gaze.

"Did becoming a werewolf fix any of that?"

He barked a broken laugh. "No. Not even close. Suddenly, I was more alone in a way I'd never expected. But I kept telling myself I was going to fix it. A pack would fix it. Power would fix it. So fucking stupid."

"Yet now you have a pack."

"No, Neoma, you have a pack. I am simply part of it." His eyes shown, yellow flooding them for a blink. Now her breath caught.

"Can you handle this, Tobin? Not being top dog?" She squinted at him, his answer might break this tenuous new bond.

"For you, I will endure anything." His hand caught hers, a light grip, not a cage. It was a promise of connection.

"Why? Why change for me? That never seems to go well for people. You need to change because you want to. Otherwise, you put yourself in the position of the martyr, the victim. I refuse to be the cross you hang yourself on."

He gave a weak laugh. "Can't I be your apostle, your devotee?"

"This isn't funny, Tobin. We just made this impossible link with the four of us. I don't want this pack to go to shit because someone suddenly remembers he needs to be top bitch." She glared at him, but he was giving her this dopey little smile. An expression she'd never seen on his face. With the leaves still stuck in his hair, he was borderline adorable. *When did Tobin become fucking adorable?* Neoma thought, resisting swooning as they held hands.

"Nae, you are the catalyst to my change, not the evolution itself." His eyes went distant for a second. "Look, because of you, I finally see someone outside of myself. I'm caring about what could happen to you. To Martín. And if I'm being brutally honest, I've always looked to my brother as someone to save me. Which left me not knowing how to help him, how to love him back when he needed it. I feel that shift now." He sat up, inching a little closer to her until their knees were touching, and he put one hand over his chest. "And this new feeling is fucking terrifying because I know I'm going to blunder. The cost of damaging these bonds is high. I've never liked putting myself at risk when I can't calculate the outcome."

"That's what I'm asking, Tobin. Why would you choose to risk yourself now? And why for me?"

"Because I trust you, Neoma." His words rippled heat along her skin, his expression so raw it chafed at her heart. "You are worth this risk. Even if I lose this bond between us, having experienced it has made me better." His gaze dropped to their clasped fingers, he wanted something.

Naoma raised her unbound hand to his face, stroking his cheek. Tobin nuzzled into her palm, scenting her, marking her. When his eyes cracked open again, there was yellow seeping into the hazel. He was panting. "I'm going to make mistakes, Nae. Probably terrible, ignorant, stupid mistakes. Heck, I've never fully understood being human. And now this? Becoming a friend? A packmate?"

"Maybe something more?" she whispered. "When you're ready." He squeezed her hand, and she could feel the need within him creeping down their link, this amorphous desire, yet it was laced with uncertainty. "Tobin, I don't have a stellar track record with relationships either. Let's take this slow. There are no expectations on my part. Hell, I just turned into a bear. I'd like to get a handle on that before, I don't know...tackling dating?"

He laughed, a full body release of emotions that brought her along for the ride. They dissolved into giggles until they were leaning against each other, wiping tears from their eyes and trying to catch their breaths.

"Okay," Tobin chuckled. "Supernatural stuff first, relationship stuff later?"

"That seems like the right order. But maybe I'm being a wimp and going after the easier problems first?"

They both snorted a laugh, and Neoma realized she was practically lying in his arms. Suddenly uncomfortable, she sat up. The space between them was tender. "I should go."

Tobin didn't move.

"Tobin?"

"Are we going to be okay, Nae? You and I?"

"I don't know, but I know I'm willing to explore this with you, as far as you're willing to go. Is that enough?" She held out her hand, but he shook his head.

"Nae, can I–can I just try holding you?"

Surprised, she nodded. "Sit back, Tobin," she commanded. He immediately did as she asked. It took some wiggling, but she finally turned in the seat, letting her back come to rest against his chest and shoulder. He carefully placed his arms around her, burying his nose in her hair. The inhale made her rise, and as he breathed out her scent, Tobin's body fully relaxed behind her, their connection thrumming with a new emotion. Peace.

For now, this was more than enough. Neoma let herself melt into the arms of her packmate, and together they watched the sun paint the sky the golden shade of a wolf's gaze.

CHAPTER 43

Unveiling Art and Hearts

Neoma & Tobin

Neoma checked her phone again, there were no new messages in the last thirty seconds, but she couldn't help herself. Meg's ability to be cryptic had reached new levels, it was as if she worked for the government on some classified project. The text exchange from three weeks ago had left Neoma feeling uneasy.

Meg: *What did you see in the woods? Did you believe it? Are you okay? We need to talk. In person.*

Nae: *Something big has happened. Something you won't believe. Call me, please, I need to talk to you.*

Meg: *I can't. It's too important, it needs to be in person. I'll figure out a way to come home. Soon.*

And that was the end of it. Neoma had been listening to crickets ever since. If Megan had been the only friend introducing stress into her life, Neoma wouldn't have been as annoyed. Yet there were others.

Robin was another issue. Or to be more accurate, the lack of Robin was causing anxiety. The boy had been missing for a few weeks now, and the police had gotten involved. That inevitability, although not a surprise, had been making Neoma sweat. Both her and Martín kept holding their breath, waiting to be hauled in for questioning despite Tobin's assurances that it wouldn't happen. "Trust me," he'd told them. "The cops have no reason to look at any of us. If anything, they'll come and talk to me. Robin might have left information behind that he was supposed to meet with me. But I highly doubt that. He didn't want anyone to ridicule him if I'd pranked him. It's okay, it's going to be okay."

Sure, Tobin was being a rock on *that* issue, but the man was providing his own brand of frustrating, toe curling, tension. She was ready to throttle him in the most supportive way possible. *I'm trying to be patient with him, trying to give him the time he needs, but I want to touch him so badly I'm ready to skin him and wear him as a coat!* Neoma yanked her mind from that unhelpful line of thinking, returning to the hormone cooling effect of Robin.

There had been a tip about an abandoned car that had led the police to investigate Robin's disappearance. They'd doubled down on the search when his work confirmed that he'd been absent. Unfortunately for the cops, someone had plundered the sad little Geo, and only the license plates had linked Robin to the vehicle. Without a missing person's report, the police weren't bothering to investigate further. Besides, they were busy looking for the hiker that had been lost shortly after they'd discovered Robin's car. The lost hiker, a young woman, had been reported missing, and even Martín had been recruited for that search of the surrounding forest. As of yet, no one had been found.

Taking a deep breath, Neoma focused on the madness bubbling around her with a tight smile. The bookstore was filled past capacity with the public, leaving her feeling amazed and overwhelmed in equal measure. She'd had no idea so many people were invested in her little business, but the grand unveiling of the store's mural had drawn a crowd. She had Stewart, her mom, and even Lukas helping to stay ahead of the book hungry hoards. Of course, the selection of treats from her mom's bakery were a big hit, and she suspected that Martín was responsible for a large part of that decimation.

She couldn't really blame him; her appetite had skyrocketed since the full moon a few weeks ago. It was playing hell on her grocery bill and confusing the heck out of her family. But she couldn't help it, she was constantly hungry.

"Neoma?" Small hands tugged on her dress, and she looked down to see all four of Martín's sister's gazing at her expectantly.

"What can I do for you? Because if I give you any more cookies, your mom is going to murder me."

They gave a collective sigh, but Sofía piped up with enthusiasm. "Do you have any graphic novels with vampires and zombies?"

"Sofía, you're eight." Neoma squinted at her. The little girl only giggled at her maniacally. Neoma rolled her eyes and pointed. "That way, third shelf down. And don't you dare tell your mother on me!" she hissed as the gaggle of girls scattered, weaving in between a group of White Haired Wonders who were loading up on romance novels.

"Excuse me," the voice caused Neoma to turn.

"Trisha? Oh my gosh!" Neoma acted on instinct and reached out to give the other woman a hug, careful not to squeeze the baby bundled to Trisha's chest. "Is this her?"

"Yes, this little munchkin is Alisa Rose, Rosy for short." Trisha tenderly gazed down at the squished face with large dark eyes taking in the world. Neoma reached out, letting Rosy grab her finger, her tiny chubby fist squeezing hard.

"She has one tight grip!" Neoma laughed.

"You think that's impressive, you should hear her scream," another voice joined the conversation. Neoma blinked as Paris walked up behind Trisha, her daughter Starla holding onto her mom's skirt. "I think I have hearing loss after that last squall."

Neoma felt shock race through her, but she grabbed it and crumbled it into small pieces. *We're all capable of change,* she sternly reminded herself. *And I need to give people a chance to show me who they are now.*

"Thanks for coming. Both of you." Neoma said, and Trisha beamed, while Paris gave a small nod. "I wasn't sure if you'd want to bring Rosy into so much madness, but I figured I'd ask. And I set aside a few books for the girls in case you showed. I'm not sure if you both already have them, but they're fantastic. Feel free to ask Stewart behind the desk, he'll get them to you." Neoma gave Trisha another hug and waved at Starla, who waved back. Paris's expression softened, and she nodded again.

"Thanks for having us. I'm so proud of what you've built here." Trisha said, squeezed her arm and moved on, waving to her mother in line to buy books. Paris followed.

"Look at you making friends." Martín said from behind her.

"Well, *friends* might be a stretch for Paris and me, but I'll take a ceasefire for now." Neoma mused.

"Hey, you gotta start somewhere. Now, what did you tell my sisters? They looked way too happy as they dove back into the bookstacks" Martín asked, rubbing her shoulder with his. He was eating cupcake number five by Neoma's count.

"I'm not responsible for your sister's taste in books, I'm just not. Especially if they're left unattended in my store." Martín chuckled, and it sent a warm feeling all the way to Neoma's toes. She shut it down.

"Knock that off." She swatted him.

"I can't help it. Your whole face softens when you feel happy. Besides, anything to take the edge off your stress will keep me from eating more cupcakes." Martín said.

"Somehow I doubt that." Neoma's tone was dry. He shrugged. "Am I really that stressed?" She asked.

As if proving a point, Martín held up his cupcake. "It's either this, or I might eat my sisters."

"Martín, for the thousandth time, you are not going to eat your sisters!" Neoma put a hand over her face. "We've talked about this, Tobin's talked to you about this. Even if the little monsters deserve it, you're not going to lose it and eat them."

"You say that now only because I have cupcakes. Stress does strange things to people, and you're worrying all over my heightened awareness, riling my beast which needs to be sedated with sugar. This is my coping strategy, so I can withstand the mental pacing, and longing, you're doing inside your head."

"Really?"

Martín nodded. "Relax, he'll be here. And you two will figure this out." He gave her a side hug. "And if he wimps out, we'll hunt him down together." He raised the last bite of cupcake in a promise and slipped through the crowd after his sisters. He flowed without thinking about it, while she still battled some pain in her joints. Yet they both moved more like predators, quiet, careful, purposeful. But with Martín, Neoma could see the most change. The broad man had walked stiffly, like a bull, pushing his way through the world. Now he prowled, rhythmic in his movements, like she had before RA. Neoma felt a small pang. Her RA pain still haunted her like an unwelcome spirit. Or a poltergeist.

After she'd shifted back to human, there had been twenty-four hours of glorious pain-free movement. Neoma thought the magic of the change had cured her, but a dull ache resumed in the joints that had been most affected. At least the pain was different; it wasn't the angry onslaught of her body attacking itself, more of an echo, or scarring due to restriction. A pain that didn't outright limit her actions but dogged them. It was an annoying reminder of her disease that otherwise seemed to be in remission. That meant Neoma didn't get to glide across the ground like Martín without putting in the conscious effort, but she no longer shuffled either, a trade she was more than willing to contend with.

All magic has a price. She reminded herself. *I wonder what price Martín is paying?* She hadn't wanted to ask him; she knew he would tell her when he was ready.

The bell over the door chimed again, and Neoma's attention drew towards the entrance like a compass needle. He was here! He came! Dressed in a chocolate t-shirt that hugged his arms and chest and brown cargo shorts paired with his dark rimmed glasses, he looked like a librarian's dream. He scanned over the heads of the milling patrons until their eyes met. Neoma's whole body thrummed with connection. It made her ache and feel seen all at once. However, there was a frustration there she was learning to contend with, this pull towards him that she had to keep reining in. Their conversation in the truck had been clear, neither of them were ready for more. Yet lately, damn she wanted to touch him, while he still seemed reluctant.

"Okay everyone!" she hollered over the noise, pulling on that well of coldness to give her voice more authority. "It's time for the reveal, let's take this party outside!"

A small cheer went up and people joyously filed out. Neoma fell back out of the way as the crowd exited. Tobin lingered, then slowly picked his way through the press of bodies. He halted in front of her. His brow furrowed in confusion, making his glasses dip. "You're," he concentrated, "you're irritated, but also relieved to see me?"

This pack bond thing was going to drive her mad in no time. She huffed at him. "Don't make a big thing of it. I've got to get out there and see what Carter did to my building. If it has to be repainted, I'm going to force the pack to help me." Matrix scooted up to her and melted against her leg with a sigh. His big tail thumped against the floor as he leaned on her while she scratched his ears, taking comfort in the big dog's presence. "Not you, you big goof. I don't think any of us could explain you with a paint brush in your mouth."

Matrix smiled as only a dog could, and Neoma brushed by Tobin, inhaling his scent while feeling the warmth of his skin as she departed. It made her smile despite her fluctuating emotions. Maybe she could keep lying, keep telling herself this was enough? He'd shown up, it was sufficient, a good start. *Oh who the fuck am I kidding?* Neoma bit her lip and forced herself not to think about her fingers trailing over Tobin's scars. Not to imagine the scent of his skin enhanced by her improved scenes. She had speeches to give, books to sell. *I just want to touch him. And smack him. And it's not his fault.* She rolled her eyes.

Outside, the party continued. People stood in groups awaiting the unveiling. Carter and his two lackeys had somehow managed to find enough sheets to keep the wall covered from prying eyes. The young men now stood off to the side with expressions that bordered on nausea. Carter bounced on his toes like a prize fighter about to enter a ring.

Neoma could relate. The sensation winding through her belly was a potent mix of excitement, anticipation, soured with a touch of trepidation as she took her place facing the shrouded wall. Pulling in a deep breath, she turned to the crowd and addressed them.

"Welcome everyone, and thank you for coming to the unveiling of Rainy Day Books art wall. I also want to take this moment to announce that Books After Dark will be continuing forward and all are welcome to come by. We will be expanding our little store and putting in more tables for additional reading, writing, and gaming opportunities. And we're partnering with Darkly Roasted Slightly Sweet to offer mobile orders delivered to the store along with treats. Reading is hungry work after all." The crowd laughed, and Neoma continued. "I want to thank this amazing community. Who knew we had such a plethora of book dragons in Kelso?" Another chuckle rippled through the audience. "Seriously though, your support has made these new dreams and endeavors possible. Thank you all, from the bottom of my heart. Now, let's witness what these talented young men have been up to." Her face hurt with the strength of her smile as she turned and nodded to Carter.

The teen grabbed a length of rope and yanked. The whole wall of fabric shuddered like it might tumble into the crowd before letting go of its tethers and fluttering down. Neoma gasped, her mind playing tricks on her. It was as if the wall had vanished, leaving a window in its place. The shift in perspective pulled the viewer into the store through the back wall. But it was more than that. The table where the group had been gaming for the last couple months had figures sitting there, each one a werewolf holding up cards, scribbling on note pads, and eating cookies. Even Matrix was painted in place, slowly sneaking a treat off the table.

As her eyes wandered the rest of the mural, the details and wonder didn't stop. Neoma picked out different creatures hidden in the stacks. Elves reading, fairies trying to take a book off a shelf, a vampire hidden in a dark corner. Stewart presided over the cash register wearing a wizard's cape and holding a staff. And the view through the windows showed the outside raining, the words under the sign reading "Rainy Day Books, where imagination comes to life."

• • ◆ • •

TOBIN WAS STILL INSPECTING THE MURAL WHEN NEOMA found him.

"What do you think?" she asked, her voice full of emotion. There was color in her cheeks, giving her tan skin a richer dimension as she beamed. She wore a long dress of blues and greens that swam with geometric shapes and fish. The same fabric made up the headband holding back her thick curls as they bounced in the slight breeze. The dress made her sea green eyes shine in the evening light. Tobin swallowed, suddenly a little nervous.

"I think the kid sees too much." Tobin said, indicating the werewolf gaming group and trying to keep his emotions in check.

Neoma shrugged. "Well, he knew what game we were playing. Lukas told him. I kind of like the werewolf wearing glasses, although he got the color wrong." She crossed her arms, brushing his shoulder as she looked at the gray wolf.

Tobin tried for a smile, but it slipped away. The last three weeks had tussled him up in emotional knots until he couldn't discern reality from fear. He wanted to touch her, but he couldn't untangle if that was the bond or his own feelings, and that terrified him. One moment he was content with how everything had worked out, completely devoted to living within a pack and deferring to Neoma. The next moment, his mind would turn to thoughts of being manipulated, again, by something magical. When those dark doubts descended, he would curl in on himself cold and sweating, wanting to run. Those moments just compounded his sensation of being trapped.

These bouts of fear were held in check each time he was with the pack, and worse when he was alone. *Surprisingly,* Tobin thought to himself, *I'm not very good at being my own support system.* Yet what was real? Was he still him? Still in control of his own decisions? He had to know in order to be Neoma's partner, not a prisoner. This amazing, hard-headed, tantalizing woman wanted more from him, and he wanted to give it, the question was how.

Neoma's face drained of good humor as she frowned at him. Grabbing his hand, she pulled him away from the crowd and back behind the store to employee parking, only stopping when they were tucked on the far side of Stewart's minibus, secluded in dim moonlight. The sounds of celebration muffled as people returned to the store, or drifted off home, giving them shadowed privacy.

"Enough. Talk to me." She leaned against her car, crossing her arms again over her chest. "I think I've been very patient, all things considered."

"What do you mean?" Tobin asked, honestly baffled. As her glower got worse, he could feel his heart rate increase. Somehow that didn't deter him but made him want to move closer. *This can't be a normal reaction.*

"How dense are you?" Neoma threw up her hands.

Tobin was beginning to wonder that himself. "I…" he started to say but then had nothing to follow up with. Fortunately, Neoma had plenty of words to cover his lack.

"Three weeks ago, we all," she looked around, "changed, in case that slipped your mind. Followed by some deep bonding moments. Those seemed pretty life altering to me at least. Then we regained our humanity, left Robin's car for dead, and returned home to act as if we'd simply gone to a movie. Then you asked me for time, and I've been doing everything I can to give it to you. Yet you show up and this heat builds between us, and I feel you pull back, pull away."

Tobin hung his head, still bereft of words. Neoma kept going.

"Meanwhile, Martín and I are developing bottomless appetites and have taken up cooking. You know how many Food Network shows I've watched in the last two weeks?" She didn't wait for him to guess. "I've discovered a new passion for honey and am now considering bee keeping, and Martín keeps wondering if he's going to unexpectedly eat his sisters! Especially when they deserve it! Did I mention we can now both grow fur at will? Tobin, our lives have changed. Every day I keep freaking out that I transformed into a bear. A blue freaking bear," she hissed. "What I'm trying to tell you is that I understand that there's a lot going on in our personal lives but pulling away every time things start to heat up between us is driving me nuts! There's this pull towards you that gets worse every time we're together and it's taking all I have not to touch you."

Tobin's eyes widened. "You're feeling that too?"

A small squeal escaped Neoma, like a teapot brought to boil. "We. Are. Linked." She pulled in great gulps of air. "It's not just the pack bond. I mean, Martín and I need you here, with us. But for me, it's more. When I can't…touch you, I feel like I'm missing something, something important." She gestured with her hands at him. "I'm trying so, so hard to give you some space, but it's wearing on me, Tobin, especially when I feel you reach for me, then pull away again." Her annoyance and desperation were a cold wind over his mind. He wondered idly if she was going to shift and start batting him around just to take the edge off her compressed feelings. He had to diffuse this, and she deserved the truth.

"I'm afraid," Tobin ground out, turning his head away.

Neoma's frustration dampened. "Of what?"

His eyes darted to her expression, and he took a deep breath. What else did he really have to lose at this point?

"I'm afraid of this pack bond. I'm afraid that what I feel isn't real. I'm afraid of…you." It was as if he had ripped off a Band-Aid, and yet relief spilled out of him.

"Me?"

"Yes. And I know we talked a lot, and I still trust you. But I don't want to be controlled by anyone or anything, and my fear is stemming from this. That you could control me…like Aithne." Tobin cringed as the words left his mouth because he could taste the weakness in them. This bond wasn't a shackle like the Fey's had been, and in his heart, he knew that. "It's an irrational fear, but I can't seem to get a handle on it." Still, there was something more to his feeling about control, something he wanted, and felt depraved for harboring that desire. He leaned against the minibus, then rubbed his temples to combat the confusion and yearning that was pounding in his skull.

"I see. Tobin, you know it's not illogical to be afraid of something that happened to you. You were enslaved, twice by the sounds of it." Her voice was kind. "That's a major trauma. It would mess with anyone. You are allowed to feel this way. I just need you to communicate about what's happening. Please."

"I know!" He threw his hands up in the air and started pacing. "I did the research. I understand PTSD and all that. Yet I'm getting hung up on this not being rational, it's emotional, and I told you, I suck at this stuff."

Neoma gave a small laugh. "Tobin, research can't fix everything. Sometimes you actually need to explore the emotions."

"Then help me. How do I do this?"

"Oh Tobin, I'm no expert. But..." Neoma tilted her head to the side as she rubbed her chin watching him pace.

"What? I'll give anything a try," he pleaded with her, feeling the pull to touch her, feeling this urge to—to do what? Somehow, physical proximity didn't seem to be all of it. *What is the last piece that I'm missing?*

"Oh, fuck it, why not. Look, I keep thinking about our night in the bookstore," Her face actually flushed, and Tobin stalled his pacing. "Was I controlling you then?" she asked, her lip quirking.

Tobin watched her like a cornered animal. "No, I..." *Wanted that,* his internal voice moaned.

"I told you to do things, and you complied, willingly, yes?" Tobin could only nod.

"Okay, so now, give me my book back," she demanded.

"What?" He blinked. "The book? *My* book? Not a chance." He was confused but a small smile escaped.

"That's what I thought." She took the tiniest step forward and spoke again, her voice lowering.

"Tobin, get on your knees."

Her order was so random he simply gaped at her, yet his body responded. Memories of crouching before her, breathing in her delicious scent turned his knees to water, heat flooding him. Yet he kept standing. "What did you just do to me?"

"I didn't do anything to you, I just proved a point. See, you didn't do what I told you to do. I don't control you." She looked smug. "So, what's your logic now?" She was teasing him, testing him. He could feel her amusement through the bond. Her desire for him tangled around it. She wanted him, her scent of blueberries filled the air.

Neoma uncrossed her arms and stepped up to him further, their bodies inches apart, her head tilted up to meet his gaze. "Now Tobin, I'm going to ask you to do something, and you're only going to do it if *you* want to." Her voice was husky, making his whole body hum with new anticipation. "Kneel for me. Now."

Tobin went weak, heat and longing rushing through him in a way he'd never experienced. The world around them faded, and he sank to his knees, panting slightly as he peered up at her. This is where he wanted to be. That missing piece had clicked into place. His brain hummed, on fire, yearning. He'd finally let go of that thing he'd held so tightly…all the damn time. His control. He was free of responsibility for a moment, and it was euphoric.

"Good boy," she said, running a hand over his head and down his cheek. She removed his glasses and placed them on the car. "Did I force you to do this?" Her voice was sultry, dark, and honey in his ears as her fingernails moved over his scalp. She grasped his hair, and he wanted to howl her name to the sky.

"No," he choked, realizing it was true. He wanted to do this, give over control to…her. He'd trusted her with the pack and his place in it, but now he discovered he also trusted her with a greater responsibility: his heart. "No, Neoma, I did this because you asked."

She smiled, and he smelled vanilla.

EPILOGUE

Matrix

M atrix trotted through the shadows with purpose, a paper bag swinging from his jaws as he followed the scent trail leading away from the party. He'd checked the bonds of his pack before leaving, feeling Martín happy with his family, and Tobin and Neoma, well, occupied. He was relieved that they were working out their relationship, but he didn't need the details.

The small park up ahead was draped in dusk, the tall pines that bordered the edges of the green space were mixed with hardwoods while the river flowed beyond like black ink. The odor pooled across the ground, telling him his quarry still lingered nearby. Matrix sat in a bare spot, the light of the waxing crescent moon giving off a sliver of illumination, granting him definition from the dark. Placing the bag at his side, he patiently held his position. He didn't have to wait long.

A tree trunk moved, and a shape slogged from the gloom until it, too, was granted form by the weak moonlight. Robin wore a huge trench coat that fluttered around him like an ill-fitting dress. A battered wide brimmed hat was crushed down over his head, hiding his face in deeper shadows, and his hind paws were somehow stuffed into large rubber boots. Where the man-wolf had gotten his attire, Matrix could only guess. But it wasn't the pilfered clothes that bothered the dog, it was the sight of Robin still transformed that concerned him. He gave a small whine, and Robin flinched.

"I can't turn back," he admitted, hunching deeper in the jacket before realizing what he was doing and straightening himself. "But why would I want to? This is amazing."

Matrix could smell the lie.

With great care, Matrix retrieved the bag and crossed half the space between them before setting it down again. Robin waited until the dog backed away before approaching. The man-wolf squatted down and opened the crumpled paper that was damp with dog slobber, his claws only ripping it slightly. Like a surgeon reaching into a body cavity, Robin extracted the treat inside, bringing the slightly smushed cupcake into the light.

Matrix could now see his yellow eyes, and they swam with emotions as the werewolf beheld the pastry.

"Did Neoma send this?" he growled as he asked, giving the frosting a tentative lick.

Matrix shook his head.

"Did you bring this?"

Matrix wagged his tail.

"Why?" Robin looked suspicious.

The big dog's frustration built as his stunted means of communication limited his response. Concentrating, he pulled up words and barked. *You. Alone. Unnecessary.* The effort cost him, especially this far from the deeper forest. But he had to help Robin, he couldn't leave the young man trapped in his current state. He knew all about being trapped. Besides, the Fey couldn't be trusted, and he was unwilling to leave an innocent alone with her tender madness.

Robin's eyes went wide. He dropped the cupcake back in the bag and stood, towering over the dog with his six foot plus height.

"I'm not alone. I have Aithne. She cares about me. She wanted me when you were all turning your backs on me. And she's giving me power," he growled, and it echoed off the trees, their needles seeming to whisper with his rising anger.

Matrix sighed and tapped the ground with his paw, the trees soothing. He gave Robin a sympathizing look.

"No, don't you dare pity me," Robin snarled. "I came because I wanted to report on what the pack was up to. To be useful to her plans moving forward. The art wall was just a convenient way to get everyone in one place." He looked smug, like he had planned this himself. Then his mask of confidence slipped, and Matrix could see the longing flutter in Robin's eyes like an ensnared moth. "She has plans, you know.

She wants to claim this wild territory and make it hers. She says there's a bigger threat coming, and if we don't defend these lands, he will take it and enthrall us all under his rule."

Matrix shook his head, making his ears flop.

"To avoid falling into his power, to protect herself, I'm worried about what she might do. Align with her. Join her—join us, together we would be unstoppable. Besides, it's not as bad as you think, and her power is incredible."

Robin drew himself up further, looking righteous as only a man-wolf in a floppy hat and trench coat could.

"You all think she's the monster, but she's not. She's the victim. He bound her true powers a century ago and now she burns with the pain of it. It's awful." He gulped before resuming what sounded like a prepared speech. "Look, he's willing to bind us all until he gets what he wants. Aithne says he's so close to that goal, and he won't stop until it's realized. I believe her, Matrix, I've seen her scars." He snatched the bag from the ground and turned to go, his steps faltering. "Tell them," his voice wavered. "Tell them not to play the game without me."

Matrix lunged forward, trying to snag Robin's leg, trying to stop him, to keep him from…from what? What could he do? How could he help? Even in those rubber boots, Robin moved faster than Matrix expected, and he wasn't willing to hurt the man-wolf to stop his retreat. The young man had made his choice, and the dog could not change his mind. At least not tonight.

Turning back, Matrix left the park. A breeze off the water cradled a hint of the changing season, the scent of brittle leaves and waking mushrooms, trees priming for slumber. A climax which nature had been preparing for all summer. The dog paused and looked up at the crescent moon. She whispered to him about the future to come, braided equally with friends and foes. And he understood, they had also been marshaling for this next chapter, growing together as a pack, putting down roots, connections that made them stronger. They would be ready when the seasons changed.

He would be ready when the forest called.

* · ● · ·

THE WOMAN AT THE BASE OF THE RED CEDAR LEAKED saltwater from her eyes. It blessed the tree. One final gift before the transformation. Aithne could not hold off any longer. She needed this tree to accept some of her burden, her power. Cedars were known to many Indigenous people as "the tree of life," might that also include rebirth?

"Do not worry sweet one," Aithne cooed to the woman as she stroked her face. More roots rose to wrap around the hiker, pulling her deeper into the alcove made by the branching trunk. The Fey nestled in, cradling the woman, and whispered against her bound lips. "This hurt will only be a temporary thing."

The night flickered with orange and yellow light as muffled screams were eaten by the trees. Aithne smiled, she hadn't lied, death only took a moment.

SPECIAL THANKS

W ell, here I am again, at the end of a book, wow what a crazy two, three(?) years this has been. This story grew in unexpected ways and refused to be trimmed down despite my best efforts. With more pages came the demands for more people to be pulled into this project. Please join me as I thank those tireless souls who poured over this manuscript out of the kindness of their hearts. And remember, this part has not had the loving touch of an editor. It is me, in my raw dyslexic glory. Have fun.

Let's start with the readers. My writing group, the Story Dogs, Aliya Hall, Melissa Nelson, Julia Back, Navit Berman, and Mike Harris, without the lot of you, I would probably not move as quickly as I do (which is not fast), and this manuscript would not be nearly as strong. Thank you all for being patient with me as I question my worthiness, and word choices. Your talents and friendships are unparalleled. Next are the intrepid Beta readers, two of whom had never read my work before. Betas, you transformed this manuscript for the better with your critiques, Natile Jones, Lori Albertson, and Stephanie Hoffman. Stephanie, I can't believe you did it all in one night, you get the Wonder Woman award, hands down. Finally, it was my great honor to have Maria Vale lay eyes on this story when it was still a fledgling with no feathers. Your insights were priceless, thank you for fielding my novice questions in the most random moments along this journey. Oh, and I must include a special thanks to my sister, Paige, who listen's tirelessly to my troubles, and always asks how things are going. Thanks Little Sis, I love being on this creative path with you.

Now for behind the scenes, to the people who help make these pages look good! Jenny Sliger @ Owl Eyes Proofs & Edits waded in to fix my comma usage and so much more. Ravven did the breathtaking cover art and created that werewolf from scratch, thanks for bringing the visual magic to my covers. Becky @ Platform House Publishing came to my rescue and formatted this beast in record time. Becky your kindness with my timeline was so supportive, big hugs! And Ashly McLeo, you were amazing at helping me with the blurb, and every single publishing question I tossed at you last minute. I owe you a coffee at the very least.

Final thought and thanks. To my husband Tom, your unwavering support through every strange book conversation is noted, seen, and adored. And to Loki, my constant fuzzy muse, who is always by my side. I am blessed to have such love in my life.

ABOUT THE AUTHOR

A.B. HERRON was introduced to books and adventure early by her father and never let go. Her love of science and daydreaming was born deep in the dark mines of Death Valley and while snorkeling secluded reefs in Hawaii. In this second sequel to her debut novel, *Watching Water,* Herron breaks the rules of a series and follows a morally gray werewolf into an adventure within the forests of Washington, much to the confusion of her writing group. Yet this story needed to be told. Herron lives in the Northwest with her husband and Buhund, Loki.

Find out more about her adventures at

www.ABHerron.com